CW00429628

The Ones That Got Away

►►►

Other Books by Stephen Graham Jones

▶ ▶ ▶

The Fast Red Road—A Plainsong

All the Beautiful Sinners

The Bird Is Gone—A Manifesto

Bleed into Me: A Book of Stories

Demon Theory

The Long Trial of Nolan Dugatti

Ledfeather

It Came from Del Rio

The Ones That Got Away

Stephen Graham Jones

PRIME BOOKS

The Ones That Got Away

Prime Books
www.prime-books.com

ISBN: 978-1-60701-235-1

for Sulac

and for Detective Bruiseman

Man has gone out to explore other worlds and other civilizations without having explored his own labyrinth of dark passages and secret chambers, and without finding what lies behind doorways that he himself has sealed.
—Stanislaw Lem

It's close to midnight and something evil's lurking in the dark
—Michael Jackson

Table of Contents

▶ ▶ ▶

Introduction: No Escape, *Laird Barron*...13

Father, Son, Holy Rabbit...17

Till the Morning Comes...25

The Sons of Billy Clay...36

So Perfect...45

Lonegan's Luck...68

Monsters...93

Wolf Island...107

Teeth...118

Raphael...147

Captain's Lament...169

The Meat Tree...176

The Ones Who Got Away...203

Crawlspace...211

Story Notes...241

Acknowledgements...253

► Introduction: No Escape
by Laird Barron

A finger bone vomited into park grass. A snake oil salesman traveling through the land of the dead. A primeval island where the human population of one is about to tick over to zero. A baby monitor that transmits on a damned frequency. Cannibalism. Black magic. Murder. Man's best friend, until the end. First love. True love. Childhood. Machetes. The Dark.

Brace yourself.

The Ones That Got Away is a slippery collection; it resists and gnaws at the bonds of genre, yet may be the most pure horror book I've come across. The cumulative effect of these stories induces dislocation and dread—the manner of dread that arises from what is known by our soft, weak, civilized selves through rote and sedentary custom and symbolic exchange of cautionary fables, as well as a deeper, abiding fear of the ineffable that's the province of the primordial swamp of our subconscious. *The Ones That Got Away* acts as a literary taproot intercepting the delta waves of humanity's ancestral lizard slumbering in muck. The beast dreaming a future where it has shed scale, fang, and claw, and goes forth on two puny legs, an organism evolved and refined, albeit eternally fettered to its savage provenance via genetic memory and vestigial apparatuses.

Homo sapiens haven't come very far, not really. We are quick to anger, quick to draw blood; quick to breed, quicker to flee. From the slopes of our brows to the shelves of our breastbones humans are designed to withstand death from above. While our savage instincts have atrophied, the beast merely sleeps, its lusts and rages merely sublimated, its fears merely quieted. Our collective blissful ignorance of the awesome nature of the universe and our amoebic place therein, as Lovecraft opined, shields us from gibbering madness while leaving intact the basic intellectual curiosity that defines us, elevates us from the beasts. Driven by curiosity and greed, but protected in equal measure by cowardice and short memories, what a contradiction is man.

Stephen Graham Jones is tuned into the phenomena of this duality—the fault line running through rationality, the divide between animal and man, and what we know and the actual truth. With this book he's acquired a distress signal emanating from the prehistoric brain and committed it to paper, produced an artifact that satisfies the requirements of literature as entertainment while translating on the subliminal register. It is a crystal clear message: all is not well, nothing has ever been, nor will ever be, and that we begin this life covered in blood, screaming. Ultimately, we don't, can't, escape the circumstances of our origins.

Childhood lost. Youth corrupted is the touchstone, the recurring theme in *The Ones That Got Away*. Everything, *everything*, begins and ends with childhood, for as children Jones's protagonists dwell closest to the animal state that powers the overmind, are thus privy to, albeit powerless against, the terrible truth, have not developed a thick, insulating shell of incredulity, and are thus scarred, if not damned to be receivers and carriers of horror. Children, with their partially-formed consciousness and absent morality, their natural affinity for the inexplicable, their essential vulnerability, get it, the essence of horror, you see. The wounded ones get it double.

Jones's adult characters who remain forever those damaged children on the inside, yet devastatingly estranged from any shred of youthful innocence, get it too. These mature protagonists bear the formative wounds and are especially sensitive to the darkness that seeps between cracks, alive as a raw nerve to the intrusion of the supernatural. Cursed with perspective, that bitter fruit of age and wisdom, such men and women cannot help but apprehend the existence of something larger than themselves, its encroachment, how it stains and deforms the fabric of reality, stains and deforms their own flesh and spirit. They are forced to come to grips with the hideous realization that the inequities of childhood, its attendant suffering and imbalances of power, are relative, a socio-economic parallax that persists from birth to death. Good and evil are empty words against the inchoate energies that twist the material world, tears it to ribbons without notice. Like the song says, there ain't no good guys, there ain't no bad guys, there's only you and me. Perhaps the darkest hour anyone will endure is that which succeeds the epiphany that the sublime and monstrous are equally inheritable traits. Behind the faces of good and evil, ruination and corruption, lies an insensate, inchoate vista of blind stars sprinkled across the maw of vast, lightless space.

The pieces herein radiate the dark energy of fairy tales. The good kind, the kind with sex and cannibalism, occultism and murder, awe and wonder. Horror. That Jones appropriates this ancient mode, deconstructs and flenses it with his high-pressure stream of consciousness narratives, is grimly appropriate. In his hands, the fairy tale isn't simply a trifle or diversion, nor at heart the sanitized parable so popular in public education, but a fragment of cosmic code, a warning and a promise, the mesmerist's chime that snaps a mind from one plane to another. Fairy tales, the down and dirty ones courtesy Black Forest campfires of ages past, are frightful correspondence with the dark, nightmare communications from the primal wellspring.

Indeed, the power of nightmares defines this collection. Jones's stories are nightmarish for the clarity of their manifest terrors often hatched from scenarios we've envisioned in the wasteland hours between falling into bed and crawling from it. Jones's stories are also nightmarish for their moral ambiguity and their juxtaposition of the seedy, grimy dirt-in-the mouth taste of reality with that of the supernatural, the diabolical and the numinous. Yet the experience of them rapidly escalates from reading accounts of discrete nightmares to actually participating in the grotesquerie, becoming entangled, infected, scarred. He's fractured the big, black picture window that overlooks the benighted regions of the soul. Each story is a fragment of that glass, and some of the imagery is jagged as the hell it evokes.

You can't go home, can never go back where you started from, is what they say like it's a tragedy, a curse. There are those who don't get to leave in the first place. The ones caught in the ankle-hold traps of poverty and abuse, corrupted by the dark days of bad childhoods, the ones who get lost in the haunted forests that surround suburb and city, backwoods shack and brownstone alike. All those kids—now grown into men and women—who dwell on the fringes of the mythical Great American dream carry on as shadows of themselves cast down through the long years. Predators and victims by turn. The ones who dream the ancient dream, who can't quite shake it upon waking and thus remain ensnared, body and soul. The ones who almost got away, but didn't.

An animal will chew off its own leg to escape the trap, but there's no escape from a following shadow. There's your tragedy, there's your curse. There's the beating heart of *The Ones That Got Away*.

—Laird Barron, author of *Occultation*
30 April 2010, Olympia, Washington

► Father, Son, Holy Rabbit

By the third day they were eating snow. Years later it would come to the boy again, rush up to him at a job interview: his father spitting out pieces of seed or pine needle into his hand. Whatever had been in the snow. The boy had looked at the brown flecks in his father's palm, then up to his father, who finally nodded, put them back in his mouth, turned his face away to swallow.

Instead of sleeping, they thumped each other in the face to stay awake.

The place they'd found under the tree wasn't out of the wind, but it was dry.

They had no idea where the camp was, or how to find the truck from there, or the highway after that. They didn't even have a gun, just the knife the boy's father kept strapped to his right hip.

The first two days, the father had shrugged and told the boy not to worry, that the storm couldn't last.

The whole third day, he'd sat watching the snow fall like ash.

The boy didn't say anything, not even inside, not even a prayer. One of the times he drifted off, though, waking not to the slap of his father's fingernail on his cheek but the sound of it, there was a picture he brought up with him from sleep. A rabbit.

He told his father about it and his father nodded, pulled his lower lip into his mouth, and smiled like the boy had just told a joke.

That night they fell asleep.

This time the boy woke to his father rubbing him all over, trying to make his blood flow. The boy's father was crying, so the boy told him about the rabbit, how it wasn't even white like it should be, but brown, lost like them.

His father hugged his knees to his chest and bounced up and down, stared out at all the white past their tree.

"A rabbit?" he said.

The boy shrugged.

Sometime later that day he woke again, wasn't sure where he was at first. His father wasn't there. The boy moved his mouth up and down, didn't know what to say. Rounded off in the crust of the snow were the dragging holes his father had made, walking away. The boy put his hand in the first, then the second, then stood from the tree into the real cold. He followed the tracks until they became confused. He tried to follow them back to the tree but the light was different now. Finally he started running, falling down, getting up, his chest on fire.

His father found him sometime that night, pulled him close.

They lowered themselves under another tree.

"Where were you?" the boy asked.

"That rabbit," the father said, stroking the boy's hair down.

"You saw it?"

Instead of answering, the father just stared.

This tree wasn't as good as the last. The next morning they looked for another, and another, and stumbled onto their first one.

"Home again home again," the father said, guiding the boy under then gripping onto the back of his jacket, stopping him.

There were tracks coming up out of the dirt, onto the snow. Double tracks, like the split hoof of an elk, except bigger.

"Your rabbit," the father said.

The boy smiled.

That night his father carved their initials into the trunk of the tree with his knife. Later he broke a dead branch off, tried sharpening it. The boy watched, fascinated, hungry.

"Will it work?" he asked.

His father thumped him in the face, woke him. He asked it again, with his mouth this time.

The father shrugged. His lips were cracked, lined with blood, his beard pushing up through his skin.

"Where do you think it is right now?" he said to the boy.

"The—the rabbit?"

The father nodded.

The boy closed his eyes, turned his head, then opened his eyes again, used them to point the way he was facing. The father used his sharp stick as a cane, stood with it, and walked in that direction, folded himself into the blowing snow.

The boy knew this was going to work.

In the hours his father was gone, he studied their names in the tree.

While the boy had been asleep, his father had carved the boy's mother's name into the bark as well. The boy ran the pads of his fingers over the grooves, brought the taste to his tongue.

The next thing he knew was ice. It was falling down on him in layers.

His father had returned, had collapsed into the side of the tree.

The boy rolled him in, rubbed his back and face and neck, and then saw what his father was balled around, what he'd been protecting for miles, maybe: the rabbit. It was brown at the tips of its coat, the rest white.

With his knife, the father opened the rabbit in a line down the stomach, poured the meat out. It steamed.

Over it, the father looked at the son, nodded.

They scooped every bit of red out that the rabbit had, swallowed it in chunks because if they chewed they tasted what they were doing. All that was left was the skin. The father scraped it with the blade of his knife, gave those scrapings to the boy.

"Glad your mom's not here to see this," he said.

The boy smiled, wiped his mouth.

Later, he threw up in his sleep, then looked at it soaking into the loose dirt, then turned to see if his father had seen what he'd done, how he'd betrayed him. His father was sleeping. The boy lay back down, forced the rabbit back into his mouth then angled his arm over his lips, so he wouldn't lose his food again.

The next day, no helicopters came for them, no men on horseback, following dogs, no skiers poling their way home. For a few hours around what should have been lunch, the sun shone down, but all that did was make their dry spot under the tree wet. Then the wind started again.

"Where's that stick?" the boy asked.

The father narrowed his eyes as if he hadn't thought of that. "Your rabbit," he said after a few minutes.

The boy nodded, said, almost to himself, "It'll come back."

When he looked around to his father, his father was already looking at him. Studying him.

The rabbit's skin was out in the snow, just past the tree. Buried hours ago.

The father nodded like this could maybe be true. That the rabbit would come back. Because they needed it to.

The next day he went out again, with a new stick, and came back with his lips blue, one of his legs frozen wet from stepping through some ice into a creek. No rabbit. What he said about the creek was that it was a good sign. You could usually follow water one way or another, to people.

The boy didn't ask which way.

"His name is Slaney," he said.

"The rabbit?"

The boy nodded. Slaney. Things that had names were real.

That night they slept, then woke somehow at the same time, the boy under his father's heavy, jacketed arm. They were both looking the same direction, their faces even with the crust of snow past their tree. Twenty feet out, its nose tasting the air, was Slaney.

The boy felt his father's breath deepen.

"Don't . . . don't . . . " his father said, low, then exploded over the boy, crashed off into the day without his stick, even.

He came back an hour later with nothing slung over his shoulder, nothing balled against his stomach. No blood on his hands.

This time the son prayed, inside. Promised not to throw any of the meat up again. With the tip of his knife, his father carved a cartoon rabbit into the trunk of their tree. It looked like a frog with horse ears.

"Slaney," the boy said.

The father carved that in a line under the rabbit's feet, then circled the boy's mother's name over and over, until the boy thought that piece of the bark was going to come off like a plaque.

The next time the boy woke, he was already sitting up.

"What?" the father said.

The boy nodded the direction he was facing.

The father watched his eyes, nodded, then got his stick.

This time he didn't come back for nearly a day. The boy, afraid, climbed up into the tree, then higher, as high as he could, until the wind could reach him.

His father reached up with his stick, tapped him awake.

Like a football in the crook of his arm was the rabbit. It was bloody and wonderful, already cut open.

"You ate the guts," the boy said, his mouth full.

His father reached into the rabbit, came out with a long sliver of meat. The muscle that runs along the spine, maybe.

The boy ate and ate and then, when they were done, trying not to throw up, he placed the rabbit skin in the same spot he'd placed the last one. The coat was just the same—white underneath, brown at the tips.

"It'll come back," he told his father.

His father rubbed the side of his face. His hand was crusted with blood.

The next day there were no walkie-talkies crackling through the woods, no four-wheelers or snowmobiles churning through the snow. And the rabbit skin was gone.

"Hungry?" the boy's father said, smiling, leaning on his stick just to stand, and the boy smiled with him.

Four hours later, his father came back with the rabbit again. He was wet to the hips this time.

"The creek?" the boy said.

"It's a good sign," the father said back.

Again, the father had fingered the guts into his mouth on the way back, left most of the stringy meat for the boy.

"Slaney," the father said, watching the boy eat.

The boy nodded, closed his eyes to swallow.

Because of his frozen pants—the creek—the father had to sit with his legs straight out. "A good sign," the boy said after the father was asleep.

The next morning his father pulled another dead branch down, so he had two sticks now, like a skier.

The boy watched him walk off into the bright snow, feeling ahead of himself with the sticks. It made him look like a ragged, four-legged animal, one long since extinct, or made only of fear and suspicion in the first place. The boy palmed some snow into his mouth and held it there until it melted.

This time his father was only gone thirty minutes. He'd had to cross the creek again. Slaney was cradled against his body.

"He was just standing there," the father said, pouring the meat out for the boy. "Like he was waiting for me."

"He knows we need him," the boy said.

One thing he no longer had to do was dab the blood off the meat before eating it. Another was swallow before chewing.

That night his father staggered out into the snow and threw up, then fell down into it. The boy pretended not to see, held his eyes closed when his father came back.

The following morning he told his father not to go out again, not today.

"But Slaney," his father said.

"I'm not hungry," the boy lied.

The day after that he was, though. It was the day the storm broke. The woods were perfectly still. Birds were even moving from tree to tree again, talking to each other.

In his head, the boy told Slaney not to keep being on the other side of the creek, but he was; the boy's father came back wet to the hip again. His whole frontside was bloodstained now, from hunting, and eating.

The boy scooped the meat into his mouth, watched his father try to sit in one place. Finally he couldn't, fell over on his side. The boy finished eating and curled up against him, only woke when he heard voices, like on a radio.

He sat up and the voices went away.

On the crust of snow, now, since no more had fallen, was Slaney's skin. The boy crawled out to it, studied it, wasn't sure how Slaney could be out there already, reforming, all its muscle growing back, and be here too. But maybe it only worked if you didn't watch.

The boy scooped snow onto the blood-matted coat, curled up by his father again. All that day, his father didn't wake, but he wasn't really sleeping either.

That night, when the snow was melting more, running into their dry spot under the tree, the boy saw little pads of ice out past Slaney. They were footprints, places where the snow had packed down under a boot, into a column. Now that column wasn't melting as fast as the rest.

Instead of going in a line to the creek, these tracks cut straight across.

The boy squatted over them, looked the direction they were maybe going.

When he stood, there was a tearing sound. The seat of his pants had stuck to his calf while he'd been squatting. It was blood. The boy shook his head no, fell back, pulled his pants down to see if it had come from him.

When it hadn't, he looked back to his father, then just sat in the snow again, his arms around his knees, rocking back and forth.

"Slaney, Slaney," he chanted. Not to eat him again, but just to hold him.

Sometime that night—it was clear, soundless—a flashlight found him, pinned him to the ground.

"Slaney?" he said, looking up into the yellow beam.

The man in the flannel was breathing too hard to talk into his radio the right way. He lifted the boy up, and the boy said it again: "Slaney."

"What?" the man asked.

The boy didn't say anything then.

The other men found the boy's father curled under the tree. When they cut his pants away to understand where the blood was coming from, the boy looked away, the lower lids of his eyes pushing up into his field of vision. Over the years it would come to be one of his mannerisms, a stare that might suggest thoughtfulness to a potential employer, but right then, sitting with a blanket and his first cup of coffee, waiting for a helicopter, it had just been a way of blurring the tree his father was still sleeping under.

Watching like that—both holding his breath and trying not to focus—when the boy's father finally stood, he was an unsteady smear against the evergreen. And then the boy had to look.

Somehow, using his sticks as crutches, the boy's father was walking, his head slung low between his shoulders, his sticks reaching out before him like feelers.

When he lurched out from the under the tree, the boy drew his breath in.

The father's pants were tatters now, and his legs too, where he'd been carving off the rabbit meat, stuffing it into the same skin again and again. He pulled his lower lip into his mouth, nodded once to the boy, then stuck one of his sticks into the ground before him, pulled himself towards it, then repeated the complicated process, pulling himself deeper into the woods.

"Where's he going?" one of the men asked.

The boy nodded, understood, his father retreating into the trees for the last time, having to move his legs from the hip now, like things, and the boy answered—*hunting*—then ran back from the helicopter forty minutes later, to dig in the snow just past their tree, but there was nothing there. Just coldness. His own numb fingers.

"What's he saying?" one of the men asked.

The boy stopped, closed his eyes, tried to hear it too, his own voice, then just let the men pull him out of the snow, into the world of houses and bank loans and, finally, job interviews. Because they were wearing gloves, though, or because it was cold and their fingers were numb too, they weren't able to pull all of him from the woods that day. Couldn't tell that an important part of him was still there, sitting under a blanket, watching his father move across the snow, the poles just extensions of his arms, the boy holding his lips tight against each other. Because it would have been a betrayal, he hadn't let himself throw up what his father had given him, not then, and not years later—seconds ago—when the man across the desk palms a handful of sunflower seeds into his mouth all at once, then holds his hand there to make sure none get away, leans forward a bit for the boy to explain what he's written for a name here on this application.

Slade?

Slake?

Slather, slavery?

What the boy does here, what he's just now realizing he should have been doing all along, is reach across, delicately thump the man's cheek, and then pretend not to see past the office, out the window, to the small brown rabbit in the flowers, watching.

Soon enough it'll be white.

The boy smiles.

Some woods, they're big enough you never find your way out.

➤ Till the Morning Comes

It was supposed to stop after that summer. My mom told me it would, and when she told my dad about it—him just home from third shift, his whiskers all grown back in already, eyes hungry for something none of us ever had for him—he just licked his lips and told me to get on back in there. That he wished he had the luxury of being scared.

Because my mom couldn't help me then, because all she could do was sit on the couch, I'd do it, I'd walk down the hall to my room. Or, our room then, mine and Nicholas, my little brother, who my dad called Señor Accidento, like the Spanish was supposed to hide what he meant.

Before Easter that year, it had been my room and only mine. But that Good Friday, Uncle Jamison was at the door, smiling a guilty smile. He was just turned twenty-six. I only knew it because I heard my dad say to my mom that twenty-six was too old to be living like he was. My mom didn't disagree, but still, Jamison was her little brother, and he didn't have anywhere else to go. And anyway, his plan wasn't to stay forever. He was just going to work for a couple of months, maybe get enough bread saved to move on to the next thing, whatever that was going to be.

I know I should have idolized him or something, let him be everything I planned on being, but already with Jamison you could tell he was a walking public service announcement. I guess I should thank him, really. I might never have gone on to college without the warning he'd been.

But I'm not going to thank him.

For his room, the one that had been Nicholas's—the one that my dad had had pool table plans for, before Señor Accidento—Jamison unboxed all his old high school stuff that my mom had been keeping in the attic for him. It was mostly old crackly posters and flags and T-shirts too ratty to wear anymore, but—his words—"good for display," to remind him who he was, to show that he was still being loyal to his old plans.

Four years after what happened happened, I'd find one of those memory T-shirts in the rag box in the garage, and hold it to my face and not let myself cry.

As for his posters, though, they're gone. I burned them myself, especially the velvet ones that felt like the fur of some animal not quite from our world. Band posters, from when Jamison had been on the road, all over the country. They had intricate, stoned designs all over them, and always skeletons, skeletons, skeletons.

That summer I was twelve. The skeletons were the reason I was afraid to go back to my room anymore. To mine and Nicholas's room. They didn't glow, quite, but they held the light from the hall in a way that made me want to look away.

I knew they were just pictures, paintings, whatever, but still, the way Jamison had them on either side of Nicholas's bed, like guards, they were always looking at me when I walked past, their mouths somehow smiling like they didn't care at all about this being dead thing.

I'd tried walking close to Jamison's side of the hall then just darting across at the last moment for my room, but it didn't help. And running— that was the worst. The one time I'd tried, I'd been sure those long spindly fingers were just skating down the back of my shirt, waiting for a bunch in the fabric to grab onto, pull me in.

I'd started wetting the bed again, yeah. After two years dry.

Every time it happened, Nicholas would be sure to announce it at the breakfast table. My dad's bleary eyes settling on me, some Spanish name for me forming in his head, I knew: El Pissorino, Pancho Yellowpants, Señor Wetsheets.

I hated him.

But, my mom said, she'd had the same problem until fifth grade herself. It would pass, it would go away, and everybody would forget.

And Uncle Jamison, he was on her side about it, almost by default, just because my dad was tolerating him so poorly. Making such a show of it, how encumbered he was. How much he wanted to be playing pool. Every day he'd circle classifieds or advertisements for eight-foot tables, and leave them where we could all see how put upon he was being here. How Jamison was just one more nail in the coffin of my dad's dreams.

But I'm not stupid, either. He was just a dad, like all the rest. You check your dreams at the door, pretty much.

Uncle Jamison, though.

The job he got, from his time in the army, it was driving an ambulance. In a perfect world, he'd have worked the day shift, so been gone when my dad was home, then been home when my dad was working. But they both worked nights that summer. And every breakfast—dinner for them, in their backwards world—after Nicholas had announced that I'd "tee-tee'd the bed," Jamison would draw what attention he could away from me, regale us with stories of the last night's calls.

There were home abortions, there were knife fights, and, twice, there was a woman standing on the median with a human ear in a plastic baggie, like she was just the delivery girl.

But the story I remember most is about a family.

The call Dispatch got was second-hand somehow, just that somebody'd seen some headlights dying way down the hill, like maybe a drunk had missed the turn. But that was over by the tracks, where the ground just fell straight away like cliffs in the movies. You didn't drive down there, you slammed down there, and only came back up on a towrope. According to Jamison, when the cars nosedived off there, after the riders had been declared dead, they'd wait until the car'd been winched back up to even peel the people up from the seats and headliners.

Anyway—you've got to picture Jamison telling it, his spoon full with eggs (he hated forks), the way he'd lean forward, his hair shaggy, his eyes hot and staring at all of us, trying to make it real—Jamison took his paramedic Robbie out there, and they found the headlights like they didn't want to, and it was an old VW bus, all painted paisley with flowers. Hippies. Deadheads. Jamison's old running buddies, pretty much. Where he was headed, anyway.

"And?" I heard myself saying, even though I had to pee again, bad.

He smiled, had me.

It wasn't a busload of Deadheads at all, as it turned out. Well, just one, one who'd grown up, got out, had kids now, but just had never sold his old three-hundred thousand mile bus, because that would be like cashing in his past, trading it for a used dishwasher. Not all dads leave their dreams at the door, I guess. Some hide them in the closet. And, Jamison, he was talking about this dad, sure, this Deadhead, but he was really making an argument for his posters, that he insisted to my mom would just scare me more if we packed them away with the sheets and towels. Better to leave them out on the wall, let me get used to them, let me beat them, learn to walk down that hall, right into manhood.

"You mean to tell me some of you actually and really grow up?" my dad said then.

Jamison grinned and looked the opposite direction.

It wasn't a real grin. Not at all. More like he was giving my dad this one free, just because it was morning, just because the sun was shining.

My dad snorted and threw his balled-up napkin down onto his plate, clattered off to the morning news, the volume jacked as high as it would go.

"Jamison," my mom said then, when it was safe. She was warning him about this story, about his audience here—*us*—but he held his hand up that it was harmless, that this was nothing.

"And when I turned the ambulance off, we could both like *hear* it," he said, "coming through the window and all. Singing. Somebody down there was *singing*, man, just real light, real perfect like."

"Singing," Nicholas repeated, as if tasting it, hearing it like Jamison had.

"But when we got down there, that's when we saw it," Jamison went on, his voice dropping to a whisper now, because my mom was all the way over at the sink, with my dad's dishes. "The two kids, this old reformed hippie's two kids, they were in back, seatbelted in like they should have been, not hurt at all, hands in their laps just like they were at church, man."

" 'Who was that singing, y'all?' my medic Robbie asked," Jamison said, his face somehow even closer to us now, then he nodded, getting us to already believe the next part: " 'It was Dad,' the kids said, like it was the most obvious thing in the world."

Only, as Jamison told it, the dad here, this old freeze-dried hippie out to show his kids the way it used to be, he'd been dead-on-impact five or six hours ago, the steering wheel coring his heart right out of his body.

But the song.

Here Jamison started snapping, just slow at first, and then humming it in his chest, and when I heard my own voice falling in—I knew the song from somewhere, must have heard it leaking under his door once—I pushed away from the table, tried to swallow whatever was in my mouth, and stifflegged it back to mine and Nicholas's room, only—

This is the part I hate.

As I passed Jamison's room, trying to avert my eyes from the posterspace above his bed, I saw something stepping neatly into his closet, something only still there because I wasn't supposed to have walked down the hall as fast as I had.

A heel, bone white, no sound at all.

My heart fell into my stomach and I peed myself right there, started crying until my dad came back to stand over me, disappointed again, enough that it came off him in waves.

For the next week, I slept maybe four hours total, each minute of that by accident, so that I woke shuddering.

"Was it real?" Nicholas asked me once—Jamison's story about the singing dad who was already dead—and I told him no, and then he asked why I was doing that, then?

"What?"

"With your—" He did his throat to show: I was humming. The song. It was the only way to keep myself awake.

Because Jamison worked at night, his room was empty, and because of the air conditioner in his window, my dad wouldn't let my mom keep his door closed, so all night, sitting in my bed, I could see his room with the light off. Part of the room.

If it would have been school, my grades would have dropped, but as it was, the only thing that fell off was my eating.

"He'll snap out of it," my dad told my mom, staring at me over her shoulder because it wasn't a prediction he was making here, but a threat.

"Sixth grade will be here before you know it," my mom promised, whenever he was at work.

I hummed to myself instead of answering, and Jamison—sent by my mom—made the effort, tried to sit me down, tell me he'd just been joshing, that of course the music never stops, that it had probably been the radio, some old 8-track or another, the kids had been confused, in shock from losing their dad, but it was too late. I already knew the song. The words had even started to come to me, some, from a place inside me I didn't even know I had.

Nine days after the breakfast story, deep in the watchful night, something crossed again, moving from alongside the bed to Jamison's closet.

I couldn't even pee myself this time.

And then my dad was standing there in the doorway.

He'd been drinking, was home early, too early.

He just stared down at me, lying there breathing all wrong, so obviously not asleep.

Nothing crossed behind him.

I wanted to sneak out, sleep in the living room, and did once, but woke to Nicholas tugging on my blanket. He'd got scared.

I went back and we both slept in my bed together, front-to-back, instead of him in the cot, and in the morning he told on me again, about having an accident, and this time I hit him. It was supposed to be on the side of the head but caught him on the neck. He held the pain down under his hand and glared at me, his lips tight, but didn't tell. It was the end of him crawling into my bed, though. The end of me using him as a shield. The end again of anything like sleep.

At night my sheets, they were starting to feel furred, velvety, so that I'd have to turn my lights on to be sure they weren't, then turn them off again, in case my dad pulled up, saw my window glowing, wasting electricity, trying to light the whole neighborhood.

By the time summer was halfway over, I'd convinced myself it was all made-up, that I was scaring myself, and even managed to sleep with my back to the door a time or two, but then I heard the humming again. The song. And it wasn't coming from me.

Nicholas. In his sleep.

I shook him until he cried, never really waking up, then I was secretly relieved when my mom came to sit by his cot until he went to sleep again. She made it safe enough to close my eyes. Her feet swished on the carpet as she left.

Except, when I opened my eyes, she was still there, her head on Nicholas's cot, her breath regular.

Meaning that those footsteps—

I shook my head no, no, and the days started to blur into the nights, the breakfasts into the dinners, my days and nights upside-down now too, and some afternoons I even stood right there on the edge of the doorway to Jamison's room, and watched the skeleton faces watch me back.

What I was doing was willing myself to grow up.

But that was coming.

And my mom was right, probably: it would have all passed, been over with the summer, or at least with Jamison moving on to his next big scheme.

Except one night, the smell of urine rising from my bed again, me breathing harder than I should have been, I heard the footsteps again, that bone smoothness across the carpet.

It was Nicholas, groggy.

"I'm telling dad," he said, and I reached out, grabbed his arm.

He looked down to it, up along it to me.

"No," I told him, and then felt it for the first time: the breeze, the wind, the pull.

It was crossing me, moving towards Jamison's room.

I breathed in, breathed out. Shook my head no but could still feel it.

"What?" Nicholas said, trying to pull away, and I closed my eyes, said it to him, what I never should have: "Just get me the extra sheets, okay?" Our linen closet, it was the second closet in Jamison's room. The far door.

To seal the deal, I promised him a little car I didn't play with anymore, the one I always caught him playing with, had to hide.

"The red one?" he said, falling asleep again just standing there.

"The red one," I nodded, and then he slouched away, stepped across the hall into the velvet darkness, and, moments later the air stopped crossing my bed, and the next thing I knew, my mom was shaking me, then my dad was, until he felt the stickiness on my skin, pulled back in disgust.

"Where is he?" my mom was saying, insisting.

My dad just looked at me, waiting.

I sat up, pushed back into the corner, and nodded across the hall, to Jamison's room, and in two strides my dad was over there, turning it over, ripping it down, until Jamison got back, stood there, and that's when my dad did what he did to Jamison, that the cops had to come stop, finally, and Jamison's paramedic Robbie had to clean up even though it wasn't his shift anymore.

And then all of us forgot how to sleep.

Me and my mom sat in the living room watching nothing on television, her crying in her chest every few minutes—her son gone with no explanation, her brother in a coma, her husband in jail for the weekend, her other son a bedwetter, a fraidy cat, a traitor.

Every light in the house was on.

Three nights later my dad knocked on his own front door, waited for my mom to open it back for him.

We went to see Jamison together, as a family.

His face was a mummy face, plastic tubes taped all over him, his life reduced to an electric green beep on a monitor.

"They shaved his beard," my mom finally said.

It had been one of my dad's complaints.

And as far as Nicholas, the police had nothing. They were waiting for

Jamison to wake up, explain it all somehow, but were ready to write it off as another runaway too.

On the way back to the house we stopped at Nicholas's favorite place, the hamburger joint that used to be the concession stand for the drive-in, when there'd been a drive-in.

We chewed the food and swallowed the food and never tasted any of it.

Halfway home, my mom motioned my dad to stop so she could throw up. He reached across, held her hair up for her, and in that moment it was good between them again. Good enough.

That night they ushered me back to my room in a way that I didn't take to mean that my brother was gone, but that I'd lost him. That I'd traded him. And I had. Then my mom squeezed my hand goodnight, my dad patted my headboard, and they closed their bedroom door, chocked the chair under the knob like they did. I knew the sound, what it meant: another ritual. For Nicholas.

Before, when they'd start—but this time was going to be quiet, I knew, both of them probably crying the whole time—I'd cross into Nicholas's room, wrench the dial on the air conditioner over, to drown them out.

This time, though, it was already on, already blowing.

For maybe five minutes I made myself stand at the door, feeling that coolness wash past, staring into the wreck of Jamison's stuff, but I still couldn't cross over.

Instead, I got the wooden bat from my closet, held it backwards to hook the butt of the handle on the edge of the door, and pulled it shut. Told Nicholas I was sorry sorry sorry. Prayed at first that he could hear me, and then a more guilty prayer: that he couldn't.

Before going to my bed, I stood over the toilet until I finally peed a trickle, like that was the trade I was offering.

It didn't work.

Because my parents still had their door shut, I shut mine too, laid a pair of pants down along the bottom to hide the light I was leaving on.

I had to sleep, I mean.

Already there were fuzzy, moving things at the edge of the tunnels I was looking down. The tunnels that were getting skinnier and skinnier, turning more into straws, pinholes, the world farther and farther away. Or maybe it was me who was backing away.

When the sounds started from my parent's room finally, I rolled over on my bed, wound the sheets tight and pressed my pillow over my head, and somewhere in there, for the first time in I didn't know how long, I fell asleep.

I didn't know it, of course, or, only knew it in the past tense, when I woke up all at once staring not at the wall like I'd meant, like I thought was safe, but at my door.

What?

It was still shut, there was nothing wrong.

But there was.

I felt the yellow warmth pooling under me: the pair of jeans I'd stuffed along the bottom of the door, they were gone.

And the cold air I'd felt washing past me before, it was going the other way now. Again. Pulling.

And there was the humming, the song.

It was coming from me, I was making it without meaning to, but it was larger too. I was singing *with* the song that was already happening.

I shook my head no, pushed as far into the back wall as I could.

The light in the hall was on too. Or, worse, light was spilling from Jamison's room.

"Mom," I creaked, hardly even a whisper, and immediately wished I hadn't.

There were two shadows on the other side of the door. Feet.

"Mom?" I said again, shaking my head no, my bladder emptier than it had ever been.

It was like I was at the old drive-in before they tore it down. Like I was watching the close-up of some doorknob starting to twist, everybody in their cars holding their breath, only watching through their fingers.

But there were no bugs dying in the cone of projected light here, and nobody was about to honk, kill the moment.

It was really happening.

"Dad," I finally whispered, my last, lastmost resort.

It wasn't him either, though.

When this door opened, it was Jamison standing there. Jamison with his shaggy beard, his too-long jeans like always, but different too. His skin loose on him somehow, and crackly, like paper that's been rained on then dried in the sun. His eyes already falling back into his sockets.

In his arms, sleeping, Nicholas.

I stood from my wet bed, faced him and shied away both at once. Wanted to hug him and scream at the same time.

Behind his beard, Jamison was mouthing the words of the song.

I nodded, understood somehow, hummed my part, filling the empty shapes he was making, the shapes he was leaving out there in the air for me to color in with my voice.

It was a kind of magic, I think.

The only way it could be.

"Tell Sissy, tell her—" he said, grinning that same grin from the day he'd first shown up, and then just held Nicholas across the threshold, like there was some rule about that too, that he could come no farther, that I was the one who was going to have to finish this.

I shook my head no, that I couldn't, that I wasn't stro—that Nicholas was too heavy.

But then he was my brother, too.

I crossed the room on robot legs, took him from my uncle's arms, and only staggered under the weight a little at first, like I could do this impossible thing, but then it was too much, just all at once.

I turned for a place to lay him down, knew it couldn't be my wet bed, knew his cot had all my little cars on it already, in offering, and I fell. First to one knee, then forward, trying to cradle Nicholas as best I could. Like a brother should.

It worked.

When he hit the carpet he came awake, looked up at me and then behind me.

I looked too but Jamison was already gone, the door across the hall sucking shut harder than should have been possible.

The next morning my dad found Nicholas and me sleeping back to front again, on the floor, and kept his boots on and laid down beside us, held us both so tight, nodding something to himself I think, wiping his face maybe, and at some point the phone started ringing.

My dad still didn't let us go. The three of us listened to my mom's footsteps crossing the kitchen, the phone cutting off mid-ring, the murmur of her saying okay to the hospital, of her thanking them for the call, for telling her this news that was probably for the best, and then we cringed from the sound of her hundred pounds falling into the stove, clattering down with the pans, not getting back up from that sheet of curled-at-the-edges linoleum.

"Jamison," I said.

"Jamison," Nicholas said too, but different than I had.

My dad just shook his head, pressed his closed eyes into my back, and did he start playing pool that next year, staying out later and later until he finally just stayed gone one night, and did Nicholas try twice to kill himself four years later, each time in the closet of his bedroom? Did my mom ever get up from the kitchen floor, let one of us pick the pans up for her? Years later, burning a pile of posters, would I think I saw Jamison, just hunched over real small in the velvet, walking away?

It doesn't matter.

All that matters is right then, that morning, having Nicholas back, our dad with his arms around us like it should have been, and that my mom was right: after that summer, I never wet the bed even once, even when I wake in my own house with that hum in my chest some nights and feel my way to the sink, fumble the light on—always the light—and find there in the soap tray, or balanced on the lip of the medicine cabinet, a little red car that wasn't there before.

Because they don't know. Because they think that can still work.

You can hide them in boxes, though, if you want, the little cars, and then put those boxes in the attic or the basement, and not tell anybody, just walk through your life with a song in your head, one that scares you, but you can't stop singing it either, because if you ever do—

Most nights, after fumbling the light over the sink on, I make it to the toilet, I mean, don't have to explain anything to my wife.

For those other nights, though, I've tiled the bathroom floor, and in front of the sink, and when I finally make myself lie back down, I'm always sure to have left the closet door behind me open, so that if Jamison wants to stand there, keep me safe for one more night, he can. Please.

➤ The Sons of Billy Clay

Because it was still his first week, Walter made Sandro bring the burgers. Because Sandro probably still believed the stories—that Walter had once left another guard down at the other end of C Block, alone, in population—Sandro clocked out like you had to when leaving the complex, went through all the security checks, then drove the six miles to the only place with decent burgers at three in the morning.

"Get lost, *kimo?*" Walter said. He'd been in the break room twenty minutes already.

Sandro set the $14.72 of burgers down, made no eye contact.

"Don't be a baby now," Walter said, unrolling the bag.

There were four burgers. He took three, slid the other one across the table for Sandro.

"What the hell?" Sandro said.

"I'm older," Walter said, "need the calories."

Sandro pushed the bag back across the table.

"Have it your way," Walter said, tearing into the first burger. "More for me, yeah?"

Three bites in, though, a glob of ketchup splattered onto the front of Walter's uniform shirt.

He stared at it, his teeth bared, nostrils flaring.

"That my fault too?" Sandro said.

"You watch it, kid."

Walter stood, peeled his shirt off and twisted the stain up to a point, let it soak in the sink.

"Go ahead," he said, his back still turned. "Eat one. Long time till sun-up."

"It going to stain?" Sandro asked.

Walter came back in his undershirt, killed the burger in two bites he had to close his eyes to get swallowed all the way down.

"Thought I told you it was the place with the yellow sign?"

"I went to the place with the yellow sign."

Walter unwrapped the next burger like he was a detective.

"Got that glass front, just south of the oil change place?"

"You don't have to eat them," Sandro said.

"Like I said," Walter said, biting in again, "long time till sun-up."

"What's that?"

"What?"

Walter's shoulder. Sandro was pointing with his chin.

Walter snorted a laugh out. "Used to be a guy, a lifer. I got him infirmary duty and he did the ink. Took five weeks, all told."

"But what is it?"

"You blind?"

Walter pulled the strap of his shirt to the side. It was a rodeo bull, kicking its hind legs at the sky, like used to be on beer cans.

"You rode?" Sandro said, smiling with disbelief.

Walter closed his eyes in disgust, finished the burger and offered the third one to Sandro. Sandro crossed his arms, set his teeth.

"Fine by me," Walter said, and peeled the wrapper.

He'd never eaten four at once before, but he'd be damned if he wasn't about to.

"So what?" Sandro said. "You're some ex-cowboy or something? Yee-haw, all that?"

Walter chewed, swallowed.

Probably Sandro had spit on the burgers, that's what it was.

"You and me," he said, "you know what they used to call us, forty years ago?"

"Stupid? Degenerates?"

"Bulls. *Gun* bulls. What the prisoners used to call the guards."

"So you never really rode?"

"Not this one," Walter said, tapping his shoulder, "not him. Nobody did. Ever. That's the thing."

Sandro looked over to the shirt in the sink, Walter was pretty sure.

Walter huffed a bit of a laugh out his nose. His eyes weren't smiling though.

"Billy Clay," he said, almost at a whisper. Like reverence.

Sandro came back to him.

Walter tapped the tattoo again.

Sandro shook his head, said, "What time's break over?"

"It didn't start until you just got back," Walter said around a bite.

Sandro leaned forward, his elbows on the table now.

"But you tried, right?" he said. "To ride that one?"

"Billy Clay? Notice how I'm still alive, sitting here?"

Sandro shrugged.

"It's how you can tell," Walter said. "Nobody ever sat Billy Clay for eight full seconds."

Sandro stared at him, his eyes flat like you used when laying down the law to the prisoners just off the bus. "Billy Clay," he said. "That's not any bull name."

"Exactly," Walter said.

The fourth burger actually hurt, going down, but Walter didn't show it.

"Hot water'll set it," Sandro said across the break room.

Walter was at the sink, working on the stain. "Thanks, Grandma," he said. "Hungry yet? I know a boy over in C Block's that's usually up about now, he could probably feed you something."

Sandro straightened his leg under the table, sent a chair clattering into the counter.

Walter smiled, kept rubbing the stain.

"Don't worry," he said. "You'll figure things out soon enough."

"Turn into you, right?"

"If you're lucky."

"Get pictures drawn on my body of things I never did."

Walter set his teeth together, scrubbed harder.

"I rode," he said. "Just not him."

"Like putting a notch in your bedpost for girls you've never—"

Walter turned around, the shirt still twisted in his hands.

"Nobody rode Billy Clay. They kicked him off the circuit, had him destroyed before he could even get any stud fees."

"Because he was so good?"

"Because he was . . . "

Walter squeezed his eyes shut, shook his head no, but did it anyway: sat down across from Sandro again.

"What I'm telling you, you shouldn't be knowing yet, okay?"

A smile ghosted the corners of Sandro's mouth. He shrugged, leaned back in his chair.

"Who am I going to tell? The rodeo police?"

Walter stared at him, let the joke die.

"Do you believe in the afterlife?" he said, finally. "That a man's spirit can leave his body, go somewhere else?"

Sandro shrugged.

"Yes or no?" Walter said, slapping his hand on the table.

"Okay," Sandro said. "Sure. Yeah."

"Well then," Walter said, flicking his eyes to the break room door, to be sure it was all the way shut. "Imagine this. 1946, right after the war. This one soldier, he comes back home but forgets to stop killing. Like he's doing it for fun now. Just whoever, and hiding them in his daddy's barn. Sick stuff, I mean. Even dragging people in from the graveyard. Pieces of them."

"I thought Billy Clay was a bull?"

"Now this soldier, you can guess he's not the only soldier to have come back, right? Only, when he went in, he was the only one in his town who signed up to beat a murder rap. He'd been doing it before the war too."

"My cousin went in the Army for breaking into this old lady's—"

"This isn't about your cousin. This is about Billy Clay. Finally some of those other soldiers and their dads, they figured out what Billy was up to, and locked him in his barn, lit it all four corners. Only, they forgot to let the livestock out first. So the horses and cattle, when the smoke got too thick, they came busting through the door. The first few got shot, just from itchy triggers, but the rest just, bam, went, gone."

"Billy Clay?"

"Burned to a crisp. Along with his kills. Except instead of burning alive, he'd hung himself from the hay loft, before the flames could even get to him."

"I don't get it."

"Yeah. Nobody else did either. At first. But then a bull turned up on the rodeo circuit, its horns black from fire."

"It was one of the ones that got out."

"And crazier than all get-out, yeah. Good stock for bucking, I mean. Only, it turned out, *too* good. He stomped two dead just in the chute, then gored another, threw him back into the pens, and he couldn't ever be put in the trailer with the other stock. He'd kill them too. But when everybody really knew was when there were some soldiers in the stands once, still in uniform. Billy Clay, that's what everybody was calling him by then, he chucked his rider, only, instead of going after that cowboy like he usually did, or hooking a clown or two, he charged the stands, and got up in the middle of those soldier uniforms, and made them wish they'd never come back."

"So you're saying—"

"I'm not the one who said it. Everybody knew. Billy Clay's spirit had left his body when he hung himself, and fell down into the stalls. Into a bull."

"But they killed him. That bull."

"Had to chase him clear through town, but yeah. Shot him down I don't know how many times, just to be sure, then used a tractor to drag him off."

"This is all real, too?"

"What do you mean?"

"You saw it or something?"

Walter shook his head again, ran his fingers through his grey hair.

"I just told you the *story* of it," he said.

"Yeah," Sandro said, shrugging. "It was neat, too. Like Goldilocks or something."

Walter slammed his palm down on the table again, used it to help him stand, lean over Sandro.

"Do you think I'd get Billy Clay tattooed on my shoulder if he *wasn't* real?"

"People do some stupid shit, I guess."

Walter spun around, went back to the sink, the cold water.

"He's real," he said. "Don't you worry about it."

"*Was* real, you mean," Sandro said. "Right?"

Walter leaned over, spit into the sink, watched it trail away down the drain.

"Ever hear of C Bar T?" Walter said, buttoning his shirt back up.

"Over in Allenville, that college kid bar?"

"They're a contractor," Walter said, tucking in now. "For the rodeo. Their specialty is bulls."

"Good for them, I guess."

"Yeah," Walter said. "Good for them. Their bulls, though, they're not like the rest of them. Ever hear of Whirlwind Baby, or Run Amok?"

"They were in that barn too or something?"

"Or something, yeah."

Walter cut his eyes to the break room door again.

"What?" Sandro said.

"Nothing. Break's over."

"So you're just going to leave it there, then? Isn't this the part where you scare me?"

"We're not at a campfire, kid."

"Whatever. Thanks. Been a real education."

With that Sandro stood, looked away, at the sink again, maybe. It didn't matter. Just *away*, long enough for Walter to step in, take him by the shirt front and slam him against the wall, so their mouths were now inches from each other.

"In 1998, Run Amok killed three riders and one clown. Whirlwind bucked off four riders in the nationals, and two of them got carted off to the hospital. One didn't come back."

By now Sandro had his hands around Walter's wrists.

"You're spitting on me," he said.

"But Run Amok and Whirlwind Baby weren't their real names, you know that?"

"What?"

"Their real names."

With that Walter pushed Sandro into the wall again and stepped back, breathing hard.

"You knew them as Bill and Frank, I guess?" Sandro said. "Tom and Marty?"

"0786388126 and 0438576399."

Now Sandro was just staring at Walter.

"Prisoners?"

Walter stared at him, turned his head to the side to rub his nose with his forearm.

"Their names were Matley Knowles and Randall Perkins. Knowles killed six people on the outside, three in here that we knew about, maybe more. Perkins, he had a thing for eating people's fingers. Didn't really care if they lived or not, just so long as he got some good old finger meat."

"I don't—" Sandro said, "what are you saying here?"

"When they drug Billy Clay, the *bull* Billy Clay, when they drug him out to rot in the fields, that same night a man named Charlie Tinker, a butcher by trade, went out and carved him up. Put the meat on ice."

"Charlie Tinker. C Bar T."

"And here I thought you were stupid."

"So he's been feeding it to his stock all these years?"

Walter shook his head no, rubbed his nose again. When he talked, it was lower now, almost a whisper. "It doesn't work like that, kid. No."

Sandro shrugged, waiting.

"'Then how does it work?'" Walter said, for Sandro.

"It's your bullshit story, man," Sandro said back.

"There's been more, too," Walter said. "Bulls, I mean. That nobody could ride. From here."

"Prisoners."

"Prisoners, yeah. Charlie Tinker found out they make the best ones. But they have to be in for a while first, to go the right kind of crazy. The patient kind. The saving-it-all-up-for-the-ride kind."

Sandro shook his head, laughed to himself, and put his hand to the door. "Got to make rounds," he said. "Right?"

"Red Eye, Sailor's Moon, Caught in the Middle, Barn Burner."

Sandro stopped with his hand to the knob. Closed his eyes then opened them.

"All from here, right?"

"Thanks to me, yeah," Walter said.

Now Sandro looked up to Walter.

Walter nodded.

"I don't understand," Sandro said.

"You couldn't. I know. Let him with the ears to hear, hear."

"What?"

"Billy Clay," Walter whispered, putting his hand over Sandro's, on the door knob. Then he hooked his chin, for Sandro to follow him. They went to the freezer, to a package of frosted-over brussels sprouts way in the back. In the box under all the burned green was a glass tube with a cork in the end.

Walter held it up, said it again: "Billy Clay."

In the tube was meat.

"What do you mean?"

"C Bar T," Walter said. "They keep me supplied. The old man, Tinker, he figured it out somehow. What you have to do, what they pay me five grand a *pop* to do, is slip a bit of this into some prisoner's grub. Then, after he gets shanked while we're not looking, you just collect whatever he's thrown back up, get it on ice, overnight it to them."

"And they feed that to—"

"They feed *them* to the bulls, yeah. It's the only way it works. The soul gets trapped in there, in the meat."

"Are you serious?"

"It's just prisoners. Their chance to be famous. To escape, kill again, all that. They'd probably pay me to do it, if they knew."

Instead of saying anything, Sandro just studied Walter's face. Finally Walter shrugged. "Next time, I'll let you watch. Maybe put it in their food or something. Last meal them, on death row. It makes collection easier."

Now Sandro smiled a bit. "You don't go to the rodeos anymore, do you?" he asked.

"I read about it."

"Yeah, well. It's changing, *kimo*. Regulations. Helmets, padded vests. Points. Celebrity announcers."

"You can still die, or worse."

"Or get barred."

Walter licked his lips, studied Sandro.

"Barred?"

"Like if your stock is too mean."

"But they're supposed to be mean."

"Not killers, though. Not anymore. The television, they want mad, yeah. But more like athletic. Like the bull's part of the performance. Like it understands, but just wants out, wants it to be over."

"The old man would have told me if he was looking for more docile prisoners, if he wanted . . . "

Sandro was trying not to smile was the thing.

"What?" Walter said.

"C Bar T, right?" Sandro said back.

Walter shrugged, looked to the break room door again, like he expected a bull to come crashing through at any moment now. When he turned back to Sandro, Sandro had pulled his shirt to the side, to show the scar tissue from a brand that covered the right side of his chest: c—t.

Walter backed up a step, into the counter.

"He heard you were telling people about it, Walter. Getting *tattoos* about it."

"No, wait, I—"

Before he could finish, Sandro stepped forward, slammed his fist hard into Walter's stomach.

The hamburgers came back up. The meat. It made Walter throw up more, and more, until there were red and black strings of it everywhere.

Sandro held it in his hand, let some of the bloody vomit run down into one paper cup, then another.

"They don't call him Tinker for nothing," Sandro said, and he folded a paper towel over the paper cups.

Bleary-eyed now, Walter stared at the cups. They'd never be enough, he knew. You had to keep it *fresh*. If Sandro'd been doing this for half his life already, he might have at least the glimmer of a—a . . . but then Walter felt something collapsing inside him, and realized that whatever wet cavern had been holding his spirit for forty-six years, it was caving in now, taking him with it.

"The old man figured out that you can pull the soul out without even knifing the guy first, yeah? Oh, and guess what else."

Walter coughed. Sandro kicked him in the side, so that Walter fell over.

"Guess what *else*," Sandro said.

Walter looked up.

"When you pull the soul like this, the host, whatever bull eats it, it remembers, man. Yeah. Everything. But it can't say anything about it. Only in the ride, man. Eight seconds of pure expression . . . "

Walter fell to his knees, tried to hold himself up with the counter. Reach for Sandro, at the sink now, washing his hands. "Oh, and boss?" Sandro said.

Walter opened his mouth but couldn't get any breath out.

"Thanks for the burgers, man," Sandro said, and threw the balled-up paper towel at Walter's face then swung wide around him, back into the real world, leaving Walter alone on the floor, his body already bucking and twisting, blood frothing at his nostrils.

The cameras were going to love him.

▶ So Perfect

The killers here are Tammy and Brianne. They're seventeen. Well, Tammy's seventeen, but Brianne always lies that she's seventeen. They're both juniors at the new Danforth High School, "Home of the Titans," rah rah rah. As to where "Titans" comes from, none of the students really know. The complete name of the school is Susan B. Danforth High School. They're not really sure who she is either. The suburb they live in isn't old enough to have any history. The year Tammy and Brianne were born, the land their Geography class would someday sit on probably had a cow standing on it, if anything. No titans, anyway.

As for Tammy and Brianne, you've seen them before, at all the malls and department stores. Here's a typical Tammy/Brianne conversation:

"And did you see her nametag?"

"Don't even start."

"Like I would be using somebody else's credit card, though? Please."

"Shh, shh. She might be listening. Her dad's got to be in prison or something, right? To let her work at a register like that?"

"You're making excuses for her."

"No. I just don't want my car to get keyed. You know how these people—"

The girl they're talking about here is Joy Kane, known in the halls of Danforth as "Candy Cane" because of the red-and-white striped stockings she wears every day. Her job is adding tax to the purchases of her classmates, and checking identification. And her father isn't in prison; he's dead.

But Joy will be up soon enough. Right now it's Tammy and Brianne. They're taking the long way out of the mall, to swing by the display window of the pet shop. Not because they want to hold the puppies or kittens, and especially not the birds or lizards, but so—this is a game they play—they can bend over at the waist to tickle the glass, like all they can think about are these cute little adorable animals.

The reason they do this is so they can waggle their peel-off lumbar tattoos. Today Tammy has the typical blue curlicues, Brianna a baseball with the word Focus as the brand, but they've also tried the IF YOU CAN READ THIS, YOU'RE TOO CLOSE one, to great effect.

On a good day they can fill the sitting area behind them in fifteen minutes, and then pretend to be oblivious, shake their way out to the parking lot to laugh and laugh in Tammy's car.

On a bad day, though, all they'll attract is the junior high crowd.

Today is a bad day.

After the pet shop they glide through their favorite purse store, study themselves in the three-way mirror for an explanation.

"What'd you have for lunch?" Tammy asks Brianne.

This is also a typical conversation for them.

"Just coffee."

"You're lying. It had whipped cream on it."

"Pig."

"Slut."

"You wish."

Still, they leave together.

As for Joy, her shift goes over four hours later, and, walking to the corner where her mom will pick her up when she gets off, she doesn't key anybody's car, has forgotten all about Tammy and Brianne, really.

Two days later is a Friday. Tammy and Brianne are having a tanning contest on Brianne's back porch. Her dad, home early from work, is washing the Irish setter. The dog's name is Frederick.

Because it's funny to her, Tammy keeps arranging her bikini so as to make Brianne's dad have to look somewhere else.

"Did you see her today?" Brianne says, her voice bored and hot.

"Who?"

"Candy Cane."

"From the other day?"

"She remembered you, I think."

"Probably wanted to see my driver's license."

Brianne laughs about this, adds, "Like she doesn't know that horizontal stripes aren't really helping those tree trunks she calls legs?"

"They're probably supposed to distract from that sweater she always wears."

"Distract whom?" Brianne says, turning herself over on the chair, her skin glistening.

After that they just watch Brianne's dad wrestle with Frederick. It's the best kind of comedy, as it pretty much confirms everything they think about the class of people he represents.

"What's he doing now?" Tammy asks after about twenty minutes.

"He's not supposed to do it while the hair's still wet."

"Perfume?"

"It's for, like, ticks, I think."

Tammy sits up, lowers her glasses. "It keeps them off, you mean?"

"Something like that."

"Just from that part of Fred's *neck*?"

"It goes everywhere, I don't know. He's not supposed to do it while the hair's wet, though," Brianne repeats louder, for her dad's benefit. "It waters it down or something."

Tammy keeps her sunglasses tilted to watch. She's never seen anything like this—shouldn't the gardener be doing it, maybe? It is entertaining, though, Frederick squirming out again and again, his eyeballs white and desperate against all that shiny bronze fur.

But then Tammy has to turn over. Brianne follows. Now they're both staring through the plastic slat of their lounge chairs, into the grass.

"I've petted Fred, though," Tammy finally says.

"What? No, it doesn't—you can't get it on you. It says so on the package, I think. Safe for children."

"You've done it . . . *applied* it or whatever?"

"Of course not. He keeps the box in the garage, by my mom's extra keys."

"Beamer or Volvo?"

"They're in the same place."

"But—you . . . he wouldn't need to put that on Fred if there wasn't a problem, right?"

"A problem?"

"Ticks," Tammy almost whispers, as if saying it might attract them, or make them real enough to hear her anyway.

Brianne laughs to herself, says, "He's a dog, T. Why don't you try to be paranoid or something for a change?"

Tammy shakes her head in mock amusement, but is really studying the grass, for bugs.

Where she should be looking is on her towel, though.

One corner of it is trailing into the grass.

Crawling up it, still flat and brown and coppery, a tick.

That night while Tammy and Brianne are in the parking lot of the pool with all the other Danforth students, Brianne's dad starts throwing up, can hardly catch his breath.

Brianne's mom calls them, tells them to meet her at the emergency room.

This messes up everything they had planned for the night.

"You go on," Tammy tells Brianne.

She's standing by Bo Richardson, and never stops smiling as she says it.

"You're driving, T," Brianne says, smiling too, her eyes so pleasant.

"Show me later," Bo says to Tammy, pushing her lightly away, his hand large on her shoulder.

What he's talking about are the tan lines Tammy's promised him.

The whole way to the hospital Tammy doesn't say anything, and neither does Brianne.

"Well?" Brianne says to her mom, finally.

Her mom is eating a pastry from the snack machine. It sickens Tammy.

"It's poison," Brianne's mom says, leaning forward to touch both of them, as if she used to be them or something. "From the, y'know. Frederick."

"The tick medicine," Brianne says.

"He got it on his skin," Brianne's mom nods.

"He'll live though?" Tammy says.

"Yes, dear. Don't worry about—"

By this time they've already stopped listening, are already, in spirit, back at the parking lot with Bo and Seth and the rest, Joy at the edge of that crowd, rubbing out cigarettes with the toe of her Wicked Witch of the West boot. At least that's what Brianne calls it.

And of course, the rest of the weekend, except for when they sneak out, they're at Tammy's mom's house. Just because Brianne's dad is too gross to be around. The next time they see him is Monday morning, before school. They're only there to pick up Brianne's belt for Tammy to wear. Like every time, Tammy makes a production of cinching the belt in over and over again, like it won't get small enough for her.

"What have you been eating?" she says to Brianne, on the way down the stairs.

"Bo Richardson," Brianne tosses back quietly, and Tammy pushes her. It's in play—well, half in play—but Brianne stumbles forward anyway, into her dad, just rounding the corner.

"Girls, girls, girls . . . " he says, adjusting his tie.

It's the only thing he ever says to them anymore.

"Dad," Brianne says, stepping back, studying him up and down. "You look—how old are you?"

This has to be a joke, though. Or an insult. Both. Her dad shakes his head like a sad clown and leaves. They get the story from Brianne's mom later: over the last forty-eight hours, Brianne's dad has lost thirteen pounds.

Thirteen *pounds*.

Neither of the girls can say anything.

At the fitting for their bridesmaid dresses two days later (Brianne's slut cousin Clarice is pregnant, and doesn't have any real friends), they have the seamstress pin their dresses tighter and tighter.

"It's supposed to *hang*, though, sweetie," the seamstress says to Tammy.

Tammy's studying herself in the mirror.

"It will," Tammy says back, and then her eyes catch Brianne's, and they look away.

In the ashtray of Tammy's car, now, where it's been since lunch, is the tick medicine.

In what should be Texas History the next day, a Thursday, they're standing in the girls' locker room together. Nobody else is there. It's just them and, on the plastic bench between them—wood would be unsanitary—one dose of Frederick's tick medicine.

"How much do you want to lose?" Tammy asks.

"From where?" Brianne says back.

They're talking like they're in church.

Tammy smiles, nods to herself, then, all at once, moving fast so she won't have time to think, she breaks the tip off the applicator and turns it over onto her fingertip, daubs a print of it behind each ear. Like perfume.

The fumes burn her eyes a little.

She blinks fast, pretends it doesn't hurt, and passes the applicator to Brianne.

"Thirteen pounds," she says.

Brianne, trying to be careful, turns the vial upside down once, fast, on the thin skin of each wrist.

And then it's over.

"Trig?" Tammy says, holding her breath a little.

"You can't smell it, can you?" Brianne asks, trying to nevertheless.

" 'Safe for children,' " Tammy recites, and then it's Trigonometry, and, an hour later, the nurse. Because they've each started throwing up. From the Chinese food they ate at lunch.

The nurse doesn't smile, just sends them home.

By Saturday, the next time they see each other, Tammy's lost eight pounds, Brianne six.

"You've been eating," Tammy accuses.

"Could you?" Brianne says back.

The answer is no.

That night they float through the parking lot like runway models, their bellybutton rings glinting in the moonlight, and, this time when Bo and Seth and Davis ask them if they want to hit the Yogurt Shack, they do, and order all they want, and even pretend that it makes them a little drunk.

Really it's the fourteen collective pounds they've shed.

From across the parking lot Joy watches them, and at one point Tammy sees her watching, and keeps smiling anyway, maybe even smiles more, then drapes herself across either Seth or Davis or that other guy from Ashworth or wherever.

It doesn't matter.

On Wednesday, they're going in for the second fitting for their dresses.

To make it to size, on Sunday night in Tammy's basement they lock themselves in the pool room and tap the tick medicine out from Brianne's hollowed-out old lipstick tube.

"The notes will still be good," Tammy says, the applicator in her hand again.

The notes are the ones the nurse wrote for them; they're good until they're well again.

"Like I'll miss Trig," Brianne says, smiling with one side of her face.

"Or ever need it," Tammy adds.

The blouse Brianne's wearing is Tammy's.

A week ago, she'd have been able to fit into it, sure, but it wouldn't have fit, either.

Now, though—even Seth had taken a second look.

This time they each lose seven pounds in forty-eight hours, and Tammy doesn't ask if Brianne's been eating anything.

At school on Friday, Tammy sees Joy watching them again, and nudges Brianne.

They're in the cafeteria. *Eating.*

The only thing Joy's touched on her tray—she doesn't ever go off-campus for lunch—is her pudding. The foil is peeled back.

Tammy scratches at a spot under her hair and says, "I bet she's got a whole closet full of those tights. One for Monday, one for Tuesday . . . "

Brianne laughs into her Dr Pepper, has to look away.

"Maybe she wants to kill us," she says behind her hand.

"By committing fashion suicide then hoping we catch it too?" Tammy says back, and then they have to leave the cafeteria altogether. Not to the bathroom, though; this is an eating day.

That afternoon in their lounge chairs in Brianne's backyard—the pool boy's there, and he's even more fun to bother than Brianne's dad—Frederick keeps trying to chase a butterfly. Either the same one or the first one's twin, they can't tell. It always dives for the bushes though, then flutters back up a few minutes later, its shadow on the grass torturing Frederick.

It gets him thirsty enough that he has to come over, lick the sweat from the sides of their legs.

"The salt," Brianne explains.

"Pervert," Tammy says down to Frederick, scratching the top of his head with her long nails.

Frederick eats it up, finally creaks his body around to hook a hind leg up behind an ear, motorboat a furrow into his fur.

"I thought he was fixed," Tammy says, shaking her head away.

"I don't think you can get pregnant just by touching them, T," Brianne says, lowering her leopard print sunglasses to see what Tammy's talking about.

"The stuff's supposed to keep him from scratching like this, right?" Tammy says, sitting up, her top starting to slide off, the pool boy suddenly very still.

"I told you," Brianne says. "It all got on my dad's hand. Not on Frederick."

"He didn't do it again?"

"You want me to remind him?"

"What, you think he counts how many he's got left?"

"He's kind of scared of it now anyway."

"Can't you make him stop, though?"

By that time the pool boy's come to the rescue. Tammy just points down to Frederick.

"What's he doing?" she says to Brianne, drawing her legs up now.

The pool boy smiles, kneels down by the dog and comes up half a minute later with a plump grey tick, its black legs pedaling the air.

Tammy squeals and climbs the back of her chair. Brianne laughs.

"Kill it!" Tammy's saying, working up to a shriek.

"Why?" the pool boy says, holding it out before him—Tammy's forgotten about her swimsuit by now, and does have some stark tan lines—"When they're like this, they're full of babies, yeah?"

"Then—then—?" Tammy says, the back of her hand to her mouth.

"The toilet," Brianne says for the pool boy, who still hasn't looked away from what Tammy's not worried about. *"Right?"*

Which is when Brianne's mom steps out to see what's going on.

Instantly, the pool boy's posture changes and he's already heading for the bathroom they've let him use once before.

That night after dinner, stepping into the guest bathroom herself to check her face before Bo drops Tammy off, Brianne sees, smeared on the toilet seat, on purpose, the tick.

Without the medicine, even, she throws up into the sink until her eyes are hot.

When she steps into the dining room ten minutes later, Tammy's waiting.

"Start without me?" she says, touching the right corner of her mouth to show what Brianne's missed.

Brianne doesn't answer, just calls out to her mom that she's taking the Volvo and, instead of taking just one application from the shelf in the garage, she takes them all.

"Why?" Tammy asks, far enough away from Brianne's house that it's safe.

Brianne shakes her head no, doesn't say anything.

▶ ▶ ▶

That Saturday between trips to Tammy's upstairs bathroom, her mom calls up to the girls that Jill is pregnant too, now.

"Slut," Brianne says, smiling, teasing a fleck of vomit from her hair.

"Three, two, one . . . " Tammy smiles back. It's the launch sequence; staying unpregnant is all about timing, they know.

As her mom explains to them the next morning, though, what this means is that Jill is out of the wedding party. Because she's only fifteen. "It wouldn't look right."

"She's *showing*?" Tammy says, stacking her plate with French toast she's not going to eat.

"It's the principle, honey," her mom says back, fixing both girls in her eyes for a second longer than absolutely necessary.

"Then it's off?" Brianne says.

"The wedding?" Tammy's mom falsettos, blinking fast to show what she's meaning here, "heavens no. We just need an understudy."

"By Saturday?" Tammy whispers, incredulous.

"I'm sure you have just scads of friends . . . " her mom trails behind her, off to wherever. Church, maybe, after two hours of make-up and a handful of pills.

In her wake, Tammy and Brianne are silent, and then the bite of toast Brianne tried to sneak works its way up her throat and she's bent over the sink, dry heaving, Tammy guarding the door, waiting her turn.

That night, showering before the parking lot, and whatever might happen after the parking lot, Tammy's fingernail breaks off while washing her hair and the blood from her scalp seeps down over her face. The only reason she realizes its blood, even, is that it's gritty. And then she's throwing up again, and more, until her mom knocks on the bathroom door with the palm of her hand.

At her house, her hair still in her towel, her body too, Brianne walks through her living room to the garage.

What she's carrying is the box the tick medicine was in.

All that's left in it now is one half-application. The other eight are in the secret pocket of her purse.

The pool boy's in the backyard again, too, doing his thing.

Brianne smiles to herself, holds the towel on her head tighter than the one on her new body.

In the garage it's easy to see where the cardboard box had sat for however many months. It's a small square of light-colored wood. The rest, all around it, is stained brown, and greasy. Brianne looks behind her, like the pool boy's suddenly going to be standing in the door, and then follows the stain up the wall to the next shelf, all the gardening stuff.

The bottle of fertilizer her dad bought off the infomercial is leaking.

"Surprise," she singsongs to him, in her mom's voice.

It's why the cardboard was so greasy. It makes her look at her fingertips. With a spade she nudges the box into place, steps away, and then finds a reason to step outside. What she's pretending to look for is an earring she lost the other day.

What she's thinking about, though, on her knees in the grass with the pool boy, her towel barely there anymore—"Thinking about Tammy *now*?" she wants to say—is the blood on the toilet seat.

If he would do that when her parents weren't looking, what else might he do?

Ten minutes later, her towel all the way off now, she finds out, and wonders if he's even washed his hands since touching that toilet seat, and somehow that makes it even better.

At the parking lot an hour later, Tammy appraises her and finally says, "You've been eating again, haven't you?"

"Something like that," Brianne shrugs, no eye contact, and then the night swallows them again.

Three days later, the Wednesday before the wedding, Tammy and Brianne are standing at Joy's register again.

"Like you don't know me," Tammy is saying.

"It's, y'know, policy," Joy says back, watching a rounder of clearance shirts out by the aisle.

The y'know was funny to her, anyway.

"I see you at school," Tammy says.

Joy doesn't say anything back.

"You could be pretty, y'know?" Tammy adds, offering her license, holding it like it's the most boring thing ever.

Joy takes it, compares it to the signature on the card, and hands it back.

"Gee, thanks," she says, wanting to drill a dimple into her cheek with an index finger. "Who wouldn't want to be prettier?"

"Thinner, I mean," Tammy says like a secret, flashing her eyes to Brianne. But Brianne's not following yet.

"How would you like to be in a wedding with us?" Tammy says then, now not letting Brianne catch her eyes.

"This is a joke," Joy says back, sliding the receipt across to Tammy.

"No," Tammy says. "The wedding's a joke. The dress is already ready, though. It's—you. Just about ten pounds lighter."

"It would look good with your boots," Brianne adds, the muscles around her mouth tense like a smile.

Tammy kicks her a little where Joy can't see.

"Bo's going to be there," Tammy says. "And the rest of them."

"And I care about that?" Joy says, too fast.

"I wouldn't know," Tammy shrugs, signing the receipt, pushing it back. "Have you ever been in a wedding?"

Joy just stares at her.

Her mother's, Brianne just manages to hold back.

"Everybody's looking at you the whole time, you know?"

"At the bride," Joy corrects.

"Not this time," Tammy says. "Let's just say she's . . . carrying more baggage into the ceremony than—"

"The engagement photos were from the face up," Brianne interrupts, in step at last.

"It's the part of her most guys prefer, really," Tammy adds.

Joy rings the register open, stuffs the receipt in, says, "So what are you trying to say here?"

"I'm saying that you're not . . . what? 'Candy Cane'?"

"Right," Brianne chimes in, biting her top lip.

"I don't want to be like you, if that's what you're thinking," Joy says.

"Of course not," Tammy says, her voice a bit colder now. "I'm just saying. The final fitting is at seven tonight. Here."

She writes the address on the back of her customer copy, slides it to Joy.

"This is a joke," Joy says again. "You said the dress was too little anyway."

Tammy smiles. "No," she says. "The dress is just about the right size, I think. You just need to slender down a bit."

"By Saturday," Brianne says.

"Ten pounds?"

"It's not impossible."

"Look at us," Brianne says, striking a mock-glam pose.

"I'm not going to be there," Joy says, sliding the address back.

"Of course not," Tammy says, but doesn't take the address back either.

Thirty minutes after they're gone, Joy studies herself in the three-way back in the dressing rooms.

A bridesmaid?

She laughs at herself.

But then she remembers the way that Brianne-one had angled her body over, to show how little extra she was carrying.

Joy looks in the mirror again, and then turns sideways to look, and then shakes her head no, just keeps collecting clothes from the stalls.

A bridesmaid, yeah.

Except—it's stupid and she knows it's stupid—what if Bo Richardson really is there?

It could be like all the movies, where the charity case loser girl finally puts on mascara, shows up at the dance, the air suddenly different around her, charged.

Which Joy laughs at as well.

She's not twelve years old, after all.

But what if she gets to keep the dress, too?

This stops her.

Is that how it works at weddings? It would be cut specifically for her, after all.

Not that she would ever wear it again, of course.

But it might be fun to burn at the parking lot or something.

First she's going to have to fit into it, though.

Just in case Bo's really there.

"What's that about?" her mom asks at five, nudging Joy's smile with the knuckle of her index finger.

"Nothing," Joy says.

Just to show that she's not taking it seriously, Joy shows up to the fitting twenty minutes late. With a friend, Lacy.

"So this is it?" Lacy says to Tammy, fingering a peach-colored spaghetti strap out from a rack.

"Where'd you get those boots?" Brianne asks back.

Everybody grins uncomfortably, and then Brianne keeps Lacy in the waiting room while Tammy leads Joy by the arm back to the curtained stalls and the fitting pedestal.

"So what do I do?" Joy says, smiling with one side of her face.

"Nothing," Tammy says, "this is all me . . . " and starts taking measurements with a tape from what looks like a tackle box.

"You mean I don't try it on now?"

"Not like—not like you are, no," Tammy says, her lips tight around a straight pin she's not going to be using.

"What do you mean?"

"We don't want to, you know, stretch it or anything."

"Listen, I don't—"

"No, I say that in the nicest way. But, you can make a dress smaller, but you can't really let it out. That's all. There's not enough material. That's why you always start big."

"Then I can't do this, right? Is that what this is about? God, I don't even know why I'm here."

"Because you want to be beautiful," Tammy whispers up to her. "Now, what size shoe do you wear?"

Joy stares down at her for a long moment, then finally looks away, to the idea of the waiting room.

"Seven," she says.

"Is that men's or women's?" Tammy asks, her voice syrupy with innocence.

Joy smiles with her eyes.

"Even if I don't eat for the next two days—" she starts.

"Leave that to me," Tammy says. "Did you see what I ate in the cafeteria today?"

"I wasn't watching, sorry."

"A piece of *pizza.*"

"Crust and all?" Joy asks.

Tammy smiles, isn't stupid.

"I'm just saying," she says, measuring from the point of Joy's shoulder to the round bone of her wrist, "there are ways."

Joy looks down along her arm.

"I thought they were sleeveless," she says.

"Just being sure," Tammy says back, and then does the other arm.

"You're naturally dark, too, so that's good. It'll be a nice contrast against the fabric."

"It?"

"Your sk— Your *tan*."

"This is a joke," Joy says again, after the necessary lull.

"If you're not coming, you might let us know," Tammy shrugs, stepping back, threading the pin from her teeth. "I mean, I know another girl."

"She needs to lose ten pounds too?"

"No. She's perfect."

"Then why me?"

"Because—I can't be telling you this. But . . . God. I saw Bo looking at you the other day. I think he likes your tights or something. He said something about—it was gross. Licking, and a candy cane?"

On accident then, Joy smiles.

"So tell me," she said. "If I were going, I mean. What's this trick?"

"To what?"

"Ten pounds," Joy says, her voice perfectly even, and Tammy looks up, as if to make sure she's serious.

Tammy had come up with the plan in the department store, right there at Joy's register, and then whispered it to Brianne in the aisle before they were even out of the store.

All she had at first, standing there having her license checked, was the image of Joy, throwing up in the middle of the ceremony. Because Clarice was a slut of a bride, obviously. Because of the example she definitely wasn't (to say nothing of Jill, the whore), Tammy's mom had been tightening the reins the last few days. Joy throwing up during the vows, then, it would be like a sign. Like revenge, or justice. Same thing.

The problem was getting to that image, though.

Like Brianne said all the way to the car, it was complicated. If they were in a movie, maybe. But this was real life. Susan B. Danforth Detention Unit and Vomitorium. It was a word she'd heard in World History last year.

Tammy knew it was complicated, she said. But she knew Joy, too. Her kind. She was jealous of what Tammy and Brianne had, of how Bo and Seth and Davis would all lift their chins and smile when they walked in.

She didn't want to be Tammy and Brianne, so much, but she did want Bo to notice her like that. At least once.

Anybody would, right?

He was Bo after all.

There was nothing complicated about that.

After the measurements, Tammy leads Joy into one of the fitting rooms and pulls the curtain shut behind them.

"What?" Joy says. "This where you cut my arm off?" She holds it out as if weighing it in her mind.

"This way's better," Tammy says, flashing the applicator between her thumb and index finger.

Joy narrows her eyes, then has to squeeze over against the wall as Brianne wedges herself in.

"What is it?" Joy asks.

"Just some diet stuff," Tammy says, nodding to Brianne. "We stole it from her mom. She got it in Greece or somewhere."

"On a cruise," Brianne chimes in. "Then it's not legal?" Joy says, her eyes watering from the fumes.

"You're really worried about illegal substances?" Brianne says back.

"FDA illegal," Tammy clarifies. "Not DEA illegal."

Joy smiles. *With* them, for the first time.

The punch line of the joke is supposed to be giving Joy enough antacids or something the day of the wedding that she stops throwing up, and then give her another just before the ceremony. Only that last tablet is something else. Red food dye, maybe, so it looks like she's dying, turning inside out at the altar.

It's going to be perfect.

"Well?" Tammy says, holding the applicator up, and, to show it's not dangerous, she dots her fingertip with it, swirls that finger behind each ear.

"That's all?" Joy says.

Brianne has it now, is rubbing a drop between her wrists. "We just need to, y'know, burn off a couple of pounds by Saturday, yeah? I mean, I lose anymore, I'm going to be back to an A cup. Freshman year all over again."

Joy takes the plastic applicator.

"Greece?" she says.

"They don't wear tops to their bikinis over there," Tammy says, like that can be the clincher: Greek women, proud enough to go topless.

Joy laughs to herself about this, studies the applicator, and says, "So, what? One drop is two pounds?"

"Here," Tammy says, and pinches the applicator away, upends it on Joy's wrist until her skin is slick with it, "now just hold it and count to twenty."

At ten seconds Joy starts coughing from the fumes, but doesn't let go.

"Ten pounds," Brianne's saying, smiling.

By Friday morning, the stomach bug the nurse had diagnosed Tammy and Brianne with (again) has run its course (again), and they make it to school in time to breeze through lunch.

Sitting on her side of the cafeteria, hunched over the table, is Joy. She's pale, looks clammy even from this far away, and, Tammy and Brianne can't be sure, but it looks like her tights aren't even so tight anymore.

"She'll thank us," Tammy says, holding her books tight to her chest.

"If she keeps it off," Brianne adds.

They don't talk to her, though, and Joy doesn't look up to see that they aren't talking to her.

"Maybe her dad makes her come to school anyway," Brianne says on the way to Trigonometry.

"What, he makes that call from prison?" Tammy asks with a smile, then slows for Seth at his locker, which turns into Davis and Bo as well, which turns into being five minutes late.

Brianne glares at her when she finally waltzes in.

Tammy glares back, adds some oomph to it.

On the other side of the classroom, hiding, is Joy. She isn't lifting her head from her desk.

Tammy shrugs to Brianne about it and Brianne shrugs back, makes the eeek! shape with her mouth.

Halfway through class is when it happens, the thing that will spark an investigation that will span four high schools and never once interrogate either Tammy or Brianne, the real killers here.

All at once, in the middle of Mr. Connors taking up last night's problems, Joy slings her head up from her desk. A line of vomit strings down from her lip. And there's more coming.

She's trying to hold it down, though. Trying just to look over at Tammy and Brianne for help, her fingers clenched around the edge of her desk.

When she can't talk, she finally lurches to a half-stand of sorts, lifts her arm to point across the room. At Tammy.

Tammy opens her mouth as if to say something then looks behind her, at the chalkboard.

"Wha—?" she starts to say, her fingertips touching her chest now in consternation, but then Joy is losing everything she's been trying to hold down, only it isn't just the bile and whatever that Tammy and Brianne already know so well. This time it's blood, like's supposed to happen at the wedding, clumpy and dark, and when her throat isn't big enough to turn her inside out, it starts seeping from the corners of her eyes too, and her nose, maybe even beading up through her scalp.

For a half-second Tammy is too shocked to react, but then her instincts kick in and she slams her open palms onto her desk and screams. Not in terror so much as in protest. Of having to be witness to this. It infects the classroom, the hall, and even the nurse when she gets there.

Though Joy is unconscious by now, there's still blood gurgling past her lips, her sides contracting over and over.

Somehow Brianne thinks to raise her hand, ask without being called upon if what Candy—what *Joy* has is catching, or what?

The nurse just keeps staring down at the blood, finally has to support herself with the chalkboard, which gives under her weight, sends her toppling into the brown metal trash can.

By two-thirty, classes are cancelled.

It's so the paramedics can carry Joy down the quiet hall and out the door, a sheet draped across her face because it doesn't matter anymore if she has air.

Tammy and Brianne watch, their eyes saucers, and then they get in the car and put their seatbelts on and creep away, both Tammy's hands on the wheel.

"Shit," she says, minutes later.

"Exactly," Brianne says back, then looks over to Tammy. "Can Deborah still fill in, you think? She Candy Cane's size?"

"Deborah?"

"Tomorrow," Brianne says, her tone all about how obvious this is.

Tammy nods once, then again, yes: Debbie, her sister's ditzy friend.

The ride home is silent, no radio even, but then, standing from the car, using it to steady herself, Tammy gets out a shaky "Hungry?"

Brianne laughs, doesn't even answer.

▶ ▶ ▶

The day of the wedding is also the first day of Joy's viewing. There's going to be more of a crowd at the wedding, though, Tammy and Brianne know. And anyway, except for Lacy, who's already been kicked out of Danforth twice in the short time it's existed, nobody knows that they've ever even *known* Joy, much less stood in a dressing room with her. And anyway, it had been mostly to help her, really. It wasn't their fault she'd turned out to be a pig, slopped so much of the stuff on.

And, while Tammy had promised Bo a show at the wedding if he showed up, she's confident she can still give him something to remember, anyway.

All days are salvageable, if you're really committed. If you can still smile.

Of course, Tammy doesn't know what Brianne doesn't even know she knows: the super fertilizer compound from the infomercial.

At the bottom of the leaky container is a warning not to eat any of the fruit this fertilizer has helped grow. It's for pageants only. The fruit and vegetable kind.

Brianne's late to the dressing room of course, but that's just because her mom's made her go stand around the flagpole at school and hold a candle.

Because Joy was in Tammy and Brianne's grade, Clarice of course cancelled the rehearsal dinner last night. "In honor."

Tammy had thanked Clarice for both of them and then gone to the parking lot alone. It was empty, everybody already at one of the memorial services.

Twenty minutes later Brianne showed up in the pants she was only just now fitting into right. She stood from her mom's Volvo, smoothed her pants down along her hip and looked across all the empty asphalt. Even the pool was in mourning.

"They think she was a saint or something," Tammy said when Brianne was close enough.

"Maybe I should try some red and white tights," Brianne said back.

Walking through Brianne's living room an hour later, Frederick growled at them like he knew.

But that was stupid.

"It won't . . . she must have been on something else too," Brianne finally whispers to Tammy, the next morning. Not over breakfast—they're going to be on *display*, after all, right?—but at the long vanity in the holy holy dressing room at the church.

"At least they'll be able to keep the flies off her now, yeah?" Tammy smiles back in the mirror, then turns before Brianne can register the joke.

Their dresses fit so perfect they each almost cry.

"Well?" Tammy says, shrugging in anticipation, her eyelashes tittering.

Brianne takes Tammy's hands in hers and bites her lower lip, and then the music's started and their groomsmen—nothing special—are walking them up the aisle, and every note the organ plays is for them.

It's perfect. Even better than that. Like bathing in the silvery flash of cameras, in the powdery scent of groomed flowers. The ashy taste in the air is candles.

Tammy scans the audience for Bo, and he's there with the rest. But, on their lapels, they're all wearing black—*ribbons*?

For Joy. Of course.

The bitch.

She can't even let Tammy and Brianne have this one day.

"Bend your knees," Brianne whispers to Tammy and Tammy just keeps smiling. In heels like she's got on, what other choice does she really have?

Moments later Clarice is waddling up the aisle on her father's arm, and Brianne is laughing without smiling, and Tammy almost gives in as well, at the corners of her mouth. Instead her eyes just cry a little, but that's to be expected.

Except—and this is where things start going wrong—as Clarice gets closer, Tammy looks over to Brianne to be sure they're seeing what they're seeing: under Clarice's dress, her lace and ivory *wedding* dress, is she really wearing motorcycle boots?

No wonder she got pregnant.

But there's something . . .

Tammy closes her eyes.

Joy again. The boots are the same. "In *honor.*"

Tammy grits her teeth, smiles past it, then, when it's time to rotate forty-degrees over, to witness this travesty, she sees a flash of red and white stripes somewhere in the pews, but can't keep her eyes there without drawing attention.

She's dead, though, Joy.

Dead dead dead.

Maybe not next year, but the year after that anyway, the kids are even going to be calling her "Killjoy" or something, Tammy knows, and then she'll just be a plaque in front of a tree that probably won't even make it two summers.

So, instead of being paranoid, Tammy smiles and stares past Brianne's hair, up to Clarice and her catch of the day, and is only just starting to get bored with all the preaching that comes before anything can even happen—the reception is what matters, she keeps telling herself—when she sees something shiny and brown grope out from under the left strap of Brianne's dress.

A tick, its body impossibly flat.

Tammy looks away, dipping her chin as if swallowing.

Five seconds later, the tick's gone.

But.

Tammy closes her eyes, holds her tissue to her nose as if trying to control herself. Or, not as if, just not for the reason everybody thinks.

In her hair in the shower that day.

The reason she could never find the scratch in her scalp was because it hadn't been a scratch at all, but one of those pregnant ticks, bursting. The grittiness in the blood, in the tick's blood, had been—it had been baby ticks.

Tammy lowers her tissue to her mouth, is breathing faster than she wants to. Finally she has to reach out for Brianne's back just to keep from losing her balance.

Brianne turns around pleasantly, sees the danger Tammy is in, then turns back around just as pleasantly. Takes a polite half-step forward, even.

Tammy shakes her head no, just a little—there are two-hundred and twelve invited guests, after all—but then it starts to rise in her throat anyway, everything she hasn't eaten that morning.

"I can't—" she starts, and loses the rest all over the back of Brianne's peach dress, and it's red, even, and she was right: it does look perfect against that silk. Classic.

For a second Tammy tries to believe that she's imagining all this, torturing herself, that this is a side-effect of Frederick's drops, but then the blood still coating her teeth, it's gritty.

Tammy shakes her head no, her hand rising to her mouth.

For the worst instant of her life, Tammy looks out to the crowd again, for Bo to . . . she doesn't know. *Help* her? Not see her? Please?

But, instead of Bo or Seth or Davis or any of them, what she sees instead, staggered in a pew behind an old couple, is Joy. Just sitting there alone, her milksop hair tucked behind each ear.

Slowly then, so Tammy has to see, Joy opens her mouth, her head turned just sideways enough for Tammy to see that she's lifting her tongue, trying to show Tammy something.

"What?" Tammy says weakly, and is on her knees now, her fingertips to the front of her own lower teeth like Joy's showing, and then past them, to where the floor of her mouth meets the base of her tongue.

Lined there like pigs at a trough are the engorged bodies of nine ticks. And they're bigger than the one from Frederick, too, are like grapes, or cherry tomatoes, or plums, or, or—

It doesn't matter.

All that does is that they have to come out.

Starting at the left, Tammy pulls on the first one until it pops, flooding her mouth with blood, and then the second one's torso tears away as well, and she's crying now—*two hundred and twelve people!*—and by the time the first of the groomsmen's fathers are able to rise from their pews, offer medical assistance, Tammy has pulled her tongue out by the root, and has started on the large tick hanging by its mouth from the back of her throat.

Standing above her, Brianne is in a kind of shock, she knows. Like this is all happening on the other side of thick, soundproof glass.

For her there's no stockings or boots or faces in the congregation.

Instead, in her lower stomach, there's just a—not a kick, but a surge of sorts. Like life, raising its wet head. From the pool boy, she knows. Out in the grass, which had to have been infested.

How could she not have remembered that?

Over the next few months of therapy and sympathy and dieting she'll try to hide it, of course, her stomach, and then, with the last application, she'll even try to kill it, but the only thing that finally works is Frederick, lunging for her in the kitchen one afternoon, trying to dig it from her swollen midsection with his teeth and his claws. It's a suicide mission for him, of course—Brianne's dad has him put down that afternoon, in a ceremony nobody attends—but it also makes things awkward for a moment in her curtained room at the hospital, when the doctor steps in with the blood results. Behind him on wheels is an ultrasound machine.

Brianne firms her lips and looks away.

When the image resolves on screen, instead of the hazy outline of a giant tick like Brianne expects, it's a baby girl.

"Just like Joy," Brianne's mom whispers, her hands in cute little grandmotherly fists under her chin, her eyes wet.

"Joy?" Brianne hears herself say, all other noise suddenly gone.

"Clarice's girl . . . " her mom says, her voice hesitant like how could Brianne not know this? "Fattest little thing you've ever seen."

Brianne breathes in deep once, twice, thinks of Tammy in her padded room, and then the doctor has the ultrasound all over her slick lower stomach, trying every angle.

The noise that was suddenly gone a moment ago was the heartbeat.

Brianne's mom stands, the stool clattering away behind her.

"What?" Brianne says.

"It's—it's . . . I'm sorry," the doctor stammers, looking at his ultrasound wand like it might really have been a knife. "It wasn't even in distress. I don't—"

Brianne smiles a sleepy smile, like she's more drugged than she is.

"It's okay," she says, "just . . . do you get it out now?"

Already she's thinking of the jeans she wore to the parking lot that last night. Because of Tammy, everybody's going to crowd around her.

The doctor focuses in on her, then on a spot beside her, Brianne is pretty sure.

"In cases like this," he says, "your body just reabsorbs the—the . . . "

Brianne's mom is already crying, though, her dad pulling her close, hiding her face in his chest.

Brianne swallows, nods, and looks up to the doctor.

"How many—" she starts, unsure how to phrase it even though it's the most obvious question in the world, "how many calories is that, do you think?"

When nobody answers she decides it must be a lot, a truly unmanageable amount, so, later that week, locked in the basement, hunched over with an art knife, she does the procedure herself, and then decides that she might just want to shorten those intestines too, maybe even loop them together front to back, so they're a closed system.

It's makes so much sense that Brianne laughs a little, and then looks up when the light above her lowers to almost nothing.

It means the garage door is grinding up on its long chain. Her parents are home.

But she still has time.

"Just . . . here," she says to the assistant she can see now, in the dark. The assistant is standing beside her, holding a silver tray, her red and white tights inadvisable against that nurse dress, except—except she's kind of pulling it off too, no?

Brianne doesn't let herself think about that, just balances a piece of her lower intestine on the blade of the knife, deposits it on the tray with a plink, and then pushes the sharp point deeper into her stomach, her assistant leaning down over her shoulder to help, saying over and over *there, and there too.*

There's more fat than Brianne ever would have guessed.

Things will be better once it's all out, though.

She'll be perfect then.

"There," the nurse says again, pointing to a section Brianne really should have seen, and Brianne smiles—of course—reaches down for it with the knife just as her parents' footsteps are crossing the ceiling above her, a world away.

► Lonegan's Luck

Like every month, the horse was new. A mare, pushing fifteen years old. Given his druthers, Lonegan would have picked a mule, of course, one that had had its balls cut late so there was still some fight in it, but, when it came down to it, it had either been the mare or yoking himself up to the buckboard, leaning forward until his fingertips touched the ground and pulling, pulling.

Twenty years ago, he would have tried it, just to make a girl laugh.

Now, now he took what was available, made do.

And anyway, from the way the mare kept trying to swing wide, head back into the shade of town, this wasn't going to be her first trip across the Arizona Territories. Maybe she'd even know where the water was, if it came down to that. Where the Apache weren't.

Lonegan brushed the traces across her flank and she pulled ahead, the wagon creaking, all his crates shifting around behind him, the jars and bottles inside touching shoulders. The straw they were packed in was going to be the mare's forage, if all the red baked earth ahead of them was as empty as it looked.

As they picked their way through it, Lonegan explained to the mare that he never meant for it to be this way. That this was the last time. But then he trailed off. Up ahead a black column was coming into view.

Buzzards.

Lonegan nodded, smiled.

What was dead there was pungent enough to be drawing them in for miles.

"What do you think, old girl?" he said to the mare. She didn't answer. Lonegan nodded to himself again, checked the scattergun under his seat, and pulled the mare's head towards the swirling buzzards. "Professional curiosity," he told her, then laughed because it was a joke.

The town he'd left that morning wasn't going on any map.

The one ahead of him, as far as he knew, probably wasn't on any map either. But it would be there. They always were.

When the mare tried shying away from the smell of blood, Lonegan got down, talked into her ear, and tied his handkerchief across her eyes. The last little bit, he led her by the bridle, then hobbled her upwind.

The buzzards were a greasy black coat, looked like old men walking barefoot on the hot ground.

Instead of watching them, Lonegan traced the ridges of rock all around.

"Well," he finally said, and leaned into the washed-out little hollow.

As he approached, the buzzards lifted their wings in something like menace, but Lonegan knew better. He slung rocks at the few that wouldn't take to the sky. They still didn't, just backed off, their dirty mouths open in challenge.

Lonegan held his palm out to them, explained that this wasn't going to take long.

He was right: the dead guy was the one Lonegan had figured it would be. The thin deputy with the three-pocketed vest. He still had the vest on, had been able to crawl maybe twenty paces from where his horse had died. The horse was a gelding, a long-legged bay with a white diamond on its forehead, three white socks. Lonegan distinctly remembered having appreciated that horse. But now it had been run to death, had died with white foam on its flanks, blood blowing from its nostrils, eyes wheeling around, the deputy spurring him on, deeper into the heat.

Lonegan looked from the horse to the deputy. The buzzards were going after the gelding, of course.

It made Lonegan sick.

He walked up to the deputy, facedown in the dirt, already rotting, and rolled him over.

"Not quite as fast as you thought you were, eh deputy?" he said, then shot him in the mouth. Twice.

It was a courtesy.

Nine days later, all the straw in his crates handfed to the mare, his jars and bottles tied to each other with twine to keep them from shattering, Lonegan looked into the distance and nodded: a town was rising up from the dirt. A perfect little town.

He snubbed the mare to a shuffling stop, turned his head to the side to make sure they weren't pulling any dust in. That would give them away.

Then he just stared at the town.

Finally, the mare snorted a breath of hot air in, blew it back out.

"I know," Lonegan said. "I know."

According to the scrap of paper he'd been marking, though, it was only Friday.

"One more night," he told the mare, and angled her over to some scrub, a ring of blackened stones in the packed ground.

He had to get there on a Saturday.

It wasn't like one more night was going to kill him, anyway. Or the mare.

He parked the buckboard on the town side of the ring of stones, so they wouldn't see his light, find him before he was ready.

Before unhooking the mare, he hobbled her. Four nights ago, she wouldn't have tried running. But now, for her, there was the smell of other horses in the air. Hay, maybe.

And then there was the missing slice of meat Lonegan had cut from her haunch three nights ago.

It had been shallow, and he'd packed it with a medley of poultices from his crates, folded the skin back over and stitching it down, but still, he was pretty sure she'd been more than slightly offended.

Lonegan smiled at her, shook his head no, that she didn't need to worry. He could wait one more day for solid food, water that was wasn't briny, didn't taste like rust.

Or—no: he was going to get a *cake*, this time. All for himself. A big white one, slathered in whatever kind of sugar coating they had.

And all the water he could drink.

Lonegan nodded to himself about this, leaned back into his bedroll, and watched the sparks from the fire swirl up past his battered coffee pot.

When it was hot enough, he offered a cup to the mare.

She flared her nostrils, stared at him.

Before turning in, Lonegan emptied the grains from his cup into the edges of her opening wound and patted it down, told her it was an old medicine man trick. That he knew them all.

He fell asleep thinking of the cake.

The mare slept standing up.

By noon the next day, he was set up on the only street in town. Not in front of the saloon but the mercantile. Because the men bellied up to the bar would walk any distance for the show. The people just in town for flour or salt though, you had to step into their path some. Make them aware of you.

Lonegan had polished his boots, shaved his jaw, pulled the hair on his chin down into a waxy point.

He waited until twenty or so people had gathered before reaching up under the side of the buckboard, for the secret handle.

He pulled it, stepped away with a flourish, and the panel on the buckboard opened up like a staircase, all the bottles and jars and felt bags of medicine already tied into place.

One person in the crowd clapped twice.

Lonegan didn't look around, just started talking about how the blue oil in the clear jar—he'd pilfered it from a barber shop in Missouri—how, if rubbed into the scalp twice daily and let cook in the sun, it would make a head of hair grow back, if you happened to be missing one. Full, black, hair. But you had to be careful not to use too much.

Now somebody in the crowd laughed.

Inside, Lonegan smiled, then went on.

The other stuff, fox urine he called it, though assured them it wasn't, it was for the women specifically. He couldn't go into the particulars in mixed company though, of course. This was a Christian settlement, right?

Finally, he looked around.

"Amen," a man near the front said.

Lonegan nodded.

"Thought so," he said. "Some towns I come across . . . well. Mining towns, need I say more?"

Five, maybe six people nodded, kept their lips pursed.

The fox urine was going to be sold out by supper, Lonegan knew. Not to any of the women, either.

Facing the crowd now, the buckboard framed by the mercantile, like it was just an extension of the mercantile, Lonegan cycled through his other bottles, the rest of his jars, the creams and powders and rare leaves. Twice a man in the crowd raised his hand to stop the show, make a purchase, but Lonegan held his palm up. Not yet, not yet.

But then, towards mid-afternoon, the white-haired preacher finally showed up, the good book held in both hands before him like a shield.

Lonegan resisted acknowledging him. But just barely.

They were in the same profession, after all.

And the preacher was the key to all this, too.

He went on, hawking, selling, testifying, the sweat running down the back of his neck to wet his shirt. He took his hat off, wiped his forehead with the back of his sleeve, and eyed the crowd, shrugged.

"If you'll excuse me a brief moment," he said, and stepped halfway behind the ass-end of the buckboard, swigged from a tall, clear bottle of nearly-amber liquid.

He swallowed, lifted the bottle again, and drew deep on it, nodded as he screwed the cap back on.

"What is that?" a woman asked.

Lonegan looked up as if caught, said, "Nothing, ma'am. Something of my own making."

"We don't tolerate any—" another man started, stepping forward.

Lonegan shook his head no, cut him off: "It's not *that* kind of my own making, sir. Any man drinks whiskey in the heat like this is asking for trouble, am I right?"

The man stepped back without ever breaking eye contact.

"Then what is it?" a boy asked.

Lonegan looked down to him, smiled.

"Just something an old—a man from the Old Country taught this to me on his deathbed. It's kind of like . . . you know how a strip of dried meat, it's like the whole steak twisted into a couple of bites?"

The boy nodded.

Lonegan lifted the bottle up, let it catch the sunlight. Said, "This is like that. Except it's the good part of water. The cold part."

A man in the crowd muttered a curse. The dismissal cycled through, all around Lonegan. He waited for it to abate, then shrugged, tucked the bottle back into the buckboard. "It's not for sale anyway," he said, stepping back around to the bottles and jars.

"Why not?" a man in a thick leather vest asked.

By the man's bearing, Lonegan assumed he was law of some kind.

"Personal stock," Lonegan explained. "And—anyway. There's not enough. It takes about fourteen months to get even a few bottles distilled the right way."

"Then I take that to mean you'd be averse to sampling it out?" the man said.

Lonegan nodded, tried to look apologetic.

The man shook his head, scratched deep in his matted beard, and stepped forward, shouldered Lonegan out of the way.

A moment later, he'd grubbed the bottle up from the bedclothes Lonegan had stuffed it in.

With everybody watching, he unscrewed the cap, wiped his lips clean, and took a long pull off the bottle.

What it was was water with a green juniper leaf at the bottom. The inside of the bottle cap dabbed with honey. A couple drops of laudanum, for the soft headrush, and a peppermint candy ground up, to hide the laudanum.

The man lowered the bottle, swallowed what was left in his mouth, and smiled a particularly vacant smile.

Grudgingly, Lonegan agreed to take eight dollars for what was left in the bottle. And then everybody was calling for it.

"I don't—" he started, stepping up onto the hub of his wheel to try to reach everybody, "I don't have—" but they were surging forward.

"*Okay,*" he said, for the benefit of the people up front, and stepped down, hauled a half-case of the water up over the side of the buckboard.

Which was when the preacher spoke up.

The crowd fell silent like church.

"I can't let you do this to these good people," the preacher said.

"I think—" Lonegan said, his stutter a practiced thing, "I think you have me confused with the kind of gentlemen who—"

"I'm not confused at all, sir," the preacher said, both his hands still clasping the Bible.

Lonegan stared at him, stared at him, and finally nodded, stepped forward. "What could convince you then, Brother? Take my mare there. See that wound on her haunch? Would you believe that four days ago that was done by an old blunderbuss, fired on accident?"

"By you?"

"I was cleaning it."

The preacher nodded, waiting.

Lonegan went on. "You could reach your hand into the hole, I'm saying. Right down to the joint of her hip."

"And your medicine fixed it?" the preacher anticipated, his voice rising.

Lonegan palmed a smoky jar from the shelves, said, "This poultice, yes sir. A man named Running Bear showed me how to take the caul around the heart of a dog and grind—"

The preacher blew air out his nose.

"He was Oglala Sioux," Lonegan added, let that settle.

The preacher just stared.

Lonegan looked around at the faces in the crowd, starting to side with the preacher. More out of habit than argument. But still.

Lonegan nodded, backed off, hands raised. Was quiet long enough to let them know he was just thinking of this: "These—these snake oil men you've taken me for, Brother. People. A despicable breed. What would you say characterizes them?"

When the preacher didn't answer, a man in the crowd did: "They sell things."

"I sell things," Lonegan agreed.

"Medicine," a woman clarified.

"Remedies," Lonegan corrected, nodding to her respectfully.

She held his eyes.

"What else?" Lonegan said, to all.

It was the preacher who answered: "You'll be gone tomorrow."

"—before any of our hair can grow in," an old man added, sweeping his hat off to show his bald head.

Lonegan smiled wide, nodded. Cupped a small bottle of the blue oil from its place on the panel, twirled it to the man.

He caught it, stared at Lonegan.

"I'm not leaving," Lonegan said.

"Yeah, well—" a man started.

"I'm *not*," Lonegan said, some insult in his voice now. "And, you know what? To prove it, today and today only, I'll be accepting checks, or notes. Just write your name and how much you owe me on any scrap of paper— here, I've got paper myself, I'll even supply that. I won't come to collect until you're satisfied."

As one, a grin spread across the crowd's face.

"How long this take to work?" the bald man asked, holding his bottle of blue up.

"I've seen it take as long as six days, to be honest."

The old man raised his eyebrows. They were bushy, white.

People were already pushing forward again.

Lonegan stepped up onto his hub, waved his arms for them to slow down, slow down. That he wanted to make a gift first.

It was a tightly-woven cloth bag the size of a man's head.

He handed it to the preacher, said, "Brother."

The preacher took it, looked from Lonegan to the string tying the bag closed.

"Traveling like I do," Lonegan said, "I make my tithe where I can. With what I can."

The preacher opened it.

"The sacrament?" he said.

"Just wafers for now," Lonegan said. "You'll have to bless them, of course."

Slowly at first, then altogether, the crowd started clapping.

The preacher tied the bag shut, extended his hand to Lonegan.

By dinner, there wasn't a drop of fox urine in his possession.

When the two women came to collect him for church the next morning, Lonegan held his finger up, told them he'd be right there. He liked to say a few prayers beforehand.

The women lowered their bonneted heads that they understood, then one of them added that his mare had run off in the night, it looked like.

"She does that," Lonegan said with a smile, and closed the door, held it there.

Just what he needed: a goddamn prophetic horse.

Instead of praying then, or going to the service, Lonegan packed his spare clothes tight in his bedroll, shoved it under the bed then made the bed so nobody would have any call to look under it. Before he ever figured this whole thing out, he'd lost two good suits just because he'd failed to stretch a sheet across a mattress.

But now, now his bedroll was still going to be there Monday or Tuesday, or whenever he came for it.

Next, he angled the one chair in the room over to the window, waited for the congregation to shuffle back out into the streets in their Sunday best.

Today, the congregation was going to be the whole town. Because they felt guilty about the money they'd spent yesterday, and because they knew this morning there was going to be a communion.

In a Baptist church, that happened little enough that it was an event.

With luck, nobody would even have noticed Lonegan's absence, come looking for him.

With luck, they'd all be guilty enough to palm an extra wafer, let it go soft against the roofs of their mouths.

After a lifetime of eating coarse hunks of bread, the wafer would be candy to them. So white it had to be pure.

Lonegan smiled, propped his boots up on the windowsill, and tipped back the bottle of rotgut until his eyes watered. If he'd been drinking just to feel good, it would have been sipping bourbon. For this, though, he needed to be drunk, the kind you could smell at ten paces.

Scattered on the wood-plank floor all around him, fallen like leaves, were the promissory notes for yesterday's sales.

He wasn't going to need them to collect.

It was a funny thing.

Right about what he figured was the middle of lunch for most of the town—he didn't even know its name, he laughed to himself—he pulled the old Colt up from his lap, laid the bottom of the barrel across the back of his left wrist, and aimed in turn at each of the six panes in his window, blew them out in the street.

Ten minutes and two reloads later, he was in jail.

"Don't get too comfortable in there now," the bearded man Lonegan had made for the law said. He was wearing a stiff collar from church, a tin star on his chest.

Lonegan smiled, leaned back on his cot, and shook his head no, he wouldn't.

"When's dinner?" he slurred out, having to bite back a smile, the cake a definite thing in his mind again.

The Sheriff didn't respond, just walked out.

Behind him, Lonegan nodded.

Sewed into the lining of his right boot were all the tools he would need to pick the simple lock of the cell.

Sewed into his belt, as back-up, was a few thimblefuls of gunpowder wrapped in thin oilcloth, in case the lock was jammed. In Lonegan's teeth like a make-do toothpick, a sulfur-head match that the burly man had never even questioned.

Lonegan balanced it in one of the cracks of the wall.

He was in the best room in town, now.

That afternoon he woke to a woman staring at him. She was sideways—*he* was sideways, on the cot.

He pushed the heel of his right hand into one eye then the other, sat up.

"Ma'am," he said, having to turn his head sideways to swallow.

She was slight but tall, her face lined by the weather it looked like. A hard woman to get a read on.

"I came to pay," she said.

Lonegan lowered his head to smile, had to grip the edge of his cot with both hands to keep from spilling down onto the floor.

"My father," the woman went on, finding her voice, "he—I don't know why. He's rubbing that blue stuff onto his head. He smells like a barbershop."

Lonegan looked up to this woman, wasn't sure if he should smile or not.

She was, anyway.

"If'n you don't see its efficacy," he said, "then you don't got to pay. ma'am."

She stared at him about this, finally said, "Can you even spell that?"

"What?"

"Efficacy."

Now it was Logan's turn to just stare.

"Got a first name?" she said.

"Lonegan," Lonegan shrugged.

"The rest of it?"

"Just Lonegan."

"That's how it is then?"

"'Alone again . . .'" he went on.

"I get it."

"Regular-like, you mean?"

She caught his meaning, set her teeth but then shook her head no, smiled instead.

"I don't know what kind of—what kind of affair you're trying to pull off here, Mister Alone Again."

"My horse ran off," Lonegan said, standing, pulling his face close to the bars now. "Think I'm apt to make a fast getaway in these?"

For illustration, he lifted his right boot. It was down at heel. Shiny on top, bare underneath.

"You meant to get thrown in here, I mean," she said. "Shooting up Molly's best room like that."

"Who are you, you don't mind my asking?"

"I'm the daughter of the man you swindled yesterday afternoon. I'm just here to complete the transaction now."

"I told you—"

"And I'm telling you. I'm not going to be indebted to a man like you. Now how much is this going to cost me?"

"Say my name."

"How much?"

Lonegan tongued his lower lip out, was falling in love just a little bit, he thought. Wishing he wasn't on this side of the bars, anyway.

"You like the service this morning?" he asked.

"I don't go to church with my father anymore," the woman said. "Who do you think swindled us the first time?"

Lonegan smiled, liked that.

"Anyway," the woman went on. "My father tends to bring enough church home with him each Sunday to last us the week through. And then some."

"What's your name?" Lonegan said, watching her.

"That supposed to give you some power over me, if you know?"

"So you think I'm real then?"

Lonegan shrugged, waiting for her to try to back out of the corner she'd wedged herself into.

"You can call me Mary," she said, lifting her chin at the end.

"I like Jezebel better," he said. "Girl who didn't go to church."

"Do you even know the Bible?" she asked.

"I know I'm glad you didn't go to church this morning."

"How much, Mister *Lonegan*?"

He nodded thanks, said, "For you, Jezebel. For you—"

"I don't want a deal."

"Two dollars."

"They sold for two bits, I heard."

"Special deal for a special lady."

For a moment longer she held his stare, then slammed her coin purse down on the only desk in the room, started counting out coins.

Two dollars was a full week's work, Lonegan figured.

"What do you do?" he said, watching her.

"Give money to fools, it would seem," she muttered.

Lonegan hissed a laugh, was holding the bars on each side of his face. She stood with the money in her hand.

"I *bake*," she said—spit, really.

Lonegan felt everything calming inside him.

"Confectionary stuff?" he said.

"Why?" she said, stepping forward. "You come here for a matrimony?"

" . . . Mary Lonegan," Lonegan lilted, like trying it out.

She held the money out, her palm down so she'd just have to open her fingers.

Lonegan worked it into a brush of skin anyway, said at the last moment, "Or you could just—you could stay and talk. In the next cell, maybe."

"It cost me two more dollars not to?" she said back, her hand to her coin purse again, then stared at Lonegan until he had to look away. To the heavy oak door that opened onto the street.

The Sheriff was stepping through, fumbling for the peg on the wall, to hang his holster on.

"Annie," he said to the woman.

Her top lip rose in what Lonegan took for anger. Not directed at the lawman, but at her own name spoken aloud.

"Annie," Lonegan repeated.

"You know this character?" the man said, cutting his eyes to Lonegan.

"We go back a long ways, Sheriff," Lonegan said.

Annie laughed through her nose, pushed past the lawman, stepped out into the sunlight.

Lonegan watched the door until it was closed all the way, then studied the floor.

Finally he nodded, slipped his belt off with one hand, ferreted the slender oilcloth of gunpowder out.

"For obvious reasons, she didn't bake it into a cake," he said, holding it up for the lawman to see.

"Annie?" the lawman said, incredulous.

"If that's the name you know her by," Lonegan said, then dropped the oilcloth bag onto the stone floor.

The lawman approached, fingered the black powder up to his nose. Looked to the door as well.

By nightfall, Annie Jorgensson was in the cell next to Lonegan's.

"Was hoping you'd bring some of those pastries you've been making," he said to her, nodding down to the apron she was wearing, the flour still dusting her forearms.

"Was hoping you'd be dead by now," she said back, brushing her arms clean.

"You could have brought something, I mean."

"That why you lied about me?"

"What I said, I said to save your life. A little courtesy might be in order."

"You think talking to you's going to save me?" she said. "Rather be dead, thanks."

Lonegan leaned back on his cot, closed his eyes.

All dinner had been was some hardtack the Sheriff had had in his saddlebag for what tasted like weeks.

Lonegan had made himself eat all of it, though, every bite.

Not for strength, but out of spite. Because he knew what was coming.

"You're sure you didn't go to church this morning?" he said to Annie Jorgensson.

She didn't answer. It didn't matter much if she had though, he guessed, and was just lying to him about it, like she had with her name. Either way there was still a wall of bars between them. And he didn't know what he was going to do with her anyway, after. Lead her by the hand into the saloon, pour her a drink?

No, it was better if she was lying, really. If she was a closet Baptist.

It would keep him from having to hold her down with his knee, shoot her in the face.

Ten minutes after a light Lonegan couldn't see the source of was doused, the horses at the livery took to screaming.

Lonegan nodded, watched for Annie's reaction.

She just sat there.

"You alive?" he called over.

Her eyes flicked up to him, but that was all.

Yes.

Soon enough the horses kicked down a gate or a wall, started crashing through the town. One of them ran up onto the boardwalk it sounded like, then, afraid of the sound of its own hooves, shied away from them, into some window. After that, Lonegan couldn't tell. There was gunfire, for the horse maybe. Or not.

The whole time he watched Annie.

"Mary," he said to her once, in play.

"Jezebel to you," she hissed back.

He smiled.

"What's happening out there?" she asked, finally.

"I'm in here," Lonegan shrugged back to her. "You saying this doesn't happen every night?"

She stood, leaned against the bars at the front of her cell.

One time before, Lonegan had made it through with a cellmate. Or, in the next cell, like this.

He'd left that one there, though. Not turned, like the rest of the town, but starved inside of four days anyway. Five if he ate the stuffing from his mattress.

It had been interesting, though, the man's reactions—how his back stiffened with each scream. The line of saliva that descended from his lip to the ground.

"I've got to piss," Lonegan said.

Annie didn't turn around.

Lonegan aimed it at the trap under the window, was just shaking off when a face appeared, nearly level with his own.

It was one of the men from the Saturday crowd.

His eyes were wild, roving, his cheeks already shrunken, making his teeth look larger. Around his mouth, blood.

He pulled at the bars of the window like the animal he was.

"You're already dead," Lonegan said to him, then raised his finger in the shape of a pistol, shot the man between the eyes.

The man grunted, shuffled off.

"That was Sid Masterson," Annie said from behind him. "If you're wondering, I mean."

"Think he was past the point where an introduction would have done any good," Lonegan said, turning to catch her eye.

"This is supposed to impress me?" Annie said, suddenly standing at the wall of bars between them.

"You're alive," Lonegan told her.

"What are they?" she said, lifting her chin to take in the whole town.

Lonegan shrugged, rubbed the side of his nose with the side of his finger.

"Some people just get caught up when they're dying, I guess," he said. "Takes them longer."

"How long?"

Lonegan smiled, said, "A day. They don't last so long in the sun. I don't know why."

"But you can't have got everybody."

"They'll get who I didn't."

"You've done this before."

"Once or twice, I suppose. My oxen gets in the ditch like everybody else's . . . "

For a long time, Annie just stared at him. Finally she said, "We would have given you whatever, y'know?"

"A good Christian town," Lonegan recited.

"You didn't have to do this, I mean."

"They were asking for it," Lonegan said, shrugging it true. "They paid me, even, if I recall correctly."

"It was that poppy water."

Lonegan raised his eyebrows to her.

"I know the taste," she said. "What was it masking?"

In reply, Lonegan pursed his lips, pointed with them out to the town: that.

"My father?" Annie said, then.

Lonegan kept looking at the front door.

Her father. That was definitely going to be a complication. There was a reason he usually passed the night alone, he told himself.

But she was a *baker*.

Back in her kitchen there was probably all manner of frosting and sugar.

Lonegan opened his mouth to ask her where she lived, but then thought better of it. He'd find her place anyway. After tonight, he'd have all week to scavenge through town. Every house, every building.

Towards the end of the week, even, the horses would come back, from downwind. They'd be skittish like the mare had been—skittish that he was dead like the others had been, just not lying down yet—but then he'd have oats in a sack, and, even if they had been smart enough to run away, they were still just horses.

Or, he hoped—this time—a mule.

Something with personality.

They tended to taste better anyway.

He came to again some time before dawn. He could tell by the quality of light sifting in through the bars of his window. There were no birds singing, though. And the smell. He was used to the smell by now.

Miles east of town, he knew, a tree was coated with buzzards.

Soon they would rise into an oily black mass, ride the heat into town, drift down onto the bodies that would be in the street by now.

Like with the deputy Lonegan had found, the buzzards would know better than to eat. Even to them, this kind of dead tasted wrong.

With luck, maybe one of the horses would have run its lungs bloody for them, collapsed in a heap of meat.

With luck, it'd be that mare.

They'd start on her haunch, of course, finish what Lonegan had started.

He nodded, pulled a sharp hank of air up his nose, and realized what had woke him: the oak door. It was moving, creaking.

In the next cell, Annie was already at the bars of her cell, holding her breath.

"They can't get in," Lonegan told her, pulling at his bars to show.

She didn't look away from the door.

"What were you dreaming about there?" she said, her voice flat and low.

Lonegan narrowed his eyes at her.

Dream?

He looked at his hands as if they might have been involved, then touched his face.

It was wet.

He shook his head no, stood, and the oak door swung open.

Standing in the space it had been was the Sheriff.

He'd seen better days.

Annie fell back to her cot, pulled the green blanket up to her mouth.

Lonegan didn't move, just inspected. It wasn't often he got to see one of the shufflers when they were still shuffling. This one, he surmised, he'd fallen down in some open place. While he was turning, too, another had fed on him, it looked like. His face on the right side was down to the bone, one of his arms gone, just a ragged sleeve now.

81

Not that he was in a state to care about any of that.

This was probably the time he usually came into work on Monday.

It was all he knew anymore.

"Hey," Lonegan called out to it, to be sure.

The thing had to look around for the source of the sound.

When he found it, Lonegan nodded.

"No . . . " Annie was saying through her blanket.

"He can't get through," Lonegan said again. "They can't—keys, tools, guns."

For a long time, then—it could sense the sun coming, Lonegan thought—the thing just stood there, rasping air in and out.

Annie was hysterical, pushing on the floor with her legs.

Lonegan watched like she was a new thing to him.

Maybe if he was just seeing his first one too, he figured. But . . . no. Even then—it had been a goat—even then he'd known what was happening. It was the goat he'd been trying all his mixtures out on first, because it would eat anything. And because it couldn't aim a pistol.

When it had died, Lonegan had nodded, looked at the syrup in the wooden tube, already drying into a floury paste, and been about to sling it out into the creek with all the other bad mixes when the goat had kicked, its one good eye rolling in its skull, a sound clawing from its throat that had pushed Lonegan up onto his buckboard.

Finally, when the horse he'd had then wouldn't calm down, Lonegan had had to shoot the goat.

The goat had looked up to the barrel like a child.

It was the same look the thing in the doorway had now. Like it didn't understand just how it had got to be where it was.

The front of its pants were wet, from the first time it had relaxed into death.

Lonegan watched it.

In its other hand—and this he'd never seen before—was one of the bottles of what Annie had called poppy water.

The thing was holding it by the neck like it knew what it was.

When it lifted it to its mouth, Annie forgot how to breathe.

Lonegan turned to her, then to the thing, and got it: she knew what that water tasted like, still thought it *was* the water, doing all this to her town.

He smiled to himself, came back to the thing, the shuffler.

It was making its way across the floor, one of its ankles at an angle not intended for distance, or speed.

Now Annie was screaming, stuffing the blanket into her mouth. The thing noticed, came to her cell.

"You don't want to—" Lonegan started, but it was too late.

Make them take an interest in you, he was going to say.

Like anything with an appetite, jerky motions drew its attention.

Annie was practically convulsing.

Lonegan came to the wall of bars between them, reached for her hand, just to let her know she was alive, but, at the touch she cringed away, her eyes wild, breath shallow.

"You should have gone to church," Lonegan said, out loud he guessed, because she looked over, a question on her face, but by then the thing was trying to come through the bars. It wasn't strong enough to, of course, but it didn't understand things the way a man would either.

Slowly, as if *trying* to, it wedged its head between two of the bars—leading with its mouth—and started to push and pull through.

The first thing to go was its one good eye. It ran down its cheek.

Next was its jaw, then its skull, and still it kept coming, got halfway through before it didn't have anything left.

Annie had never been in danger. Not from the thing, anyway.

She wasn't so much conscious anymore either, though.

For a long time, Lonegan sat on the edge of his cot, his head leaned down into his hands, the thing in the bars still breathing somehow, even when the sunlight spilled through, started turning its skin to leather.

It was time.

Lonegan worked his pantsleg up, slid the two picks out, had the door to his cell open almost as fast as if he'd had the key.

The first thing he did was take the shotgun off the wall, hold the barrel to the base of the thing's skull. But then Annie started to stir. Lonegan focused in on her, nodded, and turned the gun around, slammed the butt into the thing until its head lolled forward, the skin at the back of the neck tearing into a mouth of sorts, that smiled with a ripping sound.

When the thing fell, it gave Lonegan a clear line on Annie.

She was dotted with black blood now.

He might as well have just shot the thing, then. Same mess.

"Well," he said to her.

She was crying, hiding inside herself.

"You don't catch it from the blood," he told her, "don't worry," but she wasn't listening anymore.

Lonegan shrugged, pulled the keys up from the thing's belt, and unlocked her cell, let the door swing wide.

"But—but—" she said.

Lonegan shrugged, disgusted with her.

"*What?*" he said, finally. "I saved your life, Mary, Jezebel. Annie Jorgensson."

She shook her head no, more of a jerk than a gesture.

Lonegan twirled the shotgun by the trigger guard, held it down along his leg.

The easy thing to do now would be to point it at her, get this over with.

Except she was the cake lady.

For the first time in years, he wasn't sure if he'd be able to stomach the cake, later, if he did this to her now.

"What's the name of this town?" he said to her.

She looked up, the muscles in her face dancing.

"Name?"

"This place."

For a long time she didn't understand the question, then she nodded, said it: "Gultree."

Lonegan nodded, said, "I don't think I'll be staying in Gultree much longer, Miss Jorgensson. Not to be rude."

She shook her head no, no, he wasn't being rude.

"I'm sorry about your father," he said then. It even surprised him.

Annie just stared at him, her mouth working around a word: " . . . why?"

"The world," he said to her, "it's a—it's a hard place. I didn't make it. It just is."

"Somebody told you that," she said, shaking her head no. "You don't . . . you don't believe it."

"Would I do this if I didn't?"

"You're trying to convince yourself, Mister Alone Again."

Lonegan stared hard at her, hated Gultree. Everything about it. He was glad he'd killed it, wiped it off the map.

"Goodbye then," he said to her, lifting the fingers of his free hand to the hat he'd left . . . where?

He looked around for it, finally just took a sweated-through brown one off the peg by the door.

It fit. Close enough.

For a moment longer than he meant to, he stood in the doorway, waiting for Annie to come up behind him, but she didn't. Even after the door of her cell made its rusty moan.

Lonegan had to look back.

Annie was on her knees behind the thing the Sheriff had become.

She'd worked his revolver up from his holster, was holding it backwards, the barrel in her mouth, so deep she was gagging.

Lonegan closed his eyes, heard her saying it again, from a few minutes ago: "But—but—"

But she'd drunk the poppy water too. Thought she was already dead like the rest of them.

She only had to shoot herself once.

Lonegan narrowed his lips, made himself look at what was left of her, then turned, pulled the door shut.

Usually, he took his time picking through town, filling saddlebags and feedsacks with jewelry and guns and whatever else would sell.

This time was different, though.

This time he just walked straight down main street to his buckboard, folded the side panel back into itself, and looked around for a horse.

When there wasn't one, he started walking the way he'd come in. Soon enough a horse whinnied.

Lonegan slowed, filled his stolen hat with pebbles and sand, started shaking it, shaking it.

Minutes later, the mare rose from the heat.

"Not you," he said.

She was briny with salt, from running. Had already been coming back to town for the water trough.

Lonegan narrowed his eyes at the distance behind her, for another horse. There was just her, though. He dumped the hat, slipped a rope over her head. She slumped into it, pulled for the water.

"Go then," he told her, pushing her away. Walking behind.

All around them were the dead and nearly dead, littering the streets, coming half out of windows.

Ahead of him, in the straight line from the last town to this one, there'd be another town, he knew. And another, and another. Right now, even, there was probably a runner out there from this town, trying to warn everybody of the snake oil man.

Lonegan would find him like he'd found the last, though. Because anybody good enough to leave his own family to ride all night, warn people twenty miles away, anybody from that stock would have been at the service Sunday morning too, done a little partaking.

Which meant he was dead in the saddle already, his tongue swelling in his mouth, a thirst rising from deeper than any thirst he'd ever had before.

Lonegan fixed the yoke on the mare, smeared more poultice into her wound.

If things got bad enough out there this time, he could do what he'd always thought would work: crush one of the wafers up, rub it into her nostrils, make her breathe it in.

She'd die, yeah, but she'd come back too. If she was already in the harness when she did, then he could get a few more miles out of her, he figured.

But it would spoil her meat.

Lonegan looked ahead, trying to figure how far it was going to be this time. How many days. Whether there was some mixture or compound or extract he hadn't found yet, one that could make him forget Gultree altogether. And Annie. Himself.

They'd been asking for it, though, he told himself, again.

If it hadn't been him, it would have been somebody else, and that other person might not have known how to administer it, then it would have been one half of the town—the live half—against the other.

And that just plain took too long.

No, it was better this way.

Lonegan nodded to himself, leaned over to spit, then climbed up onto the seat of the buckboard. The mare pulled ahead, picking around the bodies on her own. The one time one of them jerked, raising its arm to her, Lonegan put the thing down with the scattergun.

In the silence afterwards, there wasn't a sound in Gultree.

Lonegan shook his head.

At the far edge of town was what he'd been counting on: a house with a word gold-lettered onto the back of one of the windows: WM. JORGENSSON.

It was where Annie lived, where she cooked, where she'd been cooking, until the Sheriff came for her.

Lonegan tied the mare to a post, stepped into Annie's living room, found himself with his hat in his hands for some reason, the scattergun in the buckboard.

They were all dead, though.

"Cake," he said aloud, trying to make it real.

It worked.

In the kitchen, not even cut, was a white cake. It was smeared with lard, it looked like. Lard with sugar.

Lonegan ran his finger along the edge, tasted it, breathed out for what felt like the first time in days.

Yes.

He took the cake and the dish it was on too, stepped back into the living room.

The father was waiting for him, a felt bowler hat clamped down over his skull. He was dead, clutching a Bible the same way the Sheriff had been carrying the bottle.

The old man was working his mouth and tongue like he was going to say something.

Lonegan waited, waited, had no idea what one of these could say if it took a mind to.

Finally he had to say it for the old man, though, answer the only question that mattered: Annie.

"I got her out before," he said. "You don't need to worry about her none, sir."

The old man just creaked, deep in his throat.

Walking across his left eyeball was a wasp.

Lonegan took a step back, angled his head for another door then came back to the old man.

If—if the buzzards knew better than to eat these things, shouldn't a wasp too?

Lonegan narrowed his eyes at the old man, walked around to see him from the side.

He was dead, a shuffler, but—but not *as* dead.

It hadn't been a bad mixture, either. Lonegan had made it like every other time. No, it was something else, something . . .

Lonegan shook his head no, then did it anyway: tipped the old man's bowler hat off.

What spilled out was a new head of hair. It was white, silky, dripping blue.

The old man straightened his back, like trying to stand from the hair touching his neck now, for the first time ever.

"No," Lonegan whispered, still shaking his head, and then the old man held the Bible out to him.

It pushed Lonegan backwards over a chair.

He caught himself on his hand, rolled into a standing position in the kitchen doorway. Never even spilled the cake.

"You've been using the oil," he said to the old man, touching his own hair to show.

The old man—William Jorgensson: a *he*, not an it—didn't understand, just kept leading with the Bible.

Lonegan smiled, shook his head no. Thanks, but no.

The old man breathed in sharp then, all at once, then out again, blood misting out now. Meaning it was almost over now, barbershop oil or no.

Again, he started making the creaking sound with his throat. Like he was trying to talk.

When he couldn't get it out, and Lonegan wouldn't take the Bible, the old man finally reached into his pocket, came out with a handful of broken wafers, stolen from the pan at church.

It was what Annie had said: her father bringing the church back to her, since she wouldn't go.

Lonegan held his hands away, stepped back. Not that the crumbs could get through boot leather. But still.

The Bible slapped the wooden floor.

"You old thief," Lonegan said.

The old man just stood there.

"What else you got in there, now?" Lonegan asked.

The old man narrowed his half-dead eyes, focused on his hand in his pocket, and came up with the bottle Lonegan had given him for free. It was empty.

Lonegan nodded about that, got the old man nodding too.

"That I can do something about, now," he said, and stepped long and wide around the old man, out the front door.

The heat was stifling, wonderful.

Lonegan balanced the cake just above his shoulder, unhooked the panel on the side of the buckboard. It slapped down, the mare spooking ahead a step or two, until the reins stopped her.

Lonegan glared at her, looked back to the house, then did it anyway, what he knew he didn't have to: palmed up the last two bottles of barbershop oil. They were pale blue in the sunlight, like a cat's eyes.

He stepped back into the living room, slapped the wall to let the old man know he was back.

The old man turned around slow, the soles of his boots scraping the wood floor the whole way.

"Here," Lonegan said, setting the two bottles down on the table, holding up the cake to show what they were in trade for.

The old man just stared, wasn't going to make it. His index finger twitching by his thigh, the nailbed stained blue.

"And I'm sorry," Lonegan said. "Hear?"

By the time he'd pulled away, the old man had shuffled to the door, was just standing there.

"Give it six days," Lonegan said, touching his own hair to show what he meant, then laughed a nervous laugh, slapped the leather down on the mare's tender haunch.

Fucking Gultree.

He pushed out into the heat, was able to make himself wait all the way until dark for the cake. Because it was a celebration, he even sedated the mare, cut another flank steak off, packed it with poultice.

He'd forgot to collect any water, but he'd forgot to collect all the jewelry and guns too.

There'd be more, though.

In places without women like Annie Jorgensson.

Lonegan wiped the last of the mare's grease from his mouth, pulled his chin hair down into a point, and pulled the cake plate into his lap, started fingering it in until he realized that he was just eating the sweet off the top, like his aunt had always warned him against. It needed to be balanced with the dry cake inside.

He cut a wedge out with his knife, balanced it into his mouth, and did it again and again, until something popped under his blade, deep in the cake.

It was a half a wafer.

Lonegan's jaws slowed, then he gagged, threw up onto his chest, and looked all the way back to town, to the old man in the door, smiling now, lifting his Bible to show that he knew, that he'd known, that he'd been going to get religion into his daughter's life whether she wanted it or not.

Lonegan shook his head no, no, lied to the old man that—that, if she'd just waited to pull the trigger, he would have *told* her that it wasn't the poppy water, that he wouldn't have *let* her—but then he could feel it inside him, burrowing like a worm for his heart, his life.

He threw up again, but it was just thin blood now.

" . . . no," he said, trying to sling the vomit from his fingers. It didn't—it couldn't . . . didn't happen *this* fast. Did it?

But—but . . .

The oil, the barbershop oil. It was the delaying agent.

Lonegan stumbled up through the fire, scattering sparks, the cake plate shattering on a rock, and started falling towards the mare. To ride, fast, back to Gultree, back to the old man. Back to those last two bottles.

But the mare saw him coming, jerked her head away from the wagon wheel she was tied to.

The reins held. The spoke didn't.

She skittered back, still sluggish from what he'd given her, and Lonegan nodded, made himself slow down. Held his hat out like there were going to be something in it.

The mare opened her nostrils to the night, tasting it for oats, then turned her head sideways to watch Lonegan with one eye, then stepped back when he stepped forward, and again, and again, like a dance, then managed to keep this up for the rest of the night, her reins always just within reach of Lonegan's arms. Or what he thought was his reach.

➤ Monsters

When I was twelve and my parents were doing their usual thing of my dad living in an apartment to teach my mom a lesson, my mom finding something new of his each day to leave out on the lawn, I ended up spending three weeks of the summer with my grandmother and her new husband. My mother said she'd traded up for him after Granddad died, and that she deserved it. What she meant was that my grandmother's new husband had a vacation place in a town that had a beach, and filled with tourists. He'd made his money consulting or something, like I had any idea what that meant. All that mattered to me was that I wasn't going to be the go-between on phone calls for a while, and that I wasn't going to be standing at different front doors every few days, one of my parents at the curb, their car in gear, the other in the kitchen thinking up the perfect terrible thing to say across the lawn or sidewalk.

Needless to say, I'd pretty much decided to never get married.

Of course, though, it was summer, and I was twelve, and the world being what it was, a few streets over from my new granddad's house—I had to call him that, "Granddad"—there was a girl one grade ahead of me but the same age, and we kind of just fell in together the way you do no matter how old you are, when you each understand that this isn't going to last, that it doesn't have to matter.

This isn't about her, though. She doesn't even need a name here. Call her Elaine, I guess.

What this is about is the job she'd wound up with for August. Through some golf and beer circumstances, her parents, who were old enough that at first I thought she was staying with her grandparents too, had met another couple, who lived in that resort town year round, and were on the way to the mountains for their vacation. Which, yeah, I mean, it seemed to me like they were going on vacation from living on vacation, but the way it worked out for Elaine was that she got paid twenty dollars a week, in *advance*, to water their flowers and walk their dog. To prove she could do it she had to walk him up and down the street one day before they (the Wilkersons) left, but the dog, as big as he was, had been trained, so Elaine had no problem with him.

And of course, because I had nothing else to do with my days but duck my grandmother's loaded questions about my dad (my new granddad just watched me a lot, as if waiting for me to approach him, finally; I was his first grandkid, I think, so he thought I was made of glass), I'd stand with her while she drowned the flowers and then help her get Matey leashed up to make the rounds.

Which, those rounds, that *is* what this is about.

As we became more and more bold with Matey, sometimes we'd wrap his leash six or seven times around one of our fists and take him down to the boardwalk. The tourists usually gave us wide lanes to walk around. According to Elaine's parents, Sid Wilkerson had been some kind of big brass with the police department. He'd joined right after high school and then stayed on until his retirement cottage. The reason we got told this, I think, was so we wouldn't let the flowers die, and wouldn't let anything happen to Matey. It wasn't that Elaine's parents cared about the plants or the dog, but that it would be awkward to have to explain it to the Wilkersons, who they thought were good people to know, as they might have an inside line on a cheap rental next summer. I don't know. Like we had anything else going on, and were going to forget the flowers. Matey, though, he was the real fun.

Because Sid Wilkerson was ex-police, he was in some kind of retirement program for "canine units." When the bomb and drug and cadaver dogs all got too old to do their jobs anymore, Sid would take one, give it a good year or two as reward for catching so many bad guys.

And, though nobody'd left us any cheat sheet for Matey, we found out soon enough that he knew some kind of hand signals. We only ever figured out the obvious ones like "get" and "stay" and "go right," but even that was a thrill, especially after all the brainless dogs we cycled through at home.

He was like our secret, our treasure, and of course we wanted to show him off down at the beach. We each even had—at least I know *I* did— dreams of him saving a drowning lady, or smelling a bomb in a trash can and saving everybody's lives, or stopping a carjacking, something like that. It was what happened in these "What I did that summer I met that girl or guy, and we found ourselves in a mystery"-stories. Though Elaine and me lived in different states, we'd still read all the same books from the library, had the same romantic-sleuth-adventure plotlines in our heads, and would never talk about something so stupid as being in a story with a "magic" dog, of course. But that was partly just because talking about something's the best way to mess it all up, right?

When you're twelve, your superstitions are pure like they'll never be again, I'm pretty sure.

And, yeah, I did finally tell her about my parents and how stupid they were, and she listened and digested it for a day or two then showed me her dad's golf clubs in the storage closet behind their barbecue. Each of the clubs was bent perfectly in half, over the memory of a knee. I didn't ask who'd done it. It was enough to know it was us against them, and that, if we could help it, we were going to wind up different people.

We should have been more specific about that last part, though, spelled it out letter by letter, that what we meant was we weren't going to still be children when we grew up.

Instead, whoever answers these kinds of impulsive prayers just took the broad strokes into account.

We *are* different now, I mean. Definitely not our parents. But that's just because our parents, unlike Elaine, didn't have their throats chewed out the day before they were supposed to pack up and go back to their real lives.

This is why Matey is important here.

Sid Wilkerson should have told us all his commands before he left. The one we needed most was whatever one would make Matey forget all his training and just be a normal, average dog.

What happened, finally, as it had to I guess, was that we asked Elaine's parents if we could go down to the boardwalk for sausage-on-a-stick at dusk. There was a stand that faced the ocean and always had music rolling across the splintery counter. Elaine's parents said yes, provided we took the Wilkersons' dog, okay?

It kept us from having to ask.

As for my grandmother and "granddad," they were still on some schedule from 1950, where kids are supposed to stay outdoors until a half hour after dark, then sneak in, wash behind their ears, eat a cold dinner and—this was the update—watch game shows with them until bedtime. So I just went, didn't have to ask.

Because it was a Friday night, the very last one of the summer, the boardwalk was shoulder to shoulder, tight enough that the tourists weren't even making room for Matey. Not that they didn't notice him, they did, only now it was a few steps later, when they looked down at the back of their hand to see what they'd just rubbed against.

And Matey, the boardwalk was dog heaven to him. He was grinning, his tongue lolling, his eyebrows raised, tail playful like an invitation. He was what I imagined Sid Wilkerson to be like on the inside: totally content with his life, with everything he'd done, and now just enjoying retirement.

Still, Elaine kept the leash balled around her fist, just in case a cat darted through the forest of legs. As far as we knew, a hand held palm-out was enough to get Matey to stay until released, no matter what, but part of that was catching his eye, which we knew were the makings of some comedy routine we didn't want any part of, at least not in public.

Another part of being twelve is the certainty that one public embarrassment is enough to ruin the rest of your life.

Since Elaine had Matey—it was her turn—I carried the ten her dad had slipped us so he could feel like a hero.

It wasn't enough to cut through the three-deep line to the sausage stand, though.

"Well?" Elaine said, the leash between her and Matey pulled tight.

We couldn't stand in line with him for forty minutes, we knew.

"Other one," I shrugged, pointing down the beach with my chin to the place that sold sausage and drumsticks and got neither of them right. We'd only been down there once, when my grandparents were insisting on being grandparents. It involved umbrellas and complicated folding chairs and Elaine and me eating ice cream we really probably liked but had to act like we didn't. Because they were grandparents, too, they were blind to all the natural divisions of the beach that everybody else tuned into without even having to think about. What they didn't understand was that there was a senior citizen's part, way down by the parking lot—old people tended to wake up first—and then, for the next four miles, it was alternating sections of girls in bikinis and the guys they attracted and then whole families with complicated coolers and buckets for sand castles and trash bags for lunch. The only bump in all this was around the sausage and drumstick place; it ran right by the boardwalk, which meant whoever was on that beach could duck under to smoke or do whatever. So, it was the bad area, more or less, the part that when you walked through it you became aware of how you were holding your face.

And of course my new granddad, the consultant, plopped his chair right down in the middle of it, and kept telling Elaine and me to go introduce ourselves to these kids, or those kids.

That was the sausage and drumstick place we were at now.

It wasn't so much Matey that gave us the nerve we needed to go there either, but that neither of us wanted to back out. I mean, it was our last Friday night of the summer. If we were going to kiss or anything, it was now or never, and the boardwalk was right there to duck under, right?

Not that either of us knew how to start such a thing.

The line at this stand, of course, was nothing. We took our sausage-on-a-stick and gave the four dollars it cost, and I held our large drink because Elaine didn't have enough hands. By then we were sharing a straw, of course.

We sat on a utility pole bench and pulled the heat lamp skin off with our teeth and let the grease run down into our hands, and knew this adventure or romance or mystery we'd been pretending to be involved in was almost over, now. Maybe it would be better by the time school got started, though. Already I was thinking how I was going to describe Elaine to my friends, or, worse, to my dad when he was trying to get even with my mom by talking "boy-stuff" with me. Teaching me about girls, like a secret. Like he knew.

As for the mystery we were supposed to be on, the closest thing the resort town had was that it had misplaced four people over the course of the summer. None of them had washed up, though, so it wasn't a very pressing thing. Probably they'd just ducked their weekly hotel tab, slipped up the Interstate. That was what my new granddad said, at least, and he'd lived here longer than anybody else we knew except maybe Sid Wilkerson. But if Sid Wilkerson were here, he'd have probably already solved the thing. With our help, of course. And Matey's.

I still smile, thinking of it like that.

And Elaine, God. If I'd have ever got married, I'm pretty sure it would have been to the first girl who reminded me of Elaine, the first girl who looked like what Elaine might have grown up into.

I can still see her, too, sitting at the top of the stairs like she was waiting for me to save her, all the blood still, then, in her body.

I was twelve years old, though.

But that's no excuse.

This is what happened: we'd found a trash can to leave our half-eaten sausage sticks in. It was close enough to the boardwalk that people would try to drop drinks down into it, so to avoid getting splashed, we just lobbed our sticks over. Matey was trained enough that he didn't snatch them from the air. He was one of those dogs that you could put a treat on his nose and he wouldn't eat until you told him he could.

How close we were to the darkness under the boardwalk then was about four feet, I'd guess, and Matey wasn't even straining at the leash to go into it, chase down some bad guy, but we went anyway, just on a silent agreement that this was going to stand in for everything else we hadn't done. This was going to be our big adventure.

Underneath, once our eyes adjusted, it was another world—trash and smoke and cast-off clothes and seaweed the tide brought in. Because the sun couldn't get to it to dry it up, it festered and stank. And there were eyes watching us, we could tell. Too many posts to tell what was bodies, what wasn't. Just that some of the posts were blowing out pale lines of smoke. It was like walking through a dream, I suppose, the kind where you don't realize you can't breathe until you're suddenly suffocating. Matey could feel it too, I think. He didn't growl or pull against Elaine, but there was a new tenseness about him. It had to do with his ears and his tail.

Without him, we probably would have made a show of pretending to be looking for something we couldn't find, then scampered back to the safety of the beach.

Nobody approached us, or said anything to us.

My guess is that the people under there had a certain respect for the line Matey still cut. He just looked like a police dog.

Ten minutes later, breathing again, we were on the boardwalk. It was exactly forty-four minutes past the time Elaine was supposed to have been home, and there was a band taking the stage somewhere behind us, so the crowd was streaming past like water. We kept our arms close, and I went first so I could keep Matey between us, which, this is how parents are supposed to act, I'm pretty sure. They're supposed to take the knees and elbows the world has to offer, keep their kid safe, out of the way.

In our case, though, we trusted Matey, sure, but didn't want him taking a piece out of a passing hand either.

And I'm probably making these people rushing past us sound like a mob. It was nothing that big, was starting to thin out after a few seconds, even, so we could see clear concrete ahead, and past that the road that led to Elaine's and however we were going to say goodbye.

Maybe Matey could feel that, too, how we weren't exactly pushing to get to that awkwardness.

Either way, some of his training bubbled up, right at the end of the crowd.

For the first time since we'd been walking him, he exploded, real jaw-snapping, slobbering, maniac killer dog kind of stuff. Not at us either, but at somebody in the crowd. Had they touched his ear wrong? Were they carrying drugs, a bomb?

I held onto his leash with Elaine, and still, he was edging us forward.

Who he was barking at was this one guy wearing leather pants instead of the bright shorts everybody else had on.

The guy stood still, let the crowd melt ahead of him, and looked from Matey up to Elaine and me.

He was smiling.

"Yours?" he said, taking a step forward, to Matey.

I started to yell to him not to, that couldn't he see the dog hated him, but I didn't even say anything. This close to Elaine, I could smell the chlorine on her, from when we'd swam earlier in the hotel pool, when we had the whole ocean if we wanted.

"Nice doggy," the guy said like a joke, taking another step forward, and there wasn't even anything that strange about his voice or, from what I could tell, his smell, or anything, but Matey was about to choke himself on the leash.

"He's a police dog," Elaine managed to get out.

The guy nodded, said that explained it then, yeah? It was a joke to him, all of this.

"Please," I said, losing ground, "we've got to—" but the guy was stepping forward *again*, like he wanted to see what Matey was made of.

Instead of walking away to his concert, he squatted down so that Matey's teeth were maybe two feet from his face, then looked over him to us.

"Yours?" he said, and we shook our heads no just as Matey bunched his haunches and surged forward for the kill.

Though he didn't make it to the guy's throat, he did catch him in the meat just under the thumb.

The guy ripped his hand away slower than I thought made any sense. As if it were made of paper, and he didn't want to pull too fast, as that might rip it even more.

"No worries," he said, his voice a new kind of even, his eyes photographing Matey practically, and—we talked about this on the way home—for the ten or maybe twelve seconds more we were there on the sidewalk with him, the guy's hand where Matey's tooth had opened it, it was just white flesh on the inside. No blood. Like the time I'd cracked my shin on the curb next door and then sat there for maybe five minutes staring at the white I knew had to be cartilage. What I was afraid of, and never told anybody, was that I was dead, and only just figuring it out. That I would only be alive if I bled.

It kept me looking behind us all the way to Elaine's turn-off, and then made me walk past it with her too, to deposit Matey one last time. Tomorrow the Wilkersons were supposed to be back, and the town was going to just go on without us, without even remembering us, probably.

At least that's what we thought.

Back at the split in the road which went uphill to my new granddad's house, after having held hands for the width of exactly three consecutive houses, which even this late in the summer felt impulsive, like falling off some tall thing, Elaine leaned down and kissed me and then turned before I could kiss back, danced off to her house.

Our nerves were still on fire from being under the boardwalk, and from Matey biting that guy, and the night, for the first time I could remember, it was alive.

On the way home I kept smiling on accident and then rubbing it in with the side of my arm.

This year at school was going to be different, I knew. It didn't matter what was going on at my house, or houses. I was going to be a different person. I was leaving all the stupid stuff behind me.

At my new granddad's I sat at the table and watched game shows and ate some cold Tater Tots with warm brown ketchup—my grandmother had no idea that ketchup went in the fridge, not the cabinet—then went up to my room to cry with the door closed, and hit the mattress because I was being stupid but then tell myself to just get it all out now anyway, because I wasn't going to let this happen again, ever.

I went to sleep on top of the covers in my beach clothes, and the last thing I remember thinking was Sid Wilkerson, driving across all of America to get back to Matey, so that, when I started hearing him bark, I thought it was just in my head.

But then it wasn't.

I rose, parted the blinds of my room, and there on the beach, staked on a chain, was Matey, long strings of saliva arcing out from his mouth.

"I don't think he likes me," a voice said behind me.

I turned around slow.

It was the guy in the leather pants.

He was just standing there.

"You—you shouldn't—" I started to say, building up to a scream, but then he was close, his hand clamped over the lower part of my face, my back pressed into the wall, his eyes hot at mine.

His breath smelled like Matey's.

"Wanna be number five?" he said, smiling.

I tried kicking him but it was like kicking a brick wall. My tears were collecting on the top of his hand. He lifted his hand, licked them off, his other hand already keeping me quiet.

"Your little girlfriend," he said then. "She's not here, is she?"

If my heart had been pounding before, it stopped now.

"Yeah," the guy said, leaning back to study Matey.

"Don't," I told him. "She's—you can't . . . "

"You'd be surprised at what I can do, maybe," he said back. "Want a little test drive?"

It took me a bit to hear what he was saying. I shook my head no and he smiled with his eyes.

"Then you know what to do," he said.

I shook my head no, I didn't—I didn't I didn't I didn't—but he was already stuffing me deep enough into the closet that by the time I got out, he was gone.

And then I realized it was quiet for the first time since I'd woke.

I felt my way to the window.

Matey was gone.

I didn't even stop to put my shoes on or care if my new granddad heard me. I went out the window, through the bushes, and crossed lawn after lawn, to get to Elaine first.

By the time I got to her street I could taste blood in my throat, feel it on the soles of my feet, but none of that mattered.

I jumped the rail to get to her front door, stabbed the doorbell button until Elaine's dad answered, a straight golf club held low by his thigh.

I was crying and trying to talk and, finally, Elaine's mom had to call my mom in the city to get my new granddad's phone number.

Nobody was mad, but nobody understood, either.

The whole time Elaine sat at the top of their carpeted stairs, studying me. Because she was in her nightgown, her dad wouldn't let her come down.

"Sid Wilkerson gets home tomorrow," I said, like my last hope.

Elaine's mom patted me on the shoulder.

They thought—I don't know what they thought. That I was lovesick, I guess. That I was twelve years old and had fallen for their daughter and now was making up things to keep them there.

Soon enough my grandmother was at the door in her robe, and was apologizing to Elaine's parents, guiding me away, to the car with my new granddad sitting in the front seat.

"No problem, sport," he said, reaching back to clap me on the leg like I was part of the club now. Like he understood, and would cover for me if needed.

I looked away, my breath too hitched up to answer any of my grandmother's questions. After we'd gone all the way to the end of the cul-de-sac to make the wide turn home my new granddad didn't accelerate like a normal human, but crept along at senior citizen speed. I just sat in the back seat, watching all the dark houses skid by into my past, thinking to myself that this was it, then, it *was* over, maybe Matey really was back in his pen at the Wilkersons', and maybe I deserved the parents I had, maybe I deserved everything that had happened, even Elaine, the way she'd looked at me from the top of the stairs, her toes digging into the carpet. It was like, being a grade ahead, she understood too. Like she wanted to come down, let me explain it all to her.

And I would have, that's the thing. All night.

I pushed my knee hard into the back of the seat and closed my eyes and tried to hide in my arms, and only looked up when my new granddad made the sound he made when a game show answer was surprising him.

What he was seeing was the guy from the boardwalk.

He was walking our direction—to the turnaround—*away* from Elaine's house.

At his side was Matey. The way he was controlling him was he had the handle of the leash in his left hand, with his right hand cinched down to the back of Matey's neck.

As we passed him I slammed myself up against the glass and he stopped, smiled, nodded something like thanks and then opened his hands, let Matey slip away.

I was out of the car before my new granddad could even stop it, and caught Matey ten minutes later in front of a house with a motion-sensitive security light. He was crazy, even snapping at me. I calmed him down as much as I could, held his head to my chest, then looked back for the guy I knew had to have been running behind us.

There was just my new granddad in his house slippers, though.

"That's Sid's?" he said, about Matey.

I nodded, and then—because they were my grandparents, and not really that bad—they rode the brakes and lit the sidewalk ahead of me, all the way back to the Wilkersons'.

I ushered Matey into his pen then watched him check all the corners over and over, and that was the second-to-the-last time I ever saw him.

The next morning, then, along with the rest of the town, we got the news: Elaine had been killed in her own bed. Something had chewed her throat out, splashed her all over the walls.

It was like I was hearing all this through a long series of tubes. Like I could angle my head away and not any of it would be real anymore.

Over the next three days, with my grandparents' help, the police pieced the events of the night together, and decided that Elaine had become too attached to Matey, so had smuggled him up to her room—her parents said she usually didn't go to bed that early, no, especially not after a scene like I'd made—and then something had happened. Something terrible. Their proof was the blood and hair smeared on the gate of Matey's pen. According to them, he'd probably licked it all off his muzzle and feet himself, hours ago. His water pan was empty too, I heard, which somehow made it not so much his fault: if we'd only not been kids; if we'd only taken better care of him.

As for my run across all the lawns to save her, everybody just shrugged, assumed I knew she had Matey up in her room, but, out of loyalty, wouldn't say anything about it. And, after a prod or two, they didn't push me to either. The story they had was neater, I mean. Made more sense: Elaine had accidentally made some bad hand signal to him, or stumbled onto an old kill command, or worn the same hair spray as some long-gone bad guy.

Whatever she'd done, or whatever had happened, the facts were that her throat had been torn out, and Matey, her responsibility, had been running the streets around her house that night, and had even snapped at me, whom he knew and loved, when I tried to pull him close.

The last time I saw him, an Animal Control officer was leading him away from the Wilkersons' house, to be put down. He had that same grin on his face too, like this was just going to be another adventure—the boardwalk, with different smells.

Standing on the porch were Sid Wilkerson and a younger cop, who'd maybe worked with Matey before Matey started killing sixth grade girls. When Sid Wilkerson saw me he just thinned his lips, turned away. Shut the door.

My new granddad guided my away by the shoulder.

My mom and dad were already having a complicated road race to get to me, prove to each other who the real parent was.

My grandmother was making something elaborate for all of us to eat, to prove how happy she was in her new marriage.

And Elaine.

All that was left of Elaine was a black stain on Matey's fence, with stupid, hateful flies crawling over it (because I didn't believe, I went and saw). And the shape my hand still remembered, from when she'd held it for three consecutive houses, and from when it had brushed hers in that dreamworld under the boardwalk where we'd walked together, not even afraid.

We should have been, though.

We should have run out into the surf as far as we could, until the parents packing up their bags became our parents and splashed out after us, shook us by the shoulders until we woke up.

Except they never would have caught us. We were twelve.

"He thinks I made him do it," I said, not really to my new granddad but just out loud.

My new granddad licked his lips, said, "Sid, you mean?"

Across town, somebody in protective goggles was probably already pushing a needle into the back of Matey's neck, then, if they were nice, petting the fur down over it.

I kept having to make my hands into fists.

"He thinks we made Matey bite him," I said, my lower lip trembling more than I wanted to let it, so that I couldn't say there hadn't been *time* for Matey to do it, that it had to have happened *after* I caught Matey, that there never *had* been any blood on him.

My new granddad's hand was still on my shoulder. He patted me, looked ahead of us, and said it wasn't my fault, not really. I looked up to him but he was just staring down the sidewalk as if already deciding where to place each foot.

"Sid should just quit taking those in," he said, tottering forward.

By the time they came for Christmas he would be on a cane, but, that summer anyway, he was still pretending.

"Taking what in?" I said.

"Those dogs," he said. "He not tell you?"

"They're . . . police," I said like a question.

He pulled his lower lip into his mouth, took another step—it was going to take us *forever* to get back to the house—and said, "Those are—those dogs he takes. What do you call them, that smell out people who have been . . . "

He made a motion with his hand, like dumping something out.

Cadaver dogs.

Trained to find dead people.

I breathed in once and held it, remembering the way the guy in the leather pants' hand hadn't bled. How he'd smiled from what should have hurt. How cold he'd been when he'd pulled me to him, how he'd got in my room. How—how . . . His breath.

Did I want to be number five?

I swallowed, my eyes full with what had happened, with who, or what, I'd led to Elaine, with what he might be picking from his teeth right now in whatever dark place he was holed up in for the daylight hours, and then, to make up for it, to *start* making up, I draped my new granddad's arm across my shoulders, to help him up the hill, and understood a little even then, I think, about what it might be like to have spent your whole life alone, so that just one person reaching up to help you along could mean the world, and save your life, and make everything all right for a few moments.

But yeah, then we got home, and the only thing really different about the next few years, about all the years since that summer, is that I still wake at night, sure I've just heard the creak of leather, and I can close my eyes, sure, but then Elaine's waiting for me at the top of the stairs, like she understands, her gashed-open throat just white, not even bleeding.

The first girl I ever kissed.

The last girl I ever kissed.

What I'm waiting for now, I think, is for her to walk down in her nightgown, take me by the elbow and lead me back to that night the guy in the leather pants asked me if I knew what I had to do here, or if I wanted to be number five?

The first time I made that decision, I was twelve, and didn't know I was going to have to live with it.

When my mom calls these days, she tells me I should consider getting a dog, maybe. That it would be good for me. A nice first step.

Thanks, Mom, but I've already got a dog, really.

His name is Matey. He lives in my head.

Maybe we'll come see you one of these days.

➤ Wolf Island

They found each other on the second day. She thought she remembered him from the deck. He knew her at once, even in the waterlogged rags of her dress: the painter's girlfriend.

"Ronald," he said about himself.

"Where are we?" she said back, falling into him.

The horizon in every direction was featureless, the sea green and swollen. Around them the beach looked spent. The storm had dredged up muck from the bottom and left it well above the tide line. Drifting back and forth at the water's edge was the flotsam of the ship they'd been on—clothes, linen napkins, plastic jugs. A man, facedown and pale, draped in seaweed.

Ronald held her tighter, then remembered he was naked.

He tried to push her away, to go collect some pants from the surf, but she wouldn't let him go.

"Last night," she said into his chest, her voice dropping to a whisper. "Last night there was . . . I saw it. Running on the beach. A wolf."

Ronald stroked her hair down along her back and studied the trees.

The night after that she was sick, from eating the fruit. At first she'd said it was from the water in the pool, but Ronald had drunk there as well.

The next morning—she'd asked to be alone for the night, embarrassed, but then called for him between bouts—Ronald was sitting alone on the beach. The dead man in the surf had drifted farther out to sea, so Ronald could no longer make out the crabs picking at the bloated face. Soon enough a fin cut the water beside the dead man.

Ronald stood, suddenly alert.

The painter's girlfriend padded up beside him. Her name was Emma, but he was trying not to think of her like that.

"Are those—?" she said, then clapped her hands over mouth when the fin breached the water, became a spinning dolphin, the water spiraling off it.

It was followed by another, and another.

"A pod," Ronald said, lacing his fingers into hers.

"Aren't you hungry?" she said to him, then doubled over, her right fist to the sand, and started heaving again.

Ronald stepped forward to give her her privacy.

The dolphins were cavorting around the dead man.

"They're trying to wake him," Ronald said, impressed.

After a while the pod ducked under, didn't come back up.

By the time Emma came back from the woods, pale and hugging herself, nodding that it was over, Ronald had a large bird, its underside torn open, the sand soaking the blood.

"How did you?" she said.

He held up the driftwood, cracked sharp at one end.

"It wasn't scared," he told her. "I don't think it's ever been hunted."

This made Emma cry. Ronald looked from the bird to her and drew her closer to him, held him to her until she was still again.

The bird was like an oversized gull. A tern, maybe. Definitely not a pelican.

After pulling all the feathers out there was hardly any meat.

Emma shook her head no about it anyway.

Ronald nodded that he understood, and peeled the stringy meat from the bone, had his eyes closed to eat it when Emma stopped him.

"What?" he said.

She took the meat, touching it with as little of her fingertips as possible, and walked to the water line, laid the meat in the wet sand.

Within thirty seconds, two large crabs and one smaller one were snipping at the meat.

"Now," she said to Ronald, and he stepped forward, brought his foot down on one of the large crabs.

Its claws sliced the air uselessly, and then Ronald drove his bare foot deeper and the crab cracked, died.

Emma laughed nervously.

Ronald studied her, no real expression on his face.

Two nights later they found tracks in the sand. Dog, wolf, something. Running.

"What would they—what would they *eat* out here?" Emma said.

"Birds," Ronald said. "Bird eggs."

But then, searching for safe fruit, Emma came screaming out of the tree line, led Ronald back to see.

Another of the crew, dead. Except he hadn't drowned. This one's throat had been ripped out, its thighs and side eaten upon.

"Check his pockets," Ronald said out loud, and knelt, rummaged, came up with a handful of folded paper that crumbled at his touch.

The dead man's belt he gave to Emma, after washing it in the surf.

"We should bury him," she said.

"Tomorrow," he said back.

Because there was no fire, they were having to eat the crab meat raw. It had yet to make them sick, but it wasn't filling, either. Just sufficient.

"Do you remember the moon that first night?" Emma was saying.

Ronald looked over at her, studied her.

"On the ship, you mean?" he said.

"I told this girl at dinner . . . I told her that the reason it was so big was that we were getting closer to it."

Ronald chuckled.

"That was before—" she started.

Ronald let his eyes move from her to the water, though with the sun setting the surface was almost too bright, like poured gold.

"The storm," he finished for her.

Emma shook her head no, no, said, "Before the . . . you know."

The disappearances. Everybody locked in their cabins for two nights, their meals brought to them, every room searched by stern men who traveled in packs of four.

Ronald nodded.

The dolphins were still there, sewing themselves up and down through the water, the young one always beside instead of in the line.

"Do you think anyone's coming?" she said then.

Ronald chuckled again.

The next morning she caught him getting bait. Another gull, tern, whatever.

He had left his pants in the trees—they were the only pants on the whole island—then bent over to all fours, allowed his back to bow with the change.

Slathered over his muzzle was the yolk of the bird's clutch of eggs.

What he was doing, what he had found he could do, was stake out the nest and wait for the bird to return, then leap into the air, slash the bird open.

It was more than was necessary, but it felt good to move, to bound, to pounce.

Emma leaned forward and screamed.

Ronald slung his face back towards her and started to give chase, then caught himself, raced around instead to meet her.

He was himself again by the time she found him.

"It was, it was—" she struggled to say.

"Where?" he said.

He was naked again, though, his pants all the way down the beach.

This time Emma noticed, pushed away from him.

"I'm sorry," he told her.

She started to run, fell down, climbed back up, and he followed at a leisurely, regretful pace, his tracks going from man to wolf, from a jog to a lope, and when he finally took her down, it was mercy, it was tender. He sat on his haunches with his mouth and paws bloody with her and stared out across the flat water.

The moon was large again, perfect.

He was alone now.

For a week then, or two, he stayed on all fours as much as he could. The fur kept the sun off his skin, and he could soak his paws in the water to stay cool.

The meat from her lasted two days, the bones another day, and then he was back to the fatless birds, and her trick with the crabs, and slapping oily fish up out of the surf, a maddening process that made him tear at the water with his claws and roar so that the fish wouldn't return for hours, sometimes all day.

He should have controlled himself better, he knew. Not with Emma, that was her fault, but on the ship, before the storm.

There was nothing to do about it, though.

Twice he swam out into the sea as far as he could and changed back, to see if he would sink, but each time he did he would change back again, like a response, and paddle to the shallows, collapse in the surf, wake as a man, like when he first washed up.

He howled, and hated himself for it, but it made him feel less alone, just to be reaching out.

Running three times around the island in boredom, timing himself against a stick marking the tide, he cut a hind paw on a broken shell and then scented the blood in his tracks the next time around, and was able to pretend for one more lap that he was hunting, that he was on the trail, gaining ground.

But dusk found him again at the water's edge, applying his black tongue to his paw.

He knew from past injuries that now he would have to stay on all fours until the cut had healed to a certain point. Which meant staying awake, not escaping into sleep. Because if he did, the cut might be life threatening to a man's foot, and he might bleed out.

He occupied himself with another bird's nest.

Instead of slopping the eggs down this time, he watched them, tuned into them so that he could hear the stirrings under the shell, and time and again he held his breath, hearing a white wall about to crumble, a wet beak scratching it from the inside, but each time, nothing.

Finally he lowered his mouth to the clutch, ate them one by one.

Because it might help, he packed his hind paw with the yolky sand and then three-legged it up and down the beach, keeping guard. Somewhere out there a whale called, a whistle so deep he thought at first it was an attack.

No other whale called back.

Without meaning to, he changed back, was standing ankle deep in the water, the salt licking at his cut, tiny silver fish darting in to nip at the yolk.

He had no idea how long he might live here.

He had something of a beard by the time the dolphins returned, frolicking out where he knew the island's shelf dropped off into colder water.

He called out to them but they were oblivious.

He dropped down to all fours, changed even though it burned calories he was only going to be able to replace with the birds he now hated, and backed up to the tree line.

He knew from other bored days that if he ran fast enough, and light enough, he could run across the sand and skate on the water for four long steps. Once five. It wasn't really running on the surface, but it was more than a man could do anyway. In the absence of radio, it had become entertainment.

This time he made it the average four steps, then paddled in place, his tail wagging in the water.

The dolphins were gone again, though.

He paddled out farther, to where the sand rose again and he could stand as a man.

Though he waited for hours, the dolphins didn't surface where he could see them, even when he felt he had become part of the ocean.

Giving up, he reached down to scratch the hardened scab on his foot and fumbled a smooth rock up from the sand. He scratched his long fingernails on it for no real reason then turned to float and kick his way back to shore, to the birds he had no taste for.

But then, between him and the island, an adult dolphin surfaced, regarded him.

They stared at each other for long moments, then the dolphin nodded twice, flicked its tail and disappeared.

Hours later, sitting on the beach, he figured it out: the dolphin had heard his fingernails on the rock. It was how they talked to each other.

He splashed into the dark water, excited, and scrounged up another rock, worked his fingernails over it again.

Twenty seconds later, two dolphins silhouetted themselves on the water.

Their smiles almost made him cry.

After bird the next morning, he spoke his rock gibberish to the dolphins again, and tried to swim out to them. If he could just touch one, he told himself. Just feel flesh again.

The dolphins came, curious, and flashed around him, only to jump twenty and thirty yards away, as if showing off. For him.

He laughed and splashed the water and clicked his fingernails on the rock, and this went on for four full days before he was finally able to touch one.

The sensation was exquisite.

He named her Emma.

From the shore later he collected all the fruit he could and slung it out to the dolphins in thanks.

They just nosed it, played with it. But then it brought other fish, which the dolphins seemed to feed on, judging by the racket of birds they collected.

Ronald waved to them then held the rock underwater, clicked and scratched his gratefulness into the sea.

Later that night, stalking a nested bird, he happened to catch a scent from one of his front paws.

It was the lingering remnant of the dolphin.

He smelled it thoroughly, so that he knew its dimensions, its essence, and then applied his tongue, and when that was done he looked out over the water.

Behind him and to the left, the bird squawked, as if impatient to die.

Ronald didn't look back to it.

Though he continued to play with the dolphins for three more days, it was different now. He was gauging them, learning their various speeds, and agility, and nerves.

Emma was the one with the calf, and calves, of course, well. They were calves.

She was careful to always keep herself between Ronald and the calf.

He nodded to her that he understood, and took her defensiveness as a sort of permission, almost an invitation.

It took him two days after that to devise his plan.

What he did, finally, was unbury the man he'd eaten from his first night here, for his shirt, and then find the pants he had forsaken after Emma.

Into each of these he stuffed dried seaweed and linen napkins and other flotsam, and fixed the pants to the shirt with the belt, until the clothes were in the shape of a man. As seen from under the water, anyway. As silhouetted against the daytime sky.

Next, with a loop of green seaweed he had to dive for, he tied the ankle of the clothes man to the shore, so that he couldn't drift too far.

After that he only had to wait until nightfall to push the dummy out.

He was careful too, in case dolphins can see onto land somehow, to allow himself to be seen just sitting there at the tree line, a man.

After dark, however, he chose another, faster shape. One that could see better, and hear the deeper lap of water, perhaps, as it was displaced by a moving body.

On cue, unable to help themselves perhaps, the dolphins came to investigate. First the one Ronald called Jare Bear, then Santo, then Emma, as if only there to instruct her calf in some arcane dolphin matter. How these pink land dolphins would never revive, perhaps, no matter how much they were nudged.

Ronald smiled with his black lips, drew the necessary air into his lungs, and began timing the sleek noses rising from the water, the toothed mouths yawning to test this strange thing.

The second time the calf's nose broke the surface, he exploded silently from the tree line, floated across the wet sand, which never had a chance to suck at his paws, and then was running across the water, his knees only breaking through on the fourth step, which was exactly how long the vine of seaweed was.

He sunk his teeth into the dorsal fin of the retreating calf and felt himself surge out into the water, the calf racing for the deep, but Ronald was able to get his feet planted at the last hump of sand.

Emma and the other dolphins flashed by him angrily, even butted him down, but he struggled back to shore, gasping, already changing, the calf writhing in his arms.

As the bite on his dorsal was only superficial, the calf lived until the next morning, with Ronald cupping water up onto it, and stroking its forehead, talking to it. Emma and the pod surfacing again and again, calling out with their shrill whistles and clicks.

The calf lasted nearly eight days.

Forever, Ronald thought to himself.

It might be that he could live out here forever.

He had been eating birds and the hateful crabs for a week, it felt like, when the dolphins finally came back again.

"Where did you go?" he called out to them, knee deep, laughing to be unalone again.

He drifted out, collected a rock, called them to him, and they played and swam and he even touched one of them again. Jare Bear, he was pretty sure, as Santo seemed to be either missing or unaccountably shy.

From the last hump of sand he said to Emma that dolphins were supposed to be smart, right?

It was a joke.

She smiled her stupid smile.

Ronald laughed, splashed water at her, and then, just because he was happy, he fished the rest of the afternoon, finally collected two of the big silver ones with the blue fins, each as long as his arm.

He waded out, slung them to the pod then had to throw rocks to keep the birds away.

The dolphins never came for the fish, though, and finally it was night and he was sitting.

Would they eat eggs? he wondered, and then smiled: he'd forgotten to *call* them, with the rock and fingernail thing. Either that or dolphins don't eat dead things.

But isn't that what they got at the water parks?

Ronald shrugged, stood, and brushed the sand from his backside.

The next morning, crabs were picking over the two fish that had washed up.

Ronald chased them off, arranged the fish on a high black rock, for the birds. Just because.

The following day the dolphins were back.

Ronald lowered his hands under the water, scratched the rock, and Emma rose up, nodded, treading water with her meaty tail. Behind her, playful, Jare Bear came up out of the water onto his tail then skated backwards, undulating his whole body to stay up.

Ronald stood, clapped, and Santo exploded from the water, hung there in the crystal droplets.

Ronald stepped in, went out to them, and this time they were all around him, nudging him, rubbing him with their rough, pungent skin, each of them close enough that, on instinct, Ronald covered his privates, just to be safe. Not that they would hurt him on purpose, but they were curious, dumb.

Again, then, Jare Bear rose up out of the water, danced backwards on his tail—evidently he was the only one of the three who'd learned that trick—and fell in, kicked once and disappeared into the deep, over the underwater cliff's edge.

While he was gone, Emma and Santo kept Ronald occupied, showing off their few tricks, bobbing and nodding their heads, smiling until Ronald was smiling with them, clapping the palms of his hand on the surface of the water in joy.

"You don't even remember, do you?" he said to Emma, patting her. "You don't even understand me, right?"

She kept smiling, nodding.

But then.

Something electric. No, not electric, just . . . Emma and Santo, they'd each tensed in the water, Ronald could tell. As if on accident. And now they were embarrassed by it, showing off even more desperately.

"What?" Ronald said, turning to look behind him.

And he saw it: Jare Bear was racing towards him, making a straight line. No fancy swimming like usual, but moving through the water like a bullet this time.

He's going to jump over me, Ronald knew.

It was another trick, another show of trust.

Except then, yards behind Jare Bear, another, more patient fin rose, this one as long at the base as Jare Bear himself, easily, and black. And gaining. Definitely gaining.

Ronald opened his mouth in wonder.

This is where the pod had been the last few days.

Swimming across the ocean to collect *this*.

He felt himself start to change, out of fear, and was halfway there when Jare Bear flashed by impossibly fast.

An instant later, the water swelled and surged.

The orca was passing, its left pectoral fin taking out Ronald's legs. The pain made him howl. Between states like he was, he was vulnerable, had twice as many nerves in his skin.

He was left roiling, trying to breathe.

But he could make it.

Once he was changed, there was nothing that could—

When he surfaced, though, he could see that Jare Bear had escaped, by skidding up onto the beach.

The great whale had too, but, heavier, and with more surface, not as far.

Now it was twisting and flopping back.

Now, Ronald told himself, and shot off the hump of sand with his new, powerful hind legs, to dart the twenty yards to shore and run deep into the trees, only . . . what?

Emma.

She had him by the hind paw.

He came around with his other, clawed at her face so that ribbons of blood swirled up, and something softer, like an eye, but then Santo hit him in the back with his blunt nose, and then Emma was dragging him out past the hump, over the bottomless cold water, and then, just as fast, she was gone.

Ronald slapped the water where he thought she was and then felt the water surge around him again.

He only had time to get all four paws in front of him before the orca hit, driving him up in a spray of water then catching him just as he came down again, taking him deeper, and faster, so that the sun on the dark surface was the moon to him, just a pale spill on the water, already breaking up into pieces, not perfect at all. The drifting shadows around it shaped like dolphins.

Above them the birds wheeled and called, hungry.

► Teeth

There was a woman waiting for him just outside his office. Kupier nodded to her, opened his door, and shrugged out of his jacket. Tuesday, it was Tuesday. He had to say it like that until noon sometimes to get it to stick.

The woman was now standing in the door he hadn't closed behind him.

"Well," Kupier said, easing into his chair, looking across his desk at her, "don't make me start guessing, here."

The woman entered, timid.

"Detective," she said.

Kupier spread his fingers and pressed his open hands onto all the manila folders on his desk, like he was trying to keep them down against something—the shuffle of the nine o'clock shift-change the woman was letting in, maybe—but then cocked his elbows, straightened his arms, pushing himself up. Because she seemed like the kind of woman who was used to that.

"Sit down," he said, offering her a chair.

She was wearing a denim skirt, her hair fixed close to her head. Sixty-five, give or take.

"I didn't know who else to tell," she said, then flashed her eyes out the open door, at the station house. "They told me to wait . . . that you—"

"They're real comedians at eight in the morning," Kupier said. "I think it's the donuts, something in the sprinkles."

The woman hid her eyes and clenched her chin into a prune.

"You have to understand," she said. "I started out just watching birds—"

"Ms. . . . ?" Kupier led off, his pencil ready.

"Lambert," she said. "I'm married."

Kupier wrote into his notebook *Tuesday*.

"Now," he said, leaning forward like he was interested, "birds?"

Mrs. Lambert nodded, wrung her hands in her lap. They were already red and chapped from it. The bench outside Kupier's office was wallowed out like a church pew.

"It's a logical progression," Mrs. Lambert said. "You start out just wanting to know the name of one you think has unusual coloring, a unique call, and then every time you see that bird, you say its name inside and it feels good, Detective, familiar, but now the rest of the birds in the park have names too, so you learn them too, and then it's trees, what kind of trees the birds are in. It makes the world more . . . more *alive*, Detective. Instead of birds and trees, you have elms and chinaberries and grackles and thrushes and—and—"

Kupier nodded, knew not to interrupt.

"And then, one day, one day you . . . you see it."

"It?"

Mrs. Lambert tightened her mouth, embarrassed, but amused with herself too, it seemed. "Maybe I shouldn't have—"

Kupier said it again, though: "It?"

"Them," Mrs. Lambert corrected, then started to say whatever she'd come to say but stood to go instead, suddenly unsure how to hold her purse.

Kupier let her get almost to the door. "*It*, Mrs. Lambert?"

Mrs. Lambert stopped, a mouse.

Kupier smiled, could almost hear her eyelids falling in defeat.

"Pellets," she said. "Owl pellets. Detective."

Kupier tapped the eraser of his pencil on a file before him, the James one, and tried to place it, attach it to the right dead body. But there were so many. "Owl droppings?" he said.

Mrs. Lambert settled back into her chair. She shook her head no. "*Pellets*, Detective." She sounded like a piano teacher. "When an owl catches the smaller rodents, it sometimes, it doesn't chew them. But that doesn't mean it can digest them whole, either. So it, it spits the undigestibles back up a few hours later. The hair, the bones, teeth."

Kupier pictured it. "Think I've collared a few of those," he said.

It was supposed to be a joke.

Mrs. Lambert nodded. "It's the only way we can see them, Detective. The owls, I mean."

"Because the park after dark is no place for a young woman."

The blood seeped up to Mrs. Lambert's cheeks.

"Tuesday," he said aloud.

"Detective?"

Kupier waved it off, asked her about these owls, then. She corrected: the pellets. He'd been playing this game for twenty-five years, now.

"I don't want you to think I'm . . . " Mrs. Lambert started, stopped, finished: " . . . that I eat cat food or anything. Just because I collect—"

"It's under-rated," Kupier said. "Cat food."

Mrs. Lambert finally smiled, God bless her.

"After you collect the *specimen*," she said, "you soak it in a pie tin of water, Detective. And you can see the little animal that was there." She held her hands up under her jaw, in imitation, and probably wasn't even aware she was doing it.

Kupier didn't look away. "Okay," he said, dragging each syllable, leaning forward to make this thing easy for her. "But you're not here because of the little animals, Mrs. Lambert. That's a different division."

Mrs. Lambert nodded, looked down, then reached into her purse. For a moment Kupier had no control of, he wondered if she'd made it back here with a gun somehow—the mother of some years-ago collar—but then it wasn't a gun she laid on the table, but a plastic sandwich container. It sloshed after she set it down.

"I don't think this was an owl, Detective," she said, patting near the container instead of the container's lid. It was something to note.

"You saved the water," he said back.

"Forensic evidence," she said. "I watch the shows."

Kupier smiled. Of course she did.

In the silted water in the container was a human finger bone. That someone had thrown up in the park.

Tuesday, Kupier said to himself again. Tuesday. By lunch he had it down, but he wasn't hungry anymore either.

That afternoon he walked alone to the park, to the place near the dying elm by the two benches that Mrs. Lambert had explained for him. He'd looked it up after she was gone, *Lambert.* It meant grey, featureless. Kupier pictured her husband in his easy chair with the remote control, his wife ten feet away under the kitchen light, watching the fragile bones of mice and voles resolve in a disposable pan.

The scene was two days old already. There was nothing, just a bird Kupier didn't have a name for.

"See anything?" he asked it.

It flew away.

The lab came back two days later, that it had been human saliva in the water, not canine.

Kupier got out another manila folder.

There were still three years until retirement. The rest of Homicide-Robbery was leaving him alone for it, mostly. Since the cancer.

On the tab of the folder he wrote GREY OWL. It sounded like a comic book name though, or an Indian, so he changed it to FINGER, R. RING: J DOE. They didn't know if it was male or female, just that it was adult. And bitten off. A specialist was supposed to be making a cast of the teeth; he was working off striations in the bone. Kupier told his captain this wasn't a trophy-thing, he didn't think. Maybe self-defense.

"Go home, Koop," his captain told him. "It's six o'clock, man."

The next morning Kupier was watching the steam roll off his coffee and waiting for Animal Control to pick up their phone. Their number had been on his door when he'd walked up; the note was stamped with two other precincts already. It had taken a while to find him.

"Yeah," the voice on the other end said. There were all manner of dogs in the background. Or maybe a lot of the same dog, but all saying different things.

"This is Detective Kupier," Kupier said. "You called about a finger."

The man on the other end paused, paused, then told Kupier yeah, yeah, the finger. What took them so damn long?

"How long's it been?" Kupier asked. A door closed somewhere far away and the steam of his coffee eddied back down into the cup.

"Three days," Animal Control said. "She's going to die, maybe."

Kupier switched the phone to his other ear, held it closer.

"Say again," he said.

"Penny," the man said, being attacked by a cat, it sounded like. "You don't know anything, do you?"

Kupier didn't answer, just got the address from the front desk, went down to motorpool to check out a car.

"Thought you just went out on Tuesdays?" the officer at the window said, and Kupier signed his name, took the keys from the drawer, walked through the garage; didn't answer.

Animal Control was a loud place. There was no one at the front desk, just a list of animals that had been run over and collected over the last two weeks. There was one column for dogs, one for cats, with tight, ten-words descriptions of each. Someone had gone through with a pencil and circled all the Labrador-type dogs, but missed one in the second row.

Behind the front desk in a cage was a green parrot. It didn't say anything. Finally Kupier walked around the desk, past the bird—nodding to it because maybe it understood more than just words—and into the tombs, or catacombs, or bestiary, or whatever they called it down here. It was full of animals, anyway.

The man he found was in a wheelchair, spraying out cement kennels with a high-pressure hose, the water running back under him to the drain. The floor sloped down to it.

"This is about Penny," Kupier said.

The man winked at him, shot him with his finger gun, and said to follow him. His tires left thin wet trails; Kupier walked between them deeper into the place. Far off, someone was whistling.

They stopped at a stainless steel examination room.

"Not the owner, right?"

Kupier shook his head no.

"Just making sure," the man said, and did a wheelie-turn to a bank of files. On the wall behind him was the memo for their mandatory sensitivity training. It had just been last week.

What he pulled out was the temporary file on the Penny dog. She was a copper-colored Irish setter, and she was dying. The man held her film up, getting the light behind them, and nodded.

"This is her," he said.

Kupier took the X-ray, held it up too, closer to the light. It was the color of motor oil.

Lodged in Penny's stomach was the radiation shadow of another finger.

"This common?" Kupier asked.

"Maybe," the man said. "We don't shoot film on them all."

"Why this one, then?"

"Her."

"The dog," Kupier said.

The man shrugged, reached into Penny's cage. She nosed into his sleeve and he buried his fingers in her red hair, came up with a silver, bone-shaped tag with hearts engraved into the corners.

Kupier nodded: somebody might actually come get this dog. At least for the collar.

"You say she's dying?" he said.

"Wouldn't you if you had that in there like that?" the man said, cocking his own finger against his stomach.

"Well," Kupier said. "Is *she* going to?"

"Without surgery, yeah, maybe," the man said.

"I thought somebody was coming to get her," Kupier said.

The man shrugged. "X-rays are sixty bucks," he said. "And her owner's machine says they're skiing. They say it all at once, together, the whole family."

"Must have taken them awhile to get it right," Kupier said.

The man nodded, had somewhere else to be now.

Kupier stared down at Penny. "We need that finger," he said.

"You could just," the man said, "y'know. *Wait.*"

Kupier nodded. Both his hands were in his pocket.

"We need it now," he said, and turned directly to the man. "Can that be arranged?"

The man leaned back in his wheelchair, in thought, then shrugged what the hell, fingershot Kupier again. Kupier took the invisible bullet like he'd taken all the rest.

"You okay?" the man said, leading Kupier back to the waiting room, and Kupier just watched the missing dogs smear by on either side and wondered what it was like here at night. Whether they left the lights on or off.

Two nights later Kupier was eating alone at the Amyl River. It wasn't a cop place, just a bar. The preliminaries on the finger bone from Animal Control was that it wasn't an index like the one from the park. So it could still be from one person. Kupier crumbled his cornbread into the glass of milk he'd ordered. It was dessert; his wife had always only let him have it on Sundays. He left the spoon in his mouth too long. It wasn't Tuesday anymore, just Thursday or Friday or some other day. Behind him a dart thumped into its board, money changed hands, a woman met a man. Kupier stared into his glass.

Earlier in the day he'd looked up Mrs. Lambert's record. She was clean, and her kids were clean, and her husband was clean. Kupier was glad for them. He was already calling them the Grey family, picturing them standing in order from tallest to shortest. He was glad for them.

The dinner crowd left to the patter of falling coins, and Kupier moved from milk and cornbread to rye and water. It was all the detectives drank in the movies. He didn't want to have a taste for it, but he did, and that was that.

In the pocket of his jacket was the plaster cast of teeth the department had contracted out for. *Teeth,* Kupier kept saying to himself. It was the first case of his career that had to do with bite patterns. They were useless, though—a glass slipper he couldn't ask anybody to try on. All they told him was that whoever they belonged to wasn't missing any from the front. The real trick now would be to see if they fit into the bone from Animal Control. Kupier looked at his own finger, rotated it in the half light.

"So we know it's not you," a man whispered over Kupier's shoulder.

It was Stevenson. The transplant from Narcotics.

Kupier shrugged. Stevenson sat down anyway. "So this is where the old guard hangs," he said. "You on stake-out for the rat squad or what, man?"

"What are you doing here?" Kupier asked. They were both carrying their pistols in their shoulder holsters, the only two men at the bar with their jackets still on.

Stevenson lit a clove. The bartender scowled over.

"You know this guy?" he asked, nodding at Stevenson.

"We're buddies," Stevenson said. It was the precinct joke. He was already drunk, maybe more. He whispered to the bartender that they were on stake-out, too. Kupier stared at the bottles lined up before him, watching in the mirror as the bartender calmly removed the clove from Stevenson's lips, doused it in the dregs of an abandoned beer.

"Thought this was a cop place," Stevenson said.

"It is," Kupier said.

Stevenson laughed through his nose at the insult. They drank and stared and stared and drank, and then, deeper into the night, Stevenson smiled, tugged at the elbow of Kupier's jacket.

It was a man at the other end of the bar. He'd just walked in. One of his sleeves was empty. It made him carry his shoulders different.

"Your one-armed man," Stevenson said.

Kupier looked away. He should have stayed at the office, or gone home. Or to the park again.

At ten o'clock Stevenson left suddenly, like he'd just realized he was missing something. Kupier followed him out with his eyes. As he passed the one-armed man he turned to Kupier, pointed down at the man, his gestures drunk and overdone. Kupier nodded just to have it done with, and the one-armed man nodded back, raised his beer.

Instead of walking, Kupier took a cab. He wasn't committed to going back to the office yet, but wasn't going home either, and was two blocks away from the Amyl River before he recognized the one-armed man, lodged in his head. Goddamn Stevenson. He didn't even dress like a homicide detective, didn't walk like he had a shoebox full of crime scene photos tucked away in the top of his closet for his grandchildren to find someday.

Kupier stood on a corner trying to figure it all out, what he was thinking—the fingers, the one-armed man—and then a bus hissed up for him, unfolded its doors. Three gaunt faces looked down at Kupier from three separate windows.

Kupier recognized one of them from somewhere, the way the teeth fit into the mouth, or didn't. Kupier wanted to give him a cigarette for some reason, even touching his chest pocket for where they would have been, but then the bus driver had his hands off the wheel in impatience and Kupier waved him on.

Eric, his name was Eric.

Kupier said it to himself as he walked—*Er-ic, Er-ic, Er-ic*—and the easy rhythm of it almost hid his beeper, thrumming at his belt. He palmed it, aimed it at his eyes, called Dispatch back. This time it was the twenty-seven tiny bones of the wrist. They'd been found in a public toilet, floating in a latex glove that had passed through a body. Kupier looked from the phone booth back in the direction of the Amyl River, and then he got it, what he'd been thinking: this was only the beginning.

He stepped out of the cab a block down from the bar with the unflushed public toilet. So he could walk up, compose himself. Pretend he had less alcohol in him than he did. The wind was supposed to be bracing.

Forensics was already there, crowded into the stall with their tweezers and microscopes. The sign on the restroom door said PLACE YOUR ORDURE HERE. Kupier felt like Mrs. Lambert must have felt: untethered from any recognizable decade. Cannibalism? Kupier said it to himself now so that no one could catch him off-guard with it later.

He stayed there questioning regulars until last call, but nobody'd seen anything.

Kupier called his captain, told him that they should pull the liquor license at that place, because they were serving bad alcohol. It was blinding the clientele. The captain didn't laugh. Tomorrow was Saturday; it was three in the morning.

Kupier escorted the wrist bones to the lab, walked with them from table to table then woke suddenly in his office at noon. What he was picturing now was a museum skeleton, where they stain all the missing bones black for display. Only this skeleton wasn't from the Pleistocene, or whenever.

The next day Kupier went to church, sat in the back rolling and unrolling a newspaper. There was nothing in it about a hand surfacing bone by bone from under the city, reaching up like it was drowning.

On Monday they had a briefing about it, Homicide-Robbery. The table was small and Kupier sat with his back to the window. It made Stevenson have to stare into the sun with his already-red eyes.

The lab had rushed the bones overnight for two nights. They went together, more or less. It was supposed to be a male, now.

"A *one*-armed male," Stevenson said.

Kupier leaned forward, out of the sun.

"This is my case, right?" he said to the captain.

The captain nodded, said of course, of course.

"Thought you had chemo on these days," McNeel said, making a show of squinting, as if not believing his eyes that this could be Kupier, here, alive.

"No," Kupier said, instead of *Tuesday.*

McNeel held his hands up in apology.

The rest of the briefing was the usual parade of forensic pathologists and criminal psychologists. At one point someone clapped ponderously.

Two weeks later it was an ulna.

Kupier didn't tell his two grandchildren about it. His daughter had left them there with him for the afternoon. They were Rita and Thomas; Thomas was named after Kupier. He took them to the park, bought ice cream all around. They called him Grandpa K. The other grandfather was Grandpa M, probably, for Marsten. Thomas was ten, two years older than Rita. Grandchild R and Grandchild T. Kupier kept both of them in sight at all times.

"Do you know about owl pellets?" he asked them.

They looked up at him.

He sat them down and had to explain first about owls at night, and then about mice, scurrying, their whiskers sensitive to the least shift in the air, and then about the owls stumbling out of the sky, vomiting bones into the wet grass.

Thomas looked up into the four o'clock sky when Kupier was done.

Rita asked about Mrs. Lambert.

They were standing by the dying elm.

"I don't know," Kupier said.

The last time he'd seen Rita and Thomas had been in the hospital, before remission, and they'd had goodbye cards for him, drawn with pictures of him and Grandma K in heaven. They'd never met her, though, so she was just a woman with white hair and glasses. He still had the pictures.

"More ice cream?" Thomas said.

They knew they were at Grandpa K's.

He ushered them through the line again, watched the sidewalk for their mother. She was late, her body full of bones. There was no message from her on the machine, either. Just Stevenson, asking if he should say this on the recorder then just saying it anyway, that the high end of the ulna had been a green fracture, which doesn't happen so much with dead—

The tape ran out there. Rita and Thomas were standing at Kupier's legs.

"Like with trees," Thomas said, using his interlaced fingers to show the way a limb will break when it's alive.

Kupier turned on cartoons for them and stood at the window. He could hear the children's teeth rotting, and wanted to lead them into the bathroom, stand there while they brushed.

"Where is she?" Rita asked.

Kupier turned back to her and said their mom had probably just stopped for dinner. It wasn't the first time. Rita asked where. Kupier looked past her to his beeper, by his keys on the counter. It was dancing across the Formica.

It was McNeel, calling from the bullpen.

"I can't," Kupier said.

In the cartoon, a tall robot was shooting flame from his hand at a column of water. It steamed away.

"Who *can*?" McNeel said back.

There was a tibia at the fair.

Kupier stood at the phone for a long time, his finger on the plunger, the dial tone in his ear, and then shrugged into his jacket. No gun, though. Not with the children.

They took a cab out past the city limits, and the neon ferris wheel rose out of the horizon, spreading the children's mouths into grins. They were sitting on the other side of the car from Kupier, because he'd stood on the curb behind them, guiding them in, making sure the door was closed.

"How many tickets can we have?" Thomas asked.

"As many as you want," Kupier said.

The cab driver was humming something ethnic.

The sanitation engineer was waiting for them at security booth. "This way," he said, studying the children, then just led the way to the long bank of port-a-potties. Trash was blowing from blade of grass to blade of grass, strands of cotton candy drifting through the air. A clown stepped out of the fifth of the plastic outhouses, his red hair frayed up into the night, thin, vertical diamonds of greasepaint bisecting his eyes. The engineer pointed two down from him, to the third. It was cordoned off, out of service.

"Usually it's just vitamins and coins and the odd pair of glasses," he said. "But this . . . '

In the fiberglass collection tub under the floor was a human tibia.

The skeleton in Kupier's mind got less black.

"He had to carry it here," Kupier said.

"It wasn't there before," the engineer said. He was holding his hat on, curling it around his temples. They were upwind.

"I'll send them to get it," Kupier said.

"Take the whole thing if you want," the engineer said, indicating an iron hoop at the apex of the outhouse, and then looked over Kupier's shoulder at something. Kupier turned. It was the fair. Thomas rode the Ferris wheel six times in a row while Kupier stood holding Rita's hand at the gate. Kupier wondered if they'd learned tibias yet in the second grade, or third.

They took another cab back to the city, both children falling asleep, their lips stained blue.

Waiting on the stoop was Ellen.

"Where were you?" Kupier asked.

"Where was *I*?" she asked back.

One of the buttons on her blouse was still undone.

After she was gone, two twenties stuffed into her hand, Kupier sat in the living room. The cartoons were still on, muted. He dialed in the number from the photocopy of Penny the dog's tag, but didn't get the machine like he wanted, the voices all in sing-song unison.

"Yes?" the father said. "Hello?"

In the cartoon one character was whirling another over his head like helicopter blades.

"Penny," Kupier said, unsure.

"Who is this?" the father asked, his voice cupped into the phone, away from whatever living room or dinner table he was standing over.

"Just checking," Kupier said, eyes closed, and hung up.

What kept him awake some nights were the bones they weren't finding, that they were supposed to have found. Because if they didn't have a humerus or clavicle or zygomatic arch to fit into their skeleton, maybe the killer would have to supply them with one. With another one, one they could find.

Stevenson said it wasn't like that, that there was just one victim, tied up in a cellar. He explained how the gauchos in the nineteenth century used to carve steaks from the cattle they were working, then rub a poultice into the wound, slap the cow back into the herd. He was slouched in Kupier's doorway, a cigarette threaded behind his ear.

"That all?" Kupier said.

Stevenson shook his head.

"You should at least pretend to try," he said, clapping his palm on the metal doorjamb in something that was probably supposed to look like restraint. "Set a good example for us rookie types."

"Because you're taking notes, right?" Kupier said.

Then the labs came back.

The blood type from Mrs. Lambert's pie tin, mixed in with the saliva, was O-positive, another glass slipper—good in court but useless until then—but the fragments of genetic markers from the two fingerbones and the wrist bones and the ulna and the preliminaries on the tibia, they seemed to share more than they didn't. Which was statistically unlikely, narrowing the victim profile to an ethnic subgroup maybe, or an extended family. Kupier sat in his office the rest of the afternoon. It was Tuesday again. Kupier was still saying *Eric* in his head, tapping his pencil with it, and then he got it: Eric from Group.

He'd been the only one in Cancer Support who still smoked. In public at least. They'd made him sit by the door because of it, even. Kupier had always watched him sitting there and thought of scuba divers from television, how they sat the same way on the edges of boats before they rolled out: knees together, hands on their thighs.

At first, Kupier had watched him because he wanted to go with him, into the picture Rita and Thomas had drawn of heaven, but then he'd lost the drawing for a few frantic days, and when he finally found it again the James Casc had been open—a woman poisoned in her own kitchen—and he couldn't just leave it, her, so he didn't.

The tibia had striations, of course. Like the ulna. Gnaw marks. And, because it was the fair, the public, the newspapers got hold of it. Kupier had three years left, and a cast of teeth in his pocket. At the airport earlier, dropping Ellen and the kids off for a weekend trip to see their father, the teeth showed up in security as dentures. The guards were too young to know any different.

Kupier checked the car out everyday now, drove the street for bones.

He drank rye and water at the Amyl River and waited for the one-armed man.

He read the news before dawn. On the third day he was named in the C-section, second page, and the next day there was the picture he'd had in his head, of the blacked-out skeleton. That afternoon Dispatch fielded one hundred and twenty two calls about bones. They were in rain gutters, bird nests, untended lots. All but four were bogus, and one of those turned out to be another finger joint, only this one was from a funeral urn, the ashes all blown away. Kupier walked away from it to the other three. It took eight days, total. It was a twelve-year-old boy with a cardboard box and an encyclopedia set. He'd reconstructed the bones he'd found over three weeks into a fibia, a calcaneous, and most of the bones of the foot. He said ants had eaten the rest. Kupier asked him where, and the boy pointed four lots down and two weeks back, to before a foundation had been poured for a new house. Kupier stood in the frame of what was going to be a kitchen. It smelled like pine. In the trunk of his car, caulked together into the shape of a lower leg just like the illustration in the encyclopedia, were the bones. The boy's mother said she'd thought he was just gluing animal bones together to look like a foot, or a leg, or whatever.

Kupier ran the boy's non-existent sheet too, and everyone on the block, and none of them came up as registered cannibals or former serial killers.

Stevenson sent him a copy of a page from a book, about a man who, over the course of a year, had eaten a bus, piece by piece.

Kupier wrote *pelvis* into his notebook.

The next morning was his six month check-up. He was clean, still, but didn't feel like it.

"You sure?" he asked the oncologist.

The oncologist stopped on his way back into the hall. "Alright," he said. "Not supposed to lie to the police, right?" He smiled, his eyes golf balls, his voice going mock-solemn. "You've got seventy-two hours, Thomas."

Kupier's hands played along, trembling on the buttons of his shirt.

The oncologist looked at his watch when he passed Kupier, walking out through Emergency. It was too loud to do anything else. Kupier smiled with the outside corners of his eyes, stepped out the double doors, and then the world flashed silver and his hand fell to his gun, and he had it out before he could stop himself, even when he knew it was a photographer.

"You're Detective Cooper, right?" the photographer asked. "Working on the Maneater case?" He was wearing running shoes.

Kupier lowered his weapon.

Behind the photographer, a pair of paramedics were holding a patient on a stretcher, the aluminum gurney rolling away behind them, down the slope to the parked cars. The patient wasn't moving. Still thought he was being saved, maybe. That this was that kind of world.

"Detective?" the photographer was still asking.

Kupier turned back to him. "Maneater?" he asked.

The photographer shrugged, disappeared.

The following morning, Kupier just sat in his office, waiting to get thrown up against his own door. He didn't have to wait long. His captain unrolled the paper on his desk, smoothing it with deliberate strokes. In the picture, Kupier was an old, frightened man. With a gun.

That night he went back to Group for the first time in months. The poster someone had brought and taped up on the wall over the coffee machine read (re)MISSION, and the shadow the uppercase letters cast was a cross. Kupier wasn't sure what it meant. The people in the group smiled sidelong smiles at him but didn't approach. Because he might run off again, huddle around the memory of chemo in his apartment alone. He didn't ask where the other missing people were. Of the new people, one was on crutches, her sweatpants tied up at the middle of her missing thigh. Kupier held his breath and eased out the door, into the Amyl River.

"Where's your friend?" the bartender asked.

Kupier pretended to cast around for Stevenson, then looked at his watch and did the math on accident: sixty-one hours left until the doctor's joke could be funny. He tried to say *remission* the way it had been on the poster, with a cross behind it, and when he finally got the door open to his house—sure that a great, grey owl was gliding soundless down the street for him—he found Rita and Thomas sleeping on his couch, their mouths stained red from Popsicles. The television wasn't on, which meant they'd been carried in already in their blankets. Kupier wrote *Cooper* into his notebook and slept in the chair, his gun nosed down into the cushions.

Ellen didn't come back for the children until noon. Kupier didn't say anything, just listed what they'd eaten, what they hadn't.

"You're working on that investigation in the papers," she said.

Kupier nodded as little as possible.

"You were named for your mother," he told her.

She looked away, blinked.

"You going to find him?" she asked.

"Eventually."

He didn't get to the station house until three-thirty. There was a package on his desk, all the labels printed on a printer. The brown paper was grease paper, and it was tied with brittle twine. He opened it with a pair of pliers, expecting hair matted with blood, a sternum, a scapula, but it was just a twenty-five year plaque with his name on it, and a handful of Styrofoam peanuts. He asked his captain about it.

His captain held his head in his hands and stared down at his desk calendar.

"That wasn't supposed to come *to* you," he said. "It was *for* you, but not *to* you, see?"

"Surprise," Stevenson said, suddenly in the room.

Kupier didn't know what to do with it.

His teeth were still powdery from the children's toothpaste the children had said he had to use if they had to. It was like plaster, like he had the cast in his mouth. He brought it up from his pocket and looked at it. Nobody had asked him for it because it was already no good—not fitted for the ulna, the tibia.

The assumption was that the soft tissue was getting digested.

Stevenson had sent another memo, too. This one was an entry on hyenas. The passage highlighted was about how the hyena didn't have an m.o. like a lion or a leopard—teeth to the throat, the skull—but that it simply ate its victims until they were dead. Which could take awhile, Kupier thought. If you did it right.

After the dayshift was gone, Kupier thumbed through Stevenson's personnel file, but he was clean too. No proclivities for human flesh, anyway. He almost laughed: next he'd be running his own sheet.

Night came, and with it another package.

It was the second set of labs Kupier had requested. They were in an oversized brown envelope. He sat on the pew outside his office and read them and then read them again: the DNA from the blood from the saliva from that first fingerbone matched the genetic workup of the bones themselves.

Kupier leaned back. Across the room from him, on the board, was a diagram of a human skeleton. The bones they'd found so far were blacked out, and the ones that were missing were grey, presumed missing, just not found yet. The tacks stuck into the blacked-out bones were color-coded to the map alongside the skeleton—where they'd been found—and there was yarn trailing from two of the tacks, from where McNeel or somebody had tried to luck into a pattern, a pentagram or arrow or happy face or something. The drop sites were random, though, all over the city. But Kupier was looking at the skeleton, again. It was one person now. No longer a body the killer was building, but one he was taking apart. All the blacked-out bones were from the right side, too.

Kupier looked down at his own hand in a new way, spread his fingers so that the tendons pushed against the skin.

Twenty-five years, Kupier said to himself.

That night it was another homicide, unrelated. It was in a sprawling parking lot; there were witnesses, even. Evidence to bag. Kupier stood in the middle of it all and surveyed the endless series of trash cans. They were spaced twenty parking slots from each other, staggered every third row. In one of them there would be more evidence.

A uniform approached, asking what Kupier wanted him to do.

Kupier shrugged, his hands in his pockets.

He gave them McNeel's home number.

In the park later he walked until the dead elm was silhouetted against a streetlight, and then he drew his shoulders together once, twice, and on the third time his dinner came up. He leaned forward, walked his hands down his legs to the ground. Was this how it was with the killer?

When the tree shifted with the wind, the streetlight pushed through, and Kupier's hands were spattered with blood. His mouth, his lips. Like before. He started laughing around the eyes and then convulsed with it, and when he stood there was a figure watching him across the grass. Thin, gaunt—at first he thought it was the woman from the parking lot, risen to accuse him, then it was Mrs. Lambert, a pie tin in her hand for his vomit, but then it was neither of them. Just somebody with a cigarette. Eric. From group. He inhaled his cigarette and the end glowed ashen red, and then he breathed in again, deeper, and Kupier could feel it in his own chest.

Eric turned, flicking the cigarette away, and Kupier followed.

It was too late for the Amyl River, so they went to one of the all-night cafeterias instead. They sat across from each other.

"So," Kupier said.

"Why are you following me?" Eric asked. His hands were balled in the pockets of his jacket.

"I'm not," Kupier said.

Eric looked away. "I wasn't at Group," he said. "I saw you go in, though."

Kupier wiped his mouth: no blood.

Eric smiled.

"You too?" he said.

"What?" Kupier said back.

"Re-lapse . . . " Eric said, drawing it out, making it into a happy, benign song.

Kupier shook his head no.

Eric shrugged, said he didn't go anymore because Group was for people who needed support—people who needed to deal with having *had* cancer. It wasn't for people who were having it again.

"What were you doing in the park?" Kupier asked.

"It's a public place."

Kupier leaned back. "Do you need anything, then?" he asked.

Eric smiled, raised his eyebrows. "A pancreas," he said, "yeah. You?"

"I told you," Kupier said. "They got it the first time."

Eric shrugged whatever.

"I was meeting somebody," he said.

Kupier didn't bite on this like he knew he was supposed to. Instead he laid a twenty down for their two coffees, stood into the fluorescent light. He called for the waitress to give Eric the change. Eric shrugged.

"Still using?" Kupier asked.

"Asking as a cop?" Eric asked.

Kupier just stared down at him.

"Tell me why I shouldn't," Eric said.

Kupier went home to his living room and sat, going through his own file this time. He didn't throw up anymore, but he wasn't moving either, just sitting there. When his beeper shook he thumbed it off, and when his alarm clock rang he walked upstairs, killed it too, then called Natty at the front desk, told her he wouldn't be in today. He had thirty-two hours of the joke left. He saw the oncologist's golf ball receding into the sky. He ate tomato soup so that when it came back up, if there was blood in it, he wouldn't have to know.

The next time he opened his front door it was Stevenson on the stoop.

"Two days, hoss," Stevenson said.

"It's Cooper," Kupier said. "Don't you read the papers?"

Stevenson wormed his way in. He had two coffees in the crook of his arm, both sloshing over the rim, and a bagful of grease that was supposed to be breakfast.

"Captain said to hand-deliver this," he said.

It was Kupier's FINGER, R. RING: J DOE file.

"You went in my office?" Kupier said, taking it the manila folder.

"Not me," Stevenson said around his cup. "But look."

Kupier did: there was a third lab report now.

"Our first soft tissue," Stevenson said, widening his eyes with how important this was.

Kupier scanned for a location, but it looked like a misprint. "The park?" he said.

"Nearly the same-ass exact spot," Stevenson said. He'd been saving it. "And here—" He flipped the page back to a black and white photograph of a cast of a footprint.

"Who found this?" Kupier asked.

Stevenson shrugged, looked away, his off-hand pointing at himself from the back of the couch.

It was Kupier's footprint, Kupier's blood. Farther out, past the edge of the crime scene, would be another footprint. Eric's, if Eric had even been real.

"Anything else?" he asked.

"Just that he's sick or something," Stevenson said. "His blood-tox came back but loaded, man. I mean, it's like I'm working Narc again all over. Oh, oh, and this guy's not O-positive anymore, either, going by the puke. Know what I think?"

Kupier looked at the food soaking into his coffee table.

Stevenson rolled on: "—that this nutjob's like *feeding* the vics to each other, man. See?"

Kupier pushed his lower lip out with his tongue.

"Got a car here?" he asked.

Stevenson nodded.

Kupier went upstairs and got dressed. The only thing different from every other day was his shoes.

"You okay?" Stevenson asked, slumped in the driver's seat.

Kupier was looking away from whatever pill Stevenson thought he was getting away with palming into his mouth. It was yellow. In his office, the second lab report was facedown right where he'd left it. Kupier read it again, then slid it under the veneer surface of his desk, pushed the glue down around it with his elbows and held his head with his hands. The only other choice was telling Stevenson it had been him in the park, that he was sick again. But then he'd be pulled off the case, have to take another extended sick leave.

Now he was the only one who knew, though. Meaning he was the one responsible for cleaning up—stopping it all.

"What now?" Stevenson asked from the door.

Kupier stared at him for long seconds, deciding. It was obvious, though. There was only one thing. "It's a cycle," he said. "We stake out the rest of the drops, wait for him."

The next morning it hit the papers, the bloody sputum in the park.

Mrs. Lambert was waiting on line one for him.

"Is it him?" she asked.

Kupier closed his eyes.

"Yes," he said, "yes,"

The next lab report identified the particulate soft tissue as the malignant bronchial matter of a lifetime smoker. Which gave them a range of ages, from forty to maybe sixty, just because sixty was the oldest active pattern killer to date. And the spectrum of pharmaceuticals in the bloody sputum from the park broke down in the lab's pie tin as medicines for medicine—chemotherapy.

"He's dying," Stevenson said, another joke.

Kupier got in his car and drove the streets for bones, until Ellen showed up one night bruised around the face, silent, Kupier's hand dropping to the gun he didn't wear to bed.

"Ellen," he said.

She laid her head against his chest and moved in. Moved out again a week later.

"Still working on that Maneater thing?" she asked when she came back for a dress from her old closet. The kids were standing in the living room waiting for the television to warm up.

"That's just what the paper calls it," Kupier said.

Sometime after that—a week, a month, no bones, the stake-outs all dry, abandoned—Kupier saw Eric again, at the bus stop on the east side of the park. The bus came, lowered itself onto its forelegs, then stood up again, left. Eric was still there.

That he was waiting for something illegal was obvious. He had that nervous stance, moving gravel around with his toes.

Kupier eased into the diner half a block down, sat by the plate glass. When it finally happened, the drop, Kupier wished he wasn't there: it was Stevenson. He walked out into the grass with Eric, away from the streetlight. Kupier left a ten on the table and followed them, arcing wide to come up out of the darkness. They were talking low when he stepped in with them.

"K—Harold . . ." Stevenson said, stuffing both hands into his pockets.

Kupier looked away. To Eric.

"What do you want?" Eric said.

Kupier pursed his lips.

"*Harold,*" Stevenson was saying. "A little late, aren't we?"

"Just saw you here," Kupier said back, still watching Eric.

"Well here I am," Stevenson said, holding his empty hands up.

There was nothing to do, really, so Kupier rubbed his eyes, left.

The next morning Stevenson was in his office door again. "Eric Waynes," he was saying.

"I'm not—" Kupier started to say.

"It's not what you think," Stevenson was already saying, "not what I know you're thinking."

Kupier looked up. "What is it, then?" he said.

Stevenson blew a pink bubble of gum, collapsed it. "He's a . . . contact. From the old days. We've got kind of a system worked out."

"This isn't Narcotics," Kupier said.

"I know it's not Narc," Stevenson said. "I tell myself that every day, man. But listen. This guy, this Eric Waynes, he says he was in the park the other night. That he could maybe give us a description of the Maneater."

Kupier breathed in, made himself exhale.

"In trade?" he led.

Stevenson shrugged, did something with his lips.

"I don't want to know," Kupier said then, "do I?"

Stevenson shook his head no, just once, in a way that Kupier knew he used to have long, greasy bangs.

That night Kupier called Eric. He still had the number from the list they'd made at group, passed around from left to right, the pen tied onto the top of the tablet with kite string.

"What do you want?" Kupier asked.

"Relax, man," Eric said. "I'm not going to tell him anything."

Kupier laughed through his nose, hung up.

That night, drinking coffee at the cafeteria, Kupier threw up again, spilling red out onto the table.

The waitress backed away.

This was what the Maneater was in all the papers for.

Kupier made himself breathe, breathe, then rose calmly for a wet dish towel.

The night shift was all gathered around, watching him.

"You don't have to . . . " one of them said—clean it up—but Kupier did. He took the towel with him too, after wiping his cup down with it, and the seat, and the napkin holder, and the door. They knew who he was, though. If anybody came around asking.

Kupier quit going to Group again, because he thought they could see it in him, eating him, then sat in the parking lot of the clinic for as long as his nine-month check-up would have lasted.

It had been two more weeks now, and still no bones.

"He's dead," Stevenson pronounced. "Choked on a kneecap or something . . . "

But then he showed up with a sketch. It was in Eric's anonymous hand. It was Kupier in the park, a silhouette lurching from tree to tree, all in black except for the lungs, which were red C's, facing each other.

"What was he on when he drew that?" McNeel said.

"All points bulletin," Stevenson said, covering the smile on his face with the CB he didn't have.

That night Kupier called his captain at three in the morning again, after the Amyl River had closed, and asked about early retirement. His captain outlined what was involved like he was reading from an index card, like he'd had this all ready for some time now, and Kupier leaned into the phone booth and pretended he could hear the captain's wife in the bedsheets on the other end, listening to all this with her eyes closed. She was beautiful. She was there.

Next he called Eric, and asked him in another voice if he had it?

"Thought you did," Eric said, using another voice too.

Kupier drove, drove, parked in front of Penny the dog's house. Twenty-five years. His gun was on the dash. Penny was a crown of reddish hair jumping for the top of the fence every four seconds.

When the security floodlights over the garage glowed on, he pulled away.

He wrote *Rita* in his notebook. And *Thomas.*

Finger, R. Ring: J Doe was the only case he had that was still open. Kupier did the one thing he could: he drove to Ellen's, knocked on the door.

"Dad," she said.

"Just wondering if the kids—" he said.

She was clutching her robe at her neck.

"What's that in your mouth?" she said, quieter.

Kupier pulled his lips over the plaster teeth.

"You alright?" she asked. "It's late."

Kupier nodded. It was.

Thomas appeared in the doorway off the living room, dragging an old ski jacket of his mother's he'd been sleeping in. It scratched across the carpet, one arm trailing. Kupier thought of the black and white photograph of the James woman looking up from behind her washing machine.

"Just wanted to see if they wanted to stay with Grandpa tonight," Kupier finally got out.

It was too late, though. All the other excuses.

In her complex's parking lot, Kupier held the wheel with both hands. It was for the best. What he had been going to get them to do was open Penny's gate for him.

He found Stevenson instead.

Kupier rolled his car alongside, unlocked the passenger door.

"On the job," Stevenson said, after he'd climbed in. Both hands in his pocket. He smelled like sweat.

"Talked to Eric Waynes?" Kupier asked, pulling away from the curb.

The corners of Stevenson's eyes crinkled. He shook his head no as if this was the funniest question he'd had all week. "You?" he asked back.

Kupier drove. "That blood in the park," he said.

Stevenson looked at him, patted the dashboard above the radio for some reason.

"Blood?" he said.

Stevenson's hand was trembling, yellowed.

Kupier nodded.

Stevenson watched him from his side of the car.

They rolled to a stop behind Penny the dog's house.

"Should I ask?" Stevenson said.

"Personal," Kupier said back. He hooked his chin at the gate. "Just open it," he said.

Stevenson snorted. "That all?"

"I need to be in the car."

Stevenson shrugged, rolled out into the alley, leading with his shoulders. The dome light didn't come on because Kupier had already disabled it. He watched Stevenson over the hood—hunching towards the gate, his long, careless steps eating up the gravel and the weeds.

He looked back to Kupier once before he did it, to be sure, and then flipped the handle with the belt of his jacket. To leave no prints, if this was coming to that. The door swung in and a metallic flash of red exploded from the tails of Stevenson's jacket.

He smiled, held his hands up, and Kupier gunned the car.

Stevenson chased behind for a few steps, filling the rearview, then slapped the trunk bye, stood there trying to breathe.

Kupier kept Penny at the leading edge of his headlights, and, for a moment, couldn't remember if she'd lived through the surgery or not—couldn't remember what he was chasing, where she was leading him. He coasted to a stop at the end of the alley.

Minutes later, Stevenson leaned down by his side mirror.

"Let me guess," he was saying. "Ex-wife got the dog in the divorce, and you—"

Kupier looked over at him. Stevenson. Who always had morning breath in the middle of the afternoon.

He showed Stevenson the drawing of his wife Thomas or Rita had done. It was creased from his wallet.

"I'm sorry," Stevenson said.

"Where do you want to go?" Kupier said.

Stevenson stood, staring past the hood. "To hell, now," he said.

Kupier smiled, blinked. "Get in," he said.

On Tuesday, Kupier started canvassing the houses downstreet from Penny's. In the direction she'd run without thinking. Police work. It took a week, up one street, down another, his notebook clammy in his palm. He wrote down the numbers of the houses that he didn't know about—where no one answered the door—and then he came back after five-thirty, got them crossed off the list. Except for eight. Out of seventy-two. It was just him doing it.

He watched the houses at night, then. Off the clock, out of radio contact. Nobody was calling him anymore anyway. Not since the fast draw at the hospital. It was supposed to be a kindness—not opening any more files he wouldn't be able to close—but it wasn't. It gave him too much time to think.

At work on a Thursday morning he pulled the reverse directory, attached names to the eight houses in Terranova where no one was ever home. He ran their sheets. Nothing. One had various handicap privileges, so he marked him off. Another was an international something or the other. Kupier had the front desk call his employer, see if he'd been out of the country at any of the right times. He had. So had two more of the people. Which left five. Kupier crossed the woman off, got it down to four, then crossed the two married men off. So now it was two. He alternated nights, watching one then the other, until he knew Terranova's schedule, which kids would explode from which door, when. It was like being part of it.

But then his beeper interrupted.

It was another drop, an old one. Just a finger.

McNeel took multiple pictures of which way it was pointing, like it had been arranged in the grass after being vomited up.

Kupier left the two men remaining on his list to themselves, visited Penny at Animal Control.

"They know she's here?" he asked the man in the wheelchair.

The man nodded, disappointed.

"Anything show up lately?" Kupier asked.

"Like what?" the man said, wheeling back in jest, "a *skull*?"

After two weeks, Kupier paid the twenty-eight dollars to have Penny spayed, then delivered her to Rita and Thomas.

"I'm sorry," he said to Ellen.

"No," she said, watching the kids, the dog. "They need something just like this."

There was a thin scar on Penny's belly. It was like a little ridge, like she'd been cut in half, glued back together.

"She's good with kids," Kupier said.

He didn't know what he was doing anymore. He could feel a tiny homunculus of bones in his stomach—himself—waiting to be thrown up. His notebook was full of words he didn't remember writing down. He had to mark them out each morning.

After Halloween—Rita and Thomas dressed up as a race-car driver and a zombie cowboy—Kupier met his replacement. It was another transplant from Narcotics. Like they were taking over. He looked around Kupier's office, leaning back on his heels, both hands buried deep in the pockets of his oversize, probably-stylish slacks.

All Kupier's stuff was in boxes around the desk.

"Maneater," the transplant said, in appreciation.

Kupier nodded. The skeleton was still on the wall, but tacked over now with other cases, other dead people.

"Merry Christmas," the transplant said, to himself it seemed—taking in the office—then caught Stevenson flashing by, palmed his shoulder like a bike messenger will a truck, let himself be pulled down the hall.

Kupier had four days left. Early retirement. Rat off a sinking ship, McNeel said in the mornings, smiling. Kupier smiled too. The line in his toilet at home that had been sterile blue for years now—accumulated crystals you could scratch off—was red now. From the tomato soup.

Kupier clenched his fists.

For retirement someone had already left him an aluminum walker. It still had its Evidence tag wired onto it. Alone in his office at night Kupier leaned on it, tried it out, and fell over the front, crashing into the filing cabinets.

He thought of Mrs. Lambert. He pictured the man in the wheelchair at Animal Control. A dog he'd seen on television that didn't have any back legs, just a pair of strap-on wheels. And then the handicapped man in Terranova.

Kupier breathed hard, suddenly aware of the dusty smells of the floor, the light seeping in under the door, a moth flailing in his trash can.

Of course.

He took a bus to Terranova and walked up the driveway of 2285 Rolling Vista, jack o' lanterns smiling behind him. The garage was open. For a cat, evidently, the litter box up on the dryer in the corner.

The car was fitted so that all the controls were on the left side of the wheel—accelerator, brake, blinkers, horn, quadrant, lights, everything. It bristled with levers. Kupier opened the door. The key was in the ignition. He advanced it to ACCESSORY, turned the blinker for a right signal.

The wall of the garage before him glowed yellow for three intervals, then the fourth was dimmer, the fifth dimmer, and the sixth just a sound, the battery only strong enough to push the relay, not the bulb.

The car hadn't gone anywhere for months. Since the drops stopped, probably.

Kupier loosed his gun, closed the garage door. It was so loud, so heavy. But he went in, no warrant, walking slow for his eyes to adjust, feeling for the kitchen counters which were lower than usual—custom—and at last he stepped into the living room.

Leaned against the brick hearth was a man without either of his legs, and with only a left arm. He was chewing the meat of his right shoulder, strings of red connecting him to himself.

Kupier sat down across from him.

They watched each other. The man swallowed. Kupier did too.

The air of the house was fetid, rotting.

The man was eating himself.

Kupier withdrew his gun, laid the cool side of the barrel against his forehead, then closed his eyes, felt for the garage again. The plug-in battery charger. It took all of four hours, but there was still enough time before dawn for Kupier to cradle the man in his arms, place him in the backseat, then drive the one-handed car to the curb in front of his own house. He unloaded the man, locked the door behind him—the phone already disabled—then took the car back, wiped the house down of himself.

In oversize freezer bags in the guest bathroom were other body parts, and a cooler full of gauze and antibiotic and morphine.

Kupier took it all.

By the middle of December, another Narc had seeped into Homicide-Robbery. Kupier heard about it through McNeel. He was the only one who still called. In his living room, the cardboard boxes he'd brought home from his office. The boxes were still packed with cases. He didn't want to look in them anymore.

"Didn't they give you a plaque or something?" Ellen had asked, dropping the grandchildren off.

Kupier nodded.

After they left, he called the station house to ask what McNeel was already supposed to be finding out: if Eric Waynes was still listed as a criminal informant. But then Stevenson answered the phone.

The plaque was balanced on the mantel.

"Looking for Len," Kupier said.

"Detective McNeel . . . " Stevenson dragged out, then grinned through the phone somehow, hushed his voice: "I think—yeah, I think somebody spilled some Worcestershire sauce or something on him, K, then like just left him in the park, man. Real tragedy."

"Tell him I called," Kupier said.

Upstairs, Martin Roche was watching cartoons. Kupier had found a mannequin in an alley, taped the legs and the left arm to Martin, then put him in his own old clothes. It was like dressing a doll. The blond wig he already had leftover in a closet; it just needed cutting into a man's hairstyle. The sunglasses were because Martin's eyes were always going everywhere. It made Kupier nervous.

For Thanksgiving, Kupier had cut Martin's turkey up for him into small portions then pressed down on it with his fork until the meat came up between the tines in a festive paste.

Here, here.

His tongue was gone, of course, chewed off. Probably the first thing, really—the closest. When he talked it was with his tablet, the pen he kept tucked in the back of the leather glove of his one good hand. Sometimes, walking to the store for a paper or some more gauze, Kupier would think about the litter box in the garage of 2285 Rolling Vista, and apologize to the cat. But it was just a cat. No matter what kind of eyes Martin drew it with.

Christmas Eve, after the more dutiful of Homicide-Robbery had knocked on his door, caroling, guns at their hips, Ellen showed up with the kids. The presents were under the tree for them already. Kupier sat in his chair watching them. It was a sea of wrapping paper. Ellen got him a small, portable television. She'd already put batteries in it. Kupier turned it over and over in his lap.

"You look good," Ellen said.

Kupier shrugged. His cancer was upstairs in the laundry corner of his bedroom, the brakes of his wheelchair clamped down.

Rita and Thomas were spitting up bows by now. Rita paused, looked at Kupier and then back, and asked her mother what was that in Grandpa K's teeth?

"Ketchup," Kupier said, pulling it in. "Tomato soup."

Penny was there, her leash hooked under the andirons of the cold fireplace so she wouldn't go upstairs.

Before bedtime, Kupier got Rita and Thomas to singsong a greeting into his answering machine, then immediately started picturing unnecessary trips to the corner store, dialing his number from the payphone, talking to Martin through the speaker.

This is remission, he might say. *This is retirement.*

He was in the upstairs bathroom dry heaving when the andirons clunked out of the fireplace, chipping the tile. Penny was loose now, not up the stairs though—Kupier knew every sound after thirty-two years—but at the front door.

Kupier stood, steadying himself on the towel rack, and walked down the hall as if in a dream, looked down onto his lawn.

Looking back up at him, pointing grudgingly up *at* him, a strung-out Eric Waynes.

Idling at the curb, smiling behind his hand, Stevenson.

Merry Christmas.

The way Kupier looked down the stairs at Ellen made her run up to him, a kid under each arm, her eyes full.

"Who is it?" she whispered.

Kupier pushed her into his bedroom.

"Close it," he said, about the door.

She did, twisting the deadbolt into the jamb.

Kupier nodded. There was blood still on his chin, from throwing up.

Ellen picked up the phone but Kupier guided it back down.

"What?" she said. "Who is it? Is it *him*?"

The Maneater.

Kupier closed his eyes, then opened them back. Looked over at Thomas. He was just staring at him, at Grandpa K, his mouth and chin bloody.

"You're him, aren't you?" Thomas said, his voice full of wonder, and in answer Kupier held his arm out along his side in the shape of a grandson. Thomas didn't step into it.

"A misunderstanding," Kupier said, starting to cough, spattering the wall red, "she said it was just an *owl* . . . " and then was just concentrating on trying to breathe air when Rita crossed the room to gather something, one of her mother's porcelain figurines maybe, that she hadn't seen for years now. Whatever it was, it made her lead with her hand, the expression on her face the kind you have in a dream: wonder. Until an arm reached up for her from the laundry, pulled her into its lap, and for the next twenty minutes, as long as Stevenson made Eric stand there knocking, the arm drew pictures for Rita and Thomas on a notebook, sketches of all of them up in heaven now, already—Grandma and Grandpa K, Rita and Thomas as bunny rabbits holding hands, Ellen hunched over on the other side of the room screaming, her fists balled at the sides of her head, her toes pigeoned together, knees knocked.

Kupier put his hand on her shoulder and told her not to worry, that this was going to work out, and for an instant saw himself as Mrs. Lambert, gaunt at the edge of some great light, and he smiled inside, so deep that he crumbled away altogether, everything but the teeth, and the legend he was about to become.

➤ Raphael

By the time we were twelve, the four of us were already ghosts, invisible in the back of our homerooms, at the cafeteria, at the pep-rallies where the girls all wore spirit ribbons the boys were supposed to buy. There was Alex in his cousin's handed-down clothes—his cousin in the sixth grade *with* us—Rodge, who insisted that *d* was actually in his name, Melanie, hiding behind the hair her mother wouldn't let her cut, and me, with my laminated list of allergies and the inhaler my mother had written my phone number on in black marker. Three boys who knew they didn't matter and one girl that each of us fell in love with every morning with first bell, watching her race across the wet grass to make the school doors by eight.

"We're the only ones who can see us," Rodge said to me once, watching Melanie run.

I nodded, and Alex fell in. When Melanie burst through the doors we each pretended not to have been watching her.

It was true, though, that we were the only ones who could see us. And there was a power in it. It let us live in a space where no one could see what we did. The rules didn't apply to us. Maybe that freedom was supposed to balance out our invisibility somehow, even. The world trying to make up for what it had failed to give us. We used it like that, anyway: not as if it were a gift, but like it was something we deserved, something we were going to prove was ours by using it all up, by pushing it farther and farther, daring it to fail us as well.

Or maybe we pushed it just because we'd been let down so many times already, we had no choice but to distrust our invisibility, our friendship. Anything this good, after everything else, it had to be the opening lines of some complicated joke. We were just waiting for the punch line. By pushing what we had farther and farther each day, testing each other, we were maybe even trying to fast-forward to that punch line.

But, too, it just felt so good to be part of something, finally, and then act casual, like it was nothing. Even if it was the rejects club, the ghost squad. Because maybe that was where it started, right? Then, next, weeks and weeks later—homecoming—maybe one of us would understand in some small but perfect way what it felt like at the pep rally, to give a girl a spirit ribbon then watch her pin it onto her shirt, smooth it down for too long because suddenly eye contact has become an awkward thing. Or, maybe one of us would be that girl. Or, just get swept away for once in the band's music. Believe in the team, that if they can just win Friday night, then the world is going to be good and right.

More than anything, I guess, we wanted to be seen, given a chance. Not on the outside anymore. That's probably what it came down to.

And the first step towards getting seen is of course being loud, doing what the other kids won't, or are too scared to.

The days, though, they just kept turning into each other.

Nobody was noticing us, what we were doing. Even when we talked about it loud in the cafeteria, in the hall.

It would have taken so little, too.

A lift of the chin, a narrowing of the eyes.

Somebody asking where we were going after school.

If we just could have gotten that one nod of interest, maybe Alex would still be alive. Maybe Rodge wouldn't have killed himself as a fifteenth birthday present to himself. Maybe Melanie wouldn't have had to run away.

Even if whoever saw us didn't want to go with us, but just had a ribbon, maybe. For Melanie. Because she really was beautiful under all that hair. The other three, then, we would have faded back into the steel-grey lockers that lined the halls, and we wouldn't have gone any farther, ever.

But we were invisible, invulnerable.

Nobody saw us walking away after final bell. We were going to the lake. It was where we always went.

In a plastic cake pan with a sealable lid, buried in the mat of leaves that Rodge said was just above where the waves the ski boats made crashed, was Alex's book. It was one of a series off a television commercial; his mom had bought it then forgot about it. And we didn't hide it because we thought it was a Satan's Bible or Anarchist's Cookbook or anything—because it was powerful—we hid it simply because we didn't want it to get wet. If my mother ever missed her cake pan, she never said anything.

"Where were we?" Melanie said, not sitting down but lowering herself so the seat of her pants hovered over the damp leaves. She balanced by hugging her knees with her arms. She'd told us once that her father had made her take ballet and gymnastics both until the third grade, when he left, and the way she moved, I believed it. We were all invisible, but she was the only one with enough throw-away grace that you never heard her feet fall.

Sitting back on her heels like that, her hair fell over her arms to the ground.

The rest of us didn't care about our clothes. Just the book.

What we were doing was trying to scare ourselves. With alien abductions, with unexplained disappearances. Ghost ships, werewolves, prophecies, spontaneous human combustion.

The person reading would read in monotone. That was one of the rules. And no eye contact either.

The first entry that day was about a man sitting in his own living room when the television suddenly goes static. He reaches for the mute button, can't find it, but then the screen clears up all at once. Only it's not his show anymore, but an aerial view of . . . he's not sure what. And then he is: his house, his own house. Ambulances pulling up. He opens his mouth, stands, his beer foaming into the carpet, and then doesn't go to work the next day, or the next, and finally starts getting his checks from disability.

"That's it?" Alex said, when Rodge was through.

"What's the question?" Melanie said.

Part of the format of the book was that the editors would ask questions in italic after each entry.

"Was he stealing his cable?" I offered, my voice spooky.

Alex laughed, not scared either.

"Was it a warning?" Rodge read, following his index finger. "Was TJ Bentworth given that day a prophecy of his own death, and the opportunity to avoid it? And, if so, who sent that warning?"

Melanie threaded a strand of hair behind her ear, shook her head, disgusted.

The test now—and we'd sworn honesty, to not at any cost lie about it—was whether or not, that night, alone, we'd think twice with our hands on the remote control. If we thought, even for a microsecond, that that next station was going to be us.

Melanie shrugged, looked away, across the water.

"This is crap," she said. "We need a new book."

I agreed.

Alex took the book from Rodge, buried his nose in it, determined to prove to us that this book *was* scary.

I left him to it, was prepared to go to Rodge's house, raid his pantry before his brother got home from practice, but then Alex looked up, said it: "We should tell our own stories, think?"

Rodge looked down, as if focusing into the ground.

"Like, make them up?" he said.

Alex shrugged whatever, smiled, and clapped the book shut.

He was three hours from the Buick that was coming to kill him.

The story I told was one that I'd already tried hard enough to forget that I never would. It was one of my dad's stories. I was in it.

The first thing I told Alex and Rodge and Melanie was that this one was true.

Alex nodded, said to Rodge that this was how they all start.

"It should be dark," Melanie said, swinging some of her hair around behind her. Their were leaf fragments in the tip-ends. I looked past her, to the wall of trees. It was night, in a way. Not dark, but still, with the sun behind the clouds, the only light we had was grey. It was enough. I nodded to myself, started.

"I was like ten months old," I said.

"You *remember?*" Alex interrupted.

Rodge told him to shut up.

"My dad," I went on. "He was like, I don't know. In the bedroom. I think I was on the floor in the living room or something." I shrugged my shoulder up to rub my right ear, stalling. Not to be sure I had it right, but that my voice wasn't going to crack. The first time I'd heard my father tell this, I'd cried and not been able to stop. I couldn't even explain why, really. Just that, you look at enough pictures of yourself as a baby and you imagine that everything was normal. That it doesn't matter, it was just part of what got you to where you are now.

But then my dad took that away.

The story I told the three of them that last afternoon we were all together was that I was just sleeping there on the floor, my dad in his refrigerator in the garage, getting another beer or something, my mom asleep in their room. The television was the only light in the room. It was wrestling—the reason my mom had gone to bed early. Anyway, there's my dad, coming back from the garage, one beer open, another between his forearm and chest, when he feels more than sees that something's wrong in the living room. That there's an extra shadow.

"What?" Melanie said, her eyes locked right on me.

I looked away, down. Swallowed.

"He said that—that—" and then I started crying anyway. Twelve years old with my friends and crying like a baby.

Melanie took my hand in hers.

"You have to finish now," Alex said.

Rodge had his hand over his mouth, wasn't saying anything.

When I could, I told them: my dad, standing there in the doorless doorway between the kitchen and the living room, looking down into our living room, past the couch, the coffee table, to me, on my stomach on the floor.

Squatted down beside me, blond like nobody in our family, a boy, a fourth-grader maybe, his palm stroking my baby hair down to my scalp.

My father doesn't drop his beer, doesn't call for my mom, can't do anything.

"What—?" he tries to say, and the boy just keeps stroking my hair down, looks across the living room to my father, and says "I'm just patting him," then stands, walks out the other doorway in the living room, the one that goes to the front door.

" . . . only it never opens," Alex finished, grinning.

I nodded as if caught, pressed my palms into my eyes and stretched my chin up as high as I could, so the lump in my throat wouldn't push through the skin.

"Good," Melanie said, "nice," and, when I could control my face again, I smiled, pointed to Rodge, his hair straw yellow, and lied, said that it was him patting me, somehow.

Rodge opened his mouth once, twice, shaking his head no, please, but, when he couldn't get out whatever he had, Alex clapped three times, slowly, and then opened his hand to Melanie, said, "Ladies first."

"Guess I'll have to wait then," she said back, flaring her eyes, but then shrugged, wrapped a coil of hair around her index finger like she was always doing, then walked her hand up the strands, each coil taking in one more finger until she didn't have any more left.

It was one of the things Alex and Rodge and I never talked about then, but each loved about her—how she was so unconscious of the small things she could do. How she took so much for granted, and, because of that, because she didn't draw attention to the magic acrobatics of her fingers, to the strength of her hair, she got to keep it.

We didn't so much love her like a girl, desire her, though that was starting, for sure. It was more like we saw in her a completeness missing in ourselves. A completeness coupled with a kind of disregard that was almost flagrant. But maybe that's what desire is, really. In the end, it didn't matter; none of us would ever hold her hand at a pep rally, or tell her anything real. It wasn't because of her story, either, but that's more or less where it starts.

"Four kids," she said, looking to each of us in turn, "sixth graders, just like us," and Alex groaned as if about to vomit, held his stomach in mock-pain.

Rodge smiled, and I did too, on the inside.

A safe story. That was exactly what we needed.

"The girl's name was . . . *Melody*," Melanie said, arching her eyebrows for us to call her on it. When we didn't, she went on, and almost immediately the comfort level dropped. Alex flashed a look to me and I shrugged my cheeks as best I could, didn't know. What Melanie was telling us was the part *before* the story, the part we didn't want and would have never asked for, because we all already knew: the thing between her and her step-dad. What they did. Only, to amp it up for us, maybe, make it worse, Melody added to the nightly visitations Melody's mother, standing in the doorway, watching. Mad at this Melody for stealing her husband.

Desperate to not be hearing this, I latched onto that doorway as hard as I could, remembered it from my own story, and nodded to myself: all Melanie was doing was reordering the stuff I'd already laid out there. Using it again, because it was already charged—we already *knew* that bad things followed parents standing in doorways.

Or maybe it was a door I had opened, somehow, by telling a real story in the first place.

After the one rape that was supposed to stand in for the rest, Melanie nodded, said, "And then there was . . . *Hodge* . . . " at which point Rodge started shaking his head no, no, please.

"We only have an hour," Alex chimed, tapping the face of his watch.

Melanie turned her face to him and raised her eyebrows, waiting for him to back off. Finally, he did. As punishment, his character didn't even get a name. Mine was *Raphael*, what Melanie considered to be a version of *Gabriel*, I guess. But Gabe, I was just Gabe back then.

I couldn't interrupt her, though. Even when her story had the four of us walking away from school, to play our little "scare" game.

But this one was different.

In the Lakeview of Melanie's story, Lake*ridge*, there wasn't a book buried in a thirteen-by-nine Tupperware dish, but an overgrown cemetery. It was just past the football field.

Over the past week, she told us, her face straight, the dares had been of the order of lying face-up on a grave for ninety seconds, or tracing each carved letter of the oldest headstone, or putting your hand in the water of the birdbath and saying your own name backwards sixty-six times.

"They were running out of stuff, though," she added.

"I *get* it," Alex said, holding his mother's book closer to his chest.

Melanie smiled, pulled a black line of hair across her mouth and spoke through it: "But then *Raphael* had an idea," she said, looking to me.

"What?" I said, looking behind me for no real reason.

Melanie smiled, let the silence build—she had to have done this before, I thought, before she moved here, or seen it done—and told us that *Raphael*'s great idea was to take some of the pecans from the tree over in the corner, the tree that (her voice spooking up) "had its roots down with the dead people, in their eye sockets and rib cages."

"Take them and what?" Rodge said, worried.

"Look at you," Alex said to him.

"And what?" I asked, at a whisper.

"Take them to one of your basements," she said. "Then put them in a bowl with water for six days, then turn the lights off and each eat one."

The lump was back in my throat. I thought it might be a pecan.

"That it?" Alex said, overdoing his shrug.

"Six days . . ." Melanie said, ignoring him, drawing air in through her teeth, "and the four of them collect back in the basement, turn all the lights off except one candle, and then, that too."

"At midnight," Alex added.

"At midnight," Melanie agreed, as if she'd been going to say that anyway, and then drew out for us the cracking of the shells in the darkness, how they were soggy enough to feel like the skin of dead people. Then she placed the pecan meat first on the Alex stand-in's tongue—he throws up—then on the Hodge-character, who swallows it, gets stomach cancer two days later, then it's Raphael's turn. All he can do though is chew and chew, the meat getting bigger in his mouth until he realizes that, in the darkness, he's peeled his own finger, eaten *that* meat.

I laugh, like it.

And then it's Melody's turn to eat.

With her thin, beautiful fingers, Melanie acts it out for us in a way so we can all see Melody through the darkness of the basement, not so much cracking her pecan as peeling it, then setting the tender meat on the back of her tongue, only to gag when it moves.

In the darkness she's created, we all hear the splat, then, unmistakably, something rising, trying to breathe. Not able to.

The lights come on immediately, and running down Melody's chin is blood, only some it's transparent, like yolk, like the pecan was an egg, and—

"C'mon," Alex said. "You don't try to outgore the gore of Gabe here eating his own *finger*, Mel."

"I'd expect that from you," Melanie said, smiling through her hair, "it was you who was born from that dead pecan," at which point Alex hooked his head to one side, as if not believing she would say that, then he was pushing up out of the leaves, tackling her back into them, and we were smiling again, and I finally breathed.

When Rodge wouldn't take his turn, saying he didn't know anything scary, Alex went. Instead of telling a ghost story, though, he opened his mother's book again.

"Cheater, " I said. "They're supposed to be real."

"Wait," he said back, "I was just looking at this one the other—" and then he was gone, hunched all the way over into the book.

I lifted my face to Melanie, said, "Where'd you hear that piece of crap?" and she pursed her lips into a smile, said, flaring her eyes around it, "You listened."

"I heard it with a walnut, not a pecan," Alex chimed in, turning pages, only half with us.

"A walnut?" Melanie said, crinkling her nose, "nobody plants a walnut tree in a graveyard."

Looking back, now, I can hear it—how she'd used *cemetery* in the story, *graveyard* to Alex—but right then it didn't matter. What I was really doing anyway was saying it *had* scared me.

"You heard it at Dunbar?" I said.

Dunbar was her old school.

She opened her mouth to answer but then stopped, seemed to be fascinated by something out on the lake.

I followed where she was looking.

"What?"

"I don't know where I heard it," she said, still not looking at me, but out over the lake. "Somewhere, I guess."

"No, what are you looking at?" I said, pointing with my chin out across the water, and she came back to me."

"Nothing."

We were twelve years old, going to live forever.

When Alex finally got the book open to the right place, it was about witch trials all through history. Salem, the Spanish Inquisition, tribesman in Africa. A whole subsection of a chapter, with pictures of the devices used to torture confessions, pointy Halloween hats, all of it.

"I'm shaking," I said to him, trying to chatter my teeth.

"Can it," he said, following his finger to the next page.

It was one of the blue boxes framed with scrollwork. The stuff that was supposed to be footnotes, but was too important.

"How to test for a witch," he read triumphantly.

"This is scary?" I said to him.

Already, one of the blue boxes from two weeks ago had given us a list on how to become werewolves: roll in the sand by water under a full moon; drink from the same water wolves have been drinking from; get bitten by a werewolf without dying. Our assignments that night had been to try to become werewolves. Or get grounded trying, yeah.

"Weigh her against a *Bible*?" Melanie read, incredulous.

"Her," Alex said, quieter, an intensity in his voice I knew, and knew better than to argue with.

By this time, Rodge was rocking back and forth, looking up to the road each time a car passed. When the noise got steady enough, that would mean it was five o'clock, and this would be over. On a day the sun was shining, the sound of cars would slowly be replaced by the sound of boat motors, but that day, if there even was a boat, then Melanie had been the only one to see it. If she'd seen anything.

"Her," Melanie repeated, not letting it pass.

Alex smiled one side of his face, looked up to her. "How do we know?" he said.

"I'm a witch," Melanie said, "yeah."

Alex shrugged.

Melanie shook her head without letting her eyes leave him. "What do you want to do, then?"

Alex looked down to the blue box and read aloud: "Devil's mark . . . kiss of—do you, if I cut you, or stick you with a needle, will you, y'know, bleed like a real person?"

Melanie just stared at him.

"C'mon," I said, standing, pulling her up behind me. She didn't let go of my hand after she had her feet under her, either. Alex saw, looked from me to her, and, even though I was just twelve, still I understood in my dim way what he was doing here: he wanted to be the one holding her hand. And, if not him, then, at least for this afternoon, nobody.

"Do you?" he said, again. "If I stick you with a pin, will you bleed?"

"Do you have a pin?" she said back.

Alex scanned the ground as if looking for one, or trying to remember a jack knife or hypodermic one of us had in a pocket.

He shook his head no.

Melanie blew air out and then held the sleeve of her right arm up, cocked her elbow out to him. It was the wide scab she'd got three days ago, when, to scare ourselves after reading about the jogger who disappeared mid-stride, we'd each had to run one hundred yards down the road, blindfolded.

Alex curled his lip up.

"What?" he said.

"You asked," she said. "It's blood. Want me to peel it?"

"But that's not—scary," he said.

Melanie lowered her elbow, let her sleeve fall back down.

Ten seconds later, Alex raised his face from the book. He was smiling.

"How about this?" he said, and I stepped around, read behind his finger.

"We can't," I said. "It's too cold."

Alex shrugged, let his voice get spooky. "Maybe we have to, for her own sake."

"What?" Melanie said, her arms crossed now.

"Tie your hands and feet," Rodge said from below, where he was still sitting. "Tie your hands and feet and throw you in the water."

"Bingo," Alex said, shooting him with his fingergun then blowing the smoke off, the thing the football players had all been doing during class lately, because it made no real noise.

"Excuse me?" Melanie said, to Rodge.

"He's been reading it after we leave," I said. "Right, Rodge?"

Rodge nodded. I'd caught him doing it early on. It wasn't because he wanted to know, to be more scared, but because, if he'd already read it *once*, then hearing it again wouldn't scare him so much. He'd made me promise not to tell. In return, I'd walked to what had been my spot in the leaves that day, dug my inhaler out, held it up to him like Scout's Honor.

"Well?" Alex said.

"It's cold," Melanie said.

"More like you just know you'll float," Alex said back, daring her with his eyebrows.

Melanie shook her head, blew a clump of hair from her mouth.

"Just tie my feet then," she said, and already, even then, I had a vision of her like she would have been in 1640 or whenever: bound at the wrists and ankles, sinking into the grey water. Not a witch but dying anyway.

Because we didn't have any rope like the blue box said we should, Alex sacrificed one of his shoe-laces. Melanie tied it around her ankles herself.

"It's only a couple of feet deep out there," Rodge said.

He was standing now, facing the water. A defeat in his voice I would come to know over the next three years.

"Then I won't sink far, I guess," Melanie said, to Alex.

"Then we can tie your hands too," he said back.

Melanie took the challenge, offered Alex her wrists.

"Not too tight," I told him.

He told me not to worry.

"This gets me out of homework for two weeks," she said, having to sling her head hard now to get the hair out of her face, then lean back the other way to keep from falling over.

"Three," I said back.

"A month," Rodge said.

Alex didn't say anything. Just, to Melanie, "You ready?"

She was. Alex should have asked me though, or Rodge.

All the same, he couldn't lift her all by himself.

"C'mon," he said, stepping in up to the tops of his lace-less shoes. The water sucked one of them off, kept it.

"Cold?" Melanie said.

"Bathwater," he said back, grimacing, then, because her feet were tied together, gave her his hand.

"Thanks," she said.

"It's in the book," he said, smiling.

He was on one side of her, me on the other, both of us trying to pull her along, not dunk her yet. Rodge still on the bank.

"Not *too* deep," I said, but Melanie jumped ahead of us, splashing me more than I wanted. "It has to be a little deep," she said. "I don't want to hit bottom either, right?"

Right. I just thought it, didn't say, because I knew she'd hear it in my voice: that this didn't feel like a game anymore. It wasn't like rolling in the sand under a full moon or running blindfolded down a part of the road that had one of us standing at each end, to watch for cars.

Something could really happen, here.

It was too late to stop it, though, too. Or that's what I tell myself.

We followed her out until the water was at our thighs, and then Alex nodded, and she turned sideways between us, so one of us could take her feet, the other her shoulders. She leaned back into me and I held her as much as I could, but she was already wet, her hair in the water so heavy.

"If she's—" I started, taking her weight, trying not to hurt her, and when Alex looked up to me I started over: "She walked out here, I mean. Like us. Didn't float. Is that enough?"

Alex refocused his eyes on the water and silt we'd just disturbed.

"Doesn't matter," he said, "it wasn't a test, then. It was her doing it herself, not getting thrown. 'Cast,' I mean. Getting cast into the water, to see."

"But you know she's not—"

"On three . . . " he interrupted, starting the motion, setting his teeth with the effort, and I shook my head no but had to follow too, like swinging a jump rope. One as thick and heavy as a young girl's body.

If I could go back, now, I would count to three in my head and never look away from Melanie, I think. But I didn't know. Instead of watching her the whole time, I kept looking up for boats, for somebody to catch us, stop this. Meaning all I have left of swinging her is a mental snapshot of her face, all of it for once, her hair pulled back, wet, inky, her skin so pale in contrast it was almost translucent. And then we let her go, arced her up maybe two feet if we were lucky, and four feet out. Not even high enough or far enough for her hair to pull all the way out of the water.

It was enough.

Without thinking *not* to, I raised my right arm, to shield my face from the splash, but then—then.

Then the world we had known, it was over. Forever.

Instead of splashing into the water, Melanie rested for an instant on the surface in the fetal, cannonball position, eyes shut, all her weight on the small of her back, her hair the only thing under, and then she felt it too—that she wasn't sinking—and opened her eyes too wide, arched her back away from it, her mouth in the shape of a scream, and flipped over as fast as a cat. Once, twice, three times, until she was out over the deep water, where the gradual bank dropped off into the cold water. She was still just on the surface, writhing, screaming, whatever part of her that had been twelve years old dying. Finally, still twisting away, she lowered her mouth to the laces at her wrists, then her hands to the laces at her ankles, and then she tried to stand but fell forward, catching herself on the heels of her hands, her hair a black shroud around her.

She looked across the water at us, her eyes the only thing human on her anymore, pleading with me it seemed, and then whipped around, started running over the surface on all fours, across the mile and a half the lake was wide there, leaving us standing knee-deep in the rest of our lives.

Thirty-two years later, now, the two hours after Melanie ran away are still lost. There's an image of Alex, falling back into the water on one arm, of Rodge, just standing there, limp, and then it's trees, maybe, and roads. The red-brick buildings of town; an adult guiding my inhaler down to my mouth. Alex running up the side of the highway to meet his Buick.

At his funeral, Rodge held my hand, and I let him, but then I couldn't hold on tight enough, I guess. Three years later, on his birthday, he bungee-corded car batteries to his work boots, stepped off a stolen boat into the middle of the lake.

Leaving just me.

Geographically, I moved as far away from Lakeview as possible. There are no significant bodies of water for fifty miles, and my children, Reneé and Miller, they each got through their twelfth years unscathed somehow. Probably because I stood guard in their doorways while they slept. Because I only allowed history and political books into the house. Because, finally, they were each popular in their classes, unaware of the kids standing at the back walls of all the rooms they were in, their faces a combination of damaged hope and hopeful fatalism, ready to break into a smile if somebody looked their way, *at* them instead of through them, but knowing too that that was never going to happen. I didn't tell them that that kid was me. The day Reneé came home with a spirit ribbon on her sweater—SKIN THE BOBCATS—I almost cried. When she forgot about it, the ribbon, I took it from the dash of her car. It's in my sock-drawer, now. One Saturday morning I woke to find my wife, Sharon, studying it, but then she just put it back, patting it in place it seemed, as if putting it to bed, and I pretended not to have been awake. It's a good life. One I don't deserve, one I'm stealing, but still, mine. Last Sunday I dropped Miller off at basketball camp two towns over, then, on the way home, bought Reneé some of the custom film she said she needed for the intro to photography course she's taking at the local community college.

Three nights after that, a Wednesday, I took her to the carnival. Because she's seventeen, and I won't get many more chances. I even broke out the Bobcats ribbon; she remembered it, held it to her mouth. At the carnival she took picture after picture, washing the place in silver light—clowns, camels, the carousel—and at the end of the night put her hand over mine on the shifter of my car, told me thanks. That she wouldn't forget.

Like I said, I don't deserve any of this.

When I was twelve years old, I helped kill a girl. Or, according to the doctors, helped her kill herself, punish herself for what her step-father had been doing to her. I never told them about the dead pecans though, or about how her hands had been tied. Just that we'd been daring each other farther and farther out into the water, until her hair snagged a Christmas tree or something. At first, I'd tried the truth, but it wouldn't fit into words. And then I realized that it didn't have to, that, with Rodge clammed up, catatonic, I could say whatever I wanted. That I'd tried to save her, even. That something like I thought I'd seen just couldn't happen, was impossible, was what any twelve-year-old kid would insist he'd seen, rather than a drowning. Especially a twelve-year-old kid already in a "scare" club, a book buried in a cake pan under the leaves that nobody ever found, that's probably still there.

I told it enough like that that sometimes I almost believed it.

But then I'd see her again, running on the surface of the water, and would have to sit up in bed and force the sheets into my mouth until I gagged.

When I finally told my wife about her—the girl I'd had a crush on who I'd seen drown when I was in the sixth grade—I'd even called her Melody, I think, like the story, and then not corrected myself. The main thing I remembered was her hair. The sheets I stuffed into my mouth were supposed to be it, I think, her hair. An apology of sorts. Love. The way your lip trembles when your best friend from elementary tells you he's moving away forever. Or your mother tells you they found him out on the highway, crammed up into the wheel well of a Buick.

The story I told myself for years was that her body was still down there, really tangled up in a Christmas tree or a trotline. That Rodge was down there now for all of us, trying to free her, but his hands are so waterlogged that the skin of his fingers keeps peeling off. Above him, a mass of fish backlit by the wavering sun, feeding on the scraps of his flesh.

"Keep her there," I'd tell him, out loud, at odd moments.

"Excuse me?" Sharon would say, from her side of the bed, or table, or car.

Nothing.

The other story I told myself was that I could make up for it all. That I could be the exact opposite of whatever Melanie's father had been—could be kind enough to Reneé that it would cancel out all the bad that had happened to Melanie, and that Melanie would somehow *see* this, forgive me.

So I go behind Sharon's back, buy her film she's supposed to buy herself. I take her to the carnival and hold her hand. I sneak into her room the morning after and—a gift—palm the film canister off her dresser, so I can pay for the developing as well, then can't wait twenty-four hours for it so go back and pay for one hour, leave the prints on her dresser without looking at them but then have to, when she leaves for a date. Like Rodge, I'm reading the book in secret, preparing myself, cataloging points to appreciate when she finally shows them to me, proud: the angle she got the man on stilts from; the flag on top of the main tent, caught mid-flap; the carousel, its lights smearing unevenly across the frame. The . . . the *tinted* or heat-sensitive lens or whatever she had on her camera, to distort the carnival. And the shutter-speed—it's like she has it jammed up against how fast the film is, so that they have to work against each other. Like she's *trying* to mess up the shots, or—this has to be it—as if it might be possible to twist the image enough that it would become just another suburban neighborhood. Maybe it's part of the project, though. They're good, all of them. She's my daughter.

Saturday, deep in the afternoon, Sharon gone to get Miller from camp, I walk into the living room and Reneé's there. On the glass coffee table, she has all the prints out, the table lamp shadeless, lying on its side under the glass, making the table into the kind of tray I associate with negatives, or slides. I see why she's done it, though: it filters out some of the purple tint in the prints, and makes everything sharper.

She's in sweats and a T-shirt, her hair pulled back to keep the oils off her face. No shoes, her feet curled under her on the couch.

"Date?" I say.

She nods without looking up.

I'm standing on the other side of the coffee table from her. "These them?" I ask.

Again, she nods.

"They're—wrong," she says, shrugging about them, narrowing her eyes.

I lower myself to one knee, focus through my reading glasses, pretend to be seeing them for the first time.

"What do you mean?" I say.

"Daddy . . . " she says, as if I'm the thicko here.

"They're . . . purple?" I say.

"Not that," she says, and points to one of the carousel shots that, with her lens/shutter speed trick, has come out looking time-lapsed. I lift it delicately by the edge, hold it up to the light, my back old-man stiff.

"See?" she says.

I don't answer, don't remember this one from when I flipped through them the first time. It's one of the carousel shots, when she was figuring out how to move her camera with the horses. The effect is to keep them in focus, more or less. Not the children—their movements are too unpredictable to compensate for—but the horses, anyway. And some of the parents standing by the horses, holding their children in place.

I shrug.

"Look," she says.

I shrug, try, and then see it maybe, from the corner of my eye, as I'm giving up: what's been waiting for me for thirty-two years. I relax for what feels like the first time. Don't drop the picture.

"Right?" Reneé says.

I make myself look again. Tell myself it's just a trick of the light. The special *film*. It was a carnival, for Chrissake. I even manage a laugh.

What Reneé captured and the drugstore developed—maybe *that's* where the mistake was: an errant chemical, swirling in the pan—is two almost-paisley tendrils of iridescent purple breath curling up from one of the wooden horse's nostrils, the horse's eyes flared wide, as if in pain.

Somebody with a cigarette, maybe, I say, a mom or dad standing *behind* the carousel, smoking. Or cotton candy under neon light. But then I follow the high, royal arch of the horse's neck, to the crisp outline of a perfect little child sitting on its back, holding the pole with both hands.

Standing beside him, out of focus, is his mother, her hand to the horse's neck. Patting it.

All I can see of her is her hair, spilling down the side of her legs.

This time I do drop the picture.

After Reneé's gone on her date, her mouth moving, telling me her plans but no sound making it to me, I take the flashlight into the backyard.

Buried under what Sharon insists will be a compost pile someday is a cake pan I bought at the discount store. In it, a book. Not the same series, not the same publisher, but the same genre: an encyclopedia of the unexplained.

The carousel horse isn't going to be in there, I know. Because it was an accident.

But Melanie.

That's the only page I read.

Her entry is in the chapter of unexplained disappearances. The woman jogger who disappeared is on the opposite page from her, like an old friend. The title the jogger gets, because of a later sighting, is "Green Lady Gone."

The title of Melanie's entry is "Roger's Story." They forgot the *d*; for the thousandth time, I smile about it, then close my eyes, lower my forehead to the book the way Alex used to, in class. It was a joke: by then we both knew enough about Edgar Cayce that we wanted too to be able to just lay our heads on a book, absorb it.

Like every time, though, it doesn't work. Or, now, this book is already in my head. All closing my eyes to it does is bring Melanie back. Not as she was on the water, but as she was running across the wet grass for the last bell, fighting to keep her hair out of her face.

Did she even leave tracks in the dew?

If she hadn't, and if we'd noticed, it would have just been because of her ballet training, her gymnastics. That she was made of something better, something that didn't interact with common stuff like grass and water.

But that wooden horse, breathing.

The mother I always knew she would be, this is the kind of gift she would give her child, I know. If she could. If it wasn't just a trick of the light.

Rodger's story is what he left as a birthday card to himself. Not word-for-word—it's been edited into the voice of the rest of the entries—but still, I can hear him through it. It starts just like Melanie's, with four social outcasts, creating their own little society. One in which they matter. How none of the four of us knew what we were doing, really. How we're so, so sorry. We never meant for . . . for her—

Rodger places us by the lake. The reason I've never been able to stop reading his version is the same reason I was never able to forget my father's story about me as a baby, sleeping on the floor: because I'm in it, just from a different angle.

In the light-blue box framed with scrollwork, the way Rodge tells it is he was just watching us, not as if he knew what was going to happen, but as if, in retelling it, reliving it, he had become unable to pretend that the him watching hadn't been through it a hundred times already. The way he watches us, he knows about the Buick coming for Alex, about Melanie, writhing on the surface of the lake. How a car battery changes the way a boat sits in the water.

Maybe the gases that escape from the cells of the battery on the way down are iridescent, are the last thing you see, before the strings of moss become hair, smother you.

According to Rodger, Melanie *asked* us to tie her hands and feet, throw her in the lake. I shake my head: he's protecting Alex. Protecting me. And then our stories synch up, more or less, the viewpoint just off a bit: instead of an image of Melanie's face just as I let her go, I see her rising from, slipping out of mine and Alex's hands the way a magician might let ten doves go at once.

And then she hisses, throws her hair from her face, and crawls across the lake, her hip joints no longer human. Her body never recovered.

The question after the entry is *What was Melanie Parker?*

I close the book, set it on the island in the middle of the kitchen, then look down the hall when the noise starts, but don't go to it.

It's the bathtub. It's filling.

I raise my chin, stretching my throat tight, and rub my larynx, trying to keep whatever's in me down, then am clawing through Sharon's cabinets in the kitchen, spice jars and sifters raining down onto the counter.

Finally I find what I know she has: the three tins of nuts, from Christmas.

The first is walnuts, the second two pecans, still in their paper shells.

I raise the blackest one up against the light, to see if I can see through it. When I can't, I feel my chest tightening the way it used to—the asthma I've outgrown—and know what I have to do. My head wobbles on my neck in denial, though.

But it's the only way.

I place the pecan on my tongue, shell and all, afraid of what might be inside, then work it over between the molars of my right side, close my eyes and jaw at once. Make myself swallow it all. Fall coughing to the floor, have to dig out one of Miller's old inhalers, from when he had asthma too.

The mist slams into my chest again and again, my eyes hot, burning.

At the end of Rodger's birthday card to himself, which the editors chose to encase in their version of the blue-box, are the words *She's still down there.*

I envy him that.

When I was twelve, I helped kill a girl I thought I loved, helped give birth to something else, something she didn't even know about. Something that saw me before crawling away. What makes it real, maybe, undeniable, is the way, that last time she looked up, she spit out the piece of Alex's shoe lace she had in her mouth. Had to shake it away from her lip.

Her tongue was any color. Maybe the same it had always been.

Because I don't know what else to do, I sit with my back against the wall, behind my chair, every light in the living room on, random muscles in my shoulder and right leg twitching, as if cycling through the sensory details of letting Melanie go that day, above the water. My lap warms with urine and I just sway back and forth on the balls of my feet, hugging my knees to my chest, Miller's inhaler curled under my index finger like a gun

An hour later, eleven, midnight, something, I try to tell the story to the end, name the out-of-focus kid on the carousel Hodge. Give him a good life. And then the front door swings in all at once and I know I'm dying, that this is what death is, and have to bite the knuckle of my middle finger to keep from screaming.

From behind the chair, all I can see is the top of the door. It closes and my vision blurs, a grin spreading from my eyes to my mouth—that this will be finally be over, after so long—but then a sound intrudes: keys, jangling into a brass bowl. The one on the stand by the coat rack.

Reneé.

She swishes past me in slow motion, for the mess the kitchen is. Never sees me.

I stand in the doorway behind her, my slacks dark enough that she won't see the stain maybe.

Instead of putting stuff back into the cabinets, she's looking through the book I left out. Opening it to the place I have marked—marked with a spirit ribbon.

Slowly, she cocks her head to the side, studying the ribbon, then holds it to her mouth again, breathes it in.

I cough into my hollow fist to announce myself, there behind her already.

She sucks air in, pulls the book hard to her chest. Turns to me, leading with her eyes, and looks at me for too long it feels like, then past me, to the living room, so bright.

"You okay?" she asks.

I nod, make myself smile.

"How'd it go?" I ask—the date.

"You know," she says, opening the book again. "Sandy and his music."

I nod, remember: Sandy's the one with the custom stereo.

"What is this?" she says, about the book.

"Just—nothing," I tell her. "Old."

"Hm," she says, leafing through, wowing her eyes up at the more sensational stuff. Aliens, maybe. God.

"She did it to herself," I say, all at once.

Reneé holds her place in the book, looks up to me.

"She was . . . she was sad," I say. "She was a sad little girl. Her dad, he was—you've got to understand."

Reneé shrugs, humoring me I think. I rub my mouth, look away, to all Sharon's cooking utensils, spilling onto the floor. When I don't look away fast enough, Reneé has to say something about it: "A surprise?"

"Surprise?" I say back, trying to make sense of the word.

"Reorganizing for Mom?" she tries, holding her eyebrows up.

I nod, make myself grin, feel something rising in my throat again, have to raise my shoulders to keep it down. Close my eyes.

When I open them again, Reneé's sitting on the island, the book closed beside her. Just watching me.

"I could have stayed home tonight," she says, an offering of sorts, but I wave the idea away.

"You need—need to go out," I tell her. "It's good. What you should be doing."

The heels of her hands are gripping the edge of the countertop. I can't not notice this.

"Okay," she says, finally, "I guess—" but then, sliding the book back so she won't take it with her when she jumps down, her hand catches on the stiff, upper part of the spirit ribbon, pulls it from the book. "Oops," she says, doing her mouth in the shape of mock-disaster, "lost your place."

I shake my head no, it's all right, I *know* where my place is, but then she has the ribbon again, is studying it. Remembering too.

We were ghosts, I want to tell her. And then the rest, finally.

Instead, I watch as she pulls the stick pin from the head of the ribbon.

"Stacy showed me this," she says, holding her right arm out, belly-up, in a way that I have to see Melanie's again, waiting for Alex to tie his shoe-lace around it.

"No," I say, taking her hand in mine, but she steps back, says, "It's all right, Daddy."

What she's doing is placing the pin in the crook of her elbow, the part of her arm that folds in.

I shake my head no again, reach for her again, but it's too late, she's already making her hand into a fist, drawing it slowly up to her shoulder.

I feel my eyes get hot, my mouth open.

When she unfolds her arm, the pin slides out of her skin like magic. No blood.

"That's—" I say, having to try hard to make the words, "in a blue box, that's the—Devil's Mark."

She looks up to me, not following.

I smile, touch her arm. Say, "You didn't bleed," and then I'm crying, trying to swallow it all back, but it's too late: the pecan is coming up.

I step back from her and throw up between us, and was right: it's not just a pecan, but bits of shell and meat and blood. Not red blood, like the movies, but darker. Real.

Reneé steps back, raising one of her shoes, to keep it clean maybe, and I look up to her, wipe the blood from my lips with the back of my forearm.

"Daddy?" she says, and I nod, sad that it's come to this, but there's nothing I can do anymore. With trembling hands I pin the ribbon to the chest of her shirt, through her skin maybe, I don't know. It makes her pull back anyway, look up to me, her eyebrows drawing together in question.

"Skin the Bobcats," I whisper to her, unable not to smile, then, when I pick her up in my arms like a little girl, say it at last—that I'm not a good person, that I've done bad things. She doesn't fight, doesn't know to. Doesn't know that we're going down the hall to the bathtub, which is already full.

Afterwards, my shirt wet like my pants, I stand again in the kitchen, hardly recognize it. Have to go outside, onto the balcony, my face flushing warm now like my eyes, my teeth chattering against each other.

Standing at the wood railing, then, I feel it: the tip ends of hair, silky long hair, lifted on the wind, trailing down from the roof.

She's up there I know, one knee to the shingles, her long fingers curled around the eave.

"Reneé?" I say weakly, unable to look around, up, and it's not so much a question as a prayer. That this isn't real. That it's Reneé on the roof, maybe. Trying to scare me.

But then Melanie speaks back in the breathy, adult voice I knew she was going to have someday: *No, Raphael.*

I nod, see my shadow stretching out over the gravel drive, how it's split, doubling from two sources of light, and I know that this is all right, finally, as it should be, as it's always been ever since that day, and then Sharon pulls in under me, my son in the passenger seat, and I'm invisible again, a ghost. Able to do anything.

▶ Captain's Lament

My name is Quincy Mueller, but since the merchant marines I've been known almost exclusively as Muley. It has nothing to do with my character, however. Far from being obstinate or contrary, I'm in fact liberal and engaging. A more enthusiastic conversationalist you're not likely to find; sailors are lonely, I mean, and hungry for company. If anything, I suppose—and this just because I'm honest to a fault—I err toward the overbearing, as isolation is something I've had my fill of.

And yes, if you detect a hit of defensiveness in my voice, you're not far from the mark. That so much should have come from a simple misunderstanding one night twenty years ago is so far beyond comprehension that it's actually amusing, I think, or at least revealing of human nature.

But I get ahead of myself.

Never mind that you already know my story. That you more than likely grew up with it.

To begin, twenty years ago I was thirty-eight, salty and fully-bearded, recovering from a near-fatal accident which had left me convalescing for nearly fourteen months. During those weeks upon weeks in bed, the room uncomfortably *still*—I hadn't been landlocked for more than two consecutive months since my twenty-second year, when I thought marriage was the cure for loneliness—I could feel my skin growing pale and translucent, my lips becoming tender without salt to rime them. Because of the injuries to my throat, too, the doctors wouldn't allow me any tobacco; I couldn't even chew upon my pipe.

I'll spare you the fates I wished upon those doctors—curses I picked up in ports all over the world—but, looking back, I see of course that they more than likely wanted me out of their hospital as much as I wanted out myself.

Since the ninth month, I had said so little, even, that they called for a battery of tests to gauge my psychological health. Though I tried to tell them all I needed was a view of the sea, the smell of brine, still, they poked and prodded my mind until I did in fact shut down. I'm not proud of it, but, like the tarpon on the deck, his side still bleeding from the gaff, I'd flopped around as long as I could, and found that useless, so was now just staring, waiting for this ordeal to be over.

The nurses took turns rolling me from side to side to ministrate my sores and perform other indignities.

In my head, though, I was sailing. On the open sea, a boat pitching beneath me, I was beyond the reach of their needles and swabs and catheters and small, polite questions.

As the days passed, they came to my room less and less, content that my body would either heal itself in time or that I would, one day when they weren't looking, simply stop trying.

To them, I mean, even twenty years ago I was already an antique, a throwback to another century, another way of life.

And, if I'm to be honest here, yes, I did indeed stop trying, finally. But the body breathes whether you want it to or not. The heart keeps beating. Perhaps because it knows more than you do—knows that, past this experience, a whole new life will open up, and whatever infirmities persist, they can be dealt with one by one.

That's all in the future, though.

Right then, on my back in bed, miles from the shore, dose upon dose of antibiotic and painkiller pulsing through my veins, it was hard not to feel sorry for myself. To let that consume me.

It was finally a nurse by the name of Margaret whom I woke to one day. She was dabbing the wetness away from the corners of my eyes, and adjusting the various lines that went into and out of me.

"Does it hurt?" she said, her fingertips light on my right forearm.

I closed my eyes, made her disappear.

The next time I woke, however, she was there again. Evidently she'd been talking for some minutes, telling me about her social life, her family, her dreams and aspirations. I let her words flow over me like water and studied the cursive letters of her name, and watched as, in slow motion, like picture cards flipping one after the other, she pointed a syringe into one of the tubes that fed me.

How long this went on, I don't know. If I'd first seen her on a Wednesday though, her badge still new enough to be hand printed, then this was at least a Monday.

What she talked about the most was a certain boy named Billy, I think. How he'd wronged her and was continuing to wrong her, but she was going to show him.

I opened my mouth to tell her something but only emitted a rusty creak, my voice broken from dis-use.

She smiled, pursed her lips, patted my tender right arm and asked if I wanted to see the ocean?

Though I couldn't talk, still, she saw the answer in my eyes—I've always had expressive eyes—and, with the help of another nurse, maneuvered my atrophied body into a gleaming silver wheelchair, pushed me down hall after hall, my heart beating *intentionally* for the first time in months, the fingers of my left hand gripping the brown plastic armrest, her subdued laughter behind me tittering out between her closed lips.

If I could have spoken, I was going to tell her how, if she wanted, I might name my next ship the *Margo*, after her, and all the rest after that as well: *Margo II, Margo III, Margo IV,* a fleet of *Margos* fanned out across the shipping lanes from here to the South Pacific.

But of course that was just talk—I'd never owned my own ship before, and didn't have one waiting for me when I got better.

And anyway, where she was taking me was a joke of sorts.

She finally stopped our perambulations in the waiting room, with my chair pushed up to a small aquarium with exotic fish, and, every ten seconds, a treasure chest that would burp air up to the surface.

I closed my eyes, woke again to Margaret's hand on a syringe, then slept and slept and slept.

The next time I came to she was stroking the top of my left hand and talking about Billy again.

Evidently I was supposed to have forgotten about the waiting room, about the ocean.

I can remember every shoal in every port I've ever drawn water in, though.

I shut my eyes and shut my ears and let her have my hand. Just that.

How long this cycle repeated itself, I don't know. My guess would place it at two months; after a while Margaret became a practiced-enough nurse that she could haul me into my chair herself, just by leveraging me with her hips and the brakes on my bed, and I was a practiced-enough patient to believe that what she was shooting into me syringe by syringe was salt water, and that the dreams I had were just the ocean inside, bending itself to the moon.

Instead of going to the waiting room now, she was walking me outside, her voice drifting around me. The air was supposed to be good for me, I suspect. It was stale, though; there was no salt in it, no spray, and the horizon was forever blocked by trees and buildings, the sky empty of properly-winged birds.

One day, as had to happen, I suppose, Margaret asked her question again: Did I want to see the ocean?

I tried to move my left hand to indicate that I got this joke, yes, thank you, how nice, but I don't think she was looking anyway.

Back in the room this time, instead of pushing the sharp nose of the syringe into the line that went into my injured arm, she instead emptied it an inch into my mattress.

"I don't want you going to sleep just yet," she said, winking.

It made my heart beat, not with fear, but, in spite of what I knew, hope.

That night—I could tell it was night by the window—she came back for me. Her shift was over; she had her overcoat on over her thin cotton uniform.

I opened my mouth to ask a question but she just patted my shoulder and swung me down into my chair.

As you've by now of course guessed, we weren't going to the waiting room and we weren't going to the paved walking path, but the back door, and, past that, Margaret's large car.

She folded me into the passenger seat, my chair in the trunk.

"Wher—?" I tried to get out, but she guided my hand back down to my lap, eased her car down the slope of the parking lot.

Across the road there were sirens, and, walking through a pool of light, a police officer with a dog on a leash.

Margaret tensed and smiled at the same time.

"One of the slobbering maniacs, Mr. Mueller," she said, nodding to the woods. "Probably just wanted to see the *ocean*, right?"

"Muley," I tried to tell her.

Even though the road we took was more downhill than up, which is to say we were heading generally closer to sea-level, I had no illusions. After the aquarium in the waiting room, I knew I was going to be lucky to even smell the salt through her air conditioner vents, much less feel any spray on my face.

At the same time, however, if this was to be an end to my suffering, then so be it.

I pushed my back into the cup of her passenger seat and waited for whatever was to come.

As I'd expected, instead of following signs to the marina or some other place of portage, she instead wound us through a maze of residential streets I could never retrace. Billy wasn't down any of them, though, in spite of her muttering his name. Vaguely, I had the idea that her intent was to induce pity in him by pretending I was her war-addled uncle; that, for a few minutes, he was going to have to pretend to be who I was supposed to be expecting him to be. Which is to say *Margaret's*.

The profanity seeping over from the driver's side of the car, too, though vituperative and heartfelt, still it was light, amateurish. I'd heard worse in Morocco at fourteen years of age, and just over a bow line tied improperly. How that Moroccan sailor might have cursed had his intended been with someone else, it burns my ears just to think about it, and makes me smile a little too. Other people's suffering can be comical, I mean, when seen from a distance. Even mine, I suppose.

That's not to say I can't still remember the fear that rattled up through me, however, when Margaret took her car from asphalt to gravel, and then from gravel to dirt. The trees crowded around us, made the sky small. I started breathing faster, so that she had to look over, narrow her eyes.

"This isn't a good time for this," she said.

I closed my eyes.

Under her thigh was a hunting knife, the kind with a rosewood handle and a brass finger guard.

At a certain point on the dirt road, she turned the lights of her car off, and, when we saw the tail lights she evidently knew, she turned her car off as well, coasted into a slot between two large trees.

For a long time then we just sat there, the two of us, and, slowly, I tuned into a new set of sounds: the woods. And, unless as I was mistaken—as it turned out, I wasn't—the taste of salt in the now-still, un-air-conditioned air.

The sea. She was close.

I tried not to let this knowledge flash across my face.

In her lap now, Margaret had a rope. She was trying to tie a knot but making a complicated job of it. My left hand floundered over almost on its own, guided the end of the rope up and under and back on itself. She appreciated this, pulled the knot tight, nodded a reluctant thank you to me and then would no longer meet my eye. Such is the way we treat the rabbit we're about to carve for dinner, I suppose.

It had felt good though, the rope against my skin again.

Margaret patted the noose she now had and stood from the car, locking all four doors before walking away into the darkness.

What did she need me for then? The *knot*?

I stared at the spot she'd disappeared into but couldn't figure it out, and finally consoled myself trying to roll my window down to bring the sea nearer. It was electric, though, and I had no keys.

How long I sat there after she left, I have no idea. If I slept, it was only for minutes, and if I hummed, it was only to hear my own voice. In the absence of monitors and pumps and footsteps, the world was rushingly quiet, and not close enough.

At some point, anyway, Margaret strode across a bare place between the trees. The rope was no longer across her shoulder, and the knife was held in her fist, low.

I tried rolling my window down again, and was still clattering away at the button when she was suddenly at my door with the car keys.

"Your turn," she said, smiling.

Sprayed across her shirt was blood that had dried almost black.

I nodded, gave my weight to her, let her heave me into my chair, pull me backwards through the trees, tump me into a clearing behind the car I was pretty sure was Billy's.

The reason I say this is that, hanging from a thick limb above the car was a man of no more than twenty-two. A boy, really. His hands had been tied behind his back, and his throat had been carved out. From years of handling knives, I instantly understood the angles: someone had sat on his chest and worked on his neck with a blade. Calmly, deliberately.

And then he'd been strung up, with a knot only a sailor would know.

Which *was* of course what she needed me for.

She pulled the empty wheelchair back into the darkness and I looked where she was looking: to Billy's car, its vinyl roof pattering with blood.

Through the foggy glass, facing forward—away—there was a girl. Waiting for her Billy to return from his necessary sojourn into the woods.

I shook my head no, no, and, because the sea was close and because it didn't matter anymore, I found the strength to pull myself forward with my left hand. It was torturously slow, however, and filled my loose pants with twigs and dirt which nettled my bed sores. But the girl. I had to tell her, had to get her to leave, to *live*.

Because I couldn't stand, I of course latched onto her bumper with my left hand, and then on the fourth try was able to hook my right under her wheel well, pull myself forward by inches.

By this time she was aware of the sound I was, had locked the door, had, even though it wouldn't help her see, turned on the dome light and started grinding the starter.

She was saying her boyfriend's name louder and louder, and then shrieking a little.

It didn't matter, though. All I had to do was pull myself up level with her window and tell her about Margaret, that we had to go *now,* that, that—

I didn't even know what. But something.

With my left hand I gripped the ledge of her back door, and with my right, the large functional hook the doctors were trying to teach me to use, I pulled hard on her door latch, my head rising even as the car started, pulling me up, up.

I couldn't hold the car there, though.

It dragged me for maybe ten feet, and then the straps on the hook let go of the stump my forearm had become and I was rolling in the dirt, Billy swinging above me, Margaret in the darkness all around, and this is how stories begin, yes.

But none of you were there for the part after the girl left, my hook clattering in her door latch, the part where I crawled arm over arm through the trees until first light delivered to me a beach, a surf, which I rolled in for hours, and have never really left since. Not longer than overnight, anyway. And, no, the name I had then, it's not the same I have now—the world is the world, after all—but my ship, my lady, she is the *Margo.* Not in honor either, but in defiance: six years after my escape from dry-dock, I read the account of that night, and found that the authorities had managed not only to scrub any reference of Margaret from the public records, but, because of the violent, infectious nature of her crime perhaps, they'd also erased the very hospital I'd convalesced in, so that all that was left for the newspaper to report was that a patient, deeply disturbed by having had to cut off his own arm off with the neck of a bottle to escape drowning, had escaped the mental hospital the town was built around, and succeeded in killing and hanging a young boy named William Jackson before disappearing, presumably, into the sea.

I'll admit to that last part anyway.

▸ The Meat Tree

We never knew what happened to him, the missing kid, the third-grader, nobody did, but it didn't matter: our pregnant mothers saw his face at every stoplight, his name stapled to telephone poles, and drove the careful ways home then sat in the car with both hands on the wheel. Our fathers never knew, not until we came home from kindergarten with a teacher's note that we needed our last names on our lunchboxes too. Because all of us born in 1978 were named after Jeremy Michaels. It was a trade, I think—letting Jeremy live on through us, just so long as we *lived*. Didn't fade away like he had.

I became interested in him at sixteen. In Jeremy.

By college it was more than interest.

He would have been in his thirties by then. I missed a test to meet a girl who was supposed to have a vintage flyer of him from some telephone pole her uncle had stolen because it was evidence of his drunk driving, but she never showed up, and after missing the test I had to drop the class, and then the rest just fell away, like I had been wearing glass clothes all my life and was just moving wrong now, breaking a sleeve off here, a lapel there. My mother called and I told her I was taking a semester off. I could hear her holding her hand over the receiver on her end. My father lied that he understood, and I appreciated that, from him.

The girl with the flyer called me just before Christmas break, talking about how she still had that flyer, did I still have that twenty? We agreed to meet at a sports bar just off campus, Tanner's, but she stood me up again, and I watched the students walk by with their backpacks slung over their shoulders. They were all imitating each other, it seemed.

I moved across town to not have to watch them anymore—or pay college rent—and then one morning I opened my door and there she was, Lorinda. I should have known right then, too: it was a fairy-tale name, the kind a little girl would pick. But I thought it was beautiful. She was the first girl to see my place.

"So?" I asked her, after all this time.

She looked away from the question, across the bulletin boards I had balanced on the piece of molding that met the paneling halfway up the wall. It was a delicate job; I couldn't find nails that would go into the cinderblock of the upper wall.

"They're all empty," she said, the bulletin boards.

I shrugged. I'd tried putting tacks on them, but it made them over-balance. And sometimes they fell over anyway, clapping onto the linoleum in the middle of the night so that when I woke the papers on my nightstand would still be fluttering, like someone had just stepped away.

"I'm waiting to put flyers there," I told her.

She smiled.

We went to Tanner's and it lasted all afternoon. I was cynical by then, of course, nodding hello to each fratboy who passed our table, daring him to acknowledge me.

Lorinda wasn't in school anymore either, so we had that. She did lower her head some when a group of guys fresh out of poli-sci or mass-comm bunched in, but she made it look natural by adjusting and re-adjusting the hasp of her necklace. It made her hair hide her face some. I scanned the guys, trying to pick which one—see if I looked enough like any of them—but they were all clones, stamped out years ago, their childhoods mapped already, positions waiting for them at their fathers' firms.

"No," Lorinda said, about the flyer. "My uncle, I don't know. He says he thinks he burned it at Thanksgiving. The pole."

"Thinks?"

Now she shrugged. "The ash was all clumpy, anyway," she said, "from the resin or—"

"Creosote," I filled in.

In addition to being cynical, I was also self-conscious about my education. Later Lorinda would teach me I didn't have to be smart all the time. But right then the flyer was the only thing that mattered: Did she ever see it? What did Ur-Jeremy look like?

"*Ur*-Jeremy?" she asked, as if she'd missed the joke.

The group of guys across the bar exploded around a video-poker machine, falling all over each other. The machine flashed and flashed, and not one of them really needed it for rent.

"As in the first," I said. "It's . . . I don't know. The prefix means old or something."

"From the Bible," she said, "zig*gu*rat . . . "

I shrugged maybe, yeah.

She said she had seen it a long time ago, the flyer, and then apologized again for not having it with her like she'd said.

I told her I didn't have any money anyway.

She was looking at me in a different way now, though.

"He your brother or something?" she asked.

I shook my head no.

"Because you look the same"—reaching across, for the hair over my ear—"here, and something about the space between the eyes. No, it's the temples."

He'd been in third grade when he disappeared. The photo was his class photo.

I was twenty-two.

I ordered a chicken sandwich and Lorinda ordered a chef salad with the turkey on the side. When it came she slid the little container of meat across to me, and just on principle I didn't take it.

"At least let me show you," she said, finished with her salad before it was even half gone.

I looked at her and past her to the campus and said sure, anything, then that afternoon at her place—eighth floor, smallish balcony, the whole year's lease prepaid by her father, blood money she called it—Lorinda sat me in a chair in her kitchen and shaped my hair like Jeremy Michael's. I could feel myself disappearing; at one point she had to straddle my leg to get the right angle on my head, and the denim sound of her inner thighs filled the small apartment.

"So why all the corkboard?" she asked, the comb in her teeth. "Waiting for the big flood or something?"

"You shouldn't let strange guys up here like this," I told her.

"I've known you for months," she said.

I didn't tell her she was the reason I was taking the semester off. Mostly because I still didn't know how long this semester was going to be for me.

But the bulletin board, the cork.

I made up a theory for her, that the kitchen was the center of American family life not because of food, but information, cycling past under the nostalgic magnets of the refrigerator, that that was why we stood around in kitchens all the time. And it was only natural that we would eat, right? Surrounded by food like that? It was America's weight problem; I was rolling, smart, didn't need anything from any classroom. I told her that if we just had that kind of regularly-updated information—snapshots, lists, appointments, *flyers*—thumb-tacked on all the walls of the living room, the hall, the porch, then maybe as a country we could—

"—burn calories walking all over the house looking for the grocery list that should've just been in one place?" she said.

"Got to have money for groceries," I said.

"Or flyers," she said back, quieter, then before I could look up for the kind of smile she had she was leading me by the hand to the balcony, making me lean over the rail while she lifted the sheet off. My hair drifted down into traffic.

"You do look a lot like him," she said.

We were standing right across from each other. The balcony was that tight, that close.

I stepped back inside, away from her, from being that close to her and not knowing what to do with my hands, and walked through the only other door. It was her bedroom, the bath right off it. I framed my face in her medicine-chest mirror.

I wanted to write *have you seen this boy?* in soap on the mirror, but it wasn't my soap, and it wasn't 1978.

She let me stand there alone until I was done.

I found her in the living room washing vegetables in a sieve. It was more of a sink job, really, but I didn't ask; I was the one trying to look like the missing kid, after all.

"Jeremy," she said.

I nodded.

"My phone used to ring in junior high," I told her. "But nobody was there."

She looked up at me for more, and maybe that was when I fell into whatever I fell into with her.

"I knew it was him, though," I said, "*them*, I mean. The Michaels. Maybe they called all of us like that."

"You think they . . . they never stopped looking—?"

"No," I said. "Would you?"

She was washing carrots and broccoli, and looking out her eighth-floor apartment window, surrounded by the clutter I could tell was just there to show her father that this apartment would never be good enough to make up for whatever he owed her, whatever he'd done. I didn't ask. I knew he'd never been over to see it, though. Before I left, to walk the streets like Jeremy Michaels—before I *had* to leave, or risk embarrassing myself with her in some awkward way—she took a picture of me without asking.

"Now I've got you," she said, holding the camera with both hands.

I shrugged, blinked long from the flash, and walked out.

Two weeks later I saw her at Tanner's. She was moving from station to station along the salad bar. Aside from one busser, we were the only people in the room, all the students gone for Christmas.

I sat down across from her.

"Vegetarian?" I said.

"Kind of a personal question," she said back, biting a cherry tomato in half, narrowing her eyes at me in play. I ordered a chicken sandwich again and the busser mumbled it to himself all the way back to the kitchen, so he wouldn't forget.

"Personal?" I said back when I could, then went into how I could tell she was, say, white, American, female. "Maybe we should all walk around in big cardboard tubes," I added. "Write on the outside just the stuff we want people to know."

She shook her head, speared some lettuce.

"What about when it rained?" she said.

I told her we'd all lie on our sides and roll down the street. She laughed, not because it was funny or even a good answer, but because she was thinking of tubes with eye holes and umbrellas. She paid for both our meals.

"Blood money?" I asked.

"Any other kind?" she asked back.

We were walking down the street by campus. It was all tattoo shops and paddle-stores and pizza; I was morally against pizza—coffee too—but it was still too early in the relationship to tell her that.

"Why don't you go home for the holidays?" she asked.

I shrugged.

"You should go to the Michaels'," she said. "Just show up in a coat and earmuffs and say you got lost coming off the bus or something, back then."

I could see myself doing it, too.

"People are easy at Christmas," I said.

She didn't say yes and she didn't say no.

That night I would wake in her bedroom, in her bed, and the junk mail on the cardboard box she used as a nightstand would be fluttering and I would think someone had just been standing there, but when I rose to pull the balcony doors to, her hand would be on my wrist, and she would pull me back into her, saying it for me again: people are easy at Christmas.

It wasn't that I didn't want to go home, it was that I wanted home to be different, somehow. Like here, maybe, like her: she didn't know we were all named Jeremy, that we were all missing, living out different versions of his cut-short life.

"Where do you get your protein?" I asked her the next morning, standing before the garden the refrigerator was.

"You don't need as much as you're conditioned to think you need," she said.

Maybe. I took the switchback stairs down eight flights anyway though, for the plastic beef-jerky the convenience store had by the register.

The clerk watched me eat.

"Good?" he asked.

"Necessary," I said back, peeling another—an urban chimp—and then sat on the stoop in front of her building, imagining she was standing on the balcony eight stories up right then, looking for me when I was right here. It was a fairy tale; I was already in it with her.

Just like I'd done with school, I let my apartment slip too, even the bulletin boards. I told myself I was just making my life more simple, sloughing off the trappings, all that, but then over a lunch of macaroni one day Lorinda pared it down for me: what I had amounted to survivor's guilt. And all survivor's guilt was was a kind of death-envy.

She would only eat the macaroni that came from a box, because there the dairy was imitation, the powder-version of stadium cheese.

I still hadn't figured out why she was interested in me. It was more than interest though, too. Her father had done some kind of number on her, it seemed: sex for her was something to conquer, to win at. I had to eat the beef jerky down at the convenience store just to keep my strength up. And to rest. She started giving me money for it, even, the beef jerky, until I had to ask her where it was coming from. Neither of us was working.

"A trust," she said. "Insurance."

I watched her hard.

"But I thought your father—"

"He just has to sign," she said, already dismissing the subject.

I told myself it didn't matter as long as it kept coming, and in that way I was like the frat boys I used to stare down at the fringes of campus, and I knew it even then. But it was nice.

We went to her uncle's so I could see the ash pile that had been one of the telephone poles. He gave us each a bottle of beer at the front door then led us around the obstacle course the side of the house was to the backyard. It was the middle of January by now. He was leaning-back drunk, like the heels of his boots were gone, or the ground soft, or the world just spinning too fast.

We stared at the ashes and he remembered aloud his girlfriend in '78, how she thought she was psychic, could see little Jeremy floating in a septic tank just outside town. It was like we weren't even there, like *he* was channeling his old girlfriend's sessions. We left our second beers halfway full, balanced on the bed rail of an old pick-up he was using for trash storage.

"I'm sorry," Lorinda said. "Have you never seen one?"

"An uncle?" I asked.

She smiled, took my arm at the top and at the bottom, where it was important.

"A *flyer*," she said.

I couldn't remember anymore. It seemed like I had, though.

That night when I woke she was gone. The apartment was dark. I walked through it touching the walls, running my hand along the counter tops, the windowsills. The balcony door was open and I stepped outside in my underwear, trying to get sick. Death-envy; I almost said it out loud.

The only thing I'd brought with me from my place was my box of books. Just trucking them around made me feel educated, noble in a surly, down-trodden way I needed. I'd offered to sell them for grocery money, but it was just an offer. Right then the only thing I was dreading was the phone bill, because my mother was going to show up on it as ten digits. We hadn't said anything real, but still, sometimes it took hours to get even that far.

"I was worried," Lorinda said, suddenly behind me, around my sides.

"Me too," I said.

We stood together not knowing anything and watching the third shift crowd wend home, their eyes hooded against the sun.

The next morning when I woke, Jeremy Michael's flyer was taped to the medicine chest mirror. Like a delayed reflection from the first time I'd been here.

"Where'd you get it?" I asked her over her morning fruit ritual.

I did look like him.

"My uncle," she said, but it was too unfolded, too well-preserved to have come from his house.

She had an envelope of money, too.

I stared at her and stared at her then followed the handrail downstairs to the convenience store, only didn't have any change for the beef jerky. A different clerk was working—meaning no credit—so I walked along the edge of Lorinda's building until dollar bills started raining down from the sky. I caught them and caught them and forgave her for whatever I knew I should be holding against her, and then, when I pushed open the door of her apartment, she took another picture of me and ran for the bed.

I followed.

The next time she went missing I went to her uncle's house. It was the only place I thought she could be. She wasn't, though, and, standing on the porch with one of his beers in my hand I realized I didn't know her last name. Maybe in fairy tales you don't have to have last names, though, because each first name is so individual. And because you never know who your father was, what your patronym should be, what you've inherited. She was the only Lorinda I'd ever known. Her uncle called her Lindy. We sat on the couch while his wife worked in the kitchen—some kind of telemarketing she didn't have to take notes for, as she was painting her nails the whole time—and on the third beer I asked him if maybe she just got lost on the way to the bathroom, Lorinda.

"She hasn't told you?" he said.

I took another beer, shook my head no, and treated him to Tanner's. It was the only place I knew anymore. Class was back in session, and I was proud to be there with her uncle—to be there drunk with Lorinda's uncle, occupying a full corner of the bar. We were unapproachable.

He told me yes, maybe she had got lost. It wouldn't be the first time.

I didn't interrupt him with any questions, and he thumbnailed it for me: that when she was ten—1988—she'd gone missing for three weeks. The big disappearing act. Little Girl Lost. It was in all the papers; her picture was up there too, stapled to the telephone poles already bristling with staples. As he talked I was falling more and more in love with her: of course she would be drawn to me—I was still looking for the girl she'd been ten years ago. And she was helping me.

I leaned back into the dull comfort of a six-pack and Lorinda walked right into it. Or, to the edge, anyway. She was standing in the door looking at me and her uncle, her hair for an instant touching both sides of the doorjamb at once. Her uncle waved to her and some of the students noticed, and I winced inside. To show how displeased she was with the whole situation—her uncle was *her* family, not mine—she sat down with us and took a big, tearing bite of my chicken sandwich. Maybe I was the only one holding my breath, I don't know.

She paid our tab and led us out. We piled into her uncle's truck and she asked to borrow it after we dropped him off. He told us not to worry about being careful; I pictured us driving home with a telephone pole angled out over the tailgate, its butt hooked under the toolbox.

"I'm sorry," I told her.

She shrugged, no eye contact at all, and drove north until I fell asleep against the door panel. She shook me awake maybe an hour later. We were at one of those halfway diners that feed the cross-country bus crowds, that just have rows and rows of toilets. We didn't go inside, but to the far island of pumps, the handles all garbage-bagged over.

"This where you get make-believe unleaded?" I asked, chocking my door open with my foot.

"Something like that," she said.

I started to get out but she was holding my wrist again. Not looking at me, but in the rearview.

I pulled my door to and watched real casual in my mirror, but there were just truckers walking in and out, always stopping just before the door to spit, all the cold air in the place rushing past them.

"Ed told me about you getting lost that time," I told her. "It's all right."

She looked at me, didn't answer, and I rewound, played it back, what she'd heard: *all right*. As if it had been her fault.

"Where were you?" I asked, quieter.

"Here," she said.

"I mean then."

"Lost," she said, in a different voice, then stood out of the car before I could follow up, apologize.

I stood too, leaned over the hood to steady myself.

She came around to my side, reached into the squeegee bucket hose-clamped onto the pole, and pulled out a freezer bag with Jeremy Michaels' face in it. Only it was me, not the picture she'd taken earlier but one while I was sleeping. I thought of the papers on her fake nightstand rustling, closed my eyes, opened them again.

I pulled it from her, turned my back, peeled the top apart.

In a neat, non-Lorinda hand on the back of the picture were the words *yes I've seen this boy.*

It was for the Michaels. Twenty-two years after they'd asked.

I could see them in their tasteful, trying-to-be-nondescript clothes out here at the last island, pulling their son's picture up from the developing tray the bucket had to be to them; the fairy tale.

"We needed the money," Lorinda said, and then said it again.

I laughed without quite smiling, and held the picture to my face, leaving my prints all over the back of it.

When she tried to touch me I pushed her away harder than I meant to and she fell over an old gravity hose and rolled away from me, like she was expecting more. I stepped forward once and she stopped, staring up at me, and I didn't lower my hand to her, just turned for the diner instead, settled into a booth by the plate glass. All the truckers were watching me over their coffee. I stared at my hands on the table, pressed them into it to keep my fingers from shaking.

We needed the money.

The waitress wouldn't take my order because she'd seen Lorinda fall. I grinned at the stupidity of it all, didn't stop until one of the truckers settled into the booth across from me. He just stared. I looked up at him and knew what was coming, knew there was no help, so just did what I could: pushed the table hard into his chest, pinning him for a moment while I scrambled up. The front door was locked, though. I pressed my forehead to the glass then turned to see the heel of the trucker's hand coming at me, palm up, and then there was the sound of keys, and then I was outside on the asphalt.

He told me he was showing me what it felt like.

I laughed again and he sat on my stomach, holding my hair with one hand, hitting me with the other, the waitress—his girlfriend?—watching from the register, holding her finger to a key as if she could just push it and pretend this moment wasn't happening, that she'd just been standing there ringing up a customer the whole time. I tried to wave to her for some reason and the snapshot of me fluttered away, like your soul does in a book, and, to complete the scene, make it right, everything suddenly bleached itself out, got washed into paler versions of itself.

It was Lorinda, in her uncle's truck.

She rolled up until her bumper was an arm's length from my head, and I looked up at the rusted undercarriage.

"He's not worth it," one of the bus-people said to Lorinda.

She tried to pick me up and I shrugged her away again, climbed the grill myself, felt around to the passenger side.

"We needed the money," she said ten miles later, then again at twenty, and in the movie I was watching in my head now, of this, a demure Ford had pulled out of the parking lot behind us, was following us even now, Mr. Michaels holding his wife's hand across the bench seat.

How he hadn't stepped out of the car to keep the trucker off me, I had no idea. It was for the best, though; I would have screamed with him walking up out of the asphalt like that, one hand extended.

I wasn't worried about the phone bill anymore. Lorinda sat across the living room from me, in the windowsill. "We don't have to keep doing it," she said. "It was just supposed to be that one time."

I shrugged. The side of my face hurt. This was a vegan house, though: there was nothing to put on it to pull the pain out. If that even worked.

"How'd you get hold of them?" I asked.

"They never changed their number," she said, looking away, eight stories down.

Meaning she'd had the flyer all along.

I scrunched my hair at the front of my head.

"They want to meet you," she said.

"You know I can't trust you anymore," I told her.

She closed her eyes.

"I always screw things up," she said.

She was sitting on the coffee table across from me now. It was maybe lunch, but we weren't eating. I wondered for a moment if maybe I *was* Jeremy Michaels, kidnapped, eased into another neighborhood, another household.

"Where were you?" I asked her.

"I told—" she started, looking north, to the diner, but then got it: where was she when she was ten, and got lost.

"Will you trust me, then?" she asked.

I told her I didn't know, and wasn't lying. We had needed the money, though. And people are so easy around Christmas.

"You know where Deermont is, right?" she asked.

I nodded: two hours south, maybe. The opposite direction from my vigilante diner. I touched my face, looked for her to go on. She covered her eyes and said they used to camp there, her family. This time her mother hadn't been able to make it, though. It was just her and her father, and it had taken me however long I had known her then to realize that she never called him "Dad." It was always the formal term, *Father*. Like he was that far away, or, like God, that close, that inside.

"You don't have to," I told her.

She told me anyway, though.

They went to their usual place, with the rock overhang. He wrote her name in the soot by his head and said people had been using this place for centuries, because it was high, and because the scooped-out part of the cliff curled the heat back at you, and because, if you stoked your fire, you could see it for miles and miles. Lorinda fell asleep looking first at her name, then, when the flames were gone and all that was left was ember light, at the after-image of her name, until she wasn't sure if it was even there anymore.

When she woke, her father was gone.

She was twenty-two when she told me this, but I could hear the ten-year-old in her voice, looking around for which tree to pee behind, if "behind" even meant anything without anybody else there.

Of course she got lost. It was like her uncle said, like I'd not meant, really: she went to the bathroom and never came back. For three weeks, anyway.

Little Girl Lost. It was what they called her on the radio, in the paper, on the news. She even showed me a flyer with her face on it and there she was at ten, in frayed pigtails.

He was fishing, she said. Her father. Fishing. Like he always did, leaving the women in camp for the morning, only this time it was just her, Lorinda.

That first day she walked to what she thought was camp over and over, and never heard her name being called, just waited for night and how she'd see the scooped-out part of the cliff that was theirs. How her father had probably worked all day dragging wood to it for the bonfire.

She sat on the highest clear spot she could find and hugged her knees and woke that way in the velvety, unbroken black.

On the second day she found a stream and drank from her cupped hands, then followed the stream to another, smaller one, and another, until it was just a trickle, a damp spot under the woven yellow grass. There hadn't been trash in any of them. Once she heard a truck on what she knew had to be a blacktop road, its tires whirring, engine laboring, but then it was gone before she could find that road, and four more days slipped by. Her pigtails were frizzy now, straggling down onto her shoulders. She was eating the soft insides of bark she peeled off certain trees, and digging for some bulb-plant that had maybe been a turnip.

On the seventh day, she found the camp again. It was deserted. The raccoons had been at the stuffing of the sleeping bags, so everything was coated with angel hair. Her father had left the camp, forgotten it. She looked down into the basin, where he had to be looking for her. By now he wasn't supposed to just start a bonfire, but burn the whole forest down, do away with the trees and just leave her there standing from the ash.

She broke open the one can of beans that was left and fingered them into her mouth along with the leaves and dirt they'd fallen into.

This left two more weeks.

Lorinda shrugged, hugging her knees again now in the window well of her apartment, and said they didn't matter, those fourteen other days. The helicopters made their patterns, her shoes fell apart, she heard another truck—an RV—even saw a flash of a mirror or lens from across the valley. It was too far away, though, and probably lost too.

Partway through the second week, she found another can of beans. It was from the six-pack her father'd had at camp. It was sitting on a rock, right-side up. She watched it all morning, then stood, walked straight to it, and smashed it on a sharp rock in the creek. The water swirled brown for an instant with juice, but she only lost a spoonful of beans, if spoons still mattered.

Sometime after that she started seeing her father.

Telling me this, her voice became uneven, then too controlled.

I told her again that she didn't have to, but she just went on.

The first time she saw him, he was walking funny, and she thought it might be because he'd been hurt trying to find her, or had worn his good boots out, was breaking in another, better pair.

She sat in the shade of her tree and waited for him to see her, to save her, rescue her, but as he drew closer she saw why he was lifting his feet so high: hip-boots. For wading. There was even a creel strapped over his shoulder, and when he turned sideways to navigate a rock, the long, limber rod which had been invisible straight on revealed itself.

He called her name, his voice strong and clear.

She didn't answer.

He walked within twenty feet of her.

Lorinda closed her eyes after this part, refusing to let him still get to her. It wasn't an act. Even now I know it wasn't an act.

After that she followed him, watched him work the small, virgin streams, pull silver fish out of the water that glinted in the sun as they died, the green line leading out of their mouths like a slender tongue extended in pain. When he met with the rangers at lunch and the middle of the afternoon, for news, reports of her, the rangers would point along the skyline, trace grids in the dirt showing where they'd searched, where he had. They didn't brush them away when they were done with them either, so at night she could emerge from the trees, stand in the squares, a ghost of herself.

I didn't even ask where she slept, or if she did.

I did understand about when they found her, though, in the ditch of a farm-to-market road. She was just sitting, watching the cars pass by. Drawn by the hum of the tires. Which wasn't the thing that made the news that afternoon. What made the news was that the driver of the car that finally pulled over had to scramble over the fence and through the brush and deep into the woods to finally catch her, and even then she fought. Even at ten years old, after nearly three weeks in the bush.

In her living room, being smart, I told her that it's like with language: a kid can pick it up. Or lose it.

She smiled.

"Along with everything else," she said.

That her dad brought tackle with him to look for her was one thing. But that she just watched him. That she could.

"I'm sorry," I said.

"Now you know," she said, shrugging, and I did: the thing she'd been doing with Jeremy Michael's parents hadn't been about the money. It had been a test; she'd watched them coast up to the fuel island with the same eyes she'd watched her father with when she was lost. The same eyes she watched me with sometimes, in the street.

Now I knew.

"It's not Christmas anymore, y'know," I told her, my voice almost shaking. She breathed out hard, through her nose.

"Run," she said, just that, looking out the window, her back to the money divided on the coffee table, and I did, taking the close way around the building because I could feel her in the sway of my back, watching.

That night I followed a homeless man through the streets from doorway to doorway, and once when he raised his fist over his head to rail at some half-remembered injury I saw the thinnest hint of a phosphorescent line tracing delicate S-shapes in the night sky above him, and I looked away, stole across town into the graffiti-steam tunnels under the college, and up out of them into the basement of one of the resident halls, the couches and the television and the academic life. Soon enough one of the fraternity boys stumbled down in his boxers to shove change into the vending machine, then stood by my couch looking at the same program I was, tossing salted peanuts into his mouth.

"This one again?" he said—the show—and I laughed, shrugged, and betrayed everything I thought I stood for.

It was three days before I had to leave, before the rent-a-cop asked for my student ID then actually ran it through, asked me what floor I lived on. By then I'd put Lorinda together in my head some, though. Enough, anyway. It all came down to her salads, how of course she liked them. It wasn't the turnips she'd dug up, but her father. How he had to have cooked the fish he caught, their smoke wisping through the trees, their taste in the air.

With some of the money from the coffee table I bought a beer at Tanner's, waiting for Lorinda to fill the door again, or not to, and with the rest I bought a cork board from the bookstore next door, carried it under my arm through the streets, collecting abandoned tacks from telephone poles. The parts of their shafts which were buried in the oily wood were shiny and bright. The flyer I was trying to ignore was the homeless man I'd seen fishing the other night. He was gone.

By the time I found another apartment, I was Jeremy, slipping away in the third grade, watching my parents through parted bushes, Huck Finning past my own memorial service. It didn't last, though, the apartment. Or, my rent. I called my father and he breathed in deep for a lecture, and I left him talking, the payphone receiver balanced to catch the rain, drown him out.

Summer Session One started and Tanner's dropped its prices, started serving more margaritas on the patio. It's where I saw Ed again. He had his own beer in cans up the sleeve of his shirt, so that at first, his arms were stiff like a robot. But as the day wore on they were wet yarn waving before him as he wheeled from our table to the bathroom, the bathroom to our table. We drank, and drank, each revolutionaries in our own way maybe, in our minds at least, and I told him I knew about her now, Lorinda, *Lindy*, the whole Little Girl Lost thing, and he eyed me over his mug, asked if I thought it really happened, then?

"What?" I said, and turned to the door, half-expecting her to appear in ratted pigtails—summoned, her hair matted with leaf litter like she'd never been found at all.

Ed shrugged it off, but then I got a little more out of him later: Lorinda weighed more when they found her than she did when they'd gone on the trip.

In the incomplete silence he left—the *suggestion*—I closed my eyes to try to think about this, cracked the beer open on the dash of his truck we were suddenly in. The beer sloshed over my hand.

"Careful," I told him, Ed, and he wheeled through molasses over to the other curb, and we urged the earth to keep rolling under us until his house came into view at the end of the street.

"The meat tree," Ed said, spraying beer before him in a fine mist.

I focused on him. We were leaning on his dumpster-truck in the backyard.

He laughed, looked up at the trees all around, like fingers reaching into the sky, and I thought of her again, at ten, alone in the woods, then told Ed about the scam she was pulling on the Michaels. How she was using the Michaels to get back at her father. I was crying drunk by then. The trucker's fist had left an impression under my eye somehow—a ring?—and I'd taken to holding my finger there. It was like all our mothers had done with Jeremy's name: used us to fill it up.

"The meat tree," I said back to Ed, finally, and he nodded, held his can up in appreciation.

"May we all find it," he said, and without him even telling me, I could see it, dripping red.

It was what he said Lorinda said she'd fed on those three weeks.

"After the beans?" I said.

"The second can," he said back, passing whatever test I was giving him. That I'd hoped he was going to fail.

I stayed with him for four more days, ran his bill up talking to my mother, the earpiece of the phone worn down from telemarketing and flecked with nail polish, then on the fifth day I found myself again at Tanner's, waiting for her. Lorinda. I told myself it was because I needed the money, but that wasn't it. I needed her.

On her machine I said I was collecting the flyers again. Like that was healthy, would make her pick up: a sheaf of missing homeless men staring up from their faded pieces of paper, or tacked at shoulder level around the living room. The thing was, nobody knew where they were going, or being taken. Supposedly it happened every few years like this. My old Sociology professor would have flowcharted the demographics, turned it into a migratory pattern. Used it to explain what was left of the twentieth century. The few homeless men left on the street had taken to calling me the Custodian. I'd hear them behind me, speaking through their tangled beards.

No, I told them in my head. *It's Jeremy.*

My hair was longer now, though, not like cropped like his parents thought—like it had been in the photograph they'd had, of me sleeping.

I wired my mom for two hundred dollars and used sixty of it for a week's worth of hotel room, paid in advance. Local calls were fifty cents each, so I loitered in the lobby, waiting for the courtesy phone. The desk jockey watched me talk to Lorinda's machine and smiled, the corners of his mouth impossibly sharp. It didn't feel like a fairy tale anymore; all the girls on the corner had names like her: Savanna, Leiloni, Katressa.

I told my mom I was registered for Second Summer Session.

I stood under Lorinda's balcony for long minutes at a time.

The clerk at the convenience store still let me have jerky on credit. Eight dollars in, I asked him why.

"She pays it," he said, nodding his head up to the eighth floor.

She knew I was watching.

The two days after that I spent at the library, leafing through the microfiche for accounts of her ordeal; for details. There weren't any, just what she told me—less, really—then one useless article about how going feral like she'd done—running from the man who'd stopped for her—was just another variant of the Stockholm Syndrome. I read it line by line. The homeless men there for the public restrooms and free air-conditioning watched me, too. On the long walk back to my room—one day left on my tab—I stepped into a pawn shop, held a high-dollar fly fishing rig in my hand.

"Go ahead," the guy stocking sockets said, and I whipped it like the ceiling was higher than it was, my off-hand open, pointing with the palm, for balance.

I talked him down to forty dollars. He folded it up into a battered poolstick case and then I was walking again, following a man I thought looked like me in thirty years. He was wearing a demure grey overcoat, his hands deep in his pockets. I knew it wasn't, that it couldn't be, but I told myself it *was* Mr. Michaels, that he'd traced Lorinda back to here; that he was looking for me.

Finally, at an intersection, I let him go then stood under the stoplight, the faces of the missing massing on the pole behind me. I looked out from them into the stopped traffic, and there, both hands visible over the wheel, was a woman who could have been my mother twenty years ago.

She was staring at me.

I started running.

I don't know what happened to the fishing rod, but, too, now, I do: a homeless man found it, opened it, fitted it together the only way it would go together, then walked through the streets casting it over the vinyl tops of cars, the flat-faced bullbats gliding down to inspect that flashing hook. He was the man I followed that first night I left Lorinda, only he was moving the opposite direction in time.

That night the clerk at Lorinda's convenience store reached under the counter, handed me some of my books. He called it special delivery.

In the pages of Heidegger were pictures of me sleeping.

"Thanks," I told the clerk.

I looked at the pictures in my room then tacked them to my bulletin board and looked at them some more, then took them down, and the next night, the one night the front desk was extending me on credit, a spoonful of rice unchewed in my mouth, I understood: it was an invitation; a warning; a plea.

I walked across town and sat at Ed's kitchen table and let his wife cut my hair. So I'd look like Jeremy. And then I borrowed Ed's truck.

Lorinda was waiting for me in the square bushes of the Michaels' house. I'd found them in the phonebook. We were four hours away from where we were supposed to be, two hours past the vigilante diner.

"Hey," I said, sitting down beside her.

She didn't say anything.

The hollow dent under my eye was so empty. If I laid on my back, dew would collect in it maybe. I had a can of beans in my pocket. A light went on in the house, the window glowing yellow, then it went off again. It was a signal. I sat the beans next to Lorinda's leg, upside down, and she righted the can then pulled her hand away, the memory snaking up her arm.

I looked out at the street.

I didn't have to say that raccoons couldn't read the label on a can of beans, to have set it upright for her, and I didn't have to say that Ed had told me about the meat tree.

Her chin was trembling. She wiped her mouth with the back of her sleeve.

"Who was it?" I said. "Who left them for you like that?"

"Ur-Lorinda," she said, her laugh a nervous trill.

"No," I said.

She looked up at me.

"It's happening again," she said. "I can't stop it. They should have left me in that ditch. Not chased me."

"What are you doing here?" I asked.

She tilted her head back to keep from crying. Headlights washed over us and we didn't move, and then it was dark all over again. I stood into it, away from the window, and then saw it like an afterimage, written into the sill, under the eave, all the nights she'd been spending here: the seven letters of her name. Like her father had written in the soot of their overhang.

I turned back to her.

She was looking at me.

"No," I said, "don't—" but she already had the match, to start the fire.

She stood too.

"Would you want to live?" she said, "if your kid was . . . " but couldn't finish.

I cupped my hand over hers, killing the flame, but she pushed me away, backed into the yard, lighting another, and another, and dropping them like footsteps.

No lights were going on in the house.

No cars were coming.

It was just us.

Tendrils of smoke were feeling up out of the grass. I walked through them to her, held her, and in broken breaths she told me about the meat tree, how, after the upright can of beans was another, and another, leading her deeper into the woods. When she got there it was night and the bugs were chattering above her, but when the sun came she saw it: the meat tree. It was like Ed had said: flanks of steaming red meat speared on the reaching branches, dripping. For her.

She ate.

And each night there was more, and on the third night she saw it moving through the trees above her, like leather in the shape of a man, or a man who had just forgot to die.

She told herself it was her father, her real father.

The meat made her sick, but she ate it, except the skin. That she draped back over the dead branches of the tree. It was hairless.

I pulled her tighter as the lawn sprinklers came on, then did what I'd always wanted to do, I think: traded myself for the Michaels, went home with her. It was something only a son would do.

She had taken the bus there, so she rode back with me, sitting in the middle of Ed's bench seat, her face paler with each car that whipped past.

We stopped at the vigilante diner and nobody remembered us. We sat against the plate glass and she ate her salad and I ate mine, and when the waitress who'd held her finger on the register key like she could have stopped the trucker at anytime asked if we wanted anything more, a burger or something real, I looked up at her and shook my head no.

Out at the last island of pumps I was floating in the oily water, a baptism, and then my eyes slammed open and I gripped Lorinda's hand hard under the table.

I moved back in with her the next day, handing my collection of flyers out the bathroom window of my motel so the front desk wouldn't know I was skipping out. We were avoiding Tanner's for some reason, too. Like it would remind us of when we didn't know so much, make us sad about who we were now, and where. That first week passed uneventful, no sex even. Lorinda was sleeping a lot. I flipped through the stations of her television and stood on her balcony at night. The Fourth of July was six weeks behind us already, more, but kids were still lighting bottle rockets and Roman candles from the tops of roofs. It was enough.

I kept the flyers of the homeless men on the nightstand.

I called my mom and told her I was okay. She asked about Lorinda. Not by name, just generally.

"She's okay too," I said, but it was a lie.

Lorinda's hair was matted, *matting*, not anymore like she'd never been found, but like she was reverting, going back, the years falling away from her. For one bad day I thought maybe she was a ghost, that she was the girl you always hear about hitch-hiking between certain mile markers, trying to get home but not able to, but then I remembered Ed, how he'd seen her too, how the microfiche at the library had had pictures of her on the side of the road, how the napkin I'd found in the kitchen trash the other day had had real blood on it, hers, from cutting fruit probably.

So she was real, physical.

I breathed out.

The day after I thought she was a ghost, I thought she was just confused, that she was repressing. That all her talk of her time lost was a displacement or transference or something, an allegory of molestation. General Psychology was the test she'd made me miss that first time. It made sense, though, that she was just projecting someone else in the woods with her—some *thing*—because her father would never do what he had maybe been doing the whole time her mother wasn't there. The meat tree even fit, the blood; the fishing rod. Isn't that what fairy tales are, anyway? What we tell ourselves *about* ourselves, just in an indirect way, with elves and magic and monsters to make it all safe? I told Lorinda about it in the afternoon when we were just sitting there and she looked across the room at me and smiled one side of her face.

"You don't gain weight from getting molested," she said.

"You were ten," I said.

"Call it what you want," she said back.

I looked away. It had been a nice two hours at least, when the world had made sense.

"You don't have to be smart like that all the time," she told me.

I kept looking away.

The rest of the afternoon she shaped my hair more like Jeremy's, and then, later, at the convenience store, looking through bangs that weren't really there anymore, two things happened: the first was the new clerk nodded at me like he knew me, then followed me into the street, led me to a wooden pole. On it was a grainy reproduction of me, sleeping. And the phone number. And the reward. I closed my eyes, the clerk faded away, and then, before I could make the stoop, the stairs, the payphone on the side of the building started ringing.

I looked from it to the street.

It was just me.

It was *for* me.

I closed my eyes and walked back inside. I was eating candy bars then, because the chocolate was made from cocoa, which was some kind of bean, and beans had protein, I was sure. And I needed protein.

When I opened Lorinda's door, turning the knob first all the way to the right then back to the left, making the room a safe place to enter (I'd always imagined a huge windshield wiper on the other side of the door, wiping back and forth), she was waiting for me with her new camera. It blinded me, and all I could think was *silver, silver, silver*. It was good, though; as the living room faded back, its corners sharpening into furniture, I let myself believe that I was just meeting her—this girl who was supposed to have a picture of Jeremy—for the first time, that I was just coming up to her apartment. That the last ten months had been some flash-forward or something, what could have happened but didn't. Lorinda played along, snapping picture after picture, her camera pushing them out onto the coffee table and the carpet and the spaces between the cushions of the couch.

We fell into bed laughing or trying to, twined together with sheets like the dead, night feeling down around us, into us, and for a few minutes what we didn't talk about didn't exist. That next morning Ed was there, though. Standing in the bedroom door, the can in his hand catching the morning sun and turning it silver. Like the flash of the camera all over, my eyes just clearing.

He looked at Lorinda sprawled naked under the sheets.

"Your dad's in town," he said.

"I know," she said.

She never looked at him.

On the coffee table by the couch where he'd sat, waiting for us to stir, were five empty cans and then the Polaroids of me, stacked neatly in the order Lorinda'd snapped them. You could tell by the continued motion, like how you know which panel comes next in a comic book. There were all these missing moments, though. Too much happening in the deadspace between, the gutters.

Over tasteless slices of breakfast melon I asked Lorinda if she wanted to see him?

"Who?" she said.

I didn't know what to say. The classifieds were still spread on the table from the day before.

"We need money," I said.

"We need a lot of things," she said back.

It was Labor Day; nothing was easy.

She walked out onto the balcony with her melon.

I called out that I was going to get a job, a dishwasher or something, anything, the guy with the spray bottle and rag at the skin arcades downtown, but it was a lie: two hours later I was standing over her uncle. He was sleeping on his back on the couch, his wife doing her telemarketer imitation in the kitchen.

"What do you sell?" I'd asked her on the way in.

"What do you need?" she'd asked back, the receiver pinned between her shoulder and jaw.

She hadn't known where Ed's brother was, just nodded to him on the couch. I was turning to go to him when I saw it: one of the flyers of me on the table under her fingernail equipment. There was money involved.

"Who are you talking to there?" I said.

"You come here for me or for him?" she asked, then *yes'd* her way back into whatever pitch she'd been in before I'd let myself in the back door. She looked at me over her fingernails like Was I done?

I was.

Ed woke when I moved his beer.

I lied that Lorinda wanted to see him, her father.

He leaned on his knees and thinned his eyes out against the harsh forty-watt above and behind me.

It was lunch, a little after.

Ed closed his eyes and gave me directions—just another motel on another street, room 134—then patted himself down for the truck keys he didn't seem to have.

"You sure she wants to see him?" he asked.

I nodded yes and never stopped walking out the door.

Not only were his keys gone, but his truck wasn't there either.

By five, I was sitting outside room 134. I hadn't eaten all day, except the part of the melon for breakfast. It had been bitter, though; I pictured the rind shriveling up at the table, the flies buzzing eight stories up and in through the open balcony door, the melon snapping shut over them.

For two hours, he never came out. Or back. It was another room in a row of rooms.

The new homeless man taped to the metal sides of the streetlight poles was a man I thought I knew; I already had his flyer tucked into my pocket. I think I was collecting them because of their beards, because if you shaved them they might pair up with artist's sketches of missing third-graders twenty years after they'd gone missing. I wanted one of them to be Jeremy instead of me. Or, Jeremy *too*.

At dark, when no lights came on in 134, I leaned against the door and it gave—no chain—and I closed it behind me, stood in the stale air, turned the light on myself finally.

It was just me.

I sat at the two-person little table for long minutes, looking at my hands, then went into his bathroom. His electric razor was there. I shaved my head an eighth of an inch at a time with it, all the thing would take. It took maybe forty-five minutes. I left the hair on the counter, stared at myself in the mirror, ran my palm over my scalp.

On the walk back to Lorinda's I left the Polaroids of me face-in in likely windowsills, under the wipers of parked cars. It was funny; I was laughing. The streets were full, school almost back in session again.

I shouldered through the crowds knotted around the entrances to the bars and once someone called my name and I closed my eyes. It was somebody from the Psych class I'd dropped; he pushed through to me.

"Thought you were dead," he said.

My scalp was halogen-white.

"I am," I said, and touched him with my finger on the forehead like I was giving Lent, then turned and walked away.

Maybe these were the missing moments between the snapshots, I thought. Literally they were, anyway; I still had two in my pocket for somewhere up the street. I started running, and didn't stop until the foot of Lorinda's building.

In the gutter and on the sidewalk were both her cameras, the film exposed to the sodium light.

I knelt, collected them, looked up at the rounded base of her balcony. It was just concrete.

I made myself walk up the stairs.

Her door was open.

I stepped in with the lower portion of my shirt pulled out to hold the broken cameras.

There were two policemen in the living room.

"I told you she threw something," the first cop said, looking at my shirt.

"Paraphernalia . . . " the other one said, approaching.

Lorinda was behind them, on the other side of the couch. She'd been crying. She looked hard at me, trying to tell me something, but I couldn't get it, not until the police men leaned over the camera parts I had.

The flyers, my flyers, the homeless men.

They thought it was me. Because I kept them. Because I fit the profile.

The second policeman—the one leaning over for the parts—saw it in my eyes the moment I realized it myself: that I was going to run. He took one step back, cocking his arm over his stick, and I flung the camera parts over the room, and the only reason they didn't catch me right off was that I wasn't scrambling for the hall, like they expected, but the bedroom.

I grabbed the flyers off the nightstand, turned hard, and bounced off the wall back into the living room, knocking one of them over, then crashed out onto the balcony, letting all the flyers go, back to the city.

After about thirty seconds I turned around.

"You done?" the first policeman asked.

The other was shaking his head, his hand at his waist.

"Jeremy Barker?" he said.

I swallowed.

"We should take both of you in," the first officer said, flashing his eyes over at Lorinda. I saw on his pad where it said *Linda*, her real name.

"For what?" she said, her voice as small as it could get.

"The Blue Inn?" the second policeman said. "Nine days ago?"

I sagged against the rail.

"Wasn't me," I said, the usual line.

They looked at my scalp, Lorinda too, and I tried to push into their minds the Blue Inn desk jockey, describing me with *hair*, with all this *hair*, but it wasn't working, I could see it in the crook of their elbows, their arms cocked above their pads, their nightsticks, but then down on the street someone screamed, straightening all our backs.

The two policemen looked at each other, deciding, then the first held his hand out to me, index finger up. "Stay," he said, and backed out.

The second one turned to follow, his partner's footsteps already retreating hard, then asked didn't he know me from somewhere?

"Nineteen seventy-eight," I said, and he looked at me a moment longer, then left.

We were arsonists, thieves, impersonators, drop-outs. Vegetarians. We fell into bed, the weight of the day pressing on our eyes, and when I woke again it was deep night and Lorinda was shuddering beside me and I held her as close as I could and our mouths found each other and hers was slick with tears and salty and I took them away, into me, and smoothed her hair back, told her everything was going to be all right. But she was shaking her head no.

"What?" I said.

Instead of answering, she closed her eyes against my chest—I could feel the lashes, even—and I drifted in and out, and when I came to once, the flyers on the nightstand were fluttering again, and I suddenly couldn't breathe anymore.

They were back was the thing.

Someone had just left them.

I stood, groping for the bedpost, the wall, then out into the living room.

The balcony door was open, the curtains wisping through it.

I parted them, stepped out, and there on the brick was a slab of raw meat. It was almost a relief, to be in one world instead of another. But still. I backed away, to the brick of the building. There was skin on the backside of the slab of meat, I could see it, but more, too: delicate footprints in red, the barest hints of toes. Lorinda's. And then, with the tip of my tongue, I felt my mouth, my lips. They were crusted, but I corrected myself: con*gealed*.

This is where she got her protein.

It was still feeding her.

It's happening again, she had said.

The bloody napkin in the kitchen trash.

It hadn't been tears in her mouth.

I felt back through the balcony door into the darkness of the living room, and the phone was ringing, had been. Once, twice, four times. I looked to the bedroom door, expecting Lorinda to fill it at any moment, standing-still asleep, her mouth red, like all she needed was a kiss to wake up, but the thing about fairy tales is that for every princess there's a troll, leathery and slight, moving from building top to building top on fingertips and toes.

No, I shook my head no, *please,* for her not to rise, then raised the phone to my ear.

There was a long pause—nothing, nothing—then a voice, a man's voice, a father: "Jeremy?"

My lower lip trembled, the room blurred, and I nodded, said it into the phone even, *yes, yes,* then set the receiver down on the counter and followed the wall around to the molding of the front door, and the line of the jamb down to the handle, and the handle into the hall, and, stumbling out into the street at four in the morning I understood for a moment what it's like to be lost, to be in the third grade and be lost, gone, disappearing, the only part of you still left a picture on a pole at an intersection as you hunch past with a crowd of students, your backpack slung over your shoulder like the rest, a girl standing on a balcony eight stories above you, waiting to be saved.

➤ The Ones Who Got Away

Later we would learn that the guy kept a machete close to his front door. That he kept it there specifically for people like us. For the chance of people like us. That he'd been waiting.

I was fifteen.

It was supposed to be a simple thing we were doing.

In a way, I guess it was. Just not the way Mark had told us it would be.

If you're wondering, this is the story of why I'm not a criminal. And also why I pick my pizza up instead of having it delivered. It starts with us getting tighter and tighter with Mark, letting him spot us a bag here, a case there, a ride in-between, until we owe him enough that it's easier to just do this thing for him than try to scrounge up the cash.

What you need to know about Mark is that he's twenty-five, twenty-six, and smart enough not to be in jail yet but stupid enough to be selling out the front door of his apartment.

Like we were geniuses ourselves, yeah.

As these things go, what started out as a custody dispute took a complicated turn, and whoever Mark was in the hole with came to him for a serious favor, the kind he couldn't really say no to. The less he knew, the better.

What he did know, or at least what he told us, was that somebody needed to have the fear of God placed in them.

This was what he'd been told.

In his smoky living room, I'd looked to Tim and he was already pulling his eyes away, focusing on, I don't know. Something besides me.

"The fear of God," though.

I was stupid enough to ask just what, specifically, that might be. Mark narrowed his eyes in thought, as if considering the many answers. By ten, when I knew it was time to be home already, what the three of us finally hit on as the real and true proper fear of God was to think you're going to die, to be sure this is the end, and then live.

We thought we were helping Mark with his dilemma.

Sitting across from us, he crushed out cigarette after cigarette, squinched his face up as if trying to stay awake. Every few minutes he'd lean his head back and rub the bridge of his nose.

The trick of this operation was that there couldn't be any bruises or cuts, nothing that would show in court.

Of all the things we'd thought of, the knives and guns and nails and fire and acid and, for some reason, a whole series of things involving the tongue and pieces of wire, the only thing that left a mark on just the mind, not the body, was tape. Duct tape. A dollar and change at the convenience store.

This is how you plan a kidnapping.

Mark's suggestion that it should be us instead of him in the van came down to his knowledge of the law: we were minors. Even if we got caught, it'd get kicked when we turned eighteen.

To prove this, he told us his own story: at sixteen, he'd killed his step-dad with a hammer because of a bad scene involving a sister, and then just had to spend two years in lock-up.

Our objection—mine—was that this was all different, wasn't it? It's not like we were going to kill anybody.

So, yeah, I was the first one of us that said it: *we*.

If Tim heard it, he didn't look over.

The second part of Mark's argument was What could we really be charged with anyway? Rolling some suit into a van for a joyride?

The third, more reluctant part had to do with a tally he had in his head of bags we'd taken on credit, cases we'd helped top off, rides we'd bummed.

Not counting tonight, of course, he added. Because we were his friends.

The rest of it, the next eighteen hours, was nothing big. Looking back, I know my heart should have been hammering the whole time, that I shouldn't have been able to talk to my parents in the kitchen, shouldn't have been able to hold food down, shouldn't have been able to stop fidgeting long enough to concentrate on any shows.

The truth of it is that there were long stretches in there where I didn't even think about what we were doing that night.

It was just going to be a thing, a favor, nothing. Then we'd have a clean tab with Mark, and Mark would have a clean tab with whoever he owed, and maybe it even went farther up than that.

Nicholas, of course—it was his parent's front door we were already aimed at—he was probably doing all the little kid things he was supposed to be doing for those eighteen hours: cartoons, cereal, remote control cars. Baseball in the yard with the old man, who, then anyway, was still just a dad. Just catching bad throws, trying to coach them better.

At five after six, Tim called me.

Mark had just called him, from a payphone.

We had a pizza to deliver.

On the pockmarked coffee table in Mark's apartment was all we were going to need: two rolls of duct tape, two pairs of gloves, and an old pizza bag from a place that had shut its doors back when Tim and me'd been in junior high.

The gloves were because tape was great for prints, Mark told us.

What that said to us was that he wasn't setting us up. That he really would be doing this himself, if he didn't want to help us out.

Like I said, we were fifteen.

Tim still is.

The van Mark had for us was primer black, no chrome, so obviously stolen that my first impulse was to cruise the bowling alley, nod to Sherry and the rest of the girls, then just keep driving.

If the van were on a car lot in some comedy sketch, where there's car lots that cater to bad guys, the salesmen would look back to the van a few times for the jittery, ski-masked kidnappers, and keep shaking his head, telling them they didn't want that one, no. That one was only for *serious* kidnappers. Cargo space like that? Current tags? Thin hotel mattresses inside, to muffle sound?

No, no, the one they wanted, it was this hot little number he'd just gotten in yesterday.

Then, when the kidnappers fell in with him, to see this hot little number, one would stay behind, his ski-mask eyes still locked on the van.

The reason he's wearing a ski mask, of course, is that he's me.

What I was thinking was that this could work, that we could really do this.

Instead of giving us a map or note, Mark followed us out to the curb, his head ducked into his shoulders the way it did anytime he was outside, like he knew God was watching, or he had a bad history with birds. He told Tim the address, then told Tim to say it back.

2243 Hickory.

It was up on the hill, a rich place.

"Sure about this?" Mark asked as we were climbing into the van.

I smiled a criminal smile, the kind where just one side of your mouth goes up, and didn't answer him.

2243 Hickory. A lawyer's house, probably.

We were supposed to take whoever answered the door. Nothing about it that wasn't going to be easy.

To make it more real, we stopped for a pizza to put in the pizza bag. It took all the money we had on us, but this was serious business. Another way to look at it was we were paying twelve dollars for all the weed and beer and gas Mark had burned on our undeserving selves.

In which case it was a bargain.

The smell of pizza filled the van.

On the inside of his forearm, Tim had written the address. Instead of "Hickory," though, he'd just put "H." All he'd have to do would be lick it a couple of times and it'd be gone.

Like *2243H* meant anything anyway.

Then, I mean.

Now I drive past that house at least once a month.

We finally decided it should be Tim who went to the door. Because he already had a windbreaker on, like pizza guys maybe wore once upon a time. And because he had an assistant manager haircut. And because I said that I would do all the taping and sit on the guy in the back while we drove around.

How I was going to get the tape started with my gloved fingers, who knew?

How I was going to stop crying down my throat was just as much a mystery.

In the van, Tim walking up the curved sidewalk to the front door, I was making deals with anybody who would listen.

They weren't listening, though.

Or, they didn't hear that I was including Tim in the deals as well.

Or that I meant to, anyway.

▶ ▶ ▶

As for the actual house we went to, it was 2234 Hickory, not 2243 like it should have been. Just a couple of numbers flipped. Tim would probably say that they were all the same house anyway, right? Up there on the hill? If he could still say.

As to what happened with whatever custody case we were supposed to be helping with, I never knew, and don't have any idea how to find out. But I do know that the name associated with the property records for 2243 Hickory wasn't a lawyer like we thought, but a family court judge.

We were supposed to have grabbed his wife, his daughter, his beagle.

I've seen them through their front window on Thanksgiving eight times now.

They're happy, happy enough, and I'm happy for them.

All this happiness.

When I finally made it back to Mark's the week after, somebody else answered the door. He had all different furniture behind him, like the girl at the portrait studio had rolled down a different background.

What I did was nod, wave an apology, then spin on my heel—very cool, very criminal—walk away.

What I would be wearing when I did that was a suit, for Tim. Or, for his family, really, who had no idea I'd been there that night.

Anything I could have said to them, it wouldn't have helped.

This is the part of the story where I tell about meeting Tim in the third grade, I know. And all our forts and adventures and girlfriends, and how we were family for each other when our families weren't.

But that's not part of this.

I owe him that much.

We should have cruised the bowling alley on the way up the hill that night, though. One last time. We should have coasted past the glass doors in slow-motion, our teeth set, our hands out the open window, palms to the outsides of the van doors as if holding them shut.

The girls we never married would still be talking about us. We'd be the standard they measure their husbands against now. The ones who got away.

But now I'm just not wanting to tell the rest.

It happens anyway, I guess.

▶ ▶ ▶

Nicholas answers the door in his sock feet, and Tim holds the pizza up in perfect imitation of a thousand deliveries, says some made-up amount of dollars.

Then, when Nicholas leans over to see the pizza sign on the van, Tim does it, just as Mark played it out for us fifty times: spins the pizza into the house like a frisbee, so everybody'll be looking at it, instead of him and who he's dragging through the front door.

On top of the pizza, stuck there with a toothpick, is the envelope Mark said we had to leave.

Putting it inside the box was our idea.

It was licked shut, but we knew what it said: *if you want whoever we've got back, then do this, that, or whatever.*

As the pizza floated through the door, I saw me in the back of the van with Nicholas, playing games until midnight. Making friends. Tim driving and driving.

We were doing him a favor, really, Nicholas. Giving him a story for school.

But then the pizza hit, slid to its stop down the tiled hall of that house.

Mark was twelve miles away, maybe more.

I was only just then realizing that.

The way some things happen is like dominoes falling. Which I know I should be able to say something better, but that's really all it was. Nothing fancy.

Domino one: the pizza lands.

Domino two: Nicholas, who'd turned to track the pizza, turns back to Tim, like to see if this is a joke, only stops with his head halfway around, like he's seeing somebody else now.

Domino three: Tim leans forward, to hug Nicholas close to him, start running back to the van.

Domino four: what I used to think was the contoured leg of a kitchen table, but now know to be one of those fancy wooden pepper grinders (my wife brought one home from the crafts superstore; I threw up, left the room), it comes fast and level around the frame of the door, connects with Tim's face, his head popping back from it.

Domino five, the last domino: Tim, maybe—hopefully—unconscious, being dragged into the house by Nicholas's father, who looks long at the van before closing the door.

The reason I can tell myself that Tim was unconscious is the simple fact that Nicholas's father didn't come out for me too. Which is a question he would had to have asked, a question Tim wouldn't have been able to lie about, even if he tried: whether he was alone.

So what I do now is convince myself he was knocked out. That he didn't have to feel what happened to him over the next forty-five minutes, like Nicholas did. Or saw, anyway. Maybe was even forced to see.

In the newspapers, it was why Nicholas's mom left Nicholas's dad: because what he did to the drugged-up kid who broke into their home, he did while Nicholas watched, transfixed, his fingertips to the pear wallpaper so he wouldn't fall down.

It involved a kitchen chair, some tape, a hammer. Pliers for the teeth, which he pushed into Tim's earholes and nostrils and tear ducts, just making it up as he went.

How long I was in the truck was forty-eight minutes.

It's better if Tim was knocked out the whole time.

What people say now—it's still the worst thing to have ever happened— what they say now is that they understand Nicholas's dad. That they would have done the same thing. That, once a person crosses the threshold into your house, where your *family* is, that he's giving up every right to life he ever had.

This is what you do if you're a traitor and in the same break room with people saying that: nod.

This is what you do if you hate yourself and can't sleep and have your hands balled into fists under the sheets all night every night: agree with them for real. That, if anybody tries to come in your door one night, then all bets are off.

And then you're a traitor.

Nevermind that, a few months before Nicholas's harmless juvenile delinquency bloomed into a five-year stretch with no parole, you went to his apartment, to buy a bag. He was Mark all over, right down to how he narrowed his eyes as he pulled on his cigarette, right down to how he ducked his head into his shoulders like his neck was still remembering long hair. And you didn't use anymore then, hadn't since the night before your wedding, would even stop at the grocery store on the way home, to flush the bag over and over, until the assistant manager knocked on the door, asked if there was a problem.

Yes, there was.

It was a funny question, really.

The problem was that one time while your friend's head was floating across a lawn, a machete glinting real casual in the doorway behind it, a thing happened that you didn't understand for years: the life meant for Nicholas, you got. And he got yours.

That's not the funny part, though.

The funny part, the reason the assistant manager finally has to get the police involved in removing you from the bathroom, is that you can still smell the pizza from that night. And that sometimes, driving home to your family after a normal day, you think it was all worth it. That things happen for a reason.

It's not the kind of thing Nicholas would understand, though.

Nevermind Tim.

Quint calls me up on a Saturday afternoon and tells me to watch this.

I stand in my kitchen and study the stove I put in last Christmas, all my tools on the counter, and all the ones I'd borrowed from Quint. It's still crooked.

"What channel?" I say.

This is different, though.

Twenty minutes later, Sherry at home with my promise to be back before ten, I've eased down to Quint's, a broken six-pack on the seat beside me, the sole of my boot skimming the loose asphalt gravel between his house and mine.

He's waiting for me on the porch, smoking like he's twelve years old again and we only have five minutes before his aunt comes home.

"What?" I say, arcing a beer across the yard to him in a spiral so perfect it should be in a commercial.

He takes it, doesn't crack it open.

That more than anything tells me something's up.

"Is it Tanya?" I say, looking behind me for some reason.

Tanya's Quint's wife. Sunday nights she's usually on-shift at the hospital.

"Inside," Quint says, and holds the screen door open, ushers me in.

I shrug, duck into the cat smell of his house and run my finger under my nose.

Quint places his hand on my shoulder like a priest and guides me past his television through the dead part of the kitchen to the hall, then down the hall. The only room this deep into his house is Gabe's. He's six months old, maybe. Born just before Christmas. The twin that lived, big tragedy, all that. One that's supposed to be already over, that Quint's supposed have dealt with. Not so much gotten out of his system—Sherry says things like that never get out of your system—but at least grown enough scar tissue over it to function.

Until now, too, I'd assumed that was the case. That Quint was functioning.

But now. Being led back to Gabe's room.

None of the pictures I have in my head are good. Better than half of them involve me lying to the police. Or, worse, to Tanya. So, when Quint palms Gabe's door open, spilling a wedge of light across his stained crib, Gabe just sleeping there, his thumb cocked in his mouth, I relax a bit.

"Say his name," Quint says.

"What?"

"Try to wake him up. Just not very hard."

"Quint, man—"

"My responsibility."

I turn to Gabe, his lips moving, back rising with breath, and shrug, fill my mouth with beer, do what I know's an annoying-as-hell little gargle.

Gabe shifts position but doesn't wake.

"What?" I say. "You gave him some Benadryl?"

My voice makes Gabe roll over, his head screwing around on his pudgy neck, his shoulder blades drawing together.

Quint crosses the room, places a hand on Gabe's side until his breathing's even again. Before he leaves he angles the baby monitor a little bit closer to the crib.

We walk back to the kitchen.

"Sherry put you up to this?" I ask.

Quint laughs without any sound, tells me to wait.

Again I look over my shoulder, for Tanya maybe, coming home early in her nurse whites, or for Sherry, waiting for me see how cute Gabe was. How we need one.

It's just us, though.

I push off the counter with my butt, follow where Quint leads.

It's to the garage, the old recliner Tanya told him he couldn't keep in the house even one day longer. Even one minute. It's in the corner by his toolcart, surrounded by the ashes of ten thousand cigarettes.

"Real nest you got here," I say, drawing my lips back from my teeth, not in appreciation.

Quint doesn't say anything, just settles down into it.

On the makeshift table beside his recliner is the listening end of the baby monitor. Gabe's breathing comes through it like he's right here with us.

I settle back against the Chevelle Quint still hasn't fixed up.

"Just watch," he says again, and takes a paperback from the stack by his chair. It's a horror novel, like all of them. I can tell by the full moon on the front, the red lettering on the spine. And because I've known Quint for nearly eighteen years now.

He settles back into what must be reading position #1, starts reading.

I lean forward, look side to side again, this time for candid cameras, then come back to him.

"Quint, dude—"

He never looks up from the book, just holds his finger up for quiet.

I shake my head—*this* is what I had to talk my way out of the house for, what I'm going to be paying for for the rest of the week—dig through the bottom drawer of Quint's toolcart for the magazines he's always kept there. They're legal, I'm pretty sure, but still, you wouldn't want the cops stumbling onto them.

For maybe four minutes I lean against the Chevelle, study the girls in the classifieds ads after I've studied all the girls in the main part of the magazine, and Quint just sits there, hunched over his damn book.

Finally I hiss a laugh through my front teeth, roll the magazine into a tube to hammer down through my fist, and am already pushing off the Chevelle to make for the door and whatever I can scrounge from his fridge when the monitor's lights pulse red, from left to right. Like a tachometer, I think, Gabe really winding up.

"Shhh," Quint says, still reading the book, his eyes narrow from the effort.

Gabe's voice comes through the monitor. A moan, I'd call it.

"Listen," I say, "this has been exciting and all, and it's not that I'm not thankful, but—"

Gabe interrupts, screaming, all the monitor's lights flashing red now.

Quint stands, his bottom lip between his teeth. He's nodding, as if waiting for me to agree that it was worth coming over here.

I just stand there.

"Like clockwork," he says, then passes his little horror novel over to me, his index finger holding his place. Without even meaning to, I put my finger there too, and then he's gone, to Gabe.

The monitor's close enough to the crib that I hear the springs in the miniature mattress when Quint picks him up, hear what he's saying, that's it's all right, buddy. That it's not real, it's not real. Daddy just had to show his friend.

I study the red lights on the monitor, then the book in my hands. Read where Gabe must have been.

It's scene where a guy's sleeping in a bed with his wife, and this guy, he's watching his doorway like it's the most important thing in the world. But still, he's not watching close enough. He blinks once, twice, and then on the third blink—ten, twelve minutes of sleep—he wakes to a dead little kid tugging on the covers, then trying to crawl in. Then crawling in anyway.

Quint says it again to Gabe: "It's not real, buddy. It's just nothing, man. Nothing at all . . . "

I put the book down, open to the place he was, and make it back to Sherry fifteen minutes before I'd promised.

On Wednesday I meet Tanya at the regular place, the usual time. Gabe's with Sherry on our living room floor. As far as Sherry knows, Tanya's sitting with her pregnant sister at the doctor's office. Wednesdays are when he sees expectant mothers. It's a weekly appointment.

As far as where I am, it's work. The only thing different from every other day is I'm taking my lunch an hour and a half early.

The lie I tell myself in the trailer I have a key to is that the reason I'm not telling Tanya about Quint, reading to Gabe from across the house, without words, is that on Wednesdays we never have time to talk, really. It's just unbutton, unbutton, lock the door twice then test the knob to be sure.

The truth of it of course is that I don't have the words to tell her, and that it's stupid anyway.

A few nights later, Quint's at my door, baby monitor in hand.

"You didn't leave him there," I say, leaning to the side to look past him, for the stroller.

"He's safe," Quint says, insulted, eyeballing all my baseboards for an outlet.

I shake my head no, tell him not in here.

On the way to the shed in back, where the light socket doubles as a plug, where Sherry'll never come because there's spiders, Quint fills me in on Gabe. It's been a week of testing. He's been reading all different kinds of novels, from all different rooms of the house, at all times of the day and night, with all different clothes and jewelry on. What he's found is that it works best when he's lying down, the book propped on his stomach. And the book, it has to be bloody of some kind. Haunted houses, werewolves, serial killers, whatever. Nothing sappy or consoling.

"Why?" I say, holding the shed door open against the wind.

Quint shrugs, steps up onto the plywood floor, says like it's obvious, "It puts him to sleep, man. Keeps him there, I mean."

I follow him in, nod.

It makes sense is the thing.

"What about science fiction?"

"He likes it."

"Sex stuff?"

"He's nine months old."

I clean a space on the bench for the baby monitor.

"He doesn't understand the war stuff, either," Quint adds, tuning Gabe's distant breathing in. "And . . . I don't know how to explain it. I think—I think it's not so much like he's seeing the words or anything. It's like he's seeing flashes of the pictures the books put in my head, yeah?"

"No," I tell him. "I don't."

Quint pulls a thin paperback up from his back pocket.

"This'll be the farthest away I've tried," he says.

I nod—what am I supposed to say, here?—and he slips into his book, his eyes narrowing with gore, maybe, or a vampire swooping down, and then, just when I think he's forgetting this is all a big experiment, Gabe lets loose through the static.

Quint looks up, momentarily lost.

"Think you can stop now," I say, pushing the book down so he can't read it anymore.

Gabe stands, the realization washing over him, and then's gone, sprinting the quarter mile between my house and his.

By the time he gets there, he's breathing hard.

He rips Gabe up from the crib, holds him close.

"You there?" he says when he can, through the monitor.

I nod, walk the monitor down to him.

Over enchiladas Sherry tells me that Tanya's messing around on Quint.

I chew, chew, swallow.

"What?" I say, my face poker-straight, another bite ready on my fork, in case I need a stall.

"On Wednesdays she drops Gabriel off here, y'know?"

I shrug, fork the bite in.

"Well," Sherry says, looking out the kitchen window, I think, "this last Wednesday, her sister started having contractions, she thought."

"Her *sister?*"

"Ronnie—you don't remember her. She's having twins too."

"Ronnie," I say, swirling the bean juice and cheese on my plate. "But Tanya just had Gabe."

"You know what I mean."

She doesn't know I'm stalling here. Spinning out.

"It was a false alarm," she goes on. "But Tanya was supposed to be with her's the thing. As far as anybody knew."

I nod, chew some more, trying each word out fifty times before I actually say it out loud.

"Does Quint know?"

"He's your friend."

I agree with her about that, study the kitchen window too. Through it there's the aluminum pole of a streetlight. It doesn't shimmer or tremble or do anything to warrant my interest in it. Still, without it to lock onto, I'd probably be throwing up.

The next week, a Monday, I'm standing on Quint's porch, synchronizing my watch with his. What he's paying me with is two beers. Where he's going is somewhere past the range of the baby monitor. My job is to record when and if Gabe wakes up, scared, and to somehow pat him back to sleep, or at least hold him until Quint gets back.

Written on the back of my arm, upside down to me, is the payphone number of wherever he's going. Because he's trying to follow the scientific method, he says, I don't need to know where he's going. It might influence the experiment in some way neither of us could anticipate.

"Okay then?" he says from the farthest part of his lawn.

I nod, tongue my lip out some. Can see the tree in front of my house from here.

Before Quint's to the end of the block, I've got the payphone number dialed in. A kid answers. In answer to my questions the kid says he's a bagboy, that the phone is by the ice machine, not quite to the firewood— why?

"Where in the larger sense, I mean," I tell him.

The grocery store.

It's two miles away.

I thank him, hang up, check on Gabe, finally turn away from him to close the door then come back again, looking at him the way I used to, those first months before his hair came in just like Quint's. It's something I can't bring up when Sherry's wanting a baby: that I've already been through it once. From a distance. That that was why I lost twelve pounds last Christmas, even with all the Thanksgiving leftovers. Praying and praying, and hating myself for each prayer, that the one that was stillborn was the one that could have given us away. Because I saw on the news that it can work like that, each twin being from a different dad. I saw it on the news and knew that we'd been lucky enough so far that this one-in-a-million shot had to be a sure thing, to make up for everything having been so good so far.

Gabe, though, his red hair, it's a gift. Everything I could have asked for. But still. I stand in Tanya's kitchen and hold one of Quint's beers to my forehead like the hero does in the movie he's trying to get out of.

On the refrigerator is a list of each thing Quint's eaten over the last ten days. Tanya thinks he's on a diet he saw on TV. She laughed into my chest when she told me, and I smoothed the hair down on the back of her head, closed my eyes.

The first time with her had been an accident, sure. But not the second, or all the rest. And now this, Quint going telepathic or whatever. Or—or not Quint, maybe, but Gabe. Maybe Quint just has a leaky mind, is one of those people my parents wouldn't ever play Spades with, and Gabe, because they have the same blood, can tune him in better than anybody.

"Bullshit," I say out loud, alone in Quint and Tanya's hall, and peel the tab off the second beer.

Except that when I was twelve, for about six weeks I'd always been able to tell when the phone was going to ring. I didn't hear it exactly, just kind of felt it in the bone behind my ear. It was just those six weeks though, and I never went to Vegas like my dad kept saying, and some things, if you just ignore them hard enough, they go away.

Like this.

What I could do here, I know, is not write anything down for Quint. Even if Gabe does wake up screaming, pictures of zombies in his head. It'd probably be best for him, even, save him from a childhood stocked with every bloody image Quint can find on the paperback rack. Because, it's not like they're going to take this on the road or anything. You don't get rich off your father's dreams seeping into your head. Parlor tricks are supposed to be neat, small. What Quint's doing requires way too much setup, and looks fake anyway.

I sit down at the table, push the notebook into the napkin dispenser we'd stole one night from some bar, years ago. Tanya still likes to make a show of checking her lipstick in it when we're over, like this is all a game—the house, marriage, kids. I have to look away when she's like that, because Sherry's smart, too smart.

And then I think the thing I always think, when I'm not with Tanya: that this has to end. Not because it's wrong, but because we're going to get caught, and then have to live down the road from each other for the rest of our lives.

I shake my head no, that this *isn't* what I wanted, and realize at the same time that what I'm doing is trying to talk myself into doing the right thing.

I drink off all of the beer I can. See that Quint's last meal was sloppy joe mix on tortilla chips, with three jalapeños, sliced.

Right about now, he's down in the parking lot of the grocery store, oblivious, a few pages into his book, his window down to hear the phone ring. Sherry's at the garage, punching holes in people's tickets. Tanya on-shift, covering for somebody, and, for me, it's just another lunch.

While Quint reads, I make a sandwich from his deli drawer, eat it standing up, and am like that—sandwich in one hand, third beer in the other—when Gabe starts screaming like he's just seen right into the black heart of evil. Like somebody's holding his head there, making him look.

I drop my sandwich, try to pick it up before it's dirty, end up tipping beer onto it instead.

"Okay, okay," I call to Gabe, and then, just as I'm standing, I feel something in my head. It stops me, cranks my head over to the phone. Seconds later, it rings.

By the third ring I manage to draw the receiver to my ear.

It's Tanya.

When I don't say anything, she asks if I'm going to get the baby or not. I look through the doorway to the hall, can almost feel the telepathy popping in the air.

"*Q?*" Tanya says then, quieter, urgent-like, and there's a ball in my throat

I can't explain—like I'm betraying her, standing in her kitchen, collecting her kid from his crib. Letting her think I'm Quint.

I hang up softly, call Quint, get the bagboy, hear Tanya ringing back on the other line.

"What do you want me to tell him?" the bagboy asks, his voice hushed like he knows more about what's going on here than he should.

Behind him is the sound of cars rattling, women talking, doors swishing open and shut.

Gabe nestles his head into the hollow of my shoulder, gathers the fabric of my shirt in his right hand.

"Tell him I've got to get back to work," I say, then hold the phone in place long after I've hung up.

It's a form of prayer.

As apology or something, I finally take one of the books Quint's always trying to get me to read.

"You know why he likes that stuff, right?" Sherry asks.

We're in bed, the television on but muted, so we can hear the new squirrels pad around above us.

"Why he likes scary shit, you mean?" I say.

"Because it's at his level."

"Hm," I say, and turn the page.

The book is that first one I watched him read to Gabe. I spend equal time on the page and television, and fall asleep somewhere in-between, wake deep in the morning, the sheets twisted under my fingers.

"Hun?" Sherry says, from her side of the bed.

For a long time I don't answer, then, once she's breathing even again, I tell her I'm sorry too, the same way I'm telling Quint: where they can't hear.

The talk I have with Quint that Friday night over beers in my garage is stumbling and ridiculous, and I'm embarrassed for him, almost. For both of us.

It starts with me, explaining that this trick him and Gabe have, it probably isn't what he thinks.

What I'm doing is being a good friend. Saving him from himself. Saving Gabe.

"Then what is it?" Quint says, eyeing me over his beer.

"You want it to be ESP."

"What else could it be?"

I shrug, rub a spot on my chin that doesn't itch.

What I can't say is what Sherry said, when I explained all this to her: that if she'd been fired from *her* job, was sponging off her wife's double shifts, spending all day everyday with her infant son, then yeah, she might invent some special powers too. Just to cope.

What I really can't say is that maybe the twin that died's involved in all this somehow. A door I can't open around Quint, because he'd fall through.

"It's like—like those people you see on *That's Incredible*, with dogs and horses, y'know?" I tell him instead. "They want so bad for it to be real that they don't even realize they're tapping their toe on the ground seven times, after asking what's four plus three."

Quint tips some more beer down the hatch.

"I'm not saying you're tapping your foot," I add.

His eyes are red around the rims.

"Then what?" he finally says, for the second time.

I shrug, open my mouth like I have something ready, but don't, finally fall back on a half-baked version of Sherry's explanation: that Quint's spent so much time at home lately that he's cued into Gabe's sleeping patterns. That sometimes Gabe wakes up when Quint's *not* reading, right?

"He's a baby," Quint shrugs. "That doesn't mean it's not . . . extra-sensory."

I swish some spit back and forth between my front teeth.

"If it is," I finally say, "it's not like you think."

This gets Quint's attention. The way he smiles a little, too, I can tell that he can hear Sherry's voice in mine, knows I'm her sock puppet here.

"When you read," I go on, closing my eyes to try to sound only like myself, "I don't think—I mean, Gabe can't read, right? Even if he were hearing your little reading voice in your head, the way you say it to yourself, all spooky or whatever, it would just be your voice, not really words. Because he doesn't understand words yet."

"That we know of."

"He's a baby."

Quint shrugs, says where I can barely hear, "I did it in Spanish too."

I stare at the floor, finally close my eyes.

"And it worked?"

"Scientific method," Quint says, crunching his can against his thigh.

"Then that proves it," I say. "Gabe doesn't know Spanish."

"Maybe there's a language under words? One that we think in or something. A telepathic society might not have any reason to ever evolve more than one language, did you think about that?"

"*Aliens,* you mean?"

"I'm just saying." Quint shrugs, comes back. "He still woke up. When I did it in Spanish. That means something."

"Because he . . . because it's not thoughts you're shooting out of your head, or even pictures, that's what it means. It's feelings, the shapes of things. Like, however reading about a dumbass zombie book makes you *feel*—scared, grossed-out, whatever—*Gabe's* feeling that."

Quint pulls his top lip in for a long time, finally nods whatever, takes another beer.

"So you calling Child Services on me, or what?" he says.

I look away, and then he says it: "You were right, though. This does prove it."

"ESP?"

"That he's mine."

What my heart does right then is stop, cave in on itself some.

"That he's yours?" I hear myself saying, my voice wooden, hollow.

In answer, Quint pushes up from the trash can he's been leaning on, then hooks his head to the door that leads into the house. It's still closed, Sherry and Tanya in there walking on dynamite.

"I wasn't sure," Quint says, not using his lips at all.

My heart flushes itself, heats up the back of my eyes.

"What do you mean?" I say just as quietly. *"Tanya?"*

The disbelief in my voice is so real.

Quint purses his lips out, shrugs once.

"Been going on for a while, I think," he says. "If I hadn't got laid off . . . I don't know. I never would have figured it out, probably."

My mouth is moving to form questions, but I can't think of the right ones, don't have time to test them from each angle before throwing them into the ring.

"She—she couldn't," I try.

"I think that's what you always think," Quint says. "What I'm supposed to think, right?"

"Then . . . what—?"

"Just little stuff," Quint shrugs. "Like, the other day. She says she called the house, but I wouldn't talk to her or something. She asked if I still trusted her, if I was just waiting to see who she was going to ask for."

"Who else could it have been?"

Quint shakes his head no, says I'm not getting it: if she thought the guy was there, then that meant that he *had* been there, right?

I just stare at him.

He shrugs, chews the inside of his right cheek the way he's always done. His mother used to spank him for it in elementary.

"I was there," I say, weakly, the blood surging in my neck now, at the chance I'm taking.

"You would have talked to her though," Gabe shrugs, not even slowing down. "I told her it was me anyway, yeah?" Then he smiles, covers it with his hand. "She's acting guilty," he says between his fingers. "It's getting to her, I mean. Building up inside her."

"What about Gabe?"

Quint does his eyebrows, bites his lower lip now.

"He's mine," he says, "right? I mean, if he wasn't, we wouldn't be able to—we wouldn't have this connection."

I nod, try to blink in a normal fashion.

"So now I know whose side he's on," Quint adds, raising his beer to me, holding it up like that so it's the only thing in the world I can see, that I can allow myself to see.

Five days from then, it's Wednesday.

What I say into the damp hair close to Tanya's scalp is that he knows, Quint. That he knows, and it's over now, it has to be.

What she says back isn't in words, so much, but it's not ESP either. The opposite, really.

We hide in each other.

The mask I wear for the next two weeks is just like my face, only it doesn't give anything away, is always ready to smile, to take part in a shrug then look away.

The reason for the mask is that Tanya and Quint are talking to a counselor down at Tanya's hospital.

Sherry watches Gabe while they're there.

It makes me so tired, controlling my thoughts around him for those hour-and-a-halfs.

One night I finally break down, go to the store for milk we don't need, and call Quint's house from the grocery store. The bagboy watches me, his lower lip pulled between his teeth like he knows too much.

"You haven't told him, have you?" I say to Tanya when she picks up.

I've got the phone cupped in both hands, am pressing it into the side of my head.

"Trevor?" Tanya says back, a note of something bad in her voice.

Trevor is her brother. The last any of us knew, he was in Maine.

A muscle at the base of my jaw quivers.

In the background of her kitchen, I hear Quint asking her something.

"Tell me you haven't," I whisper.

"Of course not," she says, distant—to Quint, or me?—"I don't know who it is."

I hang up gently, hold the phone there with my eyes closed, then nod, go in for the milk, park in front of my house minutes later, make myself drink the whole half gallon, tell myself that if I can do it, and keep it down, then Tanya won't tell, no matter how honest their next session at the hospital gets.

Halfway to the door, though, I throw it all up, and Sherry finds me like that, starts breathing too hard herself, the phone already in her hands. Ninety seconds later Tanya is leaning over me, hugging me, helping me to stand, long strings of bubbly white leaking down from the corners of my mouth, from my nose. She breaks them off with the side of her hand, guides them away, slings them towards the street.

" . . . must have been bad," I tell her and Sherry, when I can.

At first they don't respond, and then Sherry laughs a single laugh through her nose—disgust—says, "The *gallon* of milk, you mean?"

I shrug, caught. Stare at the grass for a lie, finally find one: "That new guy at work."

"The one from prison?" Sherry whispers.

"He said milk—he drinks it for his stomach ulcer."

Sherry shakes her head at this.

"And you think you have a stomach ulcer now, right?"

When I don't answer, she apologizes to Tanya with her eyes. Because I'm one of those people who can get sick from talking to somebody on the phone. It's a joke, has been for years.

"I think you're going to be all right," Tanya says, smiling.

Her hand is on my knee.

I smile, shrug one shoulder, no eye contact.

It makes them comfortable, lets them be moms, me the little boy.

To keep them from digging my hole any deeper, I point to the kitchen to show them where I'm going, then go there, run water over my hands.

I can still hear them, though.

"So how's it going?" Sherry asks Tanya, in a way that I can see the parentheses Sherry's holding around her eyes, like a Sunday morning cartoon.

I turn off the water.

"Good," Tanya says, her hands surely in her lap, innocent.

I reach for the dishtowel, draw it to my chin.

Good.

I want to laugh. Want my fingers to stop trembling.

I wind them up tight in the dishtowel, follow Sherry and Tanya to the door.

"So where's the good knight tonight?" I say from behind Sherry.

It's what we used to call Quint back in high school. From some song.

Walking backwards into the darkness, barefoot, Tanya exaggerates her shrug, says he was going down to the store or something. He didn't say.

I feel my mask smile, lift the dishtowel in farewell, and, because the kind of telepathy *I* have makes me see Quint down at the grocery store, offering a cigarette to the bagboy, the bagboy in return pointing to the payphone, to the redial button, I hear Tanya start running through the wet grass home. To catch the phone or Gabe, I don't know.

"What?" Sherry says, holding the screen open for me.

I shake my head no, nothing. Duck back through the door.

Three days later my phone rings, and I beat Sherry to it. It's nobody. My lips are shaped around the sound of a whispered, desperate *T?* when Quint says something into his end. I can't make it out.

"What?" Sherry says, stepping half out of the bedroom, her work shirt most of the way on.

"Quint," I say, then pull the phone deeper into the kitchen.

Quint's not saying anything else. But he's not hanging up either.

Finally I thumb the dial tone button, say, loud enough for Sherry, "It's in the shed, I think. Want me to walk it down?"

When I step into the bedroom then, to say it—Quint needs his quarter-inch ratchet back, that one that's spray-painted blue so nobody'll steal it—Sherry's buttoning her shirt, her eyes already settled on me.

I tilt my head up to tell her where I'm going but then see how close she is to the nightstand. Where the other phone is.

"Quint," she says, her voice artificially light, I think. Maybe.

I tell her to have a good day at the garage, then hold her side as we touch lips, and talk to myself the whole way down to Quint's. How the only part of the conversation Sherry could have heard was me, saying that about the shed. But—would it sound different to her if the line was dead? Would it have been louder in her ear, my voice closer, because half of it wasn't getting sucked down the line?

Partway to Quint's, I remember the blue ratchet, go back for it, find it on the coffee table, Sherry already gone.

I reach for it like maybe it's hot, or electric, and, when I have it, it's light like old, dry paper. What I do with it is sit, and hold it hard to my forehead, my eyes closed, and make myself breathe, breathe. Tell myself that, whatever else, Sherry can't know anything for sure, and that Tanya's not going to tell. That Quint's not waiting in his own living room down the street, a pistol in his lap, Gabe crying in the other room.

I'm half-right: Quint is in his chair, just not the new one Tanya financed for him two birthdays ago. Instead it's the ratty one, out in the garage.

He looks up at me when I step down onto the stained concrete.

His eyes are red around the rims, and the hand he has wrapped around his paperback, the knuckles are scraped raw. The kind of rash you get from punching sheetrock, over and over.

I feel along the side of the Chevelle, lift my chin to him.

"I thought you were choking or something," I say, "on the phone, I mean."

He smiles without looking at me, says, "So you brought my ratchet down to work on me?"

I look at it blue in my hand, and see it in an evidence bag.

It makes a solid thunk when I toss it into his tool drawer. With the wrenches instead of the sockets, but Quint doesn't notice, is staring at something I can't see.

"What'd you want, then?" I say.

Quint laughs as if just now returning to the garage, shrugs, throws me the magazine I was looking at last time I was here.

I unroll it, study it too long, come back to him.

"Thanks, I guess," I tell him. "I can't take it home, though, y'know?"

Quint smiles, shakes his head no, says, "You're an antenna, I think."

"A what?"

"It works best when—I don't know. When you're around. Involved."

"With you and Gabe?"

Quint nods, his eyes suddenly glossy wet.

"What's going on?" I say.

Quint doesn't answer, just shakes his head no, brings his paperback horror novel up to his face, starts reading hard enough that his lips move.

"I've already seen this—" I start, but Quint interrupts by holding his hand up. I stare at him like that for maybe four seconds, then lean back against the Chevelle again, open the mag, see the same barely-legal girls in the same unlikely positions. Soon enough I'm watching the tiny bulbs on the baby monitor. They're black, don't even remember red.

Quint swallows loud, pulls the book closer to his face, reading as hard as he knows how, then finally closes his eyes, slings the book past me.

It brings something down from the shelf, something that falls for a long time. Snow chains, I'm thinking, or one of those hanging lamps like old ladies have, with all the stained glass. I don't look around to see. Just at Quint. He's crying, trying not to. Not wiping his face, because that would be admitting that there were tears.

"He grew out of it," I say, in explanation.

Quint shakes his head no, settles his eyes on what looks like the Chevelle's front tire.

"It's not him," he says, then looks up at me. "It's not him."

"Then—what?"

"You said he was . . . that he was picking up on how this shit made me feel."

"The books, yeah."

"They just, they don't scare me anymore, I guess."

I smile, cross my arms.

"Then *you* grew out of it," I say. "Sherry always said you would."

Quint smiles, rubs it into his face. "Sherry," he says. "You're lucky. To have her, I mean."

"So are you."

"What?"

"Lucky. Tanya."

Quint keeps the same expression on his face, but changes gears in his head. I can tell.

"So find something scarier," I say. "Romance. Algebra."

Quint doesn't laugh.

Instead, he pulls a chain up from his shirt. A necklace, like dogtags, except, instead of a little nameplate on the end, it's a silver key.

"What?" I say.

"In the . . . in the books, it's all fake. I know that now."

"What do you mean?"

"This is real," he says, holding the key up before his face.

I don't have anything to say to this.

"Dr. Jak—our therapist," Quint goes on. "He says it's Tanya's symbol that she's with me again. All the way. Like before."

"A *key?*"

"She used to it to—to meet her . . . To meet *him.*"

And then I get it: the key he's wearing, it's the one I had cut for Tanya. It fits the trailer, has unlocked more Wednesdays than I can count.

He looks up, nods.

"Yeah," he says. "I was right. She's been screwing around."

"How long?"

"Two years."

"Who?"

Quint shrugs one shoulder, looks away. "It's not supposed to be important who," he says. "Just that it's"—he holds the key up, to show—"that it's over. A name isn't going to help me move on."

"Shit." It's the only word in my head. In my whole *life.*

Quint nods, does his eyebrows up in agreement.

"Then . . . Gabe?" I finally manage.

Quint stands, runs his fingers through his hair, dislodging his cap. It falls down his back. His fingers stay in his hair, his elbows out like stunted wings.

"Either I'm not—can't get scared like I used to," Quint says, his tone all about matter-of-factness, "or . . . or the other guy, he had red hair too."

I swallow. My hair is black.

"So you're saying she—Tanya—that she was stepping out on you with somebody who looks just like you?"

Quint doesn't turn back around to me.

"It's my fault," he says. "If I would have, y'know. Not been out here all the time, I guess. Maybe she was, like, looking for me all over again, yeah? Like, how I used to be?"

"You still are like that," I try. "We all are."

Quint laughs about this. The kind of laugh you manage when your doctor tells you you have six weeks left to live.

"You know he's yours," I say then, "Gabe. You wouldn't have been able to do—that ESP shit. It wouldn't have worked."

Quint turns around, his face slack. "How do we know his father isn't the telepathic one?"

"His *red-headed* father?"

"The one Tanya's been seeing," Quint says, holding the key up again, his eyes flashing behind it, "yeah."

I stare at him until he shrugs, slams his fist down to the face of his rolling toolbox.

"You want to go somewhere?" I say. "I can call in."

Quint just closes his eyes tight. "How about we go to two years ago? You manage that, you think?"

"You want to hit somebody then?" I say, stepping forward.

Quint looks up at me and for a long moment I think he's going to do it, and that, if there's any justice in the world, my jaw will crack down some important line, or a sinus cavity will collapse, or a vertebra will snap in my neck.

Instead, he just hugs me for the first time since elementary, then holds onto me, his face warm on my chest.

The spot I stare at on the wall is where a nail is buried all the way to the head, so it's just a little metal dot.

On my way out minutes later, I pass Gabe's room.

He's sleeping, unaware. Perfect.

I am not an antenna. In the breakroom a week after the talk with Quint in the garage, I write this onto the top of the table until it's a mat of words: *I am not an antenna.*

The next day it's just a blue stain that smells like citrus.

Instead of the regulation white hose all the other nurses wear, Tanya wears thigh-highs with a lace band at top. They stop just after her skirt starts.

The number of people I can tell this to is zero.

The number of people Quint told it to two years ago was one.

When she steps off the elevator into the garage the following Wednesday, I'm waiting for her.

She smiles, looks away. Never stops walking towards me.

After myself, the person I hate most in the world is Dr. Jakobi. In addition to a marriage counselor, he's a preacher. I tell Sherry that this is a conflict of interest for him, but then can't stuff it into words, exactly why. It has something to do with his stake in other people's marriages. Like, if he'd been the one to marry Tanya and Quint nine years ago, then, now, he'd be doing anything he could to keep them together, right? Just to keep his average up.

Sherry says preachers don't compare averages and percentiles.

"Sometimes you should just give up, though," I say.

This gets Sherry looking at me harder than I want.

"You want her to leave him?" she finally says.

I smile, shake my head no, like she's talking particulars, friends, where I'm more in a hypothetical mode.

I don't want them to break up, no.

But I don't sleep so much either. And it's not just the squirrels.

Under Quint's couch now is a slender little fire safe. It has a handle like a briefcase.

He calls me up on a Tuesday to see it.

"You're wanting to test it?" I say from his doorway. I haven't carried a lighter now for years.

Quint laughs through his nose some.

"It's in there," he says.

"What?"

He chews his tongue, squinches one side of his face up.

"With the doctor the other day. I wouldn't drop it, the, y'know. Whoever it was. That's not supposed to matter."

"The other guy."

Yes.

"So?" I say.

Where I'm standing is half in, half out his screen door. My fingertips holding it open. In any television show or movie, this would be a definite sign of guilt. The audience would be howling with laughter.

"So we had to move on," Quint says, the box in his lap now. "Dr. Jakobi said I didn't really want to know. Who."

Because I don't trust my voice, I don't say anything. Either that or I can't.

"It was her idea," Quint says. "She wrote it on a piece of paper, folded it up, then Dr. J held it until I came back with a safe to lock it in."

He pats the fire safe, the slap of his hand soft, almost loving.

I swallow.

"To make it mean something, though, I had it keyed for this," Quint says, holding the key up from around his neck.

"And you haven't looked?" I say.

"It's not moving on if I do. This way, it's a . . . what? An artifact, like. An old thing. Part of the past." He pauses, studies a commercial on TV. "All that matters now is what's ahead."

These aren't his words.

I don't tell them they're lies, though, and I don't ask Tanya whose name is written on that piece of paper.

It's not because I don't want to know, but more because knowing will mean a hundred other things, none of which I can face.

So I walk through my shifts in a trance, and the next Wednesday is just another day, and if I have an extra beer after work, nobody notices, and one night, desperate, I even read Quint's little horror novel cover to cover, drinking cup after cup of coffee.

It's stupid, not scary at all, but still, Tanya calls down to ask if we have any clothes that need drying. Because she's out of laundry but still needs to run the dryer. It's where they sit Gabe's car seat when he won't sleep. When he can't.

I walk down a load of wet colors, pass them through the door to Quint. His eyes are dancing.

"What?" I say.

"It's working again," he whispers, then hooks his chin inside, like I should come see Gabe crying.

"Maybe he's sick," I offer.

"C'mon," Quint says, and jabs the screen door more open for me, turns before it can swing shut.

I don't follow.

Their lights are on until two, when I stop looking.

"What?" Sherry says, passing through the living room, on a cleaning jag.

I don't answer. My mind is shaped like a fire safe, though. One of the letter-sized ones, just for documents.

There are no people with red hair in my family.

I've even called my mom to be sure.

She thought I was joking, and we laughed fake laughs together, and then I asked again.

The only thing that consoles me anymore is the blue ratchet that made its way back to my porch somehow.

I hold it by the quarter inch bolt, spin it around seven times to the left, then reverse the head, spin it back the other way seven times.

The sound is like one click, then a series of perfectly-spaced echoes.

In the other room now, Sherry, scrubbing, smart and oblivious.

I spin the ratchet louder.

Because Quint thinks he has telepathy again, he buys a high dollar baby monitor. His old one makes its way down to our house. Like the blue ratchet—holding it in one hand, the monitor in the other, I finally make the association I'm supposed to here: the ratchet, it sounds like a rattle.

The way the monitor made it down is that Sherry asked for it. She thinks we're going to be needing it.

This makes my face warm, then cold.

Two nights later, snugged in with the groceries I'm carrying in, I see a flat box of lace-top, thigh-high hose. They're black, not white, and make my heart just thump the wall of my chest. Not because I want them on her, then off her, but because—are they a test? If I like them, will it confirm what Sherry's maybe suspecting? Or, is this how Tanya reaches me, after a week without a Wednesday: dressing Sherry up in her hose, telling her how guys love those? And, *guys*, or me in particular?

It's too much for one three-dollar pack of hose.

That night, the hose thankfully in Sherry's top drawer, I try to just read a car magazine, so Quint and Tanya can sleep—because what if *I'm* the one waking him with what I think?—but every caption and every tooltip cuts right to the center of me, until Tanya's calling again, and I'm walking a load of Sherry's uniforms down, passing them across to Quint.

"What?" he says, when I just stand there.

Not on purpose, I looked at his couch, at the firesafe tucked under it, and it shut me down some.

I shake my head no, nothing.

"You should see," he says, trying to lure me in again.

His eyes are bloodshot, his beard growing in scraggly.

"He's scared of *you*," I say. "Fucking zombie."

Quint laughs, rubs his dry bottom lip with the back of his hand, and joke-punches me on the shoulder, and for a moment it feels like I actually wasn't lying the other week—that we are all still the same. That our kids are still going to be born the same year, to grow up together like we did. That our wives are going to sit in the kitchen with weak margaritas while we burn things on the grill, one of us always running down to the store for ice and beer. Taking just whichever truck's parked closest to the road.

Sherry finds me on our porch an hour later.

Instead of asking anything or even saying my name, she just hangs up the phone—Tanya, like always when Gabe's having nightmares—and sits by me.

When her robe parts over her thigh, I see the silky black hose she's got rolled up her legs, and Tanya flashes in my head, her white nurse's shoe pushing hard into the headliner of her car.

I take the corner of Sherry's robe, pull it back into place.

That weekend, when Tanya won't, I pick Quint up from the county lock-up.

What he's in for isn't owning the kind of pornography he's been using to try to scare himself, to connect with Gabe, but for getting caught buying it downtown.

Sherry says no wonder Tanya's been stepping out, right?

I'm at the door, about to leave.

"She told you with who yet?" I say, real casual, no eye contact.

"You asking for you or for him?" she snaps back, smiling behind it so I have no idea what she might be really saying.

I pull the door to, back out of the driveway slowly, obeying every law I can remember.

Two nights ago, waking all at once from a dream, the patter of squirrel feet in my head, the first thing I saw was the baby monitor on our dresser. It was on, the red lights amping up, like someone was running the pad of their finger over the mic on the other end.

It wasn't plugged in, but did have a nine-volt battery inside, one that had leaked, scabbed over.

For the rest of the night I stared at it, the monitor, until I could make out some breathing. Gabe's? This monitor was tuned to the same band or frequency or whatever as the new one, the one that was powerful enough to push the signal all the way down here. That had to be it.

So it would wear out during the day, and because I wasn't going to be there, I left it on.

Or, really, because I didn't want to touch it.

The dream I was waking from wasn't a dream either, really. More like a nightmare. It involved the Wednesday trailer somehow, but our stubby attic too, and Gabe at twelve years old, his hair dyed black to match his clothes, chains and anger seeping off every angle of his body. The only chain that mattered was the one around his neck, though. The one Tanya's Wednesday key was hanging from.

And maybe it wasn't a dream, even.

When I woke, anyway, it wasn't like I opened my eyes to the baby monitor. More like I realized I'd been staring at it.

Getting into my truck in the parking lot of lock-up, all his possessions in a manila envelope, Quint asks what's wrong?

I just look over at him.

He's still smiling. How he lived through booking and sixteen hours in lock-up is a complete mystery. That's the kind of oblivious he can be, though. The kind of focus he's always had.

Instead of going back to our houses, he directs me downtown. Because they confiscated his cardboard box of illegal porn, wouldn't even let him tear any of the pages out.

Because his cash is all in the form of a city-issued check, I have to give him the thirty-two dollars it costs for the cigar-box of photographs he buys from a guy I try hard not to be remembering.

"Don't," I say, holding the lid of the box down when he starts to open it.

He hisses a laugh through his teeth, pours his possessions out from his manila envelope. Last, because it sticks on the brad, is Tanya's key to Wednesday.

"You should chuck it," I say as he's ducking into the chain. "Temptation, all that."

"I get points for it," he says, pulling the chest of his shirt out to drop the key down.

"Points?"

"Dr. J. It's one of the things I have to show each week. Whoever has the most points gets to go first."

"So show him a different one," I say, my arms draped over the steering wheel so I'm driving with my forearms and elbows. So it would be awkward to look directly sideways anymore.

Quint considers this.

"What if I want to know someday?" he says.

"You don't," I tell him, wincing inside because I'm agreeing with Jakobi. "I mean, what would you do, if you knew?"

Quint stares at my dashboard.

"Something bad," he finally says.

I pooch my lips out, nod. "Leaving Gabe where?" I tack on.

Quint nods, keeps nodding, then reaches over to my keys, thumbing through for one that's properly silver, and small enough that it could fool Jakobi.

The first thing I think, his finger suddenly on the key to the trailer, about to hold it up to his, to compare, is to haul the wheel over, like his hand at the ignition's scared me somehow.

We might crash into a bridge abutment or concrete pylon, yeah.

But he wouldn't find the key.

He sees it all coming though, nods ahead to the wreck I'm about to involve us in, and I veer back to my side of the road, a film of sweat breaking out all over, the cigar box of illegal porn spilling down from the dash so that I have to see splashes of skin I could probably go to jail for transporting.

What I tell Quint as he's trying to collect all his porn is that I need all my keys for work, then, after I drop him off, I vacuum the floorboard on his side for three seventy-five cent cycles. The sound of the vacuum is strong and institutional, and I think I could do this for a job, maybe. A career.

With that kind of sound in your ears, it's hard to think, I mean.

I finally come home at dark.

Sherry's waiting for me on the porch, and it's good at least not to have to make some excuse to take a shower. Instead of Tanya, I just smell like the carwash.

We eat lasagna again, forking in bite after perfect bite. Somewhere in there Sherry informs me that we're watching Gabe tomorrow night.

"Tanya's sister finally pop?" I say, chewing.

"Emergency therapy," Sherry says, stabbing through another layer of pasta. "Dr. Jakobi."

My keys are in their tin dog bowl on the table by the backdoor.

I go to sleep thinking of them, waiting for the red lights of the monitor to wrap around again, and try hard not to think of Tanya's nurse shoe pressing against any headliner. Because my head's leaky, I know, and that's not the kind of thing a son should have to know about his mom.

In trade for us giving up our Friday night, Tanya leaves a hot meatloaf on their kitchen table for us, and two rented movies on top of the TV, a twelve-pack dead center on the bottom shelf of the fridge.

Quint mopes out after her, his eyes trying to tell me something. I can't make it out, though. Maybe I'm supposed to be making some excuse for him, saving him from Jakobi. Or maybe I'm supposed to call the hospital if Quint gets scared enough in therapy that Gabe wakes up screaming. Or maybe I'm supposed to be handing him his blue ratchet now, instead of leaving it in my pocket.

I don't know.

The movies are an even split: one romance, one action.

As soon as Quint's truck is gone, Sherry has Gabe up from his crib, is cooing to him, pretending. Practicing.

I sit at the table alone, scraping off the ketchup baked onto the top of the meatloaf, listening to this wonderful absence of squirrels, and find myself four beers into the twelve-pack by the time Sherry sits down across from me, Gabe on her knee.

"He's the one I feel sorry for, really," she says, halving the piece of meatloaf I saved for her.

"He doesn't know," I say, flicking my eyes to Gabe then away.

Hanging from the rusted shower rod in the bathroom, where they don't have to be, is one of Tanya's lace-top pairs of hose.

I stand there, stand there, finally have to shut my eyes to pee. Aim by echo location.

In their dryer, still, are half of Sherry's work shirts.

After dinner I stand in the utility doorway with a beer, watch Sherry fold them into a paper bag, one after the other, Gabe undoing one for every two she can get done.

She's so patient with him, is making it all into a game.

"You should watch your movie," she says. "I'll keep him in here."

"What about yours?" I say.

"Just go," she says, already half into some peek-a-boo game with Gabe.

By the time she's through, she'll have folded everything in the utility, I know.

I collect another beer on the way to the living room, push my movie into the player, settle back into the couch, and am twenty minutes into it—eight people dead already—when the beer I'm trying to settle into the carpet dings on the firesafe.

It's like a gong in my head.

And it doesn't draw Sherry.

Using more beer as an excuse, I get up, deposit my two empties in the trash, carry the last of the twelve-pack back to the living room, and study the street through the gauzy front curtain.

It's empty. Nobody watching, no Quint-truck idling in the drive, him and Tanya talking about their marriage.

To be sure, I lock the door, then, to be even more sure, ease down the hall.

Sherry's in the bedroom with Gabe now, dressing him in outfit after outfit.

"We can watch your movie," I offer.

She looks up to me, her eyebrows drawing together in what I register as earnest consternation—something I don't think I've ever registered before, from anybody—then reaches forward to keep Gabe from overbalancing off the edge of the bed.

"I hope she doesn't move," she says.

"Tanya?"

"If they split up, I mean."

"It's her parent's house."

"I know. It's just—"

"They won't."

"Would you?" she asks.

"Would I what?" I say back.

"If I was, y'know. Like Tanya."

If she were like Tanya. If I'd been meeting her each Wednesday for two years. If somebody like me had. If I were Quint.

"Trying to tell me something?" I say, smiling around my beer.

This is as serious as we ever talk. As serious as I can ever let it get, anyway. It's like walking through a field of bear traps.

I tilt my beer to her, a toast, and back out, leave the hall light on behind me so I'll be able to see her shadow if she's walking towards the living room.

Still, sitting in front of my movie, the sound turned up as cover, the firesafe in my lap—I don't know.

Is this a trap too?

Has Quint spit-glued hairs around the edges, so if I open it they'll break? Was that whole thing about an artifact of Tanya's affair just something he made up, when what's really in the box is a picture of me and him, from ten years ago? Did Jakobi slip something therapeutic in there while he wasn't looking, which'll get ruined if I see it?

The box is so heavy with all this that I'm surprised I'm even able to lift it. That it's not already crushing me.

Six times, then, the movie blaring, I count to ten, waiting for truck headlights—any headlights—to wash over the curtains, and six times they don't. So I ease my key into the lock, twist. The top sighs open.

Inside is a folded piece of paper. It's been ripped from a small notebook, the kind any good therapist is going to keep handy.

My lips are trembling, inside. Not where anybody would be able to see.

Written in Tanya's hand, in pencil, a name, not mine, just somebody she made up on the spot, because she's not stupid.

I close my eyes in thanks, maybe even smile, and when I open them again Sherry's standing there, Gabe on her hip.

She's just staring at me. No expression on her face at all.

"He—he gave you the key," she says, her eyes boring right into me now, and—it's my only choice, really—I nod, once. Leave my head down.

She knows about the firesafe, the name, the special key. All of it.

"And?" she says.

"What?"

My voice is weak. I'm not built for this.

"Are you going to tell him now?"

I look down to the paper again, then back up to her.

"I don't want to know," she says. "It's none of our business, right?"

Beside her, Gabe is staring at me too. His eyes seeing I-don't-know-how deep Behind them, guns and a car exploding.

"He's my best friend," I say, trying to watch the movie now. Again. Still.

"And you think it'll be good for him, to know?"

What I'm supposed to say is built into her question, how she asks it. It usually is.

I shake my head no, it wouldn't be good for him. That, *because* he's my friend, I won't tell, will keep it inside, hold it forever, even if it gives me cancer.

Sherry shakes her head at me, turns on her heel, goes back to whatever she has going on in the other part of the house. I relock the firesafe, push it back under the couch, and watch the movie without seeing any of it. At some point the name Tanya wrote on the paper hits me—Was it a *real* name, some *other* other guy?—and then a tank blows up on-screen and Gabe cries in the other room. I turn the movie down, and the next time I move my head, I think, is when Quint's truck door shuts outside. Just one door. It means Tanya sat beside him for the drive home. A good session, then.

When they come through the screen, they're holding hands. Or, Tanya's holding Quint's. What he is is limp, like he's being dragged. But that's better than a lot of the ways he could be. You don't go to emergency therapy for illegal porn then come home happy, I don't guess.

Sherry appears in the door, Gabe in outfit number 435, or somewhere up there.

Tanya crosses the room to him, leading with the heels of her hands the ways moms do, and Sherry's watching me close, I know. Waiting for me to nod or not nod to Quint.

Instead, I just try to avoid his eyes altogether. Throw him the second-to-last beer, another impossible spiral.

"He was an angel," Sherry's saying above me, on her way to the turn the movie off.

"You like it?" Quint says, unloading his wallet onto the speaker by the door, nodding to the paused movie.

"Which one?" I say, and he laughs in his way, looks into the kitchen for some reason—it's dark in there—then does the thing that almost makes me forget how to breathe: ducks out of the chain around his neck.

He hangs it from the upslanted peg just under his hat.

Sherry sees this, I know, even directs a question down to me, her eyes hot and sad both, but doesn't say anything, and, either because she's smart or by chance—but it can't be chance—when she comes to bed later that night she's got those lace-topped hose on, and makes sure I see.

"You like?" she says, and I nod, pull her close, wonder the whole way through if the noises she's making are hers or what she imagines Tanya might sound like, and then I think that maybe, if she *can* be Tanya, *like* Tanya, then maybe she'll get pregnant like she wants, like she deserves, and then none of this will matter, and to try to make it stick, to make it take, I even whisper Tanya's name into the pillow at the end, instantly hate myself. And then we roll away to our sides of the bed.

"Gabe?" Sherry says after a few minutes of fake breathing.

"Share," I say.

There's nothing to say, though.

It took, I know. She's pregnant now, has to be. It's the only thing that can stop me from being me, the only thing that can turn me into something else, something better. A dad.

For a few tense moments there's a tremble in the bed, and I think she's crying but lie to myself that she doesn't want me to reach across, touch her thigh, her hip, her hand.

And then nothing. Sleep. Me fixed on those dead lights of the baby monitor on the dresser, waiting for them to wind up.

They do.

Just a weak glow at first, but then that first bulb's on, and the red's climbing, wrapping, opening some connection, a conduit, a fissure.

I shake my head no, please. No no no.

But then there's a touch on my thigh, my hip, my hand.

I look over, am thinking of my old German Shepherd growing up, how he'd always nose me in the morning, just nudge me awake.

This isn't my dog, though.

It's a boy, maybe three years old already—time moves different over there—his hair long and wild on his shoulders, glinting with fiberglass. Too dark to see his face, quite, but his mouth, the lower jaw, it's just hanging, so there's just this black oval. A void.

And he's tugging at my hand, like he should be.

It's Tanya's other twin. The one she buried. Mine.

He pulls on the side of my hand and I let him, stand, follow. He looks back once to be sure and I'm reaching ahead, for his tiny shoulder.

I lose him in the hallway, though, step into the kitchen where a little black body would be stark against all the white cabinets.

I open my mouth to shape his name, whatever I would have named him, but look to the phone instead.

The bone behind my ear, it's alive again.

My hand stabs out, pulls the receiver to the side of my head before it can ring.

It's Quint. He's breathing heavy, guilty, wrong.

"Hey," he says, his whole body cupped around his phone, I can tell, so Tanya won't hear, "hey, yeah, you've got to come down, man, see this. It's, it's—"

I balance the receiver on top of its cradle without hanging up, so that the connection's still there.

I came the wrong way, that's it.

There was fiberglass in his matted hair. *Fiberglass.*

From the attic, the crawlspace. Insulation.

Of course. Footsteps in the attic, not on the roof.

I feel my back into the hallway, see the silhouette of Sherry sitting up in the bed, and she sees me too, I think, but I'm just a shadow, less. I open my mouth to apologize to her, for everything, but all that comes out is the blue ratchet sound. One click, a thousand identical ones tumbling into place behind it.

It's better this way.

At the other end of the hallway is the only ceiling vent in the house. So the attic can breathe. It's ten inches by six inches, and just a cut-out in the sheetrock now, the vent already pulled up, balanced on two rafters.

Ten inches by six inches.

Just enough for me to reach up, grab onto each side, try to force my head in.

In a rush of shadow, my son pulls me the rest of the way through.

▶ Story Notes

▶ Father, Son, Holy Rabbit
Cemetery Dance #57, Spring 2007

This is one of those wrote-in-one-sitting affairs, though in the version that got published first, I never really felt like I found the proper end, the one that would both tie up the dramatic line and kind of open the narrative up, like horror's supposed to do. Like *stories* are supposed to do. I mean, it was doing what I intended, showing how much a father could care for his son—a story I'd been carrying around already for years, until it was so pure and perfect I never thought I'd get it written down to match—but that's kind of all it was doing, showing that. And stories have to be more, have to actually *do* something.

Years later, now, revisiting it, I can finally feel out some of the repercussions of that experience this kid had in the woods. Or suspect them anyway. How a story like that, it never goes away, quite. And, as bad luck or fate would have it, the same year this story ran, I got seriously lost in some big grey woods on the reservation, and was carrying around this white rabbit that was bleeding all over me, and there was bear and wolf sign everywhere, like a joke almost, like they were playing a game with me, and then my fancy compass broke, and I managed to lose my walkie-talkie. But my dad, he knew that when I'm this many hours late he should shoot his gun three times fast. Which, evidently he did for a while. Me, though, I was in some other place altogether, was walking through all these upturned trees I'd never have guessed could exist, their root pans three times as high as I could reach, blood all over me, and I kept seeing footprints that I knew had to be mine, but didn't look like it, because I'd never been to this place, had I? So, yeah, if I knew my story elements were going to pop up, take shape around me, I'd have written about a nice unicorn with a flower in its mouth, framed by a rainbow. Maybe a mermaid back in the surf, singing. Still, though, I found my dad at last, which I guess is another way this story—"Father, Son, Holy Rabbit"—could have ended. Or maybe the way it finally did.

Stephen Graham Jones

▸ Till the Morning Comes
The Storyteller Speaks: Rare and Different Fictions of the Grateful Dead, eds. Gary McKinney & Robert G. Weiner (Kearney Street Books, 2010)

Completely did not plan to write this story. Never would have either, except my good friend Rob Weiner called me up, said he was doing this horror anthology, could I write a story for it? Sure, of course, always. But then he hit me with the theme: the Grateful Dead. Which, I mean, "Touch of Grey," that's my complete warehouse of Grateful Dead knowledge. So, my first step was to wait until the very last possible minute, Rob telling me the deadline's here, it's here, me thinking It'll pass, it'll pass, but then I accidentally looked up the Dead's discography, seeing if I knew any more songs by them—nope—and I cribbed down three or four titles. But the only one that seemed to have some horror possibilities was this "Till the Morning Comes"-one. I mean, "night," it's practically there already, yeah? And night's always the worst for me. Then I looked up some of the Dead artwork, on purpose, and, man: these are all the posters I was so terrified of, growing up, the ones my uncles—we all lived in my grandmother's house—the same ones my uncles used to have in their bedrooms. So, that kid, stifflegging it past that hall, man, I know that hall, I *know* what watching your uncle's door all night's like. Still terrifies me. I so hope those posters are really burned. Or, this story, it's me, burning them, trying to. Please.

▸ The Sons of Billy Clay
Doorways Magazine 4, January 2008

I won't watch poker, can't watch golf, can hardly sit still through an NBA game, even—it has to be recorded, so I can cue through the free-throws and analysis and commercials—but bullriding, man, I can watch that all day. Probably because in high school a lot of my friends were getting into it, bullriding, but somehow I floated out of that scene. Which is definitely for the best: tall, lanky, uncoordinated guys with poor self-preservation instincts tend to bash their faces open on the horn boss, never be the same again. Closest I ever got was strapping ropes on show steers, on concrete, and getting thrown off, stomped over. And riding so many mechanical bulls to a standstill. Because I wanted to be Debra Winger, yeah. But mechanical bulls, they're miles away from the real thing, I know. There's things that are more real than bull riding, too, though. There's me, a week or two before I wrote this story. I'm on this big group camping trip out in the mesquite and scrub, and it's after the kids are asleep, so all the men are gathered around the fire, drinking beer and telling stories. Except me, of course; I'm in my tent, reading John Grisham by secret flashlight, because I don't drink beer. But the stories the guys were telling out there, it was hard not to tune in. One was how they knew this prison guard who, when the inmates wouldn't sleep, what he'd do was lug this chainsaw or lawnmower into the cellblock, put his standard-issue gas mask on, and fire it up, let the fumes put the prisoners down for the night. Cue impressed laughter from around that campfire, yeah. Kids faking sleeping all around. But that guard, he's the one who kind of has the bad ending in this story. The one I served the bad ending too, I guess. Which is definitely a proper use of fiction, I think. And, the illustration *Doorways* did for this, it's so cool, is exactly the bull one of my uncle's friends (they were sixteen, seventeen; I was six, maybe) would always draw on my grandmother's napkins, leave on the counter for me to steal, hide in my books. The bulls were from a beer can, I think. I saw one of those cans in an antique shop a few years ago, sitting back on the deep sill of the window, all faded, not for sale, just there, and man, it was like going home. But still, I couldn't reach out, touch that can, touch that bull. Except in a story.

▶ So Perfect
Grok # 8, Winter 2008

This feels like a *Heathers* story to me. Except it's really—well, not about my dad, but one weekend my dad was alone in the house, states away, and then called me up Monday, said he nearly died the last three days. Every hour of those last three days. And that he still probably was going to. Because he, like I never had either, didn't take the warning labels all over those Frontline applicators seriously. Probably because those applicators look exactly like the activators for rearview mirror glue, which, yeah, those can get messy, but you don't die from that mess. This tick-be-gone pesticide, though, that stuff'll plain tear you up. I mean, I've got enough on me to get sick before, but just small-dose strychnine sick, never three-days gonna-*die* sick. Anyway, add that whole scene to this one day I went to teach my Tuesday lit class, and I was in half-bad shape still, had had some kind of killer food poising for four days, from this greyblack, oily lump of bad-idea meat I found in the back of the fridge, that I thought I could put enough ketchup on that it wouldn't matter how old it was. Turns out, there's no amount of ketchup. Anyway, a student up front kind of noted aloud that I looked different this day (I suspect I wasn't standing up straight yet), and I said yeah, I'd been sick, lost thirteen pounds over the weekend, and this girl sitting a few rows back, she got this look of wonder on her face, and raised her hand, waited for me to call on her, asked if I could breathe on her, please. And that way of thinking, that so obvious-to-her way of getting from some A to some B, I don't know. It stuck in my head, and the only way I could try to make it make sense was to write from inside it, feel my way out, try to document what I could, and use some Redmond O'Hanlon imagery along the way (he can describe ticks in very uncomfortable ways). And, as for Candy Cane, I used to live in Denton, Texas, and I remember for a few months always seeing this girl at the edge of every scene, wearing these Seuss-looking red-and-white striped tights, like they were a statement of some kind. And so now I let her make that statement.

▶ Lonegan's Luck
New Genre 6, Summer 2009

This is me, trying to be Lansdale. Also, the way I'd planned it, this was the first of a collection of Lonegan stories, *The Alone Again Chronicles* or something, where he dies at the end of each story, but's still around for the next, and cycles through vampires and werewolves and ghosts and aliens and all of it, just trying to scam his way through the Old West, until his true nature's finally revealed. Still might do that, too. Only reason I haven't so far—or, back when I wrote this—was that nobody would publish this one, and I kind of lost heart, thought all the usual things about my writing, my stupid stories, my grand ideas. So, thank you, Adam Golaski, for taking a chance on it, and thank you, Ellen Datlow, for selecting it for *Best Horror of the Year, Volume 2*. Maybe now I can write some more awkward-length Lansdale clones, and fall in love with them just as much. And also, thank you, Louis L'Amour. Except for all the Indians your characters were always shooting, or stealing land from, or marrying into slavery. But the rest, yes. I wouldn't know how to be a person without reading all your books over and over. Or, really, your books were the ones I used to run off into the woods with in the dark, and read the first page by matchlight, then tear that page out, light it, read the next page by the burning page, and feel my way through that way, so that I'd just have a handful of burn at the end. But I'd be happy too, because the good guys won. Except I always made them secretly Indian, in my head. They were a lot more believable that way.

▶ Monsters
Niteblade Horror and Fantasy Magazine #8, June 2009

This was supposed to just be a what-I-did-over-summer-vacation story. Innocent, flighty, nostalgic. Me, trying on a different past, one where I could have been that kid who got to go beach towns for the summer, have adventures and romances. I just wanted to see if I could do that, I mean, at least on the page. Looks like not. As soon as Matey got to be a police dog, then of course he's a cadaver dog, because the other kind are boring, and then because he's trained for what he's trained for, that training's useless unless there's some walking dead dude under the boardwalk for him to sniff out, right? And it's not like I could chase that guy out of the story after he showed up. He was there to do something, evidently. I just had to run it down with words.

But still, even after I finished—another one-sitting trick—I never thought it worked until I lucked onto that now-obvious title. It's the only thing that lets the end happen right, I think. Because, I mean, that vampire dude, he's bad news, sure, but he's just doing what his kind does, too. As for the real monsters in this story, though, our narrator here, he knows where they live. I would have let him just go ahead and get infected, so he could dole out some justice, but of course, like I was saying, it wouldn't be justice, then, right? It'd just be his kind doing what his kind does. Much worse—better—if it's him doing what he's maybe going to do by *choice*. Always better that way.

▶ Wolf Island
Juked 12.17.2009

This is my second werewolf story. And I think it's somehow a rip-off of that King story "Survivor Type," where the heroin-smuggling doctor's marooned on an island, has to eat most of himself to survive. That story and "The Jaunt," they've never left me, never will. But, anyway, that story forever lodged in my head, there I am on the couch, killing Cheetos and watching a nature show, when this killer whale just *slams* up onto a beach in South America or somewhere, after a seal, and, man: Cheetos everywhere. I had never seen anything so cool. So of course my first thought was What else could possibly ever even hope to be that cool? Answer: werewolves. End result: this story. As very influenced by Barry Lopez telling me once about watching a couple—could have been one, I guess—of moose swim from some point of land in Alaska across to an island. Everything's going fine, they're thinking moose thoughts, when bam, this pod of killer whales finds them, just absolutely feasts. I could listen to that story all day every day for a week. Even just retelling it as poorly as I am now, I mean, I'm so excited my fingers are going too fast, so there's wrong letters everywhere. And, this is definitely a pattern I see in all of my stories, all of my novels: I always want things to come down to the Hulk and Thor duking it out, say. Or that rattlesnake and the mongoose in *Any Which Way You Can*. Or Jane versus the whole sick federation of planets, or whatever they were in *Xenocide*. AVP, Jason versus Freddy, Terminator versus Terminator, all of it, yes. All stories are *Highlander* stories, as far as I'm concerned: There can be only one.

▶ Teeth
Brutarian 44, Spring 2005

The weekend I sold *All the Beautiful Sinners* to Sean Coyne at Rugged Land—no: the weekend I sold the general, vague, *idea* of *ATBS* to Rugged Land, when there was no plot in place, no characters, no setting, no nothing except the suspicion that this would be thrillerish, maybe have a police car or two, I figured it wouldn't be a half-bad idea to see if I could actually maybe do something in that arena. So, in about thirty-six hours, to prove to myself—and to Coyne—that I could, I whipped out "Teeth."

Which I so wish I didn't have to suspect Raymond Carver's "Cathedral" was somehow instrumental for, as I hate that story, think it's completely useless, way over-anthologized—he's got some really excellent stuff, I mean, why not use that?—but, that idea of teeth-casts, I don't know where else I could have stumbled onto it, either. So, yeah. Thanks, Carver. And, that name, "Kupier," some article I was reading at the time—likely *Discover*, as my beloved *OMNI* was long gone by 2002—it was some asteroid belt I was meaning to write about. But, until then, I could at least sneak the name in, save it for later. And, those owl pellets, just the idea of them's always fascinated me. Couple of years ago a friend gave me one, even, and I teased it apart with probes, for the mouse skeleton inside. Very cool. And, yes, again, this story probably owes everything to King's "Survivor Type." But, I mean, c'mon. Everything I write, it owes nearly every piece of itself to King.

▶ Raphael
Cemetery Dance 55, Fall 2006

This was so far over *Cemetery Dance*'s word-limit, and from such a complete nobody—me, 2006—that I have no idea what compelled Robert Morrish to snag it from whatever leaning slushpile it was in. And, I mean, I kind of suspected it was a broke story anyway, only sent it out because I knew I couldn't make it any better, and needed it off my desk so I could move on. But then Ellen Datlow picked it up for *The Year's Best Fantasy & Horror*, and it nabbed some good award nominations, and here I am, I guess, with all these other stories too, suddenly and unexpectedly. So, first, thanks to Robert and Ellen, and, second—again—this story's just me, loving King's *It*, a book I hope to never get over, a book I crawled into twenty years ago, never quite got all the way back out of. And, that book they read, that they bury in that cake pan, it's *Reader's Digest's Strange Stories, Amazing Facts*. Probably the single most important book of my life. When I was twelve, I was addicted to *The Enquirer* and all those, never even thought to suspect they might be making this up about aliens and Bigfoot—never had any reason to doubt any of it, as all the stuff my family was involved in at the time, it was no less out-there. Really, *Enquirer* was an anchor, some sort of touchstone. Living under the stairs in our perpetually half-built house back then, I was absolutely certain there was a bald guy with green eyes, and there were nights I would wake up with deer heads fallen from the wall into my bed, and wasps biting me on the neck, and my snakes were always loose in the house, and the neighbor was always burying my dog alive, and the only thing to do, the best place to go, was running off into the empty spaces. Like Gabe and the other ghosts. It's calm out there, alone. Good. Until something like what happens with Melanie happens, yeah. That was a complete surprise to me. The way I had the story half-planned—original title: "The Gorgeous Ladies of Wrestling" (what Gabe's dad was watching)—was that one of their stories (Gabe's) would come true at the end, and they'd learn the power of storytelling. Except then there's Melanie becoming Melody, arcing her back away from the water, and I was all freaked out, had to leave the story for a while. Which is why, when it starts up again, it's thirty-two years later. I did not want to be there at that water's edge even one moment longer. Except, then, like with the rabbit story, that's the only place there is, too. As Gabe has to find out. And, going into this one just now, I thought surely I'd find a different end, thought that surely it was broke, that everybody was wrong about it, but this ending, Melanie's hair reaching down for him, man. It still scares me, makes me see things from the corner of my eye that I have to tell myself and tell myself aren't really there. But then of course I look anyway.

▸ Captain's Lament
Clarkesworld #17, February 2008

I've never been on a boat. Or, is it a "ship" if you're talking a sea-boat? I have no idea. I've never been on the sea, the ocean. My best dream is to someday see a whale, though. I think about that a lot. Enough that this voice, Muley, it's by far the easiest voice I've ever tried. His oblique, half-antique way of talking, that nautical kind of diction, it feels more natural to me than—no, the only other voice I've ever done that feels so natural would be Francis Dalimpere, from *Ledfeather*. But that's Muley. And, I wrote them both at the same time, yeah. There's something about a character with such a romantic bent that it infects his language, it just feels so right, so real, so unfettered by the usual constraints. For a long time, *Don Quixote* was my favorite-favorite book, yeah. But then of course I put him at the back of the room in *Jaws*, scratching his nails down that chalkboard. And I was fresh from another last pass through *Demon Theory* too, specifically all the *Urban Legend* notes, so that got included as well. Except—I had no idea how to tell the backstory to the most well-known of all the urban legends without both giving that legend away too early or making it suddenly unscary. So, the only solution then is to make the backstory just as horrible, just as twisted, then couch it in a diction distracting enough that nobody asks what this guy's right hand might or might not look like.

▶ The Meat Tree
Dogmatika, Spring 2006

I always think this story's in present tense, even when I'm reading it, can see all the past-tense verbs right there. Just feels so immediate to me. And, this was the first "long" story I ever wrote that didn't get away from me, I think. No, there's one other that works, "Sterling City," but that might need italics, not quotation marks—do novellas get italics treatment? Anyway, that one went long in the best way, had that glandular problem, but this one, it was able to find the end quicker somehow—likely because it's first-person instead of third, which always makes the exposition trick easier. For me, anyway. And, unlike nearly everything else I write, that starts with a voice, with a sentence unspooling in my head, this one actually started with an image: that tree with slabs of meat draped all through its limbs. And, I'd guess that's somehow really Cormac McCarthy's baby tree from *Blood Meridian*, but so be it. Much more interesting with meat, I think. Because then you have to wonder what kind of creature would leave it up there, and why? This time, the character, the narrator, he just kind of shaped himself around that, to answer those questions, then frame them in his own terms. And, maybe more than in any of these stories, this guy here, he's me at twenty. Nearly every detail (except I could never eat a Slim Jim; sorry, Randy Savage). And, talking about that missing kid Jeremy, I think that's guilt, from all the telephone poles I've half-knocked over with tractors, or at least strung their guide wires out to where they're sagging, supporting nothing. And, those telephone poles, that's where the faces of these kids go, right? It's stupid, but I always felt about bad about clipping those poles with a knifing rig, or shooting them over and over, or seeing if they would burn.

And yeah, this is the other lost-in-the-woods story of this collection. Which I wrote before the rabbit story. If I'd just re-read this one first, then I'd have seen that you always bring the woods back out with you. The experience isn't something you walk through, remember fondly, later, at your leisure. It's something you live through, take with you everywhere, no matter if it's about meat trees or tea parties. If there's ever a thesis to what I do, I suspect that's it: everything matters. Especially the stuff you don't want to.

▸ The Ones Who Got Away
Phantom, eds. Paul Tremblay & Sean Wallace (Prime, 2009)

I wrote this all the way back in 2005, I think. Maybe 2006. And it's one of those where I had zero idea where it might be going. All I had, really, was a first line, then a kid to be saying it, then a reason for him to be saying it, then that reason being a dead friend, then that dead friend dying this or that way, and suddenly I'm cruising in a stolen van past my eighth-grade bowling alley in Wimberley, Texas, where half my living up to that point had happened, it felt like, and the way things slowed down for that drive-by, it felt so final, so last-time, so perfect and forever. Still gets to me. And I miss Tim, all the Tims. And the first version of this story, from *Phantom* and from *Five Chapters*, for some reason I thought it was magic and accidental and bulletproof. But then I opened that file again, for this collection, and the first half of it felt so wandering to me, like I could see myself feeling this new storyscape out, seeing where the holes were I could slip through, that might open onto other rooms. Like holding match after match in front of a series of doorways, waiting for one of those flames to flicker more than the rest. So I printed up draft after draft after draft of this story for two days, and read it until I hated it, then read it some more, and finally, now, here, it's a way that works, I think. The first half matches the second half, I mean. And, thanks to an ex-student from forever ago, Kenneth Simpson, I think, who first cued into this, saying that two of these small sections, if they were flipped, then it's the same story, right? I looked at it at that day, had to agree with him, and that was the seed, that was my first glimmer of suspicion that, if those two could be flipped, then were either really that necessary? And, if they weren't, then what else might be extra? So, yeah, the version here, it's the same story as ran the first time, just, I hope, better.

▶ Crawlspace
(Mostly unpublished)

Or, there's a version of it out there, "Gabriel," but it doesn't work. Which is okay sometimes, except "Gabriel," it comes so so close to working, then drops everything at the end. A lack of nerve on my part, I don't know. Or just plain stupidity. But "Gabriel," it was draft two of this novella, which is the same story—it had started out as a sister-piece to "Raphael," was going to be a series of stories, but then I didn't know any more angel names— except it's in five parts, I think, of which "Gabriel" is pretty much just the first. In the novella, we get to see Gabe grow up, get evil, and Quint's living at these Forest Arms apartments, which are so haunted—or, infected by him anyway. It was really fun, but I lost the handle on it, and there was just all this stuff happening, happening for reasons that, on second read, didn't seem to make much sense, except that they were all cool things. But that's not a story. So, I'm glad I scrapped it. Twenty-five or thirty thousand words, but so what. There's always more. Except I couldn't get Quint and Gabe out of my head. And I so wanted to, so do not need them crowding my thoughts with their strange, completely understandable, really-real (trust me) ESP. But back when I wrote this the first time, I had no idea that a woman could have twins where each twin maybe had a different dad. Once I heard that on the news or wherever—*Law & Order*, probably—the way this story could work kind of clicked in my head. Usually, with any story you're telling, economy's the key; you've got to reduce the character-count as much as you possibly can, and then a couple of people more. But, here, it turned out that what was needed was for our guy's guilt and certainty and paranoia to actually have been born into the world, and to be haunting him now, letting him become something else if he could just trust it. And, as for him and Tanya, that whole bad scene, I think it's my mash-up of Robert Boswell's excellent "The Darkness of Love" story and that painful, terrible, wonderful scene Louise Erdrich plants in *Love Medicine*, where Nector leaves an I-don't-really-love-you-goodbye note on the kitchen table for Marie, his wife, then changes his mind, comes back, finds her there but the note still there as well, only, was it under the salt, or the pepper? This whole story's built on that, I think.

➤ Thanks

To Ellen Datlow, whose run with *OMNI* in the eighties was my first and by far most formative taste of what short fiction can and should be. To Sean Wallace, my editor for this, for saying that maybe we could do a collection, yeah. To Brenda Mills, for making all of these better, in spite of what they might have done to your dreams. To Paul Tremblay, for opening the door for me into this world; before, I'd always just been sneaking through windows. To Joe Hill, for showing what a collection of horror stories can be, if it tries. To Jesse Lawrence and Chris Deal, for catching, I think, every single snag in here, and at breakneck pace. To my characters, for not saying your real names. To Laird Barron, for writing like Roger Daltrey sings: with a razor line. To Stephen King and Peter Straub and Clive Barker and Robert McCammon: without your stories to keep me in my room so many nights, I'd surely be not as alive as I am now, though I might have slept better. To my agent Kate Garrick, for always making everything work. To Brian Evenson and Craig Clevenger and Will Christopher Baer, for writing so deep the paper bleeds; I can only hope for that kind of precision. To Nabokov, for a squirrel. To my brothers, Spot and Sulac and Sky and Tommy, for living through some of these stories with me, and to my sisters, Ginger and Katie and Jenny, for believing in the gore, but seeing that there's more to it than that, sometimes. To Wes Craven and Kevin Williamson, just because, and to Shooter Jennings and Bonnie Tyler and Bob Seger, for the obvious reasons. To Reader's Digest, for their book *Strange Stories, Amazing Facts*; growing up, this was my Bible, and I still believe every word, am Gabriel because of it, but not Raphael. Never Raphael. To Randy Howard and Teddy Smith and Brett Watkins and Steve Woods and my cousin Darla Graham; you're in more of these stories than I ever meant. But I'm not sorry for that. And, like always, thank you to my wife, Nancy, for reading that first story of mine when I was twenty, and then pulling it close, asking if you could keep it: yes, yes yes yes.

stephengrahamjones
boulder, colorado
5 april 2010

Stephen Graham Jones started writing in the mid-nineties, with his first novel hitting in 2000. There have been seven more books since then, among them *Ledfeather*, *The Long Trial of Nolan Dugatti*, *Demon Theory*, and, most recently, *It Came from Del Rio*. The stories in this collection have appeared in *The Year's Best Fantasy and Horror*, *The Best Horror of the Year, Vol.2*, and *The Year's Best Dark Fantasy and Horror*, and have been finalists for the Shirley Jackson Award, the International Horror Guild Award, and the Black Quill. Jones grew up in West Texas, nabbed his Ph.D. from Florida State University, and, when not writing more and more books, teaches in the MFA program at the University of Colorado at Boulder.

Lightning Source UK Ltd.
Milton Keynes UK
UKHW012335271221
396247UK00003B/25/J